Their Destinies Were Bound by the Flames of War

Léa Delmas . . . the beautiful and headstrong daughter of a wealthy vineyard owner. Her passionate resistance to the German occupation was matched only by her smoldering desire for her childhood sweetheart . . .

Laurent d'Argilat . . . handsome and noble, he shattered Léa's dreams by denying her love and marrying his gentle cousin . . .

Camille . . . quiet and sweet, she was Léa's rival in romance—and Léa's responsibility in the throes of war.

François Tavernier . . . tall, dark and determined to capture Léa's heart, he could ignite her passions—and fury—with a single touch.

THE BLUE BICYCLE

"This epic love story of World War II . . . is a moving portrait of that turbulent era."
—*Modern Maturity*

"More than 4½ million Frenchwomen must be right when they made [*The Blue Bicycle*] an 'overnight sensation' and France's largest selling book ever!"
—*Lake Oswego Review*

The Blue Bicycle

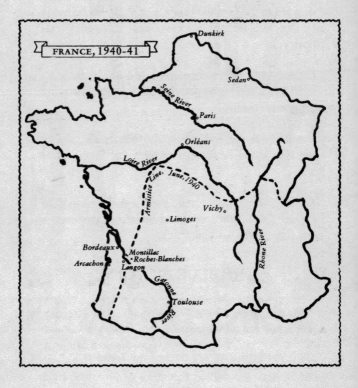

FRANCE, 1940-41

The BLUE BICYCLE

RÉGINE DEFORGES

Translated from the French by Ros Schwartz

C

CHARTER BOOKS, NEW YORK

**In memory of
Prince Yvan Wiazemsky**

This Charter book contains the
complete text of the original hardcover edition.

THE BLUE BICYCLE

A Charter Book/published by arrangement with
Lyle Stuart, Inc.

PRINTING HISTORY
Éditions Ramsay edition published 1981
Lyle Stuart edition published 1986
Charter edition/December 1987

ISBN: 0-441-06864-2

Charter Books are published by The Berkley Publishing Group,
200 Madison Avenue, New York, New York 10016.
The name "CHARTER" and the "C" logo
are trademarks belonging to Charter Communications, Inc.
PRINTED IN THE UNITED STATES OF AMERICA

10 9 8 7 6 5 4 3 2 1

Acknowledgments

The author would like to thank the following for their collaboration, often unknowingly given: Henri Amouroux, Robert Aron, Marcel Aymé, Robert Brasillach, Benoist-Méchin, Louis-Ferdinand Céline, Colette, Arthur Conte, Jacques Delarue, Jacques Delpierrié de Bayac, Jean Galtier-Bossiére, General de Gaulle, Jean Giraudoux, Jean Guéhenno, Gilbert Guilleminault, Adolf Hitler, Bernard Karenty, Jacques Laurent, Roger Lemesle, General Alain Le Ray, François Mauriac, Claude Mauriac, Henri Michel, Margaret Mitchell, Pierre Nord, Gilles Perrault, Marshal Pétain, L. G. Planes and R. Dufourg, Lucien Rebatet, P. R. Reid, Colonel Rémy, Maurice Sachs, Charles Tillon, Jean Vidalenc, Gérard Walter, Princess Wiazemsky and Prince Yvan Wiazemsky.

Prologue

As a child, Pierre Delmas used to watch the cargo ships for hours on end, coming and going from the docks at Bordeaux. He dreamed of being the captain of one of those ships, roaming the seas in the face of storms. On board, he would be master, second only to God. One day, he was found attempting to stow away in the hold of a coal ship about to set sail for Africa. In spite of threats and entreaties, he refused to reveal either how he had managed to board the ship or why he wanted to run away from his mother, whom he adored, without a word of explanation. After that incident, he never returned to the docks again to hang about the quays piled high with cargoes redolent of tar, vanilla and far-off lands.

Like his father, Pierre Delmas became a wine grower. Was it his frustrated love for the ocean that made him buy acres of pine forest swept by a westerly wind from the sea? At thirty-five, he felt it was time to get married. But, in spite of the eligible young ladies he was introduced to, he stubbornly refused to choose a wife from the Bordeaux gentry. He met Isabelle de Montpleynet in Paris at the home of a friend of his, who was a wine merchant.

He fell in love with Isabelle the moment he set eyes on her. She was just nineteen, but seemed older because of her lovely melancholy blue eyes and the way she wore her hair in a heavy black chignon. She was attentive and charming to Pierre although, at times, she seemed sad and remote. He wanted to see her smile and did all he could to amuse her. When Isabelle burst out laughing, he felt he was the happiest man alive. He was glad she had not sacrificed her splendid hair to the dictates of fashion, as the respectable ladies of Bordeaux had done!

Isabelle de Montpleynet was the only child of a rich landowner in Martinique. She was brought up on the island until she was ten, and had retained her sing-song accent and a certain gentleness of manner. Her apparent nonchalance hid a strong and proud character. When her mother, a Creole beauty, died, Isabelle's heart-broken father entrusted his daughter to the care of his two sisters, Albertine and Lisa de Montpleynet, who lived in Paris. Six months later, he too died, leaving his vast plantations to Isabelle. Shortly after Monsieur de Montpleynet's death, but with little hope of success, Pierre Delmas declared his love to Isabelle and asked her to marry him. To his astonishment and joy, she accepted. Eight weeks later, they were married in great style at the Church of St. Thomas d'Aquin in Paris. They spent a long honeymoon in Martinique and came back to settle at Montillac, with Isabelle's old nanny, Ruth, whom she could not bear to leave behind in Martinique.

Although Isabelle was a stranger to the province, she was quickly accepted by her in-laws and the neighboring families. She had a large dowry which she lavished on her new home. Pierre had lived like a typical bachelor, occupying only two or three rooms and leaving the rest to gather cobwebs. In less than a year, Isabelle had changed all that, and by the time Sabine, their first daughter, was born, the old house was no longer recognizable. Two years later, Léa was born, and three years after that, Laure.

Pierre Delmas, owner of the Montillac estate, was considered the most fortunate of men. There were many who envied his life of peaceful bliss with his wife and lovely daughters.

Montillac Château was surrounded by several acres of rich land, woods and vineyards which produced a robust red wine as well as an excellent white wine, similar to the famous Sauternes. This white wine had won several gold medals. "Château" was rather a grand word for this early nineteenth-century residence surrounded by wine sheds. There was an adjoining farmhouse with rambling barns, stables and outhouses. Pierre's grandfather had replaced the pretty, pinkish, local tiles with cold gray slate, which he felt was more stylish. Fortunately, the wine sheds and farm buildings still had their original roofing, for the gray slates gave the house a dignified and rather gloomy air that was more in keeping with the bourgeois spirit of Pierre's ancestors.

The estate was beautifully situated on a hill overlooking the entire region. A long lane lined with plane trees led up to it, past an abandoned dovecote, then the farm buildings. Just after the first barn was a path leading from the farm and the outhouses to the château. The enormous kitchen was, in fact, the main entrance to the house. Only strangers came in through the hall with its odd collection of furniture from different periods. The floor was covered with large black and white flagstones with a brightly colored carpet in the middle. On the white walls hung antique china plates, delicate watercolors and a magnificent Louis XVI mirror, which lent a note of gaiety. The visitor crossed the hall into the courtyard where there were two enormous lime trees. As soon as the fine weather came, the family spent most of their time under these trees. It was hard to imagine a more peaceful place. With its stone columns and borders of lilac bushes and privet hedges, the courtyard opened out on to a long lawn sloping down to the terrace that had a view over the countryside. To the right, there was a little wood, a flower garden and then the vineyards, stretching around the château as far as the eye could see.

Pierre Delmas had learned to love his land and now he adored it almost as much as his daughters. He was a passionate and sensitive man. His father had died very young, leaving him in charge of Montillac. His brothers and sisters had no interest in the estate, as it was too far from Bordeaux and yielded too little revenue. Pierre, however, was determined to make a success of it. In order to buy out his brothers' share of the inheritance, he had borrowed money from a friend, Raymond d'Argilat, a rich landowner near St. Emilion. That is how, though he failed to become the master of a cargo ship, second only to God, he became sole master of Montillac.

Chapter 1

August was drawing to a close. Léa, the second of Pierre Delmas's three daughters, had just turned seventeen. She was sitting on the low terrace wall at Montillac, looking out over the plains through half-closed eyes. Swinging her bare, suntanned legs, she could feel the warmth of the stone through her flimsy white cotton dress. She inhaled the fragrance of pine trees borne on the sea breeze, and delighted in the sensual pleasure of being alive. She sighed with contentment and stretched slowly, sinuously, like her cat Mona awakening in the sun.

Like her father, Léa loved the estate. She knew its every nook and cranny. As a child, she and her cousins played hide-and-seek among the rows of barrels and piles of wood. Her inseparable playmate had always been Mathias Fayard, the head storeman's son, who was three years her senior. He was utterly devoted to her and gave in to her slightest whim. Léa's curly hair was always tangled, her knees always scratched. Her face was almost engulfed by her enormous violet eyes hiding behind long black lashes. Her favorite game was putting Mathias to the test. On her fourteenth birthday, she challenged him, "Show me how to make love."

Mathias, beside himself with joy, took her in his arms and covered her pretty face with kisses as she lay back in the hay. Through half-closed eyes, she watched every movement the boy made. When he fumbled to unbutton her delicate white blouse, she wriggled to make it easier for him. Then, with a gesture of belated modesty, she covered her budding breasts while she felt a strange new feeling welling up in her.

They heard Pierre Delmas's voice booming in one of the outhouses nearby. Mathias stopped in mid-caress.

"Don't stop," murmured Léa, clasping Mathias's curly head to her.

"Your father!"

"So what, you're not afraid, are you?" she retorted.

"No, but if he caught us, I'd be ashamed."

"Ashamed? Why? We're not doing anything wrong."

"You know very well, your parents have always been very good to mine—and to me."

"But since you love me . . . "

He gazed at her for a long time. How beautiful she was like that, her tousled golden hair studded with tiny dried flowers and bits of grass. Her eyes were shining and her parted lips showed perfect little white teeth. He wanted to caress her young breasts with their hard little nipples.

Mathias reached out and then withdrew his hand. He said, as if to himself, "No, it would be wrong. Not like this." Then, he added, in a firmer tone, "Yes, I love you, and that's why I don't want to . . . You're the young lady of the manor and I'm only . . . "

He drew away and went down the ladder.

"Mathias . . . "

He did not answer and she heard the barn door close behind him.

"What an idiot!"

She buttoned up her blouse and fell asleep until evening when she was awakened by the dinner bell.

Perched on her wall, Léa was anticipating the following day's events. The thought of it filled her with joyous excitement: Monsieur d'Argilat was giving a garden party at his home, Roches-Blanches, to celebrate the twenty-fourth birthday of his son Laurent. After the picnic, there would be a ball, then dinner, then fireworks.

"It's going to be magnificent!" Léa murmured. "If I can only decide what dress to wear."

Léa enjoyed being seductive. But she really didn't have to make any effort. Her charm worked almost without her being aware of it; the choice of the dress mattered little.

"She's irresistible," the boys would say. "When she looks at us through half-closed eyes, we just want to take her in our arms."

"She's a tease," replied the girls. "As soon as she sees a man is interested in someone else, she starts making eyes at him."

"Perhaps, but you can talk about anything to Léa: horses, pine trees, the vineyards and lots of other things."

"She's a peasant. She behaves like a tomboy, not at all like a well-brought-up young lady. No young lady should go and watch cows calving and horses mating, especially not in the company of men and servants; nor should she be getting up in the middle of the night to look at the moon, with her dog. Her mother is at the end of her tether. Léa was expelled from school for misbehaving. She ought to follow her sister Sabine's example. Now there's a young lady who behaves as she should."

"But she's so boring. All she can think about is music and clothes. . . ."

As a matter of fact, Lea's power over men was absolute. None could resist her. Young and old alike, peasant or landowner, they succumbed to her charms. They would do anything for one of her smiles, and not least her father.

When she got into trouble, she would go into his study, sit on his knee and snuggle up to him. When she did that, Pierre Delmas's happiness knew no bounds and he would close his eyes to savor it all the more.

In addition to the pleasure it gave Léa to think about the garden party itself, there was another deeper and more secret pleasure: that of spending a whole day in Laurent d'Argilat's company. Laurent . . . merely saying his name made her feel excited, confused, happy. She loved him so much! And he, of course, was too reserved to say so, but he loved her too, that was obvious: just the other day, she had seen the way he looked at her and took her hand. . . .

13

In the distance, the clock struck five, at Langon or Saint-Macaire, interrupting Léa's daydream. An idea suddenly went through her mind. Her father had spent the day with the d'Argilats and would be home soon. If she hurried a little, she could meet him on the way and make him tell her about the preparations for tomorrow's party.

Pleased with this idea, she jumped down from her perch and set off, running and leaping like a young animal. As she had expected, she soon encountered her father.

"You're running as though the devil were after you. Have you quarrelled with your sisters again? Look at you, your face is all red and your hair's a mess."

Léa smiled and took her father's arm. Laying her head on his shoulder, she said in a cajoling voice:

"I'm so happy to see you, Papa darling, I was just going to come and meet you. It's such a lovely day, isn't it?"

A little taken aback by her chatter, Pierre Delmas held his daughter tight and surveyed the vine-covered slopes. The straight rows gave an impression of order and perfect calm. He sighed: "Yes, a lovely day. A day of peace; perhaps the last."

Without thinking Léa replied: "The last? But why? Summer isn't over and autumn is always the best season at Montillac."

Pierre Delmas let go of Léa and said dreamily: "Yes, it's the best season, but I am surprised you are so unconcerned. All around you war is approaching and you . . . "

"War! War!" she cut in passionately, "I'm fed up with hearing about war. . . . Hitler isn't crazy enough to declare war on Poland. And even if he does, what does it have to do with us? Let the Poles take care of themselves!"

"Be quiet! You don't know what you're talking about," he cried, grabbing her by the arm. "Don't ever let me hear you say things like that again. There's an alliance between our two countries. Neither England nor France can get out of it."

"The Russians are allied with the Germans."

"To their shame, and one day Stalin will realize that he's been made a fool of."

"But what about Neville Chamberlain?"

"Chamberlain will do the honorable thing. He'll reconfirm his wish to maintain the Anglo-Polish treaty."

"And then?"

"Then? War. We'll have no choice."

A heavy silence full of images of war fell between father and daughter. Léa broke it first: "But Laurent d'Argilat says that we're not ready, that our weapons are left over from the Great War, that they're museum pieces and our air force is useless, our heavy artillery pathetic. . . ."

"For someone who doesn't want to listen to war talk, I see that you're remarkably well informed about our military strength. And what do you have to say about the courage of our soldiers?"

"Laurent says that the French don't want to fight . . ."

"But they're going to have to. . . ."

" . . . and they'll be killed for nothing, in a war that's not their war."

"They'll die for freedom. . . ."

"Freedom! What good is freedom if you're dead? I don't want to die; I don't want Laurent to die."

She stifled a sob and looked away so that her father wouldn't see her tears. But he was so shaken by his daughter's words that he didn't notice them.

"If you were a man, Léa, I'd say you were a coward."

"I'm sorry, Papa. Forgive me. I've upset you. But I'm so afraid—"

"—We're all afraid . . ."

"Laurent isn't. He says he'll do his duty even though he's certain we'll be beaten."

"The same defeatist attitude as his father at Roches-Blanches this afternoon."

"Were you at Roches-Blanches?"

"Yes."

Léa took her father's hand in hers and pulled him along, then turned to him with her most irresistible smile.

"Come on, let's go back, or else we'll be late and Mother will be worried."

"You're right," he said, returning her smile.

They stopped at Bellevue to say hello to Sidonie who had just finished her supper and was sitting outside her house enjoying the evening air.

Sidonie was the former cook at the château; illness, more than age, forced her to stop working. To thank her for her services, Pierre Delmas had given her this cottage overlooking the whole region. Léa often came to sit and chat with the old woman, who always offered her a glass of her special homemade blackcurrant liqueur. She was extremely proud of her concoction and would eagerly await Léa's praise. She was never disappointed, even though Léa loathed blackcurrant.

"How are you, Sidonie?"

"Things could be worse, sir. As long as it's fine, the sun warms my old bones. And in a place like this, Monsieur, how can a soul be discontented?"

With a wide sweep of her arm, she indicated the magnificent countryside. On a fine day, she said, she could see the Pyrenees. The setting sun made the green vines shimmer and the dusty roads glow like gold. The roof-tiles gleamed in the light and a deceptive aura of peace enveloped everything.

"Why don't you come inside and have a drop of . . . "

The sound of the dinner-gong reached them, enabling them to get out of sampling the dreaded blackcurrant liqueur.

While they were walking back, arm in arm, Léa asked her father: "What did you and Monsieur d'Argilat talk about, apart from the war? Did you talk about tomorrow's party?"

Hoping to take his daughter's mind off their earlier conversation, Pierre Delmas replied: "It'll be a fine party; the finest party in these parts for a long time. I'll even let you into a secret, if you promise not to tell your sisters, who can't keep their mouths shut."

Léa's legs felt suddenly heavy. She slowed her step.

"A secret?"

"Tomorrow, Monsieur d'Argilat is going to announce the date of his son's wedding. Don't you want to know who he's going to marry?"

"Who?" she managed to ask.

"His cousin, Camille d'Argilat. Not that it comes as a surprise to any of us: they've been engaged since they were children. But with the rumors of war, Camille wanted to bring the wedding forward. Whatever's the matter?'' Pierre Delmas supported his daughter who seemed about to fall. "You've gone quite pale, my darling. What's the matter? You're not ill, are you? Is it because of Laurent's marriage? You're not in love with him, are you?''

"Yes. I love him, and he loves me!''

Stunned, he led Léa to a little seat by the edge of the path, made her sit down, and sat down beside her.

"What makes you think that? He can't have told you he loves you, because he's always known that he must marry his cousin. What makes you think he loves you?''

"I just know he does, that's all.''

"That's all!''

"He can't possibly marry that stupid cousin of his!''

Pierre Delmas looked at his daughter first sadly, then angrily. "First of all, Camille d'Argilat isn't stupid, she's a charming girl, very well brought up and well educated. She's just the type of wife Laurent needs . . . ''

"I'm sure she isn't.''

"Laurent has very strict principles; a young girl like you would quickly be bored with him.''

"I love him. I'm going to tell him . . . ''

"You will do nothing of the kind. I won't have my daughter throwing herself at the feet of a man who loves another woman.''

"It's not true. He loves *me*.''

Seeing his child's grief-stricken expression, Pierre wavered for a moment, and then retorted: "He does not love you. It was Laurent himself who told me how happy he was to be getting married.''

The cry which burst from his daughter's lips went through him like a dagger. His Léa, who was still a baby not so long ago, who came and snuggled under the bedclothes when she was afraid of the wolf in dear old Ruth's fairy stories, his Léa was in love.

"Please, my pet, don't cry, poppet.''

"Papa . . . oh Papa!''

"There, there . . . It's all right. Dry your eyes. If your mother sees you in this state, she'll be worried sick. Promise me you'll be sensible. You'll only make yourself look silly if you tell Laurent you love him. You must forget him."

"No, it isn't possible! It's not true!" she repeated to herself bitterly. Anyway, Camille was much too ugly for Laurent. She always looked so melancholy. How boring it must be to live with someone like her, with her delicate health and her meek ways. No, Laurent couldn't possibly be in love with Camille.

He must be in love with her. Not with that scarecrow who couldn't even sit on a horse properly or stay up all night dancing. . . . He loved her, Léa was certain. She had noticed how he held onto her hand, how he tried to catch her eye. . . . Only yesterday, on the beach, she had flung her head back. . . . She sensed how he was dying to kiss her. He hadn't, of course. . . . They were such a bore, these well-brought-up young men, they'd never touch you! No, Laurent couldn't possibly love Camille.

Léa was not listening to her father. An idea was slowly forming in her troubled mind. She took the handkerchief her father held out to her, and blew her nose noisily, "not at all in a lady-like manner," as Sabine would have said, and looked up at him with a blotchy but smiling face.

"You're right, Papa, I'll forget him."

Pierre Delmas's astonishment was so comical that Léa burst out laughing.

"I really don't understand women at all," he said to himself, feeling as though a great weight had been taken off his shoulders.

The second dinner gong made them quicken their pace.

Léa hurried up to her room, glad to have escaped Ruth's scrutiny. She splashed cold water on her face and brushed her hair. She examined her reflection in the mirror. "Not too much damage done," she thought. Her eyes seemed slightly brighter than usual. . . .

Chapter 2

Pleading a migraine, Léa stayed behind while the rest of the family went on their usual after-dinner walk. Ruth had made a fuss over her and her anxious mother had sat and stroked her forehead. They had all agreed that she seemed feverish. Léa sought refuge in what they still affectionately called "the children's room."

It was a large room in the oldest wing of the house, where the servants' quarters and the storerooms were. "The children's room" was a vast junkroom piled high with wicker hampers full of old-fashioned clothes. These had been an endless source of entertainment on rainy days, when the young Delmas girls loved to play at dressing up. There were grotesque dressmaker's dummies with large busts and exaggerated curves; and trunks overflowing with musty books— mainly school prizes won by Pierre Delmas and his brothers. It was from these often quite fascinating books that Léa and her sisters had learned to read.

This room, with its heavy wooden beams and its high windows, was another of Léa's hideouts. The floor of worn and cracked tiles was covered with old faded carpets, and it was no longer possible to make out the pattern on the discolored wallpaper.

There, among the broken toys of her childhood, she would snuggle up in the high iron bed which had been hers as a child. She would read, dream and cry, cuddling her favorite old doll, or curl up and sleep with her knees drawn up under her chin, hoping to sink into blissful oblivion like the happy, peaceful child of years ago.

The glow of the setting sun cast a feeble light over the room, leaving dark nooks and crannies. Léa, sitting up in bed clasping her knees and frowning, stared blankly at the portrait of some remote ancestor. It seemed to melt into the shadows. How long had she been in love with Laurent d'Argilat? Forever. No, that wasn't true: last year, she had not even noticed him, nor he her. It was this year that it had all begun, during the Easter holidays, when he had come to visit his ailing father. As on every visit, he had made a point of coming to pay his respects to Monsieur and Madame Delmas.

That day, she had been alone in the little drawing room, absorbed in François Mauriac's latest novel. The writer was their closest neighbor. She was so engrossed in the book that she did not hear the door open. The cool early spring air with its strong smell of wet earth made her shiver slightly and look up. She was surprised to see a tall, handsome fair-haired man looking at her with such obvious admiration that she felt a tingle of pleasure. He was dressed in a riding habit and holding, in his gloved hands, his hat and whip. In her confusion, she did not recognize him immediately. She could feel her heart beating faster. He smiled. Suddenly realizing who he was, she leaped up and flung herself round his neck, like a child.

"Laurent!"

"Léa?"

"Yes, of course it's me."

"Is it posible? Last time I saw you, you were a child— your dress was torn, your hair was a mess, your legs were covered in scratches and . . . now . . . I behold a ravishing young lady, who is elegant" (he made her turn around so he could admire her better) "with a sophisticated hair-style." (That day, she had allowed Ruth to take over her unruly curls and twist them into graceful ringlets which made her look like a medieval lady of the manor.)

"So, how do you like me?"

"Words fail me."

She fluttered her large violet eyes seductively. She had

already been told many times that it made her look irresistible.

"I can't take my eyes off you. How old are you?"

"I'll be seventeen in August."

"My cousin Camille is two years older than you."

Why did she feel so annoyed on hearing that name? She knew Laurent's relatives well and it was only polite to ask after them, but she could not bear to utter Camille's name.

Laurent d'Argilat asked after her parents and her sisters. She did not hear his questions, replying yes or no at random, listening only to the sound of his voice, which sent a thrill rippling through her.

Surprised, he stopped talking and gazed at her. Léa was convinced that he would have taken her in his arms—if her mother and sisters had not suddenly come into the room.

"Look! Laurent is here! Léa, why didn't you call us?"

The young man kissed Madame Delmas's outstretched hand.

"Léa has grown up to be as beautiful as her mother," he said as he looked up.

"Hush. You mustn't keep telling Léa she's beautiful. She's vain enough as it is."

"What about us?" chorused Sabine and Laure.

Laurent opened his arms to embrace them in an affectionate hug. "Everyone knows that the ladies of Montillac are the most beautiful women for miles around."

Madame Delmas invited Laurent to stay to dinner. Léa remained entranced even when he was droning on about the likelihood of war. When he left, he kissed her on the cheek, longer, she was sure, than her sisters. For a split second she closed her eyes. When she opened them again, she caught Sabine looking at her with spiteful disbelief. On the staircase going up to bed, her sister murmured: "You won't get your claws into him!"

Léa was so absorbed in her delightful memories that she did not even retort, and this surprised Sabine more than anything else.

A tear ran down Léa's cheek. By now, it was completely dark.

The house had been deathly silent until then, but suddenly it rang with the voices of her family back from their walk. Léa could picture her father going over to light the fire to ward off the evening damp, and then sinking into his armchair with his feet on the fender, to read the newspaper. Her mother would be working at her tapestry, her beautiful gentle face glowing in the soft light under the pink silk lampshade. Ruth, sitting nearby, would be finishing off a hem on their dresses for tomorrow's party. Laure was probable playing with a jigsaw puzzle or with one of those miniature dolls she so loved. The opening bars of a Chopin waltz floated up: Sabine was playing the piano. Léa loved to listen to her sister play. She admired her talent although she would never dream of telling her so.

Sometimes, this cozy family scene irritated her, but tonight, alone in the cold, dark children's room, she longed to be a part of it.

She would have liked, without having to move, to be sitting at her mother's feet on the little stool that was reserved for her alone. With her head in her mother's lap, she never tired of watching the flames, while dreaming of love and glory. Better still, she liked to look through the old family photo albums that were her mother's most treasured possession.

Since the beginning of summer, Laurent had come to Montillac almost every day. Together, they would gallop through the vineyards or go for a drive in the surrounding countryside in his brand-new convertible. They sped along the relentlessly straight roads of the Landes, Léa, with her head flung back, never weary of the soaring pine tops as they flew past against a postcard blue sky.

They were rarely alone on these excursions, but she was certain that the others were there only for the sake of appearances, and she was grateful to Laurent for not having the clumsy eagerness of some of her beaux. He, at least, could talk of things other than hunting, vineyards, forests and horses. She forgot that, before seeing him again, she had always loathed his subtle commentaries on

English and American novelists. To please him, she read Conrad, Faulkner and Fitzgerald in English, which was quite an ordeal, for she could not read English very well. She, who was usually so impatient, even put up with his bouts of melancholy each time he mentioned the inevitability of war.

"So many men are going to die because of a miserable second-class house painter," he would say sadly.

She made allowances for all the things she would not tolerate in others, to be rewarded by a smile, a loving look or a gentle squeeze of the hand.

"Léa, are you there?"

The door opened, casting an oblong of light into the dark room. Léa jumped when she heard her mother's voice. She sat up and the little bed creaked.

"Yes, Mummy."

"What are you doing in the dark?"

"I was thinking."

The harsh light from the naked bulb hurt her eyes. She hid her face in the crook of her arm.

"Switch off the light, please, Mummy."

Isabelle Delmas obeyed and came into the room, stepping over a pile of books. She sat down beside the bed on a broken old prayer-stool and ruffled her daughters tousled hair.

"Tell me what's wrong, darling."

Léa felt a great flood of tears well up inside her and a burning desire to confide her troubles. But knowing her mother had strict opinions on these matters, she resisted the temptation of confessing her love for a man who was betrothed to another. Not for all the world did Léa want to hurt this slightly distant woman whom she admired, worshipped and passionately wanted to resemble.

"Tell me, darling. Don't look at me like a frightened rabbit."

Léa tried to smile and talk about tomorrow's party and her new dress, but a lump came into her throat and she threw her arms round her mother's neck, sobbing and hiccuping:

"I'm so scared of war!"

Chapter 3

Early the next morning, the house rang with the cries, laughter and the bustle of the three sisters. Ruth did not know which way to turn with her three "little ones" making continuous demands. She was everywhere at once, looking for bags, hats and shoes.

"Hurry up, your uncles and cousins are here."

Indeed, three limousines had just drawn up outside. Luc Delmas, Pierre's elder brother, a renowned Bordeaux lawyer, had arrived with his three youngest children, Philippe, Corinne and Pierre. Léa was not particularly fond of them: she found them snobbish and sneaky, except for Pierre, nicknamed Pierrot to distinguish him from his godfather, for he showed signs of turning out to be quite different. By the age of twelve, he had been expelled from all the religious establishments of Bordeaux for insolence and impiety, and now went to a lay school, much to his father's dissatisfaction.

Bernadette Bouchardeau, Pierre's sister, lavished all her affection on her only child, Lucien, born shortly after the death of her husband, who had been a colonel. At eighteen, the boy had had enough of his mother's doting and was looking for the first opportunity to get away.

Adrien Delmas, a Dominican Friar, "the family conscience," was always teasing his brother Pierre. Of all the nieces and nephews, Léa was the only one who wasn't afraid of the monk, a huge man whose long white habit made him look even more impressive. He was an outstanding preacher and often travelled abroad. He corresponded regularly with religious personalities of all faiths and spoke several languages.

Father Adrien was considered a revolutionary among the Bordeaux gentry, and by his own family. Had he not sheltered Spanish refugees, men who had raped nuns and desecrated graves, then fled their country after the fall of Barcelona? Was he not a friend of the socialist writer George Orwell, whom he had found injured in Spain, wandering from café to café in the torrid heat and sleeping in derelict houses? When he managed to slip into France, it was Adrien who took him in. He was the only one of the brothers to have condemned the Munich Pact as iniquitous, and to foresee that this cowardice would not stop the war. Only Monsieur d'Argilat agreed with him.

Raymond d'Argilat and Adrien Delmas had been friends for a long time. They both liked Chamfort, Rousseau, Chateaubriand, Stendhal and Shakespeare, but differed over Zola, Gide and Mauriac. Their literary arguments would go on for hours. When Father Adrien visited Roches-Blanches, the servants used to say: "Look, here comes the good father with his Zola again. He should know by now that Monsieur doesn't like him."

Léa was the only one of the young girls wearing a dark-colored outfit, which was rather out of place on such a summery day.

She had pleaded with her mother at length to let her have this heavy black silk dress with tiny red flowers. It emphasized her slim waist, her round breasts and her curvaceous hips. She wore high-heeled red leather sandals, no stockings, and a black straw hat decorated with a little posy of flowers to match her shoes, set at a saucy angle over her eye. Her handbag was also red.

The Lefèvre brothers, Raoul and Jean, were naturally the first to rush over. It was no secret that they were both in love with Léa. Aged twenty and twenty-one, they were uncommonly strong. At school in Bordeaux, their total indifference to any form of education made them the despair of their teachers. They eventually managed to pass their exams—only to please their mother, Amelie, they said. But according to others, it was more likely to avoid being whipped, for their impetuous mother frequently did just that to her unruly offspring. Widowed at a young age with six children to bring up, the youngest of whom was only two, she took over her husband's vineyards and ran them with a firm hand.

Lucien Bouchardeau came over to embrace her next, and then whispered to Jean: "Our cousin's rather good-looking, isn't she?"

Philippe Delmas came up and blushingly embraced her. Léa quickly turned away to greet Pierrot, who flung his arms round her, knocking her hat askew.

"Pierrot, I am so happy to see you," she said, returning his kisses.

The Dominican, in his white robes, waded through the crowd of admirers and finally managed to reach Léa.

"Can I get through so I can embrace my goddaughter!"

"Oh, Uncle Adrien, you're here. I'm so pleased. But what's wrong, you look worried?"

"It's nothing, pet, it's nothing. How you've grown up. It doesn't seem long since your christening! Now it's time to find you a husband. I get the impression there are plenty of candidates!"

"Oh, uncle," she protested, adjusting her hat.

"Come on, hurry up, or we'll be late. All aboard," cried Pierre Delmas with forced heartiness.

Slowly, they made their way out to the cars. Léa wanted to drive with her godfather, to the great disappointment of the Lefèvre brothers, who had polished their old coupe in her honor.

"You go on ahead with your old wreck. We'll meet up at Roches-Blanches. Can I drive, Uncle?"

"Do you know how?"

"Yes, but don't tell Mummy. Papa lets me drive sometimes, and he's teaching me the traffic rules. That's the hardest part. I hope to take my test soon."

"But you're much too young!"

"Papa says it can be arranged."

"I'd be very surprised. Anyway, show me what you can do."

Lucien, Philippe and Pierrot went with them. Hitching up his white robes, the monk got in last after giving a few turns to the motor with the starting handle.

"What in the name of . . . "

Léa had pulled away rather abruptly.

"Sorry, Uncle, I'm not used to your car."

After shaking up her passengers with a jerky start, Léa managed to control the vehicle.

They arrived at Roches-Blanches well after the others. A long avenue of oak trees led to the elegant eighteenth-century château, which was quite distinct from the neighboring neo-gothic style château built in the late nineteenth century. Laurent and his father were very fond of this residence, which they maintained and improved devotedly.

When Léa got out of the car, her wrap-over skirt fell open, displaying a large expanse of thigh. Raoul and Jean Lefèvre could not help letting out an admiring wolf-whistle but were quickly silenced by the indignant expressions on the ladies' faces.

A servant took over the wheel and drove the car round to the rear courtyard.

As they all made their way towards the master of the house, Léa sought only one face among the dense crowd that was now gathered in front of the house: Laurent.

"Léa, at last. No party would be complete without your lovely smile," said Raymond d'Argilat affectionately.

"Good-day, monsieur. Is Laurent here?"

"Of course he is. The party is in his honor! He's showing Camille the improvements we've had done."

Léa shuddered. The sunshine went from this beautiful September day. Pierre Delmas noticed his daughter's sudden change of attitude. He took her arm and led her aside.

"Please, Léa, no scenes, no tears. I don't want my daughter to make a spectacle of herself."

Léa fought back her tears.

"It's nothing, Papa. I'm just a little tired. I'll be all right when I've had something to eat."

27

Taking off her hat, she joined her male admirers with her head held high. They were standing in front of a large table covered with refreshments: She smiled at their comments and laughed at their jokes while drinking a delicious Chateau d'Yquem, but all the time one little phrase was going round and round in her head: "He's with Camille."

It promised to be a splendid party. The sun was shining in a cloudless azure sky and the lawns, which had been watered at dawn, were a rich green. The smell of freshly cut grass mingled with the fragrance of the roses. There was a big white marquee under which a lavish buffet was served by waiters in white jackets. The lawn was dotted with tables and garden chairs under the shade of parasols. The women's pastel dresses, their fluttering and their laughter, lent a frivolous note to the occasion which contrasted sharply with the long faces of some of the men. Even Laurent d'Argilat, in whose honor all these people had gathered, seemed to Léa pale and tense when he finally appeared. Holding his arm was a young girl dressed in a plain white dress, whose gentle face was radiant with happiness. All the guests applauded their arrival, except Léa who chose that moment to tidy her hair.

Raymond d'Argilat indicated that he wished to speak.

"Dear friends, we are gathered here this first of September 1939 to celebrate my son Laurent's birthday and his engagement to his cousin Camille."

The clapping became even louder.

"Thank you, my friends, thank you, all of you for coming here. It is a pleasure to welcome you to my home. Eat, drink and be merry on this festive occasion."

At this point, Monsieur d'Argilat's voice became choked with emotion. His son stepped forward, all smiles and said: "Let the fun begin!"

Léa was sitting apart from her group of admirers. They all wanted the honor of serving her. Soon, she had enough food in front of her to keep her happy for several days. She laughed, chatted and smiled all the more under the mournful gaze of other girls who had no suitors. She had never appeared more lighthearted. But the least smile hurt her jaw, and in her fury she dug her nails into her moist palms, this new pain appeasing the one which was breaking her heart. She thought she would die when she caught sight of Laurent coming towards her group with Camille, still looking radiant, clinging to his arm. Camille's brother was not far behind.

"Hello, Léa, I haven't had a chance to say hello," said Laurent, bowing his head. "Do you remember Léa, Camille?"

"Of course I do," she said, letting go of her fiancé's arm, "How could I forget her?"

Léa got to her feet and glared at this rival whom she deemed unworthy of her. She stiffened when Camille kissed her on both cheeks.

"Laurent has told me so much about you. I'd like us to be friends."

She did not seem to notice Léa's reluctance to return her kisses. Then Camille pushed her brother forward. He was a young, shy-looking man.

"Do you remember my brother Claude? He's been dying to see you again."

How he resembled his sister!

"Come, darling, let's not neglect our other guests," said Laurent, leading his fiancée away.

Léa watched them, feeling such a strong sense of desertion that she had great difficulty in restraining her tears.

"May I join you?" asked Claude.

"Make room for him," snapped Léa, pushing Raoul Lefèvre who was seated beside her.

Surprised and hurt, Raoul went over to his brother. "Don't you think Léa's behaving oddly today?"

Jean shrugged and said nothing.

Léa offered Claude a plate piled high with hors d'oeuvres. "Here, I haven't touched it."

Claude sat down and took the plate. As he thanked her, he blushed scarlet.

"Are you going to be staying at Roches-Blanches for a while?" asked Léa listlessly.

"I shouldn't think so, with things the way they are . . . "

Léa was not listening. She was obsessed by one thought, one desire: to find Laurent, speak to him, and find out why, when he loved her, he had made this absurd decision that would tear them apart. Unable to remain sitting with the others any longer, she stood up and headed in the direction of what was known as the little wood. Claude d'Argilat and Jean Lefèvre leaped up to follow her. They were brushed aside in no uncertain terms.

"Leave me alone. I want to be alone."

They returned sheepishly to their table and rejoined the other guests.

"Do you think we're going to fight?" Raoul Lefèvre asked Alain de Russay. Being a few years older than the others, he seemed the person most likely to have an intelligent answer.

"There's no doubt about it. You heard what they said on the radio last night: the immediate handing over of Danzig to Germany, which was the ultimatum delivered to the Poles after Hitler's proposals to the Polish ambassador, expired on the 30th of August. Today is the first of September. At this very moment, you can be sure that Danzig has been proclaimed part of the Reich, and that Germany has invaded Poland."

"So, it's war?" said Jean Lefèvre in a voice that had suddenly grown older.

"Yes, it's war."

"Good, we're going to fight," crowed Lucien Bouchardeau.

"Yes, and we'll win," declared Raoul Lefèvre with childlike fervor.

"Each side always thinks it will win," Philippe Delmas said wearily.

Léa ran across the field that led to the little wood. There, under the shade of the trees, you could see the entire Argilat estate. It was good land, the soil was richer and better exposed than Montillac, yielding a better quality wine. Léa had always loved Roches-Blanches.

She surveyed these fields, vineyards and woods with a proprietorial eye.

No, nobody could understand and cherish this land better than she, apart from her father and Monsieur d'Argilat . . . and of course Laurent. Laurent . . . he loved her, there wasn't the slightest doubt about that. Then what was he doing with the scarecrow? She was so plain, so badly dressed, so awkward, as if she had just left school. And her hair-style—how could anyone wear her hair like that in this day and age? Braids wound round her head! It made her look quite Germanic, hardly suitable in these times of patriotic fervor. And that false sweetness: "I'd like us to be friends." Whatever next! No, decidedly not, Laurent could not be in love with that insipid creature! It was sheer gallantry that made him feel bound to honor a promise made when he was still in the cradle. But she, Léa, would be able to convince him to break off this ridiculous engagement and elope with her.

Léa was so wrapped up in her daydreams that she had not noticed a man leaning against a tree who was watching her with an amused smile.

Whew, she felt better! There was nothing like a bit of solitude and reflection for clearing one's head. Now she was happy. Everything would turn out the way she wanted it. She stood up and thumped her right fist on her left palm, a gesture she had learned from her father, a gesture he made when he had just taken a decision.

"I'll have him!"

A peal of laughter made her jump.

"I'm sure you will," said an ironical voice.

"You startled me. Who are you?"

"A friend of Monsieur d'Argilat's."

"You don't look like a friend of his. Oh! I'm sorry . . . "

He burst out laughing again. He was almost handsome when he laughed, thought Léa.

"Don't apologize, you're quite right. The highly respectable d'Argilats and your humble servant don't have a great deal in common. Besides, I would find their company too boring."

"How can you say such a thing? They are the most elegant and cultured men in these parts!"

"That's precisely what I meant."

Léa looked at the man with curiosity. It was the first time she had heard anybody speak of the owners of Roches-Blanches in such an off-hand way. He was very tall with carefully combed brown hair, insolent blue eyes which were enhanced by his tan, although his face was hardly handsome. He had strong features, full lips and even teeth. He was chewing a twisted cigar, which gave off a terrible smell. His beautifully cut pale-gray suit with white pinstripes contrasted sharply with his weatherbeaten look and that frightful cigar.

Léa waved her hand as if to clear the air of the sickening smell.

"Perhaps you object to my cigar? It's a bad habit I picked up in Spain. Now that I'm back in Bordeaux society, I'm going to have to get used to Havanas again," he said, carefully stamping it out. "It's true that with war on the way there's likely to be a shortage."

"War, war . . . haven't you men got anything else to talk about? Why should we go to war? I'm tired of hearing about it."

The man smiled at her as if she were a spoiled child. "You're right, I'm a bore to bother such a delightful young lady with such trivial matters. Let's talk about you instead. Are you engaged? No? A sweetheart, then? Not even that? I don't believe you. Earlier on, I saw you surrounded by a crowd of charming young men who all seemed enchanted by you, except for the lucky fiancé, of course . . . "

Léa, who had sat down again, leaped to her feet. "I'm tired, monsieur, I want to go back to my friends."

He made an exaggerated mock bow which infuriated Léa. "I shan't keep you any longer. I should hate to impose my presence on you or keep you from your suitors."

Léa walked straight past him without another word.

The man seated himself, took a cigar from a brown leather case, bit off the end and spat it out; as he lit it, he thoughtfully watched the pretty figure of the funny little girl who didn't like war walk off into the distance.

The musicians were beginning to set up their instruments under the trees, while the young guests looked on with interest.

Léa's return was greeted with shouts from her friends.

"Where were you? We looked all over for you."

"It wasn't very nice of you to sneak away like that."

"Yes, but Léa prefers the company of older, rather shady men to that of young people from good families," said her cousin Corinne.

Léa's eyebrows betrayed her astonishment. "Who do you mean?"

"You're not going to pretend that you don't know François Tavernier—you were cooing at him in the little wood."

Léa shrugged and looked at the girl pityingly. "I met the gentleman for the first time today, and have just learned his name. As far as I'm concerned, you're welcome to him. What can I say? It's not my fault men prefer me to you."

"Especially that kind of man."

"I've had enough of this! He can't be as awful as you make out since he's a guest of Monsieur d'Argilat's."

"I think Léa must be right. If Monsieur d'Argilat has invited Monsieur Tavernier, it's because he deserves to be invited," said Jean Lefèvre, coming to his friend's defense.

"They say he's a gun-runner and that he's sold tons of arms to the Spanish Republicans," muttered Lucien Bouchardeau.

"To the Republicans!" exclaimed Corinne Delmas, her eyes wide open with horror.

"So? They had to have arms to fight with, didn't they?" said Léa irritably.

Just then her eyes met those of her uncle, Father Adrien. He seemed to be watching her with a smile of approval.

"How can you say such a thing?" cried Corinne. "Monsters who rape nuns, dig up corpses, kill and torture?"

"What about the others, didn't they kill and torture?"

"But they're Communists, atheists . . . "

"So what? Don't they have a right to live?"

"How can you say such terrible things? You're a Delmas; your whole family prayed for Franco."

"Perhaps we were wrong."

"You shouldn't be worrying your pretty head about such things," said Adrien Delmas, stepping forward. "Don't you think you'd be better off getting ready for the dance? The orchestra is ready."

The group of young people surrounding Léa swooped on to the dance floor like a flock of doves. Léa stayed where she was.

"Who is François Tavernier?"

The Dominican looked surprised and embarrassed by her question.

"I'm not too sure. He comes from a wealthy family but they say he ran away because they disagreed over politics, and there was a woman involved."

"Is it true, this gun-running story?"

"I have no idea. He's very discreet. If it is true, then he's done something to save France's honor. We didn't behave very well over the Spanish Civil War."

"Uncle, how can you, a priest, talk like that? Didn't the Pope support Franco?"

"Yes, yes, but the Pope can make a mistake."

"Uncle, now you're going too far," laughed Léa, "I thought the Pope was infallible."

It was Adrien Delmas's turn to laugh. "You're a sly one! And I thought you weren't interested in all that nonsense, as you call it."

Léa took her uncle's arm and led him slowly towards the dance-floor from which the strains of a lively fox trot reached them.

"That's what I tell the others, because if they had their way, that's all they'd talk about. And as they don't know what they're talking about, I'd rather they kept off the subject. But in fact, I'm very interested in it. I read all the papers in secret, I listen to the radio, especially the BBC . . . "

"Did you listen this morning?"

"No, what with the picnic, I didn't have time."

"Léa, there you are at last! Aren't you coming? You will dance with me, won't you?" said Raoul Lefèvre.

"And me," his brother chipped in.

Léa reluctantly let go of her uncle's arm and allowed them to drag her on to the dance floor. Adrien Delmas turned around. Nearby, François Tavernier, smoking his twisted cigar, was watching Léa dance.

For nearly an hour, Léa did not miss a single dance, all the while seeking out Laurent. Wherever could he be? She saw Camille alone with Sabine. She must take advantage of the situation. Her dancing partner, Claude d'Argilat, was becoming more enamored of her every second. In the middle of a waltz, Léa suddenly faltered.

"Léa, what's the matter?"

"It's nothing. I'm just a little giddy. I feel rather tired. Would you take me somewhere quiet and fetch me a glass of water."

Claude hurried her away from the noise to the shade of a large tree, halfway between the house and the dancing. He settled her on a grassy bank with tender care.

"Don't move, just rest there. I'll be back right away."

As soon as he had gone, Léa jumped to her feet and ran towards the house. She went into the greenhouse, the pride and joy of Roches-Blanches. The humidity made her skin feel clammy. The blaring music was now only a faint noise in the background. The most exotic plants clambered across the floor, up towards the glass dome. A stone path twisted among the flower beds and ended up in an artificial grotto with clusters of orchids hanging from the walls. A door led into the château hall. Léa pushed it open. She could hear her father's voice coming from the main drawing room, and those of Uncle Adrien and Monsieur d'Argilat. She listened: it didn't sound as if Laurent was with them. He wasn't in the library, nor was he in the little drawing room. She went to the conservatory. There was a whiff of English tobacco in the air: Laurent's cigarettes. Near a tall vase overflowing with long stems studded with little white flowers that gave off a heavy fragrance, in the half- shadows, a red pinpoint glowed.

"Léa, what are you doing here?"

"I was looking for you."

"Do you like the party? Are you having a good time?"

How handsome he was, in the blue-green light. For a brief moment Léa felt her anger ebbing, the violent anger that had come over her when Laurent had asked that empty, frivolous question. But almost immediately, the anger welled up again. Her expression hardened.

"Am I having a good *time*?" she exclaimed. "You love me. You know I love you. You decide to marry that frumpy goody-two-shoes, and then you ask me if I'm having a good time? You must be completely crazy, or blind, or both!"

Laurent stood stock still, stunned by her violent attack. Léa went up close to him. Grabbing him by the arms, she thrust her face in front of his.

"I love you, Laurent, and you love me too. I dare you to tell me it's not true."

Without making the feeblest gesture to defend himself, Laurent murmured:

"Léa, what are you talking about? Nothing gives me more pleasure than our friendship, you know that."

"I don't give a hoot about your friendship!" Léa threw at him, tightening her embrace. "I'm talking about love!"

Suddenly Laurent freed one of his arms. His hand, redolent of tobacco, closed over Léa's mouth. "Be quiet, Léa, you mustn't say things you'll regret later."

"Never," she groaned, pulling at the hand over her mouth. "I love you and want you. I want you as much as you desire me. I dare you to deny it, I dare you to say you don't love me."

Léa would never forget Laurent's stricken face. Before her eyes, a world appeared and simultaneously vanished. A mixture of joy and fear battled within this soul destined for a peaceful existence where love was an uncomplicated matter.

During that moment, Léa's beauty was breathtaking. Her hair was wild, her face shone, her eyes glistened and her lips swelled; her entire being craved his kisses.

"Answer me. You love me, don't you?"

"Yes, I love you," he murmured.

Léa's face lit up with happiness, making her even more beautiful.

They fell into each other's arms, kissing. Suddenly Laurent pushed her away. Léa stared at him in tender surprise, her wet lips parted.

"Léa, we're crazy. Let's forget this."

"No, I love you and I want to marry you."

"I must marry Camille."

She searched his face wildly, and her violet eyes darkened. "But you love me. If you're afraid of marriage, let's run away. All I want is to live with you."

"That's impossible. My father has announced my engagement to Camille. It would kill them both if I broke off this engagement."

Léa struck him. "What about me, don't you care if I die?"

These words brought a wry smile to Laurent's lips. He took Léa by the shoulders and shook his head, saying: "No, not you. You're strong, nothing can shake you. You have an instinct for survival that Camille and I don't have. We belong to an old family, we're worn out. We need the peace and quiet of our libraries. . . . No, let me have my say. Camille and I are alike, we think about the same things, we like the same way of life, one that is studious and austere. . . .

"I like studying too. . . . "

"Of course you do," he replied wearily. "But you'd soon become bored with me: you like dancing, having admirers, noise, people—all the things I loathe. . . . "

"Didn't you run after me?"

"No, I don't think so. I was wrong to see you so often, and to be alone with you so much."

" . . . and to lead me to believe that you loved me."

"I didn't mean to do that. I so much enjoyed watching you live. You're so proud, so free . . . so beautiful. I was grateful to you for listening to me. Every inch of you is alive, a celebration of all that is natural . . . "

"But you love me, you said so."

"I shouldn't have. How can I not love you? But I love you the way a person loves impossible happiness . . . "

"Nothing is impossible. All you need is guts."

Laurent looked at Léa thoughtfully, but he seemed not to see her. "Guts, no doubt. But I haven't got that sort of guts."

"Coward! So that's what makes you happy—to marry that girl who'll give you a brood of sickly little brats!"

"Be quiet, Léa. Don't speak that way of Camille."

"Why not? Has that old witch ever done me any favors? Unless you happen to like hunched shoulders, a pinched face, lank hair . . . "

"Please, Léa . . . "

"Why did you make me believe you loved me?"

"But Léa . . . "

In her fury, she was incapable of conceding that Laurent had never overstepped the bounds of friendship. The shame of rejection was mixed with her anger. She hurled herself at him and slapped him with all her might.

"I hate you!"

A red mark appeared on his pale face. The violence of her gesture calmed Léa down, but left her in the grip of despair. She slipped to the ground and, hiding her face in her hands, burst into tears.

Laurent stared at her with a look of deep sorrow. He drew close to her shaking body and very gently stroked her hair. Then he turned round and slowly left the room. The door shut softly behind him.

Hearing the quiet click of the handle, Léa stopped in midsob. Now it was all over. She had ruined everything. He would never forgive her for this ridiculous scene, her insults. The bastard . . . letting her make a fool of herself like that! She would never ever get over the shame.

She got to her feet painfully, her face blotched and her body feeling bruised, as if she had fallen.

"Bastard, bastard, bastard . . . "

She gave a vicious kick to a pot containing a fragile orchid, sending it across the room before it shattered on the stone floor.

In the middle of the great white marble entrance hall, at the foot of the great staircase, Léa paced up and down as if she did not know which way to turn.

Exclamations and shouts could be heard through the walls of Monsieur d'Argilat's study, the door of which was suddenly thrown open. Léa stepped into the shadows of the doorway that led down to the cellar. Laurent d'Argilat and François Tavernier came into the hall.

"What's happening?" asked Tavernier.

"They're broadcasting Gauleiter Forster's appeal over the desecration of Danzig on the radio. Danzig supposedly agrees to become part of the Reich."

Laurent d'Argilat turned so pale that François Tavernier asked him, with more irony than he intended; "Didn't you know?"

"Of course I did, but my father, Camille, Father Adrien, Monsieur Delmas, a few others and myself decided to keep the news quiet so as not to ruin this last peacetime party."

"Well, if you think it's for the best. What about Poland? What do they say about Poland?"

"Battle has been raging since 5:45 a.m. and Warsaw has been bombed."

Raoul and Jean Lefèvre came running in. "Vincent Leroy has arrived from Langon. It's general mobilization."

Behind them the guests were crowding in, anxious for more details. Some women were already crying.

Monsieur d'Argilat came out of his study with Father Adrien and Monsieur Delmas.

"Friends, friends," he murmured, suddenly looking older.

Through the open study door, the radio could be heard crackling, then there were German voices, and Polish, then the louder tones of the interpreter.

Someone turned up the volume.

"Men and women of Danzig, the moment you have been waiting for for twenty years has arrived. From today, Danzig is part of the great German Reich. Our Führer, Adolf Hitler, has freed us. For the first time, the swastika, the flag of the German Reich, flies from the public buildings of Danzig. From today, it also flies from all the old Polish buildings and throughout the port."

Silence hung over the gathering while the announcer commented on Hitler's acceptance of Danzig back into the Reich, and described the monuments decked with flags, the public festivities.

"Article l: The Constitution of the Free City is abolished effective from this moment," Adrien Delmas recited almost to himself.

"This morning, Germany opened hostilities against Poland," continued the voice on the radio, undaunted.

"So it's war," said Bernadette Bouchardeau weakly, sinking into an armchair.

"Oh Laurent!"

Camille fell into her fiancé's arms, her eyes brimming with tears.

"Don't cry, darling, it'll soon be over."

Standing back a little, hidden by a huge basket of flowers, Léa watched them. In the general upheaval, no one noticed her pallor and her dishevelled hair. She forgot the scene in the conservatory, her rejection, and only thought of Laurent's possible death.

"Two women who love him, happy man." François Tavernier's unctuous voice whispered in her ear.

Léa jumped and wheeled around. "What do you mean?"

"My dear, you're pale, and you have eyes only for him. One doesn't need to be a mind reader to reach such a conclusion."

Léa shuddered and crossed her arms over her chest.

"Shall I warm you up, or would you like me to get you a brandy?" he offered, in the same low voice.

Léa pride was hurt by his ironical protective tone.

"If I may express an opinion," Tavernier continued quietly, "this charming gentleman is a fool to look at anyone else but you."

"You're a beast!"

"Perhaps, but if you had shown the slightest interest in me, I would have . . . "

"I cannot imagine any woman taking the slightest interest in you."

"You're mistaken, little girl. Women, real women, like a bit of rough treatment."

"The sort of women you choose to frequent, no doubt, but not well-brought-up . . . "

" . . . young ladies. Like you?"

Her wrists were held tight in his vise-like grip. He drew her towards him. Then, pinning her arms behind her back, he pressed her close. Suffused with hatred, she closed her eyes.

François Tavernier held her as though he wanted to see into the depths of her soul, while the mocking glint in his eyes disappeared.

"Let me go, you repel me!"

"Anger becomes you, my beauty."

The man's lips gently brushed those of the motionless girl. She struggled in silent fury, fearing that they would end by calling attention to themselves. Fortunately, all of those present were listening intently to the alarming news coming over the radio. The hand tightened its grip, causing Léa to let out a gasp, while the other held her unruly hair. The lips tasting of tobacco and alcohol were insistent. Léa was overcome with rage. . . . Suddenly, she realized that she was returning kisses. Why did her whole body seem suddenly weak, what was that delicious sensation between her thighs?

"No!" Screaming, she broke free.

What was she doing? She must be crazy! Allowing this man, whom she despised, to kiss her! She would rather see him dead. She who loved another! And to make matters worse, she had enjoyed his disgusting kisses!

"Bastard! I hate you!"

"Today you do, but what about tomorrow?"

"Never! I hope war breaks out and you get killed!"

"As far as war is concerned, your wish will certainly be granted, but as for my getting killed, don't depend on it. I don't intend to risk my life in a war that's lost before it's even begun."

"Coward!"

"I can do much better things for you than die. Ask me for anything you like—jewels, furs, houses—I'd give them to you on a plate, but unworthy though my life may be, I prefer to hang on to it."

41

"You're the only one who would. A bastard like you . . ."

"I know, I'm a bastard. You said so a little while ago. Your vocabulary seems rather limited."

"Be quiet, Hitler's speaking."

They both turned their attention to the broadcast.

Chapter 4

Isabelle Delmas had insisted that her husband's relatives spend the night at Montillac. They set up camp beds in the three sisters' bedrooms and in the children's room. As a special favor, Léa agreed to let Pierrot sleep in her hideout. He was fully appreciative of her noble gesture.

All evening, the cousins helped Ruth and Rose, the chambermaid, to shift and make up beds, forgetting about the war. The house rang with their shouts and laughter. Once they had finished, the young people flopped breathlessly on to the beds and cushions in the children's room. They preferred the clutter of this room, where clouds of dust raised by Ruth's vigorous sweeping hung in the air, to the drawing room where their parents were gathered.

Léa sat on her bed with Pierrot playing rummy, but her thoughts were elsewhere and she was losing. Aggravated, she pushed the cards away and leaned against the iron bedstead, looking pensive.

"A penny for your thoughts. Aren't you playing?"

"She's thinking about François Tavernier," said Corinne.

"She's the only person he talked to," added Laure.

"You're wrong, she's not thinking about François Tavernier," murmured Sabine.

"Who then?" asked Corinne.

Léa shuffled the cards and tried to appear indifferent. What was the bitch going to say? When they were little girls, Sabine could already guess what her younger sister was thinking, what mischief she was up to or where she was hiding, before anyone else. That made Léa so angry, she would hit her elder sister. How many times had Ruth had to step in and stop them from fighting. . . . Sabine could not help watching Léa's every move and running to her mother to tell tales. Isabelle Delmas hated sneaks and punished her harshly, which aggravated the rivalry between the two sisters.

"Yes, who?" repeated the two cousins.

Sabine kept them in suspense, her face jubilant with malice. "She's thinking of Laurent d'Argilat."

"But he's engaged to Camille!"

"That's impossible!"

"You're crazy!"

"You must be mistaken!"

Léa's head swam and all she could see was Pierrot's inordinately enlarged face looking at her inquisitively.

"Oh yes she is, honestly, she's in love with Laurent d'Argilat."

Léa sprang up from the bed and bounded across to Sabine with astonishing agility and, before her sister could grasp what was happening, grabbed her by the hair. Although she was taken aback, Sabine was quick to react, and dug her nails into her sister's cheek. A little blood appeared. But Léa, who was stronger, was getting the better of her. She was sitting astride Sabine, pinning her to the ground, holding on to her ears and banging her head against the floor. Everyone rushed over to separate them. When they finally managed to do so, Sabine remained motionless for a moment.

The noise and the shouting had brought their parents up.

"Léa, you're very naughty. Why did you hit your sister?" said Isabelle Delmas. "At your age . . . "

"Mummy . . . "

"Go to your room. And you can go without supper."

Léa's anger left her all of a sudden. She wanted to tell her mother that she was unhappy, that she badly wanted to be comforted. But instead her mother was scolding her and sending her away.

Léa would probably have burst into tears on the spot if she hadn't caught Sabine looking at her triumphantly. She fought back her tears and left the room holding her head high under the reproachful gaze of her aunts and uncles. Only Uncle Adrien made an affectionate sign and smiled in a way that said: It doesn't matter. Her emotions nearly got the better of her. She fled from the room.

"Poor Isabelle. She's going to be quite a handful, that one," said Bernadette Bouchardeau, her sister-in-law.

Isabelle did not answer as she left the children's room.

Léa disobeyed her mother and, instead of going to her room, she rushed into the garden, crossed the courtyard and took a short cut through the vineyards, running towards Bellevue. To avoid going past Sidonie's cottage, she climbed over the wall surrounding the estate, followed the dusty road and then the path leading to the chapel, the place of refuge of all her childhood sorrows. When she was halfway there, a muggy gust of wind made her slow down and finally stop altogether.

She crossed her hands over her chest, as if to restrain her thumping heart, and surveyed the scenery. She gradually succumbed to the enthralment of the dark threatening sky over the plain. All around her, nature was writhing in the grip of a wild wind, groaning in protest against the storm blowing in from the sea. The sky was getting darker by the second, with clouds gathering to form terrifying shapes.

Léa's hair lashed in the gale as she stood motionless, Medusa-like, contemplating the fury that calmed her own. She felt the very earth shudder as warm drops of rain began to fall, slowly releasing balmy fragrances that went to her head; she felt more intoxicated than if she had drunk the choicest wine. Her clinging dress, which was soon soaked, emphasized her curves even more than if she were naked, and the wind made her nipples hard. The raging elements took her out of herself.

A blue flash ripped through the clouds and was followed closely by an earth-shattering peal of thunder. Léa shouted out loud. Her face, wet from the rain which ran down her cheeks like tears, glowed with a primeval joy. A wild and liberating laughter welled up inside her and burst out as lightning tore the sky apart. The laughter became a cry of triumph and of the joy of being alive. She let herself sink to the ground where the path had turned into mud. She kissed the mud still warm from the sun, and sank into the soft earth. She pressed her face in the clay which seemed to hold all the perfumes of Montillac. She wished the earth would open and swallow her up so she could be absorbed by it and brought back to life in the vines, the flowers and the trees of her beloved land. She rolled over, offering up to the elements her rain- and clay-smeared face.

Léa awoke late the following morning feeling exhausted, and tried to recall the events of the previous day. Her muddy clothes flung carelessly all over the bedroom floor brought back the storm and the events that had preceded it. She felt terribly unhappy. For the first time in her life, she had not gotten her own way. She pulled the covers over her head as if to smother her distress. The sound of footsteps and voices reached her ears through the wall of bedclothes, which she threw back as she sat up.

My goodness! What would Ruth say when she saw her nightdress and sheets stained with mud? There was a sharp knock at the door.

"Léa, Léa, get up, Laurent and Claude have come to say goodbye."

She tore off her nightdress and ran into the bathroom, turned on the tap and washed all the traces of mud from her face and body. She brushed her hair vigorously. It was so tangled that it came out in fistfuls. She grabbed the first dress that came to hand, an old pink cotton dress that she was particularly fond of, but which she had now outgrown. She slipped on an old pair of slippers and flew downstairs.

The whole family was gathered in the main drawing room, clustered round Laurent and Claude d'Argilat. The two young men's faces lit up when they saw their friend come into the room. Her cheeks were flushed from being hastily scrubbed and her flaming hair was tangled. She looked like a little girl who had grown up too fast in her short tight-fitting dress.

Léa controlled her desire to hurl herself into Laurent's arms. Trembling from the effort, she managed to appear calm, and asked softly: "Are you leaving so soon, Laurent?"

"I have to join my regiment."

"And I have to join mine in Tours," added Claude.

So as to put her father, her sister and Laurent off the scent, Léa took Claude's arm and led him to one side.

"Promise me you'll be careful."

"I promise. Will you think of me sometimes when I'm at the Front?"

"I'll think of nothing else."

Claude did not hear the irony in her voice. He was overcome with sheer joy. He stammered: "So, d . . . do you care for me a little?"

Just then, Léa could hear Laurent's voice, behind her.

". . . we'll be getting married as soon as I have some leave. Camille doesn't want to wait."

His words made her bow her head in pain. A tear ran down her cheek.

Once again, Claude misinterpreted her response.

"Léa, are you crying? For me? Do you love me as much as that?"

She suppressed a gesture of irritation. How on earth could he think for one moment that she was interested in him, he was so dull, so like his sister. Oh! Revenge! To punish Laurent for his cowardice, Camille for her love and Claude for his stupidity!

She looked up and her expression hardened as she looked at the lovesick youth.

"Of course I love you."

"So, then . . . you'll marry me?"

"Naturally."

"When?"

"As soon as you get leave."

"Let's go outside."

With uncharacteristic authority, Claude grabbed Léa's hand and led her out of the drawing room into the garden. There, behind a hydrangea, he pulled her towards him and kissed her. She nearly pushed him away, but told herself that she had to put up with it. Goodness, how clumsy he was! The memory of Laurent's kisses, brutally chased away by that of

François Tavernier, caused Léa to shudder, which was misinterpreted once more by Camille's brother.

"You love me!"

Léa nearly burst out laughing.

"Would you agree?" asked Claude.

"Agree to what?"

"To my asking your father for your hand?"

Léa felt that her whole future depended on her answer. Was it so clever to marry this poor boy just to punish Laurent? Wouldn't she be the first to suffer from it?

She could make out Sabine's figure through the leaves.

"Yes, my darling," said Léa, embracing Claude.

So when they went back inside, Claude d'Argilat asked Pierre Delmas if he could have a word with him in private. When they returned from their brief discussion, Léa's father looked preoccupied.

Under a cloudy gray sky, the garden paths were a mass of evaporating puddles. Clouds of flies buzzed around the stables. Léa pushed open the door of the barn; the wooden planks were gray with age. She climbed the ladder to the hayloft, as she used to when she was a child, and flopped down in the fragrant, prickly hay.

She thought about what had just happened. Laurent and Claude had left and she had immediately run off to avoid her father's pained and questioning expression. At the thought of this, an unpleasant taste came into her mouth. She did not feel brave enough yet to discuss the matter. She closed her eyes and sought oblivion in sleep.

As a child she had always resorted to this form of release whenever her mother scolded her and she felt inexplicably weary of everything and of herself. Each time, blissful sleep would come to the rescue. But today it did not. Léa tossed and turned in the hay and felt betrayed.

A body bounced against hers.

"Mathias, what's got into you?"

Her childhood pal embraced her, covering her with kisses, and muttered: "Bitch . . . you little bitch . . . "

"Stop it! Let go, you're hurting me!"

"You didn't say that when Claude d'Argilat was kissing you."

Léa burst out laughing and pushed him away. "So that's it."

"Well, isn't that enough?"

"I don't see what business it is of yours. I'm free to kiss who I please."

"You're not going to tell me that you like that little wimp?"

"And if I do? I don't see what it's got to do with you."

Mathias glared angrily at her, and then gradually his expression softened. "You know very well I'm in love with you."

He said it so tenderly that Léa felt moved. She ruffled Mathias's hair and said, with more feeling than she intended: "I love you too, Mathias."

Quite naturally, they found themselves in each other's arms.

In her distress, Léa found comfort in his caresses. She gradually forgot Claude and Laurent and was only aware of the pleasure of kissing Mathias. She would doubtless have let herself go altogether if she had not heard her father's voice calling her, muffled by the hay. She tore herself away from Mathias and, without bothering to use the ladder, she jumped down on to the hard earth floor of the barn.

So many times in the past had Léa jumped down from the hayloft, with the agility of a cat, but this time, one of her ankles gave way. She cried out and Mathias was by her side in an instant.

"My foot!"

Her cry had been heard by her father whose tall frame appeared in the doorway. When he caught sight of his daughter lying on the ground, he rushed over, pushing Mathias aside.

"What's the matter?"

"Nothing, Papa, I've twisted my ankle."

"Let me see."

Pierre Delmas examined the injured leg, causing Léa to cry out in pain. The ankle was swelling rapidly. He carefully picked her up.

"Mathias, tell Ruth to call the doctor."

Soon Léa was installed on the couch in the entrance hall,

propped up by cushions. Doctor Blanchard arrived. After examining and bandaging the injured foot, he reassured Léa's parents.

"It's a nasty sprain, but it's not serious. Total rest for a week, and then she'll be able to run around again."

"A whole week in bed! I'll never be able to manage it, Doctor."

"Don't worry, you'll soon get used to it."

"It's all very well for you to talk, it's not your ankle," said Léa sulkily.

To make things easier, Isabelle Delmas decided that Léa would sleep downstairs on the divan in her father's study. This arrangement brought a smile back to Léa's face. She adored the room with book-lined walls and large french windows that opened out on to the most beautiful part of the garden, overlooking the vineyards and the woods.

Later that afternoon, the Lefèvre brothers came to say goodbye. Léa was so sweet and charming, so flirtatious with them, that they left each convinced that he was the chosen one.

"Isn't it enough that you chase Laurent, compromise yourself with François Tavernier, and flirt with Claude and Mathias? Must you also encourage those idiotic Lefèvre brothers?" said Sabine who had witnessed the scene. "You're just a . . . "

"Quarrelling again, children! Sabine, your sister is not well, she needs to rest. Leave her alone," said their mother firmly as she entered the room.

She sat down beside Léa.

"Does it still hurt?"

"A little. My ankle's throbbing."

"That's natural. I'll give you a sedative this evening so you can sleep."

"Mummy, it's nice being ill and having you look after me." Léa took her mother's hand and kissed it. "I love you so much, Mummy."

Touched, Isabelle stroked her daughter's hand. For a long time mother and child sat in silence, feeling close in their mutual tenderness.

"Is what your father tells me true?"

Léa withdrew her hand, her face hardened.

"Answer me. Is it true that you wish to marry Claude d'Argilat?"

"Yes."

"Do you love him?"

"Yes."

"This love seems very sudden. You hadn't seen him for more than a year. Has something happened that I don't know about?"

Léa was suddenly tempted to tell her mother everything, to admit all, and to be comforted. She fought against her feelings. She mustn't hurt her mother, she mustn't disappoint her. She had to reassure her.

"No," she said firmly, "I love him."

Chapter 5

Léa was still confined to the divan in her father's study. Her bed was cluttered with newspapers. She was listening to the end of the Premier's speech on the radio through the open door of the drawing-room.

"We are at war because war had been imposed on us. Each one of us is at his post on French soil, the soil of freedom, one of the last places where there is respect for human dignity. You will combine your efforts in a deep spirit of unity and of fraternity for the good of the country. Long live France!"

Claude d'Argilat was sitting beside the divan on a low chair, with his arm in plaster and a sling around his neck.

"If it weren't for this wretched arm, I'd show those filthy Boche what a French soldier's made of."

"Well, it's your own fault. Why did you have to play at being a jockey on your uncle's poor old mare?"

"You're right," he admitted in a pitiful voice, "I was so happy that you loved me and were going to marry me that I needed to gallop and yell to the wind how lucky I was to be loved by you."

"Poor Claude, we're a fine pair."

"You'll probably think this is awful, but in fact I'm rather pleased I had this stupid accident because I can be with you while your other suitors have all left. Have you discussed our marriage with your parents? I've told Camille all about it and she says she's delighted to have you for a sister."

"Why did you tell her about it? I wanted it to be a secret until Papa gives his consent!" said Léa angrily.

"But Camille's my sister, darling, I've always told her everything."

"Well, for once you should have kept quiet."

"You are really horrid sometimes. And yet you can be so gentle. . . ."

"I'm not gentle! I don't want the whole world to know my business."

"But Camille isn't the whole world."

"Oh that's enough. Camille, Camille, Camille. I'm sick of Camille! Go away and leave me alone."

"Léa . . . "

"Go away, I'm tired."

"I'm a brute, forgive me . . . say you forgive me."

"Yes, all right."

"Thank you, darling. See you tomorrow," said Claude, taking her hand which she held out reluctantly.

"Yes, see you tomorrow."

Shortly after he had left, Pierre Delmas came in.

"How's our invalid?"

"I'm fine, Papa, I just wish it didn't take so long to heal. I've got pins and needles all over."

"Patience, pet, remember what Kipling said . . . "

" 'Too much haste was the downfall of the yellow snake who wanted to swallow the sun.' "

"I see you haven't forgotten your old father's advice. Put it into practice, my girl, you'll see that it's true."

"No doubt it is," sighed Léa.

Pierre Delmas sat down at his desk, put on his glasses, shuffled some papers, glanced at the newspaper, opened a drawer, closed it again, became engrossed in the ceiling, got up and went over to the french windows.

"The days are getting shorter," he muttered, still looking at the garden.

Léa studied her father's tall sturdy frame. His broad shoulders seemed to stoop slightly, and his hair looked grayer. He looked strangely vulnerable. She smiled at the idea. Vulnerable? Pierre Delmas, who was capable of lifting a wine barrel unaided, of felling a pine tree as quickly and as well as the best woodcutter?

"Papa!" she cried in a burst of tenderness.

"Yes."

"I love you."

"You love me and you want to leave me," he said, turning around and coming towards her.

"It's not the same."

Pierre Delmas sighed and sat down in the low chair, which creaked under his weight.

"Are you absolutely sure you want to marry that fellow?"

Léa did not answer, but looked down sulkily.

"You wouldn't be getting married out of spite?"

Léa blushed and shook her tousled hair.

"Marriage is a serious business. It's a life-long commitment. Have you really thought about it?"

At all costs she had to make her father believe she was truly in love with Claude and that the "Laurent affair" was a thing of the past, a childish whim. "I hardly knew Claude. When I saw him at the party, I knew I loved him and that what I'd felt for his cousin had been no more than a keen friendship that I'd mistaken for love."

Pierre Delmas looked at her dubiously.

"But the other evening you sounded somewhat more passionate than you do at the moment."

Léa's stomach sank and she was afraid she would not have the strength to keep up the pretense.

"The other evening I was tired, aggravated, furious that Laurent hadn't told me about his wedding himself. I thought he was in love with me and I was enjoying flirting with him. I don't care if he gets married. Besides, he's so boring, I wonder how on earth Camille can put up with him."

"That's exactly what I feel. I think one of the Lefèvre brothers would be more suitable for a girl like you."

"But, Papa, they're just friends!"

"Friends? My dear girl, you know nothing about men. Those two are crazy about you, and they're not the only ones. Now, you need to get some sleep. Good night, kitten."

Delighted to do as she was told, Léa fell asleep quickly, thinking how lovely it was to be called "kitten" by a father she loved dearly.

Very soon, Léa was better and able to go for walks in the country. She was usually accompanied by Claude. It was nearly time for the grape harvest and Montillac was a hive of activity, as it was every year. That autumn, with the young men away, their places were taken by women. For a few days the war was of secondary importance. There could be no delay as far as the grapes were concerned—a storm was brewing. Everybody was hurrying to finish before it broke. Nobody stopped for the usual four o'clock break. They had to finish picking the grapes before it started to rain. But at five o'clock, the first drops, which soon became a heavy downpour, forced them to abandon work. It was not long before the ox-drawn carts holding the barrels full of grapes were under cover in the vast sheds.

In a barn, long tables covered with spotless white tablecloths had been set out. There was an abundant spread of pâtés, meats, chicken, cheese, steaming tureens of soup and jugs of wine. The grape-pickers washed their hands in a big barrel of water near the door before going in. Then they took their places on the benches round the tables.

Pierre Delmas presided over the meal, while Isabelle, wearing a white apron over her summer dress, served the food, assisted by Sabine, Léa, Laure and Ruth. Léa had worked so hard that her hands were blistered. She took her seat next to her father. She loved these feasts in the barn during the grape harvest. Each year the festivities lasted for several days. All the young people from the area would get together and there was laughter, singing and dancing. But this year, their hearts were not in it. Most of the guests were women and the few men present were old. The meal began in silence, and no doubt everyone was thinking of those who were away and remembering the hilarity of previous years. Aware of his guests' sadness, Pierre Delmas stood up and raised his glass, saying: "Let us drink to the health and safety of our

55

brave soldiers, and, in their absence, let us carry out cheerfully the work they aren't here to do."

"To the health of our soldiers," everyone cried.

Léa placed her hand on her father's knee and he raised his glass again, for her alone.

"I'm drinking to your happiness, my love," he added softly.

Chapter 6

"Oh, Léa, I'm so glad you're marrying my brother. You must come and stay with us in the Rue de Rennes until you've found an apartment."

"But I don't want to go to Paris" cried Léa.

"But you'll have to, darling. When the war ends, Claude will go back to his studies."

"And what will I do?"

Camille laughed charmingly.

"I'll show you Paris. I'm sure you'll love it, it's the most beautiful city in the world. We'll go to exhibitions, museums, concerts—we'll go to the opera, the theatre . . . "

"That's all very well, but I prefer Montillac."

"You're right, Montillac is wonderful, so is Roches-Blanches, but they are nothing like Paris."

"I didn't think you were so frivolous."

Camille looked astonished. "How on earth can you say that? It's not frivolous to love a city steeped in culture. Laurent is like me, he thinks we can work better in Paris, since we can find everything we need there. Libraries . . . "

"I don't like libraries, they're graveyards for books." Léa knew she was going a bit too far, but Camille was getting on her nerves about Paris and culture.

Pierre Delmas had run out of arguments and allowed Léa to have her way. He gave his consent for her to marry Claude, who thanked him so profusely that he said to himself that Léa might be happy with him after all. As for Isabelle, she simply hugged Léa very tightly.

Sabine muttered: "Beggars can't be choosers."

Only Laure and Ruth openly said they were happy about the idea, Laure because she liked weddings, and Ruth because she thought it would "knock a bit of sense into that scatterbrain."

A short while after their engagement had been officially announced, the two families received a shattering piece of news, and Léa almost gave herself away: Lieutenant d'Argilat had been injured while going to the assistance of one of his men who had been severely wounded in a minefield. Pierre Delmas and his daughter were at Roches-Blanches when a messenger brought the news. On seeing Monsieur d'Argilat turn pale, Camille guessed that something had happened to her fiancé. She stood up and went over to her uncle, trembling.

"Laurent?"

Pierre Delmas also stood up.

"Please answer. What has happened to Laurent?" begged Camille.

"Nothing serious, my child, nothing serious," Monsieur d'Argilat managed to say, "wounded in the arm."

At that moment, a servant brought in a telegram. Monsieur d'Argilat held it out to his friend.

"Pierre, open it, I haven't the strength."

Pierre Delmas did as he was asked and read the telegram.

"It's Laurent. He's perfectly fit and he'll be here tomorrow."

"Tomorrow!"

"Yes, tomorrow. Here, look!"

Camille snatched the telegram he was holding out to Laurent's incredulous father.

"Oh Uncle, it's true! Laurent will be here tomorrow," said the girl, bursting into tears.

Throughout this scene, Léa had kept out of the way, fighting her impulse to shout, and then to cry with joy. Laurent was alive! He was coming home, she would be able to see him. She closed her eyes. Her daydreams were interrupted by the sound of Camille's voice.

"Uncle, let's take advantage of this opportunity to bring our wedding forward. I'm sure that's what Laurent wants more than anything."

"As you wish, Camille. Whatever you do is fine by me."

"Léa, why don't you want to get married at Saint-Macaire like me? It would be lovely to have a double wedding."

The fool! Léa did not care two hoots about where she got married since she was not the one Laurent was marrying. The last thing she wanted was to hear the man she was in love with agreeing to take another for his wife. She said abruptly: "I insist on getting married at Verdelais. Papa, let's go. Mummy's waiting for us."

Léa had difficulty in restraining her tears on the way home. She could feel Pierre Delmas's anxious eyes on her. Usually such a chatterbox, she gave monosyllabic replies to her father's questions. He soon gave up trying to make conversation.

When they arrived at Montillac, she could not face Sabine's comments, and fled to the children's room, where she stayed until dinner time, curled up in her bed.

Léa had been awake since dawn. She could not sit still. Claude had promised to call her as soon as Laurent arrived. She had not stopped pacing up and down. Isabelle, who found this exasperating, sent her to Bellevue to see how Sidonie was.

"The fresh air will do you good."

Léa was furious as she ran towards Bellevue, stumbling along the mud path that had been churned up by the recent rains and the passing carts. She stopped, breathless, to rest on the little bench outside the house. Sidonie's old dog gave her a warm welcome, barking and frisking about. The noise brought Sidonie out.

"Is that you, child? Why don't you come in? You're all in a sweat. Come inside quickly, before you catch cold."

There was no arguing with Sidonie. Léa kissed her and followed her inside.

"There's nothing wrong up at the château, I hope, for you to have run like that?"

"No, no. Mummy sent me to see if you needed anything."

"How kind your mother is! You tell her I'm as well as can be expected at my age. Ah! Being old is the worst thing that can happen to you!"

"Come on, Sidonie, it's better than being dead."

"I'm not so sure. That's what you say when you're young, when you've got good red blood in your veins, when you can climb a ladder without being afraid of falling, when you can be of some use. Look at me now, what use am I? I'm just a burden on your father, a worry to your mother . . . "

"You mustn't say that, Sidonie, everyone at Montillac loves you, you know we do."

"Of course I do, but that doesn't stop me feeling a nuisance, especially now, with this wretched war. I can't even knit, my poor old knotty hands keep dropping the wool and the needles. I'd so like to make socks for our soldiers. They were so cold, poor things, during the last war!"

A tear ran down her crinkled cheek. With a lump in her throat, Léa watched it trickle down and disappear in the wrinkles around her mouth. She felt a rush of pity and went over and knelt at the old lady's feet, as she used to when she was a child. She would bury her face in Sidonie's apron that smelled of flour and soap whenever she felt miserable.

Sidonie's hand, which was gnarled from years of rough work, stroked Léa's golden hair, as it had done long ago.

"Don't be sad, my love. I'm just a mad old woman who moans and groans all the time. Don't take any notice. The storms make my old bones ache and I get bad-tempered. Come on, look at me. Look at the state she's in, this crybaby! Would anyone think she was a grown-up young lady who's getting married soon? What would your fiancé say if he could see you now with your eyes and nose as red as a white rabbit's? Do you remember the white rabbits? What a fuss you made when it was time to kill them. You didn't want them to be eaten, so you would stand in front of the hutch with your arms outstretched, shouting: 'No, they're princesses that have been changed into rabbits by a wicked witch.' Your father and I had to exert a great deal of cunning to catch them. We had to wait until nightfall and leave as many ribbons as there were rabbits in the hutch, so that the next day you'd think the rabbits had been changed back into princesses who had forgotten their ribbons in their haste."

The memory of that story from her childhood brought a smile back to Léa's face.

"I was silly then, I still believed in fairies."

"Don't you believe in them any more? You're wrong not to. Who was it made you so beautiful? Of course there's the good Lord, but the fairies had a hand in it too."

Léa laughed.

"Stop it, Sidonie, I'm not a baby any more."

"To me, you'll always be my little girl, the child I never had," the old woman said, making Léa get up and hugging her tight.

They remained locked together for a long time.

Sidonie was the first to break loose. She took a checkered handkerchief out of her apron pocket and blew her nose noisily, wiping her eyes.

"Come along, it's not good to get sentimental. Tell your mother not to worry, I don't need anything. Thank Miss Ruth for coming to see me yesterday . . . . What's the matter with me! You're not going to leave before you have a drop of blackcurrant liqueur."

"Thank you, Sidonie, but don't bother."

"It's no bother, no bother at all!"

Chapter 7

"Laurent d'Argilat, do you take Camille d'Argilat to be your lawful wedded wife?"

"I do."

That firmly stated "I do" boomed through the gothic church and cut through Léa like a knife. She felt her body stiffen, her blood freeze and her heart stop beating, and a deathly chill stole over her.

The sun made the colors of the stained-glass windows dance before her eyes like a kaleidoscope, casting a halo of light around Camille, in her white gown, and transforming Laurent's uniform into a harlequin's costume. "He looks like my old puppet Jonas," she thought. The church was bathed in magical hues that gradually blotted out the congregation. Then, from this mass of moving colors, a single cold gray statue emerged. Léa felt greatly relieved to be in control of the colors behind her closed eyelids. There was a humming as streams of red light, like a jet of blood, played on the vaults that emerged from the haze. A more high-pitched note scattered the blues, while the greens spread out to form a dark carpet on which the yellows, pinks and purples fell like petals. Then, while the rumbling grew louder, as if under the leadership of an invisible conductor, the colors gathered to form terrifying shapes surrounded by thick black lines which served to emphasize the horror. A diabolical glowing red figure, more terrible than all the rest, rose up before Léa. She was so frightened that she heard herself cry out.

Where was this unbearable heat coming from? Who had

beaten off the monsters? Where were the vivid dancing hues? Why was everything so dark? And that music that made her stomach churn and her head sing. . . .

"Mademoiselle, would you like to take the collection?"

What did that red-robed giant want of her? Why was this man with this grotesque costume and plumed headdress addressing her? What was this unbearable pressure on her arm?

"Léa . . . "

"Mademoiselle . . . "

She turned her head and saw, on her left, her fiancé's anxious expression. The pressure? It was his hand. She wrenched herself free. What right had he to touch her? And the other one, the fellow in red, what did he want with his basket lined with white satin? He wanted her to take the collection. . . . Whatever next? Could he not understand that the idea of going up and down between the pews, with her pale pink organdy dress hitched up in one hand and the basket in the other, was unbearable.

The verger insisted: "Mademoiselle, would you like to take the collection?"

"No thank you," she said sharply.

The man looked at her in astonishment. Usually, young ladies were delighted to be asked; it enabled them to show off their dresses. Disappointed, he asked Sabine, who was quick to accept with a defiant smile on her lips.

Mass finally came to an end. The newly wedded couple stood before the altar festooned with bouquets of white flowers to be congratulated by their families and friends.

When Léa's turn came, it was only her pride that kept her on her feet. Camille, flushed and radiant, held out her arms and hugged her to her breast.

"Léa soon it will be your turn. May you be as happy as I am at this moment."

Léa, whose thoughts were miles away, offered her cheek to Camille. She clung desperately to the phrase that was going round and round in her shattered mind: "It's not true, it's a dream, a bad dream . . . it's not true."

Claude nudged her and she found herself facing Laurent. Motionless, she gazed at him.

"Kiss him," said Claude.

The bridal procession walked down the aisle to a rousing march from the organ. Camille looked happy and beautiful beneath the slightly discolored lace veil that had been worn by generations of d'Argilat brides. Her long cream-colored satin dress gleamed in the sunlight. The young woman's hand rested lightly on her husband's black sleeve, as he slowed his pace to keep step with her. Behind them followed bridesmaids, dressed in pink organdy with matching head-dresses. Léa hated pink organdy.

Outside the church, a large crowd was waiting to cheer and applaud the newlyweds.

A long-haired photographer with a floppy bow tie made the wedding party stand in front of the church door for the traditional photograph. During one of these shots, Léa moved and her face was so blurred in the print that she was hardly recognizable; in another, she was looking down and all that could be seen was the top of her enormous hat.

As they left Saint-Macaire in her Uncle Adrien's car, with Claude, Lucien and Laure, Léa suddenly felt violently sick. She leaped out of the car and doubled up by the side of the road.

"But this child has a burning temperature," cried Uncle Adrien, as he held her head. The nausea had passed and Léa dropped down on to the grass, her face pale and blotchy.

Adrien helped her up, lifted her and carried her to the car.

"I'm cold," she stammered.

Lucien took a blanket out of the trunk and covered her up.

Doctor Blanchard diagnosed a serious case of measles and ordered a starvation diet and complete rest.

The wedding, which was supposed to take place in early November, was postponed, and Claude had to leave to join his regiment, in despair since he was not able to set eyes on his fiancée.

Her mother, her father and Ruth took turns keeping a twenty-four hour watch over her, but Léa took a long time to recover. Doctor Blanchard had never seen such a bad case of measles in all his forty years as a physician. He had nursed the fear that it might be the beginning of an epidemic. But it turned out to be no such thing and Léa's was an isolated case.

Long letters from Claude d'Argilat arrived at Montillac almost daily. They piled up, unopened, on Léa's bedside table. Each week, Isabelle Delmas informed the unhappy soldier of his fiancée's state of health. After three weeks, Léa was able to add a short note at the foot of her mother's letter.

Claude d'Argilat never read that note. When the letter reached his billet, he had been killed by a grenade that went off during an exercise.

For several days the news was kept from Léa. It was feared that she was too weak to take it.

On a fine warm December morning, Léa was trying out a few steps on the terrace, leaning on Ruth's arm. She could feel her body coming back to life and she sighed contentedly.

"It's time to go in now. That's enough for your first time up."

"Let's stay a little longer, Ruth. I feel so good."

"No, child," said the nanny, firmly.

Léa knew that there were times when you didn't argue with Ruth. She did not insist.

Who was that tiny black figure coming towards them? Why was she dressed in mourning? Horrified, Léa stood stock still watching the woman in widow's garb make her way towards them.

"Laurent!"

She let out the name she loved and hated in a cry that frightened the birds in the trees. Ruth, who had no idea what had prompted this, just stared at her.

The woman in black, her face concealed behind her veil, was now very close.

"Laurent," groaned Léa, pulling her woollen cape tightly around her.

The woman raised her veil and Camille's stricken fact appeared. She held out her arms to the invalid, who stiffened as she let herself be kissed.

"My darling, my poor darling."

"Laurent?"

"You're so unselfish always to think of others. Laurent is fine, he asked me to give you a big kiss and to tell you that our home will always be your home too."

Léa was no longer listening. After her moment of agony, she suddenly felt wildly happy. She embraced Camille with a radiant smile.

"How you frightened me! Why the black? Who or what are you mourning?"

"Oh Léa! Haven't they told you?"

"Haven't they told me what?"

Camille dropped to the ground, her face buried in her hands.

"What on earth's going on? What's the matter with you? What are you in such a state about? Ruth, why is Camille in mourning?"

"Her brother's dead."

"Her brother? What brother? Oh, you mean . . . ?"

Ruth nodded.

"Claude . . ." I shan't have to tell him I don't want to hear another word about our marriage, thought Léa instinctively, and then blushed with embarrassment at such a thing crossing her mind. Her eyes filled with tears of shame, which Camille mistook for grief.

"Oh! My poor darling."

Léa grew healthier every minute. In spite of the freezing weather which made her nose and cheeks pink, she was able to accompany her father on his long rides through the vineyards again. The war seemed very remote. Black suited her very well.

To take her mind off things, Pierre Delmas invited her to go to Paris with him. He had business there. They would stay with Isabelle's aunts: Lisa and Albertine de Montpleynet. She readily agreed. In Paris she would be able to see Laurent again, as he had just been transferred to the War Ministry.

Chapter 8

Léa and her father arrived in Paris on the evening train. The station was so dimly lit that it was barely possible to see. Outside, it was pitch black. The few street lamps with their muted lights were unable to pierce the darkness. After what seemed a long wait, they found a taxi with dimmed headlights which drove them slowly along the embankment.

There were so few cars and pedestrians that Léa felt as though she were driving through a ghost city. The occasional bluish lights made the place seem even more unreal.

"There's Notre-Dame," said her father.

Léa could make out only a dark shape that was even blacker than the sky.

"That's the Place Saint-Michel."

So this was the famous Latin Quarter that was supposed to be so gay and lively! There were only a few shadowy figures who seemed to be avoiding each other as they hurried along.

In response to her silence, her father said: "It's so sad how all of this has changed. In the old days, at this time, all the cafés would still be open."

They arrived at the Rue de l'Université without exchanging another word. Both were lost in their own morose thoughts.

Lisa and Albertine's welcome brought a smile back to their faces. A meal was waiting for them in the dining room, beautifully set out on the table. This room appeared larger than it really was because of the wallpaper: it depicted a panoramic scene of a ship about to set sail. When Léa came to visit her aunts as a little girl, this room was her universe. As soon as she caught sight of the half-open door, she would dive under the long table. From her hiding place she could see the boats, the enormous flowers with their brilliant colors and the deep blue of the sea. How many voyages had she set out on, in her magic ship made from the table and the heavy green tablecloth with its long tassels! The walls told of a whole lifetime of rainbow-colored adventure, bringing back the stories that Isabelle used to tell when her daughters wanted to hear about that far-off land that they had never seen.

"Aunt Albertine, I'm so happy nothing's changed here."

"And why should anything change, my pet? Isn't it enough that we change?"

"But, Aunt Albertine, you don't change a bit. You've always been the same, ever since I've known you."

"Which means I've always been old to you."

"Oh no, Aunt Albertine! You and Aunt Lisa will never be old!"

Albertine embraced her niece and made her sit down at the table. Pierre Delmas sat down opposite Léa.

"You must be starving. Estelle has cooked veal with morel mushrooms, specially for you, Pierre," said Albertine.

"She's the one who remembered how you love your food," simpered Lisa.

"I can see that I'm going to put on a few pounds here, and then your niece will scold me."

"Ha! Ha! He hasn't changed either, he's still a big tease," the two spinsters giggled.

Léa tucked in with gusto and, watching her eat with such a healthy appetite, Pierre could not help thinking about poor Claude, who had been so quickly forgotten.

In her room, which had once been her mother's, Léa found a huge bouquet of roses with a little card. Enthralled by the beauty of the flowers, she picked up the card and read: "Welcome to our new Parisienne, with love from Camille and Laurent."

Her pleasure was ruined. What did she care for Camille's love? As for Laurent's, if he was going to send his love together with that of his wife, he could keep it. She ripped up the card and went to bed in a bad mood.

She was awakened the following morning by the lovely smell of hot chocolate and by the sun pouring in through the window, making her hide under the covers.

"Close the curtains!"

"Up you get, lazybones, you can't stay in bed on such a beautiful morning. Do you have any idea what the time is?"

Léa poked the tip of her nose out. "No."

"It's nearly eleven o'clock. Your father went out ages ago and Camille d'Argilat has already called twice," said Albertine as she put the breakfast tray down beside the bed.

"Oh, what a bore!" grumbled Léa, but she sat up and Albertine held out the tray.

"Why do you say that? It's very sweet of Camille to be so concerned about you."

Léa preferred to say nothing. Instead she made herself comfortable.

"Aunt, how kind of you! All my favorite things!" she exclaimed as she sank her teeth into a warm golden croissant.

"Enjoy it while you can, darling. They've already announced a whole list of restrictions. Today's a cake day but there's no meat; tomorrow, the butcher will be open but not the baker. We're going to have to get used to it."

"Well, are we awake at last?" asked Lisa peering round the open door. "Did you sleep well?"

"Good morning, Aunt. I slept like a log."

Her aunts kissed her and went out.

Léa had two more croissants and drank two cups of chocolate. Feeling very full, she pushed away the tray. Then she lay down again and crossed her arms behind her head.

A gentle breeze blew in through the half-open window making the tulle curtains ripple. The spring sunlight seemed to bring the characters on the faded blue wallpaper to life.

Without any effort, Léa could imagine her mother in this room, which was calm and gentle, as she was. What did the young Isabelle dream about on spring mornings? Did she think about love, about marriage? Did she want to live life to the full, to embrace an amorous body, to be kissed and caressed? No, it was not possible. Everything about her seemed so remote from such things.

The telephone rang somewhere in the apartment. A few seconds later, there was a gentle knock at the door.

"Come in."

The door opened and a large woman in her fifties, dressed in a pale gray smock with a big spotless white apron, came into the room.

"Estelle! I'm so glad to see you. How are you?"

"I'm well, Mademoiselle Léa."

"Estelle, don't be so formal, come and give me a kiss."

The Montpleynet sisters' housekeeper did not wait to be asked twice. She kissed Léa on both cheeks: after all, she had held her in her arms as a baby.

"My poor child, how dreadful! Your fiancé . . ."

"Be quiet. I don't want to hear anyone talk about it."

"Yes, of course . . . forgive me, pet, I'm so clumsy."

"Not at all."

"Oh! I was forgetting . . . Madame d'Argilat is on the phone. It's the third time she's rung."

"I know," snapped Léa. "Is the telephone still in the little drawing room?" she went on, slipping on the dark red dressing gown her mother had given her for Christmas.

"Yes, mademoiselle."

She ran barefoot down the long corridor and went into the little drawing room, the Montpleynet sisters' favorite room.

"Oh look," Léa exclaimed, "they've changed the wallpaper! A good thing too. This one is much more cheerful."

She went over to the table where the receiver lay.

"Hello, Camille?"

"Léa, is that you?"

"Yes, I'm sorry I kept you waiting."

"That's all right, my darling, I'm so glad you're in Paris. It's a lovely day, would you like to go for a walk?"

"If you like."

"I'll come and pick you up at two o'clock. Does that suit you?"

"Fine."

"See you later. If only you knew how delighted I am to be seeing you again."

Léa hung up without replying.

The two young women dressed in mourning were sitting on a bench in the Tuileries gardens enjoying the sunshine after a harsh winter. France had lain under a heavy blanket of snow for weeks. Spring had arrived at last: all the signs were there—the mildness in the air, the softer light which made the Louvre and the buildings in the Rue de Rivoli glow faintly pink, the gardeners planting the first tulips in the flower beds, the way strollers watched women walk past, a certain languor, the shriller shouts of children chasing each other around the pond, and especially that indefinable fragrance in the air that affects even the most sober.

Like Léa, Camille was basking in a voluptuous sense of well-being which made her grief at her brother's death fade and calmed her fears that this strange war might take her husband from her too. She was brought down to earth again by a ball rolling between her feet.

"Sorry ma'am."

Camille smiled at the fair-haired child in front of her, picked up the ball and gave it to him.

"Thank you, ma'am."

Camille watched him toddle away and smiled tenderly.

"Isn't he sweet! Look, Léa, his hair's the same color as Laurent's."

"I don't think so," Léa replied brittlely.

"I would so love to have a child like that."

"What a strange idea, to want to have a child now. You must be either mad or ignorant."

The bitterness in her voice made Camille think she had upset her friend by talking about the joys of motherhood when poor Léa had just lost . . .

71

"Forgive me, I'm so selfish. Anyone would think I'd already forgotten poor Claude but . . . but I miss him so much," she said, bursting into tears and burying her face in her hands.

Two women paused and looked compassionately at the thin figure dressed in black, and racked with grief. This exasperated Léa even more.

"Stop making a spectacle of yourself."

Camille took the handkerchief Léa held out.

"I'm sorry, I don't have your courage or your dignity."

Léa refrained from saying that it was not a question of courage, nor of dignity. What was the point of making an enemy of the wife of the man she loved? She would see him again that evening, since Camille had invited her to dinner.

"Come on. Let's go. How about having some tea? Do you know of anywhere near here?"

"That's a good idea. Let's go to the Ritz. It's close by."

"The Ritz it is."

They left the Tuileries and headed towards the Place Vendôme.

"Can't you watch where you're going!" cried Léa.

A man who was rushing headlong out of the famous hotel would have knocked her over if his two powerful hands had not saved her at the last minute.

"I'm so sorry, madame . . . But it's the lovely Léa Delmas! My dear, in spite of the disguise, I would recognize you anywhere. I have unforgettable memories of you."

"Will you let go? You're hurting me."

"Excuse me, I'm a brute," he said, smiling.

François Tavernier removed his hat and bowed to Camille.

"Good afternoon, Madame d'Argilat. Do you remember me?"

"Good afternoon, Monsieur Tavernier. I have not forgotten a single person who was there on the day my engagement was announced."

"I know that your husband is going to be in Paris from now on. I don't wish to be indiscreet, but might I enquire why you are in mourning?"

"For my brother, sir."

"I am deeply sorry, Madame d'Argilat."

"What about me, nobody asks me," said Léa, furious at being left out.

"You?" he replied in a joking voice. "I imagine you're decked out in black out of vanity. One of your admirers must have told you that it suits you."

"Oh, sir!" exclaimed Camille. "How can you say such a thing. . . . My brother Claude was her fiancé."

If Léa had been more observant and less angry, she would have noticed the succession of expressions that came over François Tavernier's face: astonishment, compassion, doubt and finally irony.

"Mademoiselle Delmas, I beg your forgiveness on bended knee. I did not know that you were going to marry Monsieur d'Argilat. Please accept my sincerest condolences."

"My private life is none of your business. You can keep your condolences."

Camille broke in: "Monsieur Tavernier, take no notice, she doesn't know what she's saying. My brother's death upset her deeply. They were so much in love."

"I'm sure they were," said François, winking at Léa.

This bore, this lout, this bastard had not only seen through her, but he had the cheek to let on! Léa took Camille's arm.

"Camille, I'm tired, let's go home."

"No, not yet. Come and have a cup of tea, darling. It'll be good for you."

"Madame d'Argilat is right. I recommend tea at the Ritz. As for the cakes, they're delicious," said François Tavernier in a genteel tone that was so incongruous with his appearance that Léa nearly burst out laughing, in spite of her anger.

She could not hide a brief smile which, for a second, lit up her scowling face.

"That's much better!" he cried. "I would sell my soul for one of your smiles, fleeting though it is," he added as her face became gloomy again.

A man in a gray uniform, with cap in hand, had been standing a little apart from the group, in front of a big black limousine, since the beginning of the conversation. He now came forward.

"Excuse me, sir, but you'll be late. The minister is waiting for you."

"Thank you, Germain. What chance has a minister got compared with a beautiful woman! Let him wait! Meanwhile, ladies, I must take my leave of you. Madame d'Argilat, may I come and pay you my respects some day soon?"

"With the greatest of pleasure, Monsieur Tavernier. My husband and I will be delighted."

"Shall I be fortunate enough to see you again, Mademoiselle Delmas?"

"I shouldn't think so. I shall not stay in Paris long and I am very busy visiting friends."

"I am sure we shall see each other again. We could be such good friends!"

François Tavernier bowed once again and got into the car. The chauffeur closed the door, slid behind the wheel and slowly drove off.

"Well, are we going to have this tea?"

"I thought you wanted to go home."

"I've changed my mind."

"As you wish, darling."

In her splendid apartment on the Boulevard Raspail, where some fine pieces of Louis XIV furniture blended in with the modern furniture, giving an impression of sophisticated luxury, Camille put the finishing touch to an arrangement of flowers in the center of the table. She was so absorbed in these preparations that she did not hear Laurent come in. His kiss on the back of her neck, above the black lace collar of her crepe dress, made her cry out.

"You frightened me," she said tenderly as she turned around, with a bunch of pink primroses in her hand.

"How was your day with Léa?"

"Fine. Poor thing, she's still suffering the shock of Claude's death. One minute she's sad and the next she's cheerful, then she's exhausted and a moment later she's restless. She'll be gentle, then aggressive. I didn't know what to do to please her."

"You should have taken her to places where there were lots of people."

"That's what I did. I took her for tea at the Ritz, where we bumped into François Tavernier."

"That's hardly surprising, since he lives there."

"He was charming and sympathetic with me, but most odd with Léa."

"What do you mean, odd?"

"It's as though he's trying to tease her all the time, trying to annoy her, which he managed to do only too well. You know him better than I do—what kind of man is he?"

Laurent replied, "It's hard to say. At the ministry, some think he's a scoundrel, who would do anything for money; others feel he's one of the best judges of the current situation. Nobody doubts his courage; his wounds from Spain vouch for that. Nor is there any doubt that he is intelligent, and knows a lot of people. They also say he has many mistresses and a few loyal friends."

"That's not a very reassuring portrait—nor is it a very attractive one. What do you think of him?"

"I haven't really got an opinion. I find him both likeable and unlikeable. We agree on a number of things, notably the weakness of the military leadership and the stupidity of this waiting game which is undermining the troops' morale. I agree with his analysis of the Russian-Finnish war, in spite of his cynical attitude. . . . Whenever I meet him, I feel rather wary. I'm charmed by him and a minute later he disgusts me. It's as though he has no sense of morality, or, if he has, he keeps it well hidden. What else can I tell you? He is far too complex a character to sum up in a few words."

"It's the first time I've known you to be disconcerted by anyone."

"Yes, it's a type of intelligence that I don't understand. There's something about him that I can't put my finger on. We've had the same upbringing, we've been to the same type of schools, we have similar tastes in music and literature; we have both travelled, studied and we are both thinking men. All this makes me tolerant of human nature, makes me want to fight to defend our freedom, whereas it makes him hard to the point of indifference towards the future of the world."

"I don't think he is either hard or indifferent."

Laurent looked at his young wife tenderly.

"You are so good that you can't think ill of anybody else."

There was a ring at the doorbell.

"It's our guests. Will you let them in while I make sure everything is ready in the kitchen?"

"What a trial that dinner was." Never had Léa been so bored in her life. How can anyone stand Camille and the Montpleynet sisters' chatter for more than five minutes? All they talked about was the problem of getting food in Paris, passive defense and the servants. Lucky there weren't any children or they'd have gone on about the comparative merits of breast and bottle feeding, or the different ways of bundling the babies up. And even her father, who didn't know very much about these matters, was joining in!

Léa's heart had come to a standstill when she stepped into the apartment. How handsome, slim and elegant Laurent was! There was a look in his eye that was full of admiration for her, no matter how hard he tried to hide it. And, when he held her in his arms, close to him, longer than was appropriate, she thought, his mouth in her hair, on her cheeks . . . What was it he had said? That she was his sister. . . . Where on earth did he get such an idiotic idea? His sister! And what else did he say? "Claude would have wanted it this way." What did he know about the wishes of the dead? What about her? Didn't she have something to say on the subject? "This house is your home." Very nice too, but he'd better not insist, or she might take him up on it. The only thing she wanted was to feel his lips on hers. She had merely replied: "Thank you, Laurent."

And she had been looking forward to this reunion so much. All her pleasure had been dampened by an envy that was making her unjust towards the man she loved.

Two weeks passed, during which Léa saw Laurent almost every day. Unfortunately, they were never alone. But she put up with Camille's presence— a presence that was becoming increasingly hateful to her—for those few moments in his company. In her rare moments of honesty, she admitted that Camille was less boring than most women: she could talk about anything without sounding pedantic, and she went to great lengths to entertain Léa. In spite of her concern for propriety, had she not agreed to take Léa to the cinema, which was hardly the thing one did when one was in mourning? Léa remembered how Camille had taken off her hat with its long black crepe veil, with a deliberateness that expressed her grief more eloquently than words. She had done that to please her when Léa had announced that she was tired of behaving as if they were both widows, that it demoralized her and made her ill. . . .

One morning, Pierre Delmas came into his daughter's bedroom while she was having her breakfast in bed.

"Good morning, darling, are you enjoying your stay in Paris?"

"Oh! Yes, Papa, even though I haven't done anything very exciting."

"What do you call 'exciting'? You've been out every day; you've seen the museums, the shops, you went rowing in the Bois de Boulogne. What more do you want?"

"I'd like to go dancing, to see a show at the Folies Bergères—to have a good time."

"Do you realize what you are saying? Your fiancé died barely four months ago and all you can think about is going dancing. You sound like a woman with a heart of stone."

"It's not my fault he died."

"Léa, you've gone too far. I never believed you were really in love with poor Claude, but this time I'm truly disappointed in you."

The disgust in her father's voice felt like a slap in the face. All of a sudden, she felt so miserable, so misunderstood and unmasked, that she burst into tears.

Pierre Delmas could bear anything except his favorite daughter's tears.

"It's all right, pet, it's not serious. I understand. It's hard to have to give up your fun at your age. We'll be going home, you'll see Mummy again, we'll go out for walks together like we did before."

"I don't want to go back to Montillac."

"Why not, since you're so bored in Paris?"

Léa did not answer.

"Answer me, darling."

She looked up at her father, knowing that at the sight of her tear-stained face he would do whatever she wished.

"I'd like to enroll at the Sorbonne and study literature," she said in a tiny voice.

Pierre Delmas stared at her in astonishment.

"What an extraordinary idea! At any other time, I would have no objections, but have you forgotten we're at war?"

"It's not an extraordinary idea. Camille and several of her friends go. As for the war, it's not here yet. Please, Papa darling, please say yes."

"I'll have to discuss it with your mother, and I'll have to ask your aunts if they'd be prepared to let you stay with them," said Pierre Delmas trying to fend off Léa as she smothered him with kisses.

"You telephone Mummy, and I'll take care of the aunts," she said leaping out of bed. "Besides," she added, "Camille's invited me to come and stay with her if there's the slightest problem."

"I can see I'm faced with a veritable conspiracy. Where are you going today?"

"I don't know yet, Camille's going to phone me. What about you? What are you doing?"

"I've got a meeting and a business lunch."

"Don't forget we're having dinner at Laurent's this evening. He wants us to meet some of his friends."

"I won't forget. See you this evening."

"Yes. Don't forget to phone Mummy, either!"

When the door was safely closed, Léa started to prance around the room, certain that she was going to get her own way. Today, she was going on the offensive. The previous day, she had told Camille that she had some errands to do alone, and told her aunts that she was having lunch with Camille. How good it was to be free, to have a day to herself!

78

How lucky it was a fine day! She would be able to wear the pretty suit she had bought in secret at the elegant boutique in the Faubourg Saint-Honore. She had spent all her savings on the hat, the bag, the shoes and the gloves. Humming, she made her way to the bathroom. When she emerged, shrouded in her huge white dressing gown, she reeked so strongly of perfume that Albertine, who was passing the bathroom, asked if she had spilled the bottle.

It was almost eleven o'clock. If she was to be at the War Ministry by midday, she'd have to hurry. She dressed quickly, shuddering with pleasure at the feel of the pale pink silk blouse. The heavy black crepe skirt was a marvellous fit. As for the jacket, it emphasized her slender waist. She put her hair up and wore one of those delightful hats to be found only in Paris, a sort of black straw tambourine subtly decorated with pink flowerbuds with a little veil. She donned a pair of high-heeled shoes, gloves of the softest kid, and carried a little bag which matched the hat and completed this slightly severe outfit. But in spite of Léa's desire to look like a woman, she did not look one bit older. She threw a last-minute glance at herself in the mirror to make sure her seams were straight and that her general appearance was all right: she was so pleased at her reflection in the tall wardrobe mirror that she smiled with pleasure.

Now she had to slip out unnoticed by her aunts and Estelle, who were bound to be surprised at the sight of a fiancée in mourning wearing pink and flowers on her hat.

On the pavement of the Rue de l'Université, the porch door slammed shut behind her. Léa breathed a sigh of relief. Shivering, she headed towards the Boulevard Saint-Germain to find a taxi. How cold it was! The sunshine was deceptive. Winter had returned. Fortunately the government had authorized the use of heating until April 15th!

She had to walk to Saint-Germain-des-Prés to find a taxi. She could feel the admiring glances of the men and the envious looks of the women as she walked past. At the taxi stand, the drivers were lounging around enjoying the sunshine, smoking and stamping their feet to keep warm. Léa got into the first cab. A youngish man wearing the most extrordinary checkered cap slipped into the driver's seat.

"Where do you wish to go, mysterious lady in black?"

"To the War Ministry, please."

"The War Ministry it is."

Léa went up to the orderly. "I'd like to speak to Lieutenant d'Argilat."

"Do you have an appointment?"

"Yes," stammered Léa, somewhat overwhelmed by her surroundings where soldiers and officers of all ranks were coming and going as if in a railway station.

She looked up and saw Laurent coming down the corridor.

"Léa, what are you doing here?"

"Mademoiselle says she has an appointment with you."

Laurent raised his eyebrows, but seeing Léa's sheepish expression, he said, as he led her away: "That is so. What's happened? Nothing serious?"

"No, I just wanted to see you," she replied, watching him out of the corner of her eye, "and have lunch with you," she added hastily.

"That's a splendid idea. Luckily, I'm free. Come into my office. I'll call Camille to tell her to come and join us."

"Oh no!" she cried.

On seeing Laurent's look of surprise, Léa said gently: "Camille isn't free to have lunch today, she has to shop for this evening."

"It's true, I forgot the reception. Where would you like to have lunch?"

"In a very smart place."

"All right," he laughed, "how about Maxim's?"

"Wonderful!"

A chauffeur-driven car dropped them off outside the restaurant. Albert, the headwaiter, greeted them with his usual courteousness.

"Monsieur d'Argilat's table."

When Léa walked in, many heads turned. Her heart was thumping beneath her pink silk blouse. She sat down and looked about her without any attempt to conceal her curiosity and her pleasure at being in the most famous restaurant in the world. Everything seemed unforgettable: the flowers in silver vases, the china, the crystal glasses, the silent and efficient service, the mirrors reflecting pink light from the lamp shades into infinity, the women's jewels, their hats, the lace curtains, the red velvet and the dark wood panelling. Here, everything suggested luxury; the war was a long way away.

"That looks like Maurice Chevalier," she whispered.

"It is. And over there, in the corner, is Sacha Guitry. At the next table is the lovely Mary Marquet. . . . "

The headwaiter handed them the menu.

"What do you want to eat?"

"I don't care, I'm sure everything is delicious. You choose for me."

When they had ordered, the wine steward appeared.

"What would you like to drink, sir?"

"Champagne!" cried Léa.

"Mademoiselle wishes to drink champagne."

The wine arrived immediately.

"Here's to us," said Léa, raising her glass.

"To us and to those we love," added Laurent.

They drank in silence looking into each other's eyes. Léa blossomed under the gaze of the man she loved. The little black veil made her look mysterious, and drew attention to her sensual moist lips. She felt Laurent's eyes on her like a caress. With deliberate sauciness, she lifted the veil.

"You are beautiful."

There was emotion in his voice. Léa replied with a burst of laughter. Laurent clutched the white tablecloth. This made Léa tremble as if his hands were grasping her. She then did something she had always done as a child, but in the circumstances was sheer provocation: she played with her lower lip, twisting it between her thumb and first finger.

"Stop it!"

Her fingers froze in mid-air and Léa pouted in mock surprise. Laurent was spared having to explain by the arrival of the hors d'oeuvres. Léa set to with a hearty appetite. She finished her smoked salmon in a few mouthfuls.

"Mmm, that was so good!"

Abruptly, she added: "Do you think the fighting will start soon?"

He was so unprepared for such a question that he almost knocked his glass over.

"Yes. I have to join my regiment."

Her eyes grew round, her heart stopped: "When?"

"The day after tomorrow."

"Where?"

"Near Sedan."

"How long have you known?"

"Three days."

"Have you told Camille?"

"Not yet."

Léa hardly touched the next course, but drank several glasses of champagne. Gradually, images of Laurent dead or injured faded. Her thoughts took on an alcohol-tinged euphoria.

"Let's change the subject, shall we?" she suggested, placing her hand in his.

"You're right, let's not waste these last moments of peace and happiness. I'll always think of you, in the worst situations, as the beautiful lady in black and pink."

Her chin cupped in her hand, Léa leaned forward with half-closed eyes.

"You see, you do love me."

A blush spread over Laurent's face.

"Don't deny it, I know you do. No! Be quiet, listen to me. You'll only talk nonsense. I love you, Laurent, I love you even more than that day I told you so. I got engaged to Claude out of spite, to hurt you. Luckily, he's. . . . That's not what I meant. I mean, I'm still free."

"You're forgetting that I'm not."

"True. But you love *me*."

"That's not true. And anyway, you surely don't think for one moment I'd be coward enough to desert Camille? Especially . . . ?"

"Especially . . . ?"

"Well, well, well, it's my dear friend d'Argilat."

"Tavernier, how are you?"

He was unbearably elegant. A real upstart, thought Léa, trying to convince herself as she surveyed the tall figure dressed in an impeccably cut pale-gray suit.

"Not as well as you, I'm afraid. I'm delighted to see you again, Mademoiselle Delmas."

Léa nodded furiously, which caused the intruder to smile.

"I see that the feeling is not mutual. Allow me to take leave of you, we'll see each other at greater length this evening."

With a wave of his hand, François Tavernier walked off, greeting various people on his way out.

"I can't stand him. Surely you haven't invited him this evening?"

"Yes, we have. He's mentioned several times that he'd like to pay his respects to Camille."

"Well, it's going to be some party."

"You're rather hard on him. He can be very amusing and charming."

"You could have fooled me. He's vulgar. I've had enough of this place. Let's go!"

Outside, the weather had changed: the sun had gone and the sky was gloomy.

"It looks like snow," said Laurent walking towards the car from the Ministry which was pulling up at the curb.

"Yes, I'm cold."

"I'm not surprised, you're not dressed warmly enough. Get into the car, quickly."

Once inside, he wrapped Léa in his raincoat and put his arm around her. They drove in silence for a few minutes.

"Rue de l'Université, please."

"Hold me tight, that'll warm me up," said Léa resting her head on Laurent's shoulder.

Her eyes were closed but she could feel that the young man was as agitated as she was. Soon she could bear it no longer.

"Kiss me."

Laurent tried to ignore her waiting lips, but slowly, resolutely, Léa drew him towards her. He no longer resisted. Forgetting Camille and the presence of the chauffeur, he was engulfed in the temptress's kiss and time stood still. When he managed to tear himself away from her, the car was drawing up in the Rue de l'Université.

"What number is it, sir?" asked the chauffeur in a hushed embarassed tone.

"Stop here."

"Yes, sir."

Léa looked at Laurent in silent triumph. She looks like an animal, thought Laurent as he tried to regain his composure and ran his fingers through his hair. The car pulled up. Without waiting for the chauffeur to open the door, Léa got out, holding her hat. Laurent accompanied her to the door of the apartment.

"Forgive me for what I did."

"Why forgive you? We both enjoyed it. Don't look at me like that, it's not the end of the world being in love. See you this evening, my love."

Lieutenant d'Argilat remained motionless for a moment in front of the door that had just closed.

That evening Léa was wearing a long black satin sheath dress bought at the beginning of her stay. When her father saw her like that, her dress as tight as a shiny second skin, her shoulders and arms seeming all the more naked for the black material which heightened their whiteness, he cried: "You can't go out in that outfit!"

"Honestly, Papa, it's the fashion. All the women are wearing sheath dresses."

"Perhaps they are, but it's not proper for a young girl. Take it off."

Léa's face clouded over and she pursed her lips. "I haven't got another dress. I'll wear this or I won't go at all."

Knowing his daughter, Pierre Delmas knew that nothing would make her change her mind.

"At least wear a stole," he said, giving in.

"I've got something even better. Look what Aunt Albertine has lent me: her black fox cape."

Pendulous diamond earrings, borrowed from Lisa, completed her dress, flattering the slenderness of her neck with her hair piled high.

A young chambermaid escorted them to the cloakroom cluttered with coats. Léa left the fox cape there while her father looked on, furious. When she walked casually into the drawing room, leaning on her father's arm and swinging a black- and-white beaded evening bag, all heads turned in her direction.

"Léa, you look absolutely lovely," exclaimed Camille, who was dressed in a long plain black crepe dress with a gathered skirt, a prim white bodice fastened with a cameo, and elbow-length sleeves. "I've got a surprise for you, look who's here."

"Raoul, Jean!"

Suddenly a child again, Léa fell into the Lefévre brothers' arms. They were both in uniform.

"How wonderful! What are the two of you doing in Paris?"

"We've been on leave," said Raoul.

"We're on our way back to the Front," added Jean.

"And as our train isn't till tomorrow morning, we dropped in to see Camille and Laurent, who invited us for this evening."

"We wanted to come and see you, but Camille told us you were coming and that we should make it a surprise."

"What a lovely idea!" said Léa with a radiant smile in Camille's direction.

Léa greeted a general, a colonel, a scholar, a renowned writer, a famous painter, a pretty woman, two mature older women and . . . François Tavernier.

"You again!"

"What a charming welcome, typical of your delightful nature."

Léa curtly turned her back on him.

"The back is as good as the front."

She whipped around. "Will you stop your insolence!"

"My dear, when young women wear certain dresses, it's not for men to admire the color of the material. Do you not agree? Ask our dear friend, Laurent d'Argilat."

"Ask me what?" said Laurent stopping beside them.

"Mademoiselle was worried whether her dress suited her and whether you liked it."

"Very much," stuttered Laurent. "Excuse me, I think

Camille needs me," he said, beating a retreat.

"Beast!" exclaimed Léa, but François burst out laughing while a general came over to speak to him.

"Well, Tavernier, have you managed it yet?"

"Not yet, sir."

Léa made for the buffet, where Raoul and Jean Lefévre were deep in conversation with her father.

"We were talking about home," said Raoul. "When are you going back?"

"I think I'm going to stay here a little longer, I want to study at the Sorbonne. Papa, have you telephoned Mummy?"

"Yes."

"Did she agree?"

"She says that it's too late in the year to start at the Sorbonne, but you can stay in Paris for another fortnight if your aunts don't mind."

"Of course they don't mind! Thank you, Papa. Are you staying too?"

"I can't. I'll be leaving in two days."

Raoul offered Léa a glass of champagne and drew her to one side.

"You shouldn't stay here. The war's going to start up again. Paris could become a dangerous place."

"Can you imagine the Germans in Paris? But you'll stop them. Aren't there more of you than there are of them?"

"That's irrelevant. They're better prepared, their weapons are better adapted and their air force is superior."

"Maybe, but you're braver."

Raoul shrugged. "Bravery, you know, compared with their tanks . . . "

"Look, I'm so happy to see you. Don't spoil this evening."

"You're right. Let's drink to victory, and to your beauty."

Léa, Raoul and Jean made their way over to a little ante-room that led off the guest-filled drawing room through a double swinging door. The walls were lined with books and there was a fire in the white marble fireplace. On the mantelpiece was a magnificent bronze statue of a horse with its rider being attacked by wolves. Léa sank into one of the armchairs by the fire. The boys took their places at her feet.

The three young people sat silently watching the flames without really seeing them. Gradually they grew drowsy from the warmth, lulled by the crackling of the logs. François Tavernier had been leaning against the door jamb for a while, watching them, a glass of champagne in his hand. He felt an instinctive liking for the two brothers.

Léa stirred and stretched with a sort of contented grunt. The firelight cast a golden halo around her face, shoulders and arms. The pure line of her profile was silhouetted against a background of light that left her features in shadow. Then she lowered her head exposing a nape that just begged to be kissed or nuzzled.

François Tavernier raised his glass to his lips so brusquely that he spilled a little champagne on his impeccable dinner jacket. He had to have that girl. He could not remember ever having desired a woman so passionately. What was so special about her? Certainly, she was beautiful, very beautiful even, but she was a child, a virgin, no doubt. And he had a horror of virgins who always got so stupidly sentimental and moaned on and on about the loss of their virginity. However, this one, it seemed to him, was of a different breed. He could still remember the kiss he had snatched from her at Roches-Blanches on the day of the party, when he had surprised her behind her basket of flowers. He felt aroused. One day, she would be his.

Léa looked towards the door and caught François Tavernier's gaze upon her; there was no mistaking the look in his eye. She loved that expression on men's faces so obviously full of desire. Although she hated the man staring at her, she felt a sudden thrill and trembled with pleasure. This slight movement did not escape François Tavernier's gaze, and he smiled with male satisfaction. That smile annoyed Léa, who was not aware that it concealed a much greater emotion.

"What do you think you're doing, standing there like that?"

"I'm looking at you."

The intensity in his voice irritated Léa even further. She stood up with calculated slowness.

"Come on," she said to the Lefévre brothers, "it's impossible to be left in peace, even here."

Without waiting for them, she headed for the drawing room. As she walked past François Tavernier, he stopped her, grabbed her arm and said tersely: "I don't like being treated like this."

"Well, you'll have to get used to it if we have the misfortune to meet again. Let go of me."

"First, let me give you a word of advice. Don't stay in Paris, it could become dangerous."

"You must surely be mistaken, it can't be dangerous since you are here, instead of at the Front like any man worthy of the label."

He grew pale at her insult, his features hardened and an unpleasant glint came into his eye.

"If you were not just a little girl, I'd slap your face."

"Women must doubtless be the only enemy you are capable of fighting. Let me go! You're hurting me!"

For no apparent reason, he let out a loud laugh which drowned the buzz of conversation in the drawing room. He released Léa's arm, leaving a red mark where his hand had been.

"You're right; women are the only adversaries worthy of me. And, I must admit, I don't always win."

"I find it hard to believe that you ever win."

"You'll see."

"I've seen all I need to, sir."

Léa went and joined Camille, who was chatting with one of her guests.

"I have the impression our young friend had a bone to pick with Tavernier," said the beautiful young woman Camille was talking to.

Léa looked at her with that haughty air she often adopted when asked an embarrassing question, a habit which her mother had tried, without success, to break her of.

"I really don't know what you're talking about."

"Madame Mulstein knows Monsieur Tavernier very well and was speaking most highly of him," said Camille hastily.

Léa did not answer, waiting for her to continue, with an indifference that was almost rude.

"My father and my husband hold him in great esteem. He is the only person who can help me to get them out of Germany."

"Why do they want to leave Germany?" asked Léa, who could not help being intrigued.

"Because they're Jewish."

"So what?"

Sarah Mulstein looked at the beautiful girl who was at the same time provocative and childlike in her black satin sheath dress. It took her back a few years to when she was walking into an elegant Berlin cabaret, with her father on one arm and her husband on the other. She too had been wearing a new satin dress, only hers was white. The owner had come rushing over when he recognized her father, Israel Lazare, the world-famous conductor, and had offered them the best table. They were following him when a tall fair-haired man with a flushed face and wearing an SS uniform stood in their path. A glass of brandy in his hand, he had confronted her father: "Israel Lazare?"

Her father had stopped, smiled and bowed his head in greeting, but the man had cried: "That's a Jewish name . . ."

In the vast red-and-black room, conversation came to a halt; only the piano could be heard, heightening the tense silence. The owner had tried to intervene, but the officer had sent him flying with a blow so violent that he had fallen. A few women screamed. Then the officer grabbed Israel Lazare's dinner jacket and spat in his face, saying he did not like Jews. Sarah's husband had tried to protest but another punch sent him reeling.

"Don't you know that we don't like Jews in this country? That we consider them less than dogs? The only good Jew is a dead Jew!"

The piano fell silent. The room spun round. Sarah was surprised to find that she felt more amazed than frightened. She noticed odd details around her: the dress that suited the tall blonde so well; that gray-haired lady's beautiful pearls; the dancers with beautiful legs gathered near the red curtain. She heard herself scream:

"Papa . . ."

She was surrounded by the soldiers who were with the officer. They were saying she was not bad for a Jewess. One of these men reached out towards her white dress. As if in a nightmare, she heard the fabric tearing. Her husband, who had come round, rushed over to her. A bottle smashed over his head. He crumpled, slowly, his face suddenly covered with blood.

Her white dress was spotted with red. Incredulous, she looked down without trying to conceal her naked, blood-stained breasts. She had the strange reaction of staring at her hands. Then she began to scream.

"Shut up, you dirty Jew!"

The contents of a glass of brandy had stopped her cries, burning her eyes and nostrils. The smell had made her nauseous; she leaned forward and vomited copiously. She did not see the blow coming. The toe of the boot caught her in the stomach and sent her flying into a pillar.

"Bitch! How dare you puke over me!"

From that moment, everything became blurred: her husband lying in a pool of blood, she in her vomit, her father being dragged along by his gray hair that was slowly becoming tinged with blood, the screams, the whistles blowing, the sirens and then these last words heard as the ambulance doors were closing: "It's nothing. They're Jews . . . "

"So what?" repeated Léa.

"Well," said Sarah Mulstein softly, "Jews are put into camps where they are tortured and killed."

Léa looked at her in disbelief, but the expression in Sarah's eyes told her it was true.

"Forgive me, I didn't know."

Chapter 9

The following morning, Léa was awakened by a telephone call from Laurent, asking her to have lunch with him at the Closerie des Lilas. Léa was quite certain he would be her lover before the day was out. She dressed with great care, selecting salmon-colored silk lingerie edged with cream lace. As it was cold out, she wore a black wool shirt-dress trimmed with a white piqué collar that made her look like a demure schoolgirl. She brushed her hair and decided to wear it loose on her shoulders: the dark outfit set off her golden halo beautifully. She slipped on the black wool coat made by the dressmaker at Langon and, after trying on several hats, gave up the idea of wearing one altogether.

She had plenty of time to spare, so she decided to walk up the Boulevard Saint-Michel. The exercise made her cheeks glow and she walked into the Closerie looking radiant.

She liked the place at once, with its dark panelling, the velvet-covered seats and the barman skillfully mixing a cocktail. The cloakroom attendant relieved her of her coat. Laurent was waiting for her at the bar, reading *Le Figaro* with a worried frown. He did not see Léa until she was seated next to him.

"Bad news?"

"Léa forgive me," he said, starting to his feet.

"Don't bother to get up. I'm so glad to see you."

"Do you want a drink?"

"The same as you."

"Barman, another port, please."

Léa studied him intently. She would do anything he wished. The headwaiter came over to them. "Can I show you to your table now, sir?"

"Yes, then we'll be able to talk in peace. Would you have Mademoiselle's drink brought over."

As soon as they had made themselves comfortable, the waiter arrived with Léa's port and the headwaiter handed them the menu.

"I'm afraid we haven't been able to get meat or desserts today, sir, but we have some excellent fish."

He sounded so apologetic that Léa nearly burst out laughing.

"Perfect. Would you like some oysters to start with? It's the last of them, and they're always superb here."

"That sounds lovely," said Léa, raising her glass to her lips.

Taking the wine waiter's advice, Laurent chose a Meursault but he showed no interest in it, which was rare in a man born and bred in the vineyards.

How tired and anxious he looks, the young girl thought. "Is something the matter?"

Laurent was looking at her as if he would like to engrave every one of her features on his memory. Léa blossomed under his gaze.

"You're very beautiful. Very strong too."

Léa's eyebrows rose enquiringly.

"Yes, you're strong," he went on. "You go wherever your desires lead you, without hesitation. You're like an animal without any sense of morality, heedless of the consequences either for yourself or for others."

What was he getting at? He'd do better to tell her he loved her and forget these philosophical considerations.

"But I'm different, Léa. I wanted to see you to tell you three things and to ask you to do something for me."

The wine was served and then the oysters. Love did not affect Léa's appetite and she greedily devoured the oysters. Laurent watched her with an expression of tenderness, forgetting to eat.

"You're right, they're delicious. Aren't you having any?"

"I'm not very hungry. Do you want them?"

"Can I?" said Léa. She was so eager that Laurent's tense features relaxed in a smile.

"What did you want to tell me?"

"I'm leaving this evening."

"This evening!"

"At midnight. I have to join my regiment in the Ardennes." Léa pushed away the plate of oysters, her face suddenly clouded with anxiety.

"We're expecting a German offensive."

"Our soldiers will repulse it."

"I wish I could be so sure."

"You sound like François Tavernier."

"Tavernier probably knows more about what's going on than anyone else. Unfortunately, General Gamelin's officers won't listen to him."

"I'm not surprised. Who'd trust him? What else did you want to tell me?"

Without looking at the girl, Laurent said softly, "Camille's expecting a baby."

Léa closed her eyes and gripped the edge of the table for support. Laurent could not bear to look at her pallid face and clenched fists. He was painfully sad to be the cause of her suffering. He took her icy hands in his.

"Léa, look at me."

He would never forget that hurt look. Her silent grief was more than he could bear. And that single tear sliding down her soft cheek, disappearing in the corner of her mouth, then following the curve of her chin before making a damp trail down her neck.

"My love, don't cry. I also wanted to tell you I love you."

What did he say? That he loved her! But then all was not lost! Why was she crying? Camille was expecting a baby. That was nothing to worry about. It would make her look awful for months, while as for her . . . ! This was no time to make a mess of her face with tears. He loved her, he'd just said so. Life was wonderful.

Abruptly, she started laughing and wiped her eyes with her napkin.

"Since you love me, nothing else matters. I don't care if Camille's expecting a baby, it's you I want."

He looked at her with a weary smile. It was so difficult to make her understand that as far as he was concerned, their love could not lead anywhere. Now, he felt guilty for what he saw as betrayal of his wife.

"Tell me again that you love me."

"Whether I love you or not, it won't make the slightest difference to our relationship. I'm Camille's husband."

"I don't care about that. All I know is that I love you and you love me. you're married? So what? That won't stop us making love."

How desirable she was, uttering those provocative words. Doubtless, she did not really understand what she was saying. But what Léa went on to suggest showed that he was the innocent one.

"We could go to a hotel. There are lots around Montparnasse."

Unable to believe his ears, he blushed, and replied: "It's quite out of the question."

Léa's eyes grew round. "But why, since it's my idea?"

"I'd rather forget what you said."

"You don't know what you want. You want me, but you haven't the guts to admit it. You're pathetic."

Laurent gazed at her sadly. In front of them, the fish lay untouched. By now, it was cold.

"Mademoiselle and monsieur didn't like the fish? Would you like something else?"

"No, that'll do." Laurent cut the waiter short. "The bill, please."

"Very good, sir."

"Pour me a drink," demanded Léa.

Although she felt desperate, Léa seemed more relaxed as she slowly sipped her wine.

There was a long silence between them.

"What are you thinking about?" Léa asked.

Laurent smiled weakly, and sighed: "I'm thinking of Camille. She's not well. The doctor fears a difficult pregnancy and wants her to stay in bed until birth."

94

"Why not send her to Roches-Blanches?"

"Unfortunately, that's impossible. The doctor doesn't think she's strong enough for the journey." His voice broke. "The Germans will be here very soon. And I have to leave. . . . "

Laurent buried his face in his hands. Léa, who was touched by his distress, could not help smiling at the attitude of the man she loved.

"Very well, I'll look after your little family for you."

Laurent looked up, his eyes wet, incredulous. "You will?"

"I said I would. But don't think you're getting off so easily. I love you, and I'll do everything I can to make you forget Camille."

Chapter 10

A week after Laurent had left, Léa still did not understand what had prompted her to accept. Camille's welcome had been particularly hateful to her when, giving in to her urgent calls, she had gone to visit her.

Camille was in her bedroom, lying on the bed. When Léa entered, she attempted to get up, but nausea prevented her. She held out her thin arms towards her visitor.

"I'm so happy to see you, darling."

Léa sat on the edge of the bed and had no option but to return her kisses, in spite of the repulsion she felt. She noticed, with malicious satisfaction, Camille's pallor and the bags under her eyes.

"Laurent told you about the baby?" Camille asked, blushing, clutching Léa's reluctant hand in her own feverish fingers.

Léa nodded in silence.

"He said that you'd agreed to look after me. How can I ever thank you? You're so kind. I've felt so alone since Laurent left. When I'm not thinking about him, I think about my poor brother, whose death was such a stupid waste. I tremble for the child I'm carrying. . . . I'm ashamed to admit it—but I can tell you everything, can't I? I'm frightened, I'm so terribly frightened of suffering and of dying."

"Don't be so silly, you don't die from having a baby."

"That's what the doctor says, but I feel so weak. You can't understand, you're so strong and healthy. . . . "

"Well, complaining won't make you feel any better," cut in Léa irritably.

"You're right, forgive me."

"Have you heard from Laurent?"

"Yes, he's fine. All is quiet at the Front. He doesn't know how to keep his men's spirits up. They are bored stiff and spend their time drinking and playing cards. His only joy is that he's with his horses. In his last letter, he gave me a detailed description of Fauvette, Gamin, Wazidou and Mystérieux."

There was a knock on the door and the maid came in and announced that the doctor had arrived. Léa took advantage of his visit to take her leave of Camille, promising to return the next day.

The following day, Léa kept her word and went to see Camille. It was a beautiful day. It seemed as if everybody in Paris was out enjoying the sunshine, there were so many people on the pavements, in the cafés, sitting on the terraces. There was a terrible traffic jam-up in the Boulevard Saint-Germain. The cars were blowing their horns full blast, more for the fun of making a noise than because anyone was annoyed at the delay. On this magnificent May morning, everyone seemed happy and relaxed. If it had not been for the presence of numerous uniformed soldiers, nobody would have believed the country to be at war.

As Léa walked past the Gallimard Bookshop in the Boulevard Raspail, she decided to go in and buy Camille a book. As she had no idea of her literary tastes, she stood looking at the vast array of books, at a loss.

"Can I help you, mademoiselle?"

The man who had just spoken was wearing a pale elegant suit. He was tallish, with a wide slightly fleshy face and very blue eyes. His long thick lashes made him look a little effeminate. His mouth, with red lips, was well formed. He fidgeted with his green spotted yellow bow tie. Léa, thinking he was the clerk, answered: "Yes please. I'm looking for something to entertain a sick friend, but I don't know what she likes."

"Give her this, I'm sure she'll like it."

School for Corpses . . . Louis-Ferdinand Céline . . .

Do you think so? It looks rather morbid."

"That's obvious," he said with an ill-concealed ironical smile. "Céline is just the author for someone who is depressed. He is easy to read, his style is unique, and he is both witty and profound. He ranks among the top writers of our time."

"Thank you very much, I'll take this book. How much is it?"

"I don't know, the cashier will tell you. Please excuse me, I have to go."

He picked up a gray pen from a table, with which he waved goodbye to Léa, and bowed before leaving.

"Are you buying that book, mademoiselle?" asked a salesgirl.

"Yes, that gentleman who just went out recommended it. Is it good?"

"If Monsieur Raphaël Mahl recommends it, it must be good," said the salesgirl with a big smile.

"Is he the manager of the bookshop?"

"Oh no! Monsieur Mahl is one of our best customers. He's a very cultured gentleman who knows more about contemporary literature than anyone."

"What does he do?"

"Nobody really knows. Sometimes he's got lots of money, and sometimes he borrows left, right and center. He deals with paintings, antiques, I think, and old books. He's a writer too. He's had two books published that made a very big splash."

Léa paid and left the shop, strangely unnerved by the encounter. She walked up the Boulevard Raspail clutching her parcel.

As she arrived at Camille's apartment, a man was coming out. It was Tavernier.

"What are you doing here?"

"I've been visiting Madame d'Argilat," he said, removing his hat.

"I shouldn't think she was very pleased."

"You are mistaken, my dear, she loves my company. She finds me entertaining."

"That doesn't surprise me, coming from her, she's always wrong about people."

"Not always, only sometimes . . . like about you," he said pensively.

"What do you mean?"

"That she doesn't see you as you are, since she loves you."

Léa shrugged her shoulders as if to say "What do I care?"

"Yes, she does, she loves the woman who has sworn to steal her husband from her. Because that is what you have sworn to do in that pretty little head of yours."

Léa blushed but managed to control her temper. It was in a sweet voice with an innocent smile that she answered: "How can you say such dreadful things? That was over a long time ago. Laurent is nothing more than a dear friend who has asked me to look after his wife while he is away."

"You don't seem very happy about it?"

Léa burst out laughing, in her youthful, frank way. "You're right about that: Camille is only interested in boring things."

"And you?"

"I want to experience everything, to see everything. If it weren't for my aunts who watch my comings and goings, and this war which has mobilized all the young men, I'd be wining and dining every evening in the best restaurants. I'd go dancing at the cabarets and spend hours in cafés."

"Well, that's a fine idea. Suppose I come and pick you up at seven o'clock? We'll go for a drink, then to a show, after that we'll dine at a fashionable restaurant, and to round the evening off we'll go dancing at a cabaret, or go and listen to Russian folksongs."

As she listened to this catalogue of entertainments, Léa's eyes grew round like those of a child celebrating its first Christmas. François Tavernier had to make a superhuman effort not to take her in his arms, he was so excited by her temperamental character, her lust for life and her sensuality!

"That would be wonderful, I'm so bored."

This confession, said in such a pitiful voice, by such a pretty mouth, nearly got the better of Tavernier's resolution to behave himself. He concealed his agitation by laughing.

"He looks like a fox," thought Léa. "He's just like the

others, I'll be able to do anything I want with him."

"So, that's settled, I'll pick you up at seven. Meanwhile, I'll telephone your aunts to request their permission."

"And if they refuse?"

"Let me tell you, my dear friend, that no woman has ever refused me anything," he said with an irony that Léa took for vanity.

"Well, I'll see what my aunts have to say when I get home. Good-day."

Her change of mood did not escape François Tavernier's notice. As he left he wondered: "Perhaps she has a sense of humor?"

When Léa entered Camille's vast beige and white bedroom, Camille was up, standing by the window with her forehead pressed to the glass.

She was wearing a cream satin housecoat which blended in with the decor. When she heard the door close, she turned around.

"What are you doing up?" cried Léa. "I thought you were supposed to stay in bed."

"Don't scold me. I feel much better. Monsieur Tavernier came to visit me. He's a tonic."

"I know. I met him downstairs."

"He's worried about us and thinks we should leave Paris. I told him he was wrong to worry, that all is calm at the Front. So calm that General Huntzinger has invited the whole of Paris to his headquarters for a theatrical gala."

"How do you know?"

"Laurent told me in the letter I received today."

"How is he?"

"Very well. He told me to give you a kiss and to tell you that a few lines from you would make him very happy. Have you heard from your parents?"

"Yes, Mummy wants me to go back."

"Oh!" groaned Camille sinking into an armchair.

"Don't worry. I told her that I couldn't leave you alone, that you needed me."

"That's so true! I was saying to Monsieur Tavernier: Léa's presence comforts me and gives me courage and strength."

100

Léa did not answer but summoned the maid.

"Help Madame back to bed. You must rest now, Camille. By the way, I've brought you a book, *School for Corpses*."

"Thank you, darling. You are so thoughtful. Who wrote it?"

Someone named Céline. Apparently, he's a great writer."

"Céline! . . . Have you ever read anything by him?"

"No. What about you?"

"I've tried, but it's hard. The things he writes about are so awful."

"You must be thinking of someone else: a certain Raphaël Mahl assured me that it is a most entertaining book."

"Who did you say?"

"Raphaël Mahl."

"Now I understand. He was having fun with you. Mahl is a vile creature who dirties everything he touches and whose greatest pleasure in life is to hurt others, especially his friends."

Camille's vehemence astonished Léa. She had never heard her speak so harshly of anyone.

"What has he done?"

"Nothing to me, but he had betrayed and robbed someone very close to Laurent and myself."

"Someone I know?"

"No."

When Léa got back to the Rue de l'Université, a delivery boy had just brought three enormous bouquets of flowers. Lisa and Albertine were standing there in raptures, exclaiming: "How magnificent!"

"This Monsieur Tavernier is a man of the world. There aren't many around like him these days."

Léa found these two old ladies, who had spent their whole lives together and had never left each other's sides for even a single day, delightful. Albertine, five years her sister's senior, had become the head of the family. It was she who managed the inheritance left by their parents, ruled the servants with a firm hand, decided where to spend their holidays and

101

whether any repairs should be carried out. She was what they call a bossy woman.

As for Lisa, since the beginning of the war, she lived in a permanent state of fear, sleeping badly, waking up at the slightest sound, with her gas mask always within reach. She would never go out without it slung over her shoulder, even to go to mass on Sundays or to visit a friend who lived nearby. She read all the newspapers and listened to all the radio stations. Her suitcases had been packed since the invasion of Poland. She had nagged her sister to sell their superb old custom-made Renault and buy in its stead a faster roomier family car, a Vivastella Grand Sport. After a few drives around Paris, to enable Albertine, the only one who could drive, to get used to the new car, it was taken to a garage in the Faubourg Saint-Germain, and the mechanic was entrusted with the mission of ensuring that the vehicle was always in perfect working order. Should he ever forget, then Lisa's weekly visit, complete with gas mask, would remind him.

"Léa, my girl, dear Monsieur Tavernier has kindly offered to take you to a concert in aid of the war orphans."

"Did you accept?" asked Léa suppressing a smile.

"Naturally. As it's for charity, you may go, in spite of your being in mourning," stated Albertine.

"But is it proper?" Léa asked hypocritically as she found it increasingly difficult to stifle a giggle.

"Of course. He's a well-educated man, a friend of politicians and of the President. Besides, your friend Camille entertains him in her house, and that says it all," added Lisa.

"So, if Camille entertains him, I can go out with him without any hesitations," Léa remarked sarcastically.

"Look how delicate this rose is," exclaimed Lisa.

"Aren't you interested in yours?" said Albertine, carefully folding the wrapping paper from her deep yellow roses.

Léa tore off the wrapping to reveal a bouquet of magnificent white roses with red edges. An envelope had been slipped among the stems. She whisked it out and hid it in her pocket.

"I think Mademoiselle Léa's flowers are the most beautiful of all," said Estelle, who had just come into the drawing room carrying a heavy crystal vase full of water.

"Aunt, would you lend me your fox fur?"

"Of course, darling. Estelle will bring it to your room."

Léa was putting the finishing touches to her appearance when the doorbell made her jump. Already? she thought. She smiled at her reflection in the long wardrobe mirror. Tavernier was right, this dress suited her very well and highlighted her complexion and her figure. However, she was annoyed at herself for giving in to the request on the card that had come with the roses: "Wear the dress you wore the other day. You look so beautiful in it." Anyhow, she did not have any choice; it was her only long dress.

Before leaving her room, she slipped on the black fox fur cape to hide her bare shoulders from her aunts. When she joined them in the little drawing room, they were in fits of laughter with François Tavernier, who was leaning against the mantelpiece in a black dinner jacket.

"Hello, Léa, let's hurry. It wouldn't do to arrive after the President."

"Indeed not. Let's hurry," said Albertine, impressed.

François Tavernier opened the door of a superb red and black Bugatti which was waiting outside the house. The smell of leather inside the luxurious car was intoxicating. The engine started up with a muted roar.

"What a beautiful car!"

"I was sure you would like it. Enjoy it while you can, they won't be making thoroughbreds like this any more."

"Why not? More and more people will have cars."

"You're right, but these models represent an art of living that will disappear in this war . . . "

"Oh no! Not one word about the war, or I shall get out this minute."

"Forgive me," he said, taking her hand and pressing it to his lips.

"Where are you taking me?"

"Don't worry, I'm not taking you to a charity concert as I told your aunts. You needn't worry; tomorrow you will be able to read in the newspapers that:

103

Monsieur François Tavernier, adviser to the Minister of the Interior, attended the Charity Gala at the Opéra in the company of the ravishing and elegant Mademoiselle Léa Delmas.''

"How come?''

"I have a journalist friend who agreed to do me this little favor. How about having a drink at the Coupole before we go and listen to Josephine Baker and Maurice Chevalier at the Casino de Paris? The barman makes excellent cocktails.''

Léa thought that Josephine Baker was wonderful, but she didn't enjoy Chevalier.

"You're mistaken,'' said François Tavernier, "at the moment, he embodies the French spirit.''

"Well, I don't like that spirit of self-satisfaction and smug sauciness.''

"What a funny little girl you are, both vain and profound. What kind of woman will you become? I'd rather like to watch you grow up.''

In the big hall of the Casino de Paris, the crowd was hurrying towards the exits, commenting on the show which they had obviously enjoyed.

"I'm hungry,'' said Léa, leaning on her companion's arm.

"We'll eat soon. I wanted to take you to Monseigneur's, but there wasn't a table, not even for me. I've booked at Scheherazade, where Leo Marjane is appearing. The Russian band is wonderful. I think you'll like it.''

Whether it was the caviar, the vodka, the champagne or the violins, Léa was filled with joy of being alive, and laughed heartily and laid her head on Tavernier's shoulder. Amused, he watched the young girl bloom under the effect of pleasure. She asked the band to play a slow waltz and asked her companion to dance. She danced with such suppleness and such sensual grace that soon the whole restaurant had eyes only for the couple that was gliding slowly across the floor.

François Tavernier gestured to the headwaiter. Almost immediately, another bottle of champagne appeared. They drank in silence lulled by the music.

"Kiss me, I want to be kissed."

"Even by me?" he said, leaning forward.

"Even by you."

Close to them, an insistent little cough disturbed their kiss. A very pale young man was standing by the table, hat in hand.

"Loriot, what do you want?"

"May I have a word with you, sir? It's urgent."

"Excuse me, I'll be back in a moment."

Tavernier followed Loriot and stopped near the bar. After a short animated discussion, he came back to Léa, his face grim.

"We have to leave."

"So soon! But what time is it?"

"Four in the morning. Your aunts will be worrried."

"Of course they won't. They know I'm with you. They think so highly of you," she said sputtering with laughter.

"That's enough. We have to leave."

"But why?"

Without answering, he flung a few bills on the table and grabbed Léa's arm, forcing her to get up.

"Attendant! Mademoiselle's cape."

"Let go of me! Would you please tell me what's going on?"

"What is going on, dear friend," he said in a subdued voice, "is that at this very moment the Germans are bombing Calais, Boulogne and Dunkirk, and they're invading Belgium and Holland by air."

"Oh no! My God! Laurent!"

François Tavernier's face had been tense and now it suddenly became hostile. In the space of a second, they sized up each other. The cloakroom attendant interrupted this confrontation by helping Léa on with her cape.

They drove home in silence. When they reached the Rue de l'Université, François Tavernier accompanied Léa to the door. As she was putting her key in the lock, he forced her to turn around, took her head in his hands and kissed her savagely.

105

She bore it passively.

"I preferred you earlier."

She did not reply, but calmly turned the key, went in and closed the door behind her.

In the silence of the May night, all she could hear was the beating of her heart and the retreating sound of a car engine.

When she reached her room, she flung her clothes on the floor, picked up her nightdress waiting for her on the bed and slid between the sheets pulling the covers up over her head. Of course it wasn't as good as her little bed in the children's room at Montillac, but it was still a refuge.

She fell asleep calling Laurent's name.

Chapter 11

"Albertine . . . Estelle . . . Léa . . . the Germans are coming, the Germans are coming . . ."

Estelle rushed out of the kitchen, arms covered up to her elbows in flour, then Albertine appeared, pen still in hand, in a white woollen dressing gown, and last came Léa, her hair dishevelled and the black fox fur cape thrown over her blouse.

"What's the matter with you, what's all the noise about?" asked Albertine sternly.

"The Germans," sobbed Lisa, a pathetic figure in her pink dressing gown, "they've invaded Belgium, they said so on the radio."

"Oh my God!" exclaimed Estelle, crossing herself. She left a floury smear on her forehead.

"So I wasn't dreaming," murmured Léa.

Albertine's hand went to her throat but she said nothing.

The telephone was ringing insistently. Finally Estelle picked up the receiver.

"Hello . . . one moment please . . . Mademoiselle Léa, it's for you."

"Yes, speaking . . . Call the doctor . . . He's not there? . . . All right, keep calm, I'm coming."

Léa explained: "Camille fainted when she heard the news on the radio. The maid is panicking and the doctor isn't there so I'll go there to help."

"Shall I come with you?" asked Albertine.

"There's no need, thank you. Estelle, would you bring me a cup of coffee, please?"

When Léa arrived at Camille's, the young woman had come around.

"Mademoiselle Léa, I was so frightened, I thought that Madame was dying!"

"Come new, Josette, calm down. Did you leave a message for the doctor?"

"Yes, he'll be here as soon as he gets back from the hospital."

In Camille's bedroom it was dark; there was just the feeble glow of a little bedside lamp. Taking care not to bump into the furniture, Léa went over to the bed. There was an expression of such suffering on Camille's face that Léa felt sorry for her. She leaned over her and gently stroked Camille's cold forehead.

"There's no need to talk. The doctor's on his way. I'm here. Sleep."

Camille smiled weakly and closed her eyes again.

Léa stayed by her side until the doctor arrived in the early afternoon. When he came out of the bedroom, he seemed concerned.

"Are you Madame d'Argilat's only relative in Paris?" he asked.

Léa was about to disillusion him as to her kinship with Camille, but felt tired at the thought of the complicated explanations this would involve.

"Yes."

"I'm extremely worried. This woman must have complete rest. I trust that you will make sure she gets it."

"That's a tall order given the present situation," said Léa.

"Yes, I know," sighed the doctor as he wrote out a prescription, "but she must have as much peace and quiet as is possible under the circumstances."

"I'll do my best, Doctor."

"She must have someone with her all the time. Here is the address of somebody who is highly qualified. Tell her that I recommended her to you; I hope she is available. I'll be back tomorrow. Meanwhile, carry out the instructions on the prescription to the letter."

The nurse, Madame Lebreton, who was a widow from the Great War, arrived that evening and took matters into her hands with an air of authority that irritated Léa, but which was also a relief. The idea of spending the night in Laurent's apartment was as unbearable as having to cope with Camille's tears again. Madame Lebreton wrote down Léa's telephone number and told her to go home and not to worry.

The Montpleynet sisters' apartment was in a state of turmoil. Lisa wanted to leave immediately for Montillac, while her sister wanted to wait and see what happened.

Léa burst out laughing at the sight of her Aunt Lisa dressed for the journey, her hat askew, clutching her gas mask, standing astride one of the suitcases that were cluttering up the hall.

"I don't intend to spend the night here," she proclaimed angrily.

Albertine asked Léa to come into the little drawing room.

"I don't think we're going to be able to make her listen to sense. It looks as if we're going to have to leave. Besides, your parents telephoned and said you should come back home as soon as possible."

"I can't, Camille is ill and there's no one to look after her."

"Let's take her with us."

"She mustn't be moved."

"But I can't leave you alone in Paris, anymore than I can allow that scatterbrain Lisa to leave by herself!"

"But aunt, that's ridiculous. The Germans are a long way off and our army will stop them.

"I'm sure you're right. It's silly of us to worry so. I'll try to talk sense to Lisa."

She was helped by François Tavernier, who came to ask after Camille, having been barred from visiting her by the nurse.

He told the trembling Lisa that as long as he was in Paris, there was nothing to fear. She agreed to stay until Whitsunday, convinced that the Holy Spirit would inspire the military.

"And don't forget, ladies, are we not protected by St. Genevieve, the patron saint of Paris? The churches were crowded this afternoon and at Notre-Dame, where they were praying to the Blessed Virgin to protect France. There were a number of ministers and priests. At the Sacré-Coeur, they were playing the national anthem on the great organ. The heavens are on our side. Don't worry."

François Tavernier sounded so serious that Léa would have believed him had he not winked at her.

"You're right," said Lisa, reassured, "God is on our side."

The next day, Camille was calmer, and there was a little color in her cheeks. At her request, Léa bought a map of France so that she could pinpoint Laurent's position and follow the progress of the French troops in Belgium. A large Max Ernst canvas was taken off the wall and the map put in its place. Léa marked the positions of the French army and the German troops with little colored flags.

"Luckily, he's in the Ardennes, it's safer there," said Camille.

"But François Tavernier says that's the French army's weak spot."

"That can't be true. If it were, they wouldn't have given leave to so many soldiers recently!" said Camille vehemently.

"Madame d'Argilat, it's time for your injection," said Madame Lebreton, who came into the room without knocking. "You must rest now. The doctor will be here and he certainly won't approve of you getting worked up like this."

Camille blushed like a naughty child and stammered: "You're right."

"I must go and keep an eye on Aunt Lisa. She's in such a state that she's capable of anything," said Léa, rising.

"When I think that you're staying because of me!"

"Don't think that. I have no wish to leave now. It's much more fun here than in Langon, or even Bordeaux."

"Fun, fun," grumbled the nurse.

Léa and Camille had to stifle their giggles.

"Don't forget to bring the newspapers tomorrow."

"There won't be any papers tomorrow, it's Whitsunday," said Léa as she adjusted her hat.

"That's true—I'd forgotten. I'm going to pray that those filthy Huns will be repulsed. Don't come too late."

"All right, see you tomorrow. Do rest."

As Léa crossed the Rue de Grenelle, lost in thought, she bumped into a passer-by. She apologized and recognized the man who had advised her to buy the book by Céline. He recognized her too, raised his hat and greeted her: "Did your friend like the book?"

"I don't know, but I get the feeling you were laughing at me in recommending it."

"Really?"

"Yes, but it's of no consequence."

"Quite. Forgive me, I haven't introduced myself: Raphaël Mahl."

"I know."

He stared at her with a mixture of surprise and anxiety. "Do we have mutual friends?"

"I don't think so. Goodbye."

"Don't rush off like that. I'd like to see you again. What's your name?"

Without really knowing why, Léa heard herself reply: "Léa Delmas."

"You'll find me on the terrace of the Deux Magots café every day, around one o'clock. I'd be delighted to offer you a drink."

Léa did not answer. She strode away.

Back at her aunts', all was quiet: the apartment was empty. Léa was worried and wondered if Lisa had not panicked again and swept Albertine and Estelle away with her. She did not have much time to dwell on things, as her aunts came in followed by Estelle.

"You should have seen the crowds, the fervor! God can't desert us," exclaimed Lisa breathlessly as she removed her ridiculous pink hat trimmed with a large bunch of violets.

"It was very moving," said Albertine calmly, as she took off her gray jacket.

"To be sure, with all these prayers and parades, the Germans haven't got a chance," added Estelle making for the kitchen.

"Where have you been?" asked Léa.

"We went to Notre-Dame. Parisians have been urged to pray together," said Lisa as she tidied her hair in front of one of the Venetian mirrors in the hall.

Léa went into the little drawing room, where she found an enormous brand new radio.

"Your Aunt Lisa bought it," said Albertine in response to her puzzled niece's look.

"Isn't the other one working?"

"Yes, but she insists on having one in her bedroom, by the bed, all the time. Lisa wants to know what's happening by the hour, day and night. She even listens to the BBC in London."

Léa turned one of the knobs. After a brief silence, followed by crackling, she heard: *"The day after tomorrow, the first Belgian and Dutch refugees will be arriving in Paris by train. All those who wish to show their sympathy should come and meet them at the Gare du Nord and send donations to the French Red Cross."*

"We'll go," said Albertine, firmly. "Léa, phone the garage and ask them to bring the car around tomorrow morning. Estelle and I will sort out some food and clothing."

When Léa arrived at Camille's, she found her in tears. She was kneeling in front of the radio despite Sarah Mulstein's pleading and Madame Lebreton's scolding.

"Léave me alone, be quiet, I want to hear the news," she cried, on the verge of hysterics. "Oh! It's you, Léa, tell them to leave me in peace!"

"I'll be back later," said Sarah walking towards the door. When she had left, Léa firmly got rid of the nurse.

"Listen, they're broadcasting the communique from the French headquarters."

"Between Namur and Mezierès, the enemy has managed to establish two bridgeheads, one at Houx, to the north of Dinant, the other at Montherme. They have created a third, larger one in the Marfée woods, near Sedan."

"The Marfée woods, look at the map, Léa. That's very close to Laurent."

Léa stood in front of the map, pointed to Sedan and then to Moiry, where Laurent d'Argilat was stationed.

"No it isn't, it's at least twenty kilometers away."

"Twenty kilometers? That's nothing for an army with tanks and planes dropping bombs everywhere. Have you forgotten what happened in Poland when the cavalry charged the German tanks? It was a massacre. I don't want that to happen to Laurent," screamed Camille throwing herself down on the carpet, her body racked with sobs.

Léa said nothing. She stared at the map. The little red flag marking the position of the 18th Cavalry Division looked like a bloodstain on the green forest.

Camille was right, twenty, thirty, even fifty kilometers were nothing to tanks. Which route would they take to kill the man she and Camille loved? Through Mouzon? Through Carignan? The little village of Moiry had become the center of the world for her, the most important spot in the whole war. She had to know exactly what was going on there. Who could tell her? François Tavernier! He would know.

"Do you know where we could reach François Tavernier?"

Camille looked up, tears streaming down her face.

"François Tavernier? What a good idea! He was here and was very reassuring. He's at the Ritz Hotel. He left his phone number in my book, by the vase of flowers."

The book fell open to the right page immediately. His name and telephone number, written in fine copperplate handwriting, stood out from the others. Léa dialed the number. A woman's voice answered; she gave her name, was passed on to another woman and finally a man.

"Monsieur Tavernier? This is Léa."

"No, this is Loriot. We met a few days ago."

"I'm sorry, I don't remember."

"It was in a Russian nightclub."

"Oh!"

"What can I do for you, Mademoiselle Delmas? Monsieur Tavernier is not here."

"When will he be back?"

"I don't know. He's gone to the Front at the Minister's request."

"Where?"

"I'm sorry, mademoiselle, but I can't divulge his whereabouts, it's a military secret. As soon as he's back I'll tell him you called. You can count on me."

"Thank you, sir. Goodbye."

Léa turned to face Camile and shrugged helplessly. How she goes on, she thought at the sight of the young woman lying on the floor. "Get up," she snapped.

A slight flush crept over Camille's pale face.

"Yes. I'm sorry, I'm being ridiculous. Laurent would be ashamed if he saw me like this."

Camille struggled to her feet clutching at the armchair. Once up, she faltered, managed to regain her balance and, aware of the look of disgust in Léa's eye, walked over to the bed, and summoning up all the dignity she could muster, sat down, gritting her teeth to stifle a moan of pain. Her hands were pressed to her heart while her mouth fell open in a mute cry. Just then, the doctor appeared.

"Good God!" He ran over to the sick woman and laid her gently on the bed. "Call the nurse," he said to Léa as he opened his bag. Léa left to fetch Madame Lebreton.

When Léa returned, followed by Madame Lebreton, the doctor had just finished giving Camille an injection in her arm.

"I told you not to leave her. Madame d'Argilat nearly died, and she," he said, pointing to Léa, "was just standing there!"

Léa was going to respond angrily when Josette came in, saying that Madame Mulstein was enquiring after Madame.

"I'll speak to her."

Sarah Mulstein was half lying on a low sofa when Léa walked into the drawing room. She raised herself up and then, recognizing Léa, sank back again.

"Excuse me for not getting up, Léa, but I'm worn out. How is Camille?"

"Bad."

"What can we do?"

"Nothing," said the docter, coming into the room. "She needs total rest. Mademoiselle Delmas, can you not get in touch with her husband?"

"Doctor, he's at the Front!"

"I don't know whether I'm coming or going with this war. I can't stop thinking about the last one, with so many lives lost for nothing, and it's happening again!"

"Madame, your friend is asleep now. But it is essential that she realize that she is endangering the life of her child unless she takes proper care. I have forbidden her to read the papers or to listen to the radio. She is not obeying my orders. Good day, ladies. I'll see you tomorrow."

Léa and Sarah were silent for a few minutes.

"Poor Camille. She hasn't picked the best time to bring a child into the world," sighed Léa.

"You don't think so?" said Sarah, getting to her feet. "What are your plans for this evening? Shall we have dinner together?"

"That would be lovely but I must go home to change and tell my aunts."

"You look fine as you are. And you can have a bath at my place. Call your aunts and tell them you'll be home before ten."

Léa did as she was told. Only Estelle was in, the Montpleynet sisters were not yet back. She insisted that Léa be home no later than promised.

Since she had been in Paris, Sarah had been living at the Hotel Lutetia, so as not to have to worry about the details of everyday life, as she put it. On entering her room, two hours earlier, with Léa, she had thrown her shoes across the room and flung her coat on to one of the flowery chintz-covered twin beds.

"Make yourself at home while I run the bath."

She came out of the bathroom wearing a long blue terrycloth bathrobe.

"The bath fills up very quickly. There are bath salts on the shelf. Do you want a drink? I'm going to have an Alexander, the barman's really very good at them."

"I'll have one too," said Léa, a little in awe of this woman whom she hardly knew.

A quarter of an hour later, it was her turn to emerge, flushed, with her hair up, wearing a lilac bathrobe.

"How young you are," exclaimed Sarah. "I've never seen a complexion like yours, or such extraordinary eyes, and such a lovely mouth. I can see why men fall in love with you."

This avalanche of compliments made Léa blush; she felt embarrassed.

"Here's your drink. I've booked a table at a restaurant I'm very fond of. I hope you'll like it."

While she talked, Sarah rummaged around in one of the many open suitcases scattered around the room. She took out a set of pale blue lingerie and a pair of dark gray stockings. In another case, she found a slightly crumpled red wool dress.

"I won't be long," she said, disappearing into the bathroom again.

"What a mess," thought Léa. "To think that Mummy calls me untidy! What would she say if she had a daughter like Sarah?" She was astonished to realize that she had not thought about her mother for several days. She promised herself she would write her a long letter.

"Put the radio on," yelled Sarah through the partition.

Léa looked about her, moving piles of dresses, coats and newspapers: there was nothing that bore any resemblance to a radio.

Sarah reappeared in a short slip, drying her wet hair with a towel.

"Why don't you switch the radio on? It's time for the news bulletins."

"I can't find it."

"How silly of me! They took it away to repair it. Aren't you dressed yet?"

Léa indicated that her clothes were still in the bathroom.

"What's the matter with me this evening? I'm absolutely exhausted."

When Léa came back into the room, she found Sarah on

her stomach under the bed, looking for her shoes which eventually turned out to be in the waste-paper basket!

The little restaurant L'Ami Louis was packed. But, "because they were friends of Monsieur Tavernier's," the owner set up a little marble table behind the door, which he locked, and a young waiter hung up a sign saying *Full* and drew the grimy velvet curtains to protect the clients from the idle curiosity of passers-by.

Léa looked around, fascinated. It was the first time that she had been in this sort of place; it had little in common with what she expected an elegant restaurant to be like.

"I'm going to take you to a fashionable bistro," Sarah had said.

The light reflected from the yellowish walls made the guests look as if they were suffering from hepatitis. The floor was covered with sawdust which formed dirty little damp piles underfoot; the wooden chairs were hard and uncomfortable, and the noise and the smoke bothered Léa.

The waiter laid the table skilfully. Léa was reassured by the spotless white of the linen and the gleaming silverware and glasses. To make conversation, she leaned forward and said to her companion: "Do you often come here?"

"Quite a lot. As I told you, François Tavernier brought me here: the *foie gras,* the game and the wine are all excellent. The decor leaves a lot to be desired, but you soon forget about it with the quality of the food and the marvelous service."

"What wine would you like, madame?"

"I've forgotten the name of the wine Monsieur Tavernier always has, I find it very good."

"Indeed, it is very good, madame, it's a Château La Lagune."

"Fine, we'll drink to his health."

Léa tasted the wine like an expert.

The waiter brought over the *foie gras* and some thick slices of Bayonne ham, while the wine steward filled their glasses.

"For the next course, there's sirloin steak, Provence

casserole, loin of lamb and squab with peas.''

"Have the squab, it's delicious," advised Sarah.

Léa nodded, smiling.

"Now let's drink to the health of our friend, François," said Sarah, raising her glass.

"That's an idea after my own heart," said the amused voice of Tavernier as he approached. He seemed younger, with his slightly dishevelled hair, his turtleneck sweater and tweed jacket.

"François!" exclaimed Sarah. "What a lovely surprise! I thought you must have been buried alive under the German bombs!"

"I very nearly was," he said as he bowed to kiss her outstretched hand on which a beautiful diamond sparkled. "Good evening, Léa, has your aunt recovered from her fright?"

"Yes. She's fine for the moment."

"I hear you called. Nothing's wrong, I hope?"

"Camille wanted to get in touch with you. I thought you were at the Front?"

"I was. I came back this afternoon. As you can see from my clothing, I haven't had time to change—will you forgive me? The table is small, but may I join you?"

"What a silly question! We'll make room," said Sarah. "Waiter, bring a chair."

"You won't be very comfortable, Monsieur Tavernier."

"It doesn't matter."

"What would you like to eat, sir?"

"A sirloin steak, very rare."

The wine steward refilled their glasses. François Tavernier drank in silence; his thoughts seemed far away. Léa was dying to ask him what he had seen, but did not dare.

"Don't keep us in suspense," said Sarah, "what's happening out there?"

For a second, a look of irritation clouded François Tavernier's face as he looked from one beautiful young woman to the other: they were so different— the brunette with enormous black eyes and pale skin and her aquiline nose and generous mouth; what a contrast to the wild Léa with her dishevelled hair, her stubborn forehead, her sensual mouth, her strange eyes that made him want to plunge into their depths. That toss of her head when she was listening . . .

"Let's change the subject, I don't want to worry your pretty little heads with all that. We'll talk about it tomorrow."

"No, not tomorrow, now," said Sarah impetuously, grabbing Tavernier's arm. "I have a right to know," she continued in a low voice. "If the Nazis win this war, I'll never see my father or my husband again."

"I know, Sarah. I know."

"No, you don't know. You don't know what they're capable of . . . "

"Calm down, Sarah, I know all that as well as you do. In spite of the speed of developments, I haven't lost touch with my contacts in Germany, and the news I have is not so bad. However . . . "

"However?"

" . . . I wonder if they will be any safer in France?"

"How can you doubt it? France is a free country, an asylum, the home of the Declaration of the Rights of Man. France would never imprison Jews simply because they're Jews."

"I admire your confidence in the justice of my country. I dearly hope you are right."

"But we'll win the war," said Léa, who had not yet said anything.

François Tavernier was spared having to reply by the arrival of their meal. The three of them ate hungrily, silent for a while and then gradually, thanks to the wine and the excellent food, they tried to make small talk. The dinner ended in laughter, the women slightly tipsy, especially Léa who had drunk a lot.

"Oh! Half past ten already. My aunts will be worried," she said as she stood up.

"Come on, I'll take you home. Put that on my bill," said François Tavernier to the waiter, leaving a tip on the table.

When Léa got home, her aunts were far too exhausted to

comment on her lateness. They greeted Sarah and Francois absentmindedly; they only had one thing in mind, and that was bed.

"Keep me posted about Camille," said Sarah as she was leaving. She kissed Léa on both cheeks.

"I'll phone you tomorrow," said François flattening himself against the wall to let Sarah past.

Chapter 12

Ever since the 14th of May, when François Tavernier told Léa that France had just lost the war, events had moved too swiftly for Léa. They had followed the progress of the German invasion on their map, unable to believe it was really happening. Camille had not heard from Laurent since the offensive on the 10th of May and they feared for his life. Despite the censorship of the news, they were furious at the thought of the thousands of French soldiers who must have died for nothing on the roads in the north.

Alarming rumors were being spread by the fleeing hordes: stories of pillaging from village to village; ceaseless bombing; the Ninth Army totally crushed, with General Giraud desperately trying to pick up the pieces; the collapse of the Second Army—Laurent's—under General Huntzinger; spies everywhere; abandoned children; the old and the sick wandering about, homeless . . .

François Tavernier once again urged Léa and Sarah to leave Paris. Sarah refused, saying that if her father and her husband managed to escape from Germany, they would be able to meet in Paris. If she left, they would not know where to find her. As for Léa, she could not leave because Camille's health, after improving a little, had gotten worse.

Lisa had gotten her way. Although she had been slightly reassured by the dismissal of General Gamelin and the appointment of Marshal Pétain as Vice-Premier, two days later she was in an even greater panic. The Montpleynet sisters left their home in the Rue de l'Université, taking Estelle with them and leaving Léa in Sarah Mulstein's and François Tavernier's care. Right up until the last minute they hoped their niece would leave with them, so afraid were they of incurring Pierre and Isabelle Delmas's displeasure.

Finally, on the 30th of May, two letters from Laurent arrived. Josette rushed into the drawing room where Camille and Léa were sitting by the window, brandishing the envelopes triumphantly. "Madame, Madame, look! Two letters from Monsieur!"

Léa and Camille leaped up, their hearts pounding, unable to speak. Josette held out the two thick envelopes covered with military postmarks, surprised that the good news had not been received with more enthusiasm. Camille sat slowly down again.

"Léa, I haven't got the strength. Will you open them?"

Without replying, Léa snatched the letters, tore them open and smoothed the crumpled pages of cheap lined notepaper covered with cramped handwriting. One of the letters was dated the 17th of May and the other the 28th.

"Please read them," said Camille in a choked voice.

"My beloved wife," began Léa.

The words swam before her eyes: "My beloved wife . . . " but they were not addressed to her. To hide her agitation, she walked over to the window.

"Please go on."

Camille had no idea how much it cost Léa to continue reading. Léa went on in a flat, monotonous voice:

My beloved wife, I've been thinking of you so often these last few days, all alone, in your condition, with no word from me. In Paris you probably have more idea of what's going on than we do here. It is all so unbelievable! I have been desperately trying to understand what has happened since the Germans invaded Belgium and Luxembourg. I set out to do my duty, but we have had to withdraw. No longer soldiers, we have become runaways, joining thousands of refugees. Everywhere you look there are cars crammed with people and belongings, motorcycles, bicycles, suitcases, bags bursting at the seams. Men and women crying, children shrieking as they wend their way on foot along the endless roads under the scorching sun.

Every day the bombing gets worse. Deserted villages are sacked. All that's left are the animals—pigs and calves wandering around among terrified hens and mooing cows that follow us, wanting to be milked.

Darling, the only thing that keeps me going is the knowledge that you are safe. I should not like you to see the crowds of refugees sleeping in the fields and ditches like corpses, screaming in terror as the bombs fall all around them.

I hate war, as you well know, but I am ashamed of the way our troops have fled. I am ashamed of the weakness of our leaders. Each day, I think of you, of our child, of my father, of Roches-Blanches, of everything that gives me the will to live. And I think about honor. . . . Sometimes I feel furious at not being out there fighting, confronting the enemy, gun in hand. When I see the mountains of wounded horses, I want to vomit, to cry. These last days, I've been sleeping in the woods, in barns, eating whatever I can lay my hands on. I am exhausted and humiliated. What can I do?

Léa held the first letter out to Camille, leaving her to read the closing words of endearment that were so painful to her. "Please darling, read me the other one. We both love him so much, I want us to read it together!"

Léa started, wondering what Camille meant by her "We both love him so much." Had she guessed at her feelings for Laurent? Or did she trust her that much?

The second letter was dated the 28th of May.

My sweet love. I have come a long way since my last letter. Do you know, I'm only about fifty kilometers from Paris and the thought of being so close to you is driving me crazy. All your letters arrived at the same time. I am very happy to learn that Léa is beside you. I find it a great comfort. Tell her how grateful I am and how fond I am of her.

I also had a letter from my father. Unfortunately, the news is not good. I fear that this war that he was so afraid of, and the setbacks we have suffered, have affected his health. Our morale is very low and reading the newspapers has done nothing to improve it: the bombing of Belgium and Holland, the Allied forces virtually surrounded in Flanders, the dismissal of Gamelin and his replacement by the "young" Weygand . . . Perhaps Pétain's appointment as Vice-Premier will save French hope and honor.

I am sending the diary I have kept during these days of war. If you have the strength, read it. Perhaps it'll put you in the picture. Forgive me for boring you with the details of my food problems and my flight through the woods. But this is all that my daily life has consisted of since the 10th of May. As I said before, I'm delighted not to have to fight—not out of cowardice, please believe me, but out of a horror of seeing blood spilled. However, as I wrote in my last letter, these German victories, our inferiority, at least in my area, will be a perpetual source of shame and sorrow. I have to go now, my love, the colonel wants me to join him. Take good care of yourself, I love you.

Léa held the letter out to Camille. Camille put it in her lap, as she tried to concentrate on the first one, repeating, as if to herself: "He's all right, he's alive."

"Of course he's alive, otherwise he wouldn't be writing," snapped Léa.

Camille made no reply; she was glancing through the diary which recorded the events between the 10th and 27th of May, 1940. With an expression of incredulity, she read Laurent's day-by-day account, occasionally reading a sentence or two aloud:

La Ferté-sur-Chiers, Beaufort. . . . I'm going off in search of news. The colonel is missing and many think that he's had it . . . must find food. . . . One of my men has just been blown up by a mine. . . . A brigadier was assassinated by a drunken sol-

dier . . . Wiazemsky and I have only one idea in our
heads—to organize supplies. We manage to milk wandering cows and feed the children. . . . In the evening the
planes came whistling overhead, and the explosions
followed. It was our first experience with bombs as we
lay flat on the ground. . . . In the ditch, a solitary
sergeant was crying. . . . We're sleeping in a barn.

"Poor Laurent," murmured Camille, "he never could sleep
anywhere other than in a bed!"

Léa shot her a look of pure envy.

"Listen, Léa," continued Camille, enthralled, "on the 24th
of May he stopped at Chalons."

Unforgettable feeling of finding a large town with civilians, shops, cafés. A good supper, brandy and cigar: the
war sometimes has its good sides. What a wonderful feeling it is sleeping between clean sheets after a long bath.

Léa watched Camille finish reading, her anger reaching its
peak.

"I wish I were in his shoes. At least he doesn't have to
stay shut up indoors all day."

"How can you say such a thing?" exclaimed Camille.
"Laurent is risking his life!"

"Perhaps, but he doesn't have time to get bored."

Camille looked sadly at Léa. "Are you so bored with my
company? I know it's not much fun for you being a
nursemaid. If it weren't for me, you'd have gone home to
your parents. Oh! How you must hate me," said Camille
bursting into tears.

"Stop crying. You'll make yourself ill and Madame
Lebreton will blame me again."

"Forgive me. You're right. Why don't you go out and enjoy youself a bit more? Sarah Mulstein and François Tavernier are always asking you. Why do you refuse?"

"Because I see enough of them here every afternoon!"

"But they don't come every day!"

"Maybe, but it's still too often."

Camille bowed her head, exhausted. "I'm fond of them.

125

François is so kind, so cheerful. . . . "

"I don't understand what you see in that coward."

"Léa, you know that's not true, he has a very responsible position and the ministers often consult him."

"That's his story. Honestly, you're so gullible. As you are with Sarah. I wouldn't be surprised if she were a spy."

"Léa, you're going too far. You read too much pulp literature and see too many bad films."

"I kill time as well as I can."

"Léa, please, let's not argue. Let's just be grateful that Laurent is safe and sound."

"For the moment, it's your health that matters. Do you think the doctor will allow you to leave?"

"I really have no idea," sighed Camille. "I do wish I could be at Roches-Blanches with Laurent's father. I'm so afraid for my child!"

There was a knock at the door and Josette came into the room. "It's Madame Mulstein and Monsieur Tavernier."

"Show them in," cried Camille, her pale face lighting up with pleasure.

"Not them again!" said Léa grumpily.

Sarah Mulstein came in, holding a bunch of roses. She crossed the room to kiss Camille. She smiled when she caught sight of the pages of Laurent's letters scattered over the cream satin bedspread.

"I see that you've heard from your soldier. It must be good news judging by the color in your cheeks. You look almost cheerful."

"Yes, it's a great relief. What lovely roses! You're so good to me. Thank you, Sarah."

"Hello, Léa. You look glum, what's the matter with you?"

"Nothing. I'm bored," said Léa as she allowed Sarah to kiss her.

"Let me admire the roses in your cheeks," said François as he stooped to kiss Camille's outstretched hand. "It's quite true, you almost put your flowers to shame."

"I think you're exaggerating somewhat," laughed Camille. "What about you, Sarah, is there any news of your husband?"

Before replying, Sarah removed her elaborate black felt

hat with its long red ostrich feather. She sank down into a low armchair beside the bed and automatically smoothed her rumpled skirt.

"Yes, I had some news yesterday."

"Oh, I'm so pleased for you."

"He's been sent to a camp in Poland," continued Sarah.

"Oh no!" cried Camille.

Léa, who had been keeping to herself, went over to François Tavernier and sneered: "I thought you were supposed to be getting him out of Germany."

"It didn't work."

"François did everything in his power," said Sarah wearily.

"How can you be so sure?" insisted Léa.

"Léa!"

"Forget it, Camille, you know that our lovely friend thinks I'm a coward, and I don't give a damn," said Tavernier nonchalantly.

"Let me answer that, François. My father telephoned me from Lyons. That's how I learned of the circumstances of my husband's arrest. The Nazis are taking their revenge on him, having failed to keep in their clutches an artist who is internationally famous: if it hadn't been for François's many interventions, it's not only my husband who would have been shipped to a concentration camp. . . . Papa will be in Paris tomorrow."

A painful silence fell over the room. Léa was the first to break it: "Forgive me, François. You too, Sarah."

"I've told you before, Léa: how young you are! You're too quick to jump to conclusions without knowing what you're talking about. You must be more careful now. You see spies everywhere. Beware the fifth column," said Sarah.

Léa turned away to hide her irritation and then looked at her watch. "I'd completely forgotten, I've arranged to meet somebody. I'll see you this evening, Camille. I'm leaving you in good company."

François Tavernier followed her out and joined her in the hall, where she was putting on her hat in front of a long mirror.

"That hat doesn't suit you, it makes you look older. Ex-

127

cept for the color, it would suit your Aunt Lisa better."

Léa swung around angrily. "You don't know what you're talking about. This hat comes from one of the most elegant milliners in Paris."

"Don't act the Parisienne with me, you're infinitely more delightful as the little savage from Montillac, especially when you blush as you are doing now."

"I'm not blushing, and I don't care what you think. Leave me alone."

"No, I've got to talk to you. Let's go to your room."

"Not likely!"

"Stop putting on airs. That doesn't suit you either. Come along."

He took her arm and dragged her towards the door.

"You let me go, or I'll scream!"

"Scream away. You don't want to talk? Very well then, I'll carry you."

And so saying, he swept Léa off her feet. Contrary to her threats, she did not scream, but tried to free herself by hammering him with her fists.

"This is the virgin's lair, isn't it?" he asked, pushing the half-open door with his shoulder.

"Let me go! Will you let me go!"

"Your wish is my command, madame."

Tavernier casually flung Léa down on the bed.

Léa bounced backwards with a howl of helpless rage, her dishevelled hair in her eyes, then got up, crouching and ready to pounce. But François was too fast for her and in an instant he was on the bed, gripping her wrists.

"Bastard . . . "

"How many times have I told you, your vocabulary of insults is very limited. you should read more. All right, that's enough playing around, I've got to talk to you. Will you listen to me?"

"Let go . . . "

"Now you're going too far. If you won't keep still, I'll kiss you."

Léa immediately stopped struggling.

"You want to talk? What about?" she asked, serious now.

"About you and Camille. Leave Paris. It's no longer safe here."

"I know," said Léa, rubbing her wrists. "It's not my fault if the doctor says she can't be moved."

"I'll talk to him about it. In a few days, the Germans will be in Paris, and I'll be at the Front myself."

"Well! That's funny, I thought you didn't like lost causes."

"No, I don't, but that's not the issue."

"A question of honor, perhaps," said Léa as nastily as she could.

The look he shot her made her huddle up on the bed for fear he would hit her. But there were no blows, and she looked up and blushed with shame at his shattered expression. She was overcome with a desire to throw herself into his arms and ask for forgiveness. She might have done so if, at that moment, he had not burst out laughing.

"Honor! Perhaps . . . but I am unworthy of such a feeling! No doubt one has to be called Laurent d'Argilat to understand such things."

"Leave Laurent's honor out of this. Let's talk about our departure."

"Can you drive?"

"Yes, I learned in Bordeaux just before I came to Paris."

"I'm going to try and beg, steal or borrow an ambulance or a comfortable car in which Camille can travel lying down. You will take Madame Lebreton and Josette with you."

"What! You're letting us leave alone?"

"There's no alternative. All able-bodied men are at the Front. Anyway, you're big enough to look after yourself."

Without replying, Léa looked down. François Tavernier was touched by this gesture of helplessness. He took her face in his hands and raised her chin. Great tears were running down her cheeks. He gently kissed her eyelids and then his mouth sought her lips which offered no resistance. He sat down on the bed, let go her curls and then lay down beside Léa.

"Cry, pet, if it makes you feel better."

On hearing his solemn but soft voice that reminded her of her father, Léa burst into tears and nestled up to François.

"I want to go home. I'm so frightened that Camille will lose her baby . . . what would Laurent say? Why doesn't Papa come and get me? Is it true that the Germans rape all the women?"

"You're going home, darling, don't worry, I'll take care of everything."

"But you said you were going away . . . "

"I'll arrange everything before I leave."

François was a little annoyed with himself for taking advantage of the situation; his lips became more insistent, his hands bolder, but this had a soothing effect on Léa, who gradually began returning his kisses.

The sound of voices in the hall interrupted their brief moment of pleasure. Léa gently pushed François away from her, stood up and smoothed her crumpled clothes.

"Don't just lie there looking at me. Wipe your mouth, you're covered with lipstick. And comb your hair," she ordered, pointing to the brushes on the dressing table.

Smiling, he did as he was told.

"It sounds as though the doctor and Madame Lebreton are arguing," said Léa straining to hear what was being said.

There was a knock at the door.

"It's Josette, Mademoiselle Léa. The doctor would like to speak to you."

"Very well, tell him I'm coming. What on earth can he have to say to me?" she said turning towards François.

He shrugged. "I'm going to leave you. I have to prepare for tomorrow's meeting with Churchill and his aides."

"What do you think will come of this meeting?"

"Not much. General Reynaud hopes to obtain more RAF planes. He won't get them, nor will he get the French troops who are in Dunkirk evacuated at the same time as the British troops."

"So what's the point of the meeting?"

"To keep in touch, to try and find out the exact position of our allies, to discover what their attitude will be if there's a separate armistice."

"Separate armistice?"

"It's in the air. Try and think about other things. You

shouldn't have to worry your pretty little head about such matters. That's men's business," he said, pulling her towards him.

She complied and looked at him in a way she had never looked at him before.

"I shouldn't like anything to happen to you," he murmured.

Léa seemed disappointed at not being kissed. Her pout made him smile.

"That's enough for today. I'm going to try and find you a vehicle. I'll be in touch in two days. Go and see what Doctor Dubois wants."

Léa left the room without replying.

"And about time too, Mademoiselle Delmas, do you think I have nothing better to do than wait for you?" exclaimed the doctor when Léa walked into the room.

"I'm sorry, Doctor, I thought you were with Madame d'Argilat."

"Madame d'Argilat is very well, she's not a problem . . ."

"So we can leave?" exclaimed Léa excitedly.

"That would have been possible if Madame Lebreton had not handed in her notice over a trifling matter."

"A trifling matter!" said the nurse, whose presence had escaped Léa's notice. "I find out that my son-in-law is seriously wounded in Brittany and my daughter wants to go and join him with her two children. You call that a trifling matter!"

"Your daughter is old enough to travel without her mother," said the doctor impatiently.

"With two children under five? It's clear, Doctor, that you have never had children."

"And I'm glad of it in these troubled times."

"Madame Lebreton, you can't leave me alone with Camille, I don't know how to take care of her, how to give her injections."

"I'm sorry, I have to think of my own family. Send her to a hospital."

"Madame Lebreton, you know as well as I do that there's

not a bed to be had in any hospital, for either love or money, and that many of them have been evacuated,'' said the doctor.

"There's nothing I can do about it,'' snapped the nurse. "I'm taking the train to Rennes this evening. Mademoiselle Delmas, it's time for Madame d'Argilat's injection. If you like, I'll show you how to do it. It isn't difficult.''

Sarah Mulstein was still in Camille's room when the two women entered followed by Doctor Dubois. He endeavored to sound cheerful as he announced: "Madame Lebreton has to leave us for personal reasons. She is going to show Mademoiselle Delmas how to do your injection.''

Camille turned pale and tried to smile weakly, saying: "I hope it's not too serious. Thank you for taking such good care of me. Poor Léa, I'm such a lot of trouble.''

"Turn over,'' grumbled the nurse, who stood holding the syringe poised.

Sarah and the doctor moved away while Madame Lebreton went on: "Now watch, it isn't difficult: one sharp movement . . . you press the plunger slowly . . . ''

Chapter 13

Parisians were fleeing their city. Nearly three hundred people had been killed in the bombing of Orly, Le Bourget and Villacoublay airports, the Citroën factories and the residential Fifteenth and Sixteenth districts, on that Monday, the 3rd of June. Early in the morning, the first cars left Paris for the south. But hordes of Parisians congregated at the railway stations, mingling with the stream of refugees from the north and the east of France.

Léa was crossing the Place Saint-Sulpice on her way to the Town Hall where ration books were being allocated. The square lay silent and sluggish: it felt more like August than early summer. Without the yellow coupons stuck inside the book, it was impossible to obtain sugar. Milk, coffee and butter were already becoming scarce; Léa wondered what on earth they would be eating for breakfast soon.

When she emerged from the Town Hall after standing in line for two hours, Léa was in an extremely bad mood. She was tired from waiting for so long in corridors smelling of disinfectant, perspiration and musty papers. She sat on a bench by the fountain, drawing Camille's beige raincoat tighter around her. It was no longer so hot, and threatening clouds were gathering in the sky from which death might strike at any moment.

She recalled, with irritation, how calmly Camille had reacted when she heard the air-raid sirens and then the deafening roar of the airplanes flying over Paris, and finally the bombs exploding. Léa insisted that Camille go down to the improvised air-raid shelter in the cellar, but, stubborn as a mule, she had refused, saying she would rather see death coming than be buried alive. Léa, furious and terrified, had stayed by her, burying her head in the silk cushions.

And there was still no sign of François Tavernier! He could not have left for the Front without seeing her again, and keeping his promise that he would find a means of getting them out of Paris. It was already the 6th of June.

"A frown like that can only mean bad news," said a man coming to sit beside her.

Léa was about to rebuff him when she recognized Raphaël Mahl.

"Well, hello, haven't you left Paris yet?"

"To go where?"

"To the devil, if you like!"

"That, my dear, is where we'll all end up. Not that I mind, I've always liked blond devils, especially in uniform. Don't you? It'll be a pleasant change from all those hook-nosed Jews."

"Shut up, you're disgusting."

"Why is it disgusting? Isn't it because of Cohens and Company that we're going to lose the war? I know them well, you see, I'm half-Jewish, you know."

"I have a Jewish friend whose husband was arrested simply because he's Jewish."

"Isn't that a good enough reason?"

"You are repulsive!" exclaimed Léa, leaping up.

"Come, come, calm down, I was joking," he said, also rising and taking Léa's arm.

She broke away impatiently.

"Excuse me, I have to go home."

"Wait, I've got a friend too. She's asked me to sell one of her furs, a magnificent silver fox. I'll let you have it for a very reasonable price; it's an excellent bargain."

"I didn't know you were interested in furs?"

"In this case it's just a matter of doing a favor for a friend who needs money to be able to leave Paris. She's Jewish too, and she's afraid of the Nazis. As for me, I'm more afraid of boredom. If you're not interested in the fox fur, I've also got carpets, exquisite antique carpets."

"So now you're a carpet dealer. I thought you were a writer."

The jovial expression immediately left Raphaël Mahl's face. He suddenly looked sad and weary, and his face was suffused with a melancholy beauty emphasized by his intelligent eyes.

"Yes, I'm a writer. A writer first and foremost. You are only a woman, what can you understand of the writer's life, of his daily struggle between a desire to live and a desire to write? The two are incompatible. I'm like Oscar Wilde, I want to put genius into my life and into my work. But that is impossible. I rage, but I have to choose: to live or to write. There is a great book inside me, I know it, but my desire to take part in what is going on in the world, to get caught up in worldly passions, oppresses me so much that my work suffers from it. As the Goncourt brothers wrote in their *Journal,* I need 'a regular daily routine, peace and quiet; one's whole being must be snug, in a state of meditation, in order to give birth to something great, dramatic and full of torment. Those who spend themselves in passion or dashing around frenetically will never produce a creative work and will exhaust their lives just by living.' *Exhaust my life in living it* ... that's what happening to me. You women are protected by your lack of imagination, the only thing you create is through childbirth. Of course, there are among you sublime monsters like Madame de Noailles, or Colette—ah! there's a remarkable craftswoman for you—but there is little of that real intelligence, which is essentially masculine."

"Masculine, intelligence? How dare you say that when this country is in the hands of the only creatures who, in your opinion, have any real intelligence, and is in the process of falling apart most miserably."

"We are bing beaten by a country superior to us in strength and intelligence, and we have to give in."

"Give in to savages?"

"Your pretty little head is lovely to look at, but completely empty. All you're doing is repeating what you've heard the gossips say. This war that seems so brutal to you will be good for France. Already, in 1867, the Goncourts were writing: 'Savagery is necessary every four or five hundred years to revitalize the world. The world was dying from civilization. In the past, in Europe, when the longtime population of a cultured land had become suitably anemic, it would be overrun by great six-foot fellows from the north who would regenerate the race.' The Germans are those fellows who will give our anemic race the new blood it needs for its resurrection. Believe you me, I may be a swindling pederast, but I have been a keen observer, for the purposes of literature—and sometimes my personal needs—of that thinking animal called Man. Man, whom one day God banished from his sight and, poor creature, he has never recovered. Remember Lamartine's beautiful line: 'Man is a fallen angel, who can remember Heaven.' "

"You sound like my Uncle Adrien—he's a Dominican," mocked Léa.

"He made the right choice. For a man like him, there's nothing but the Church. I wanted to be a priest, once. I was a Jew, I converted. Friends, fervent Catholics, encouraged me. On the eve of being ordained, I ran away from the seminary and spent three days in a brothel full of young boys. It was divine! After the safe smell of ecclesiastical armpits, after the pock-marked cheeks of my dormitory companions, whose obsessive state of rut stained their pajamas and the sheets, after gloomy mornings seeing their flesh bulge under their robes, what a delight it was to be able to caress and kiss the soft perfumed bodies of those young male prostitutes. How could you understand, little girl, still a virgin, no doubt? You haven't even experienced the insipid embrace of Sappho."

"Indeed, I do not understand. You disgust me."

"It's true that I'm base and disgusting!" He burst out laughing. "Hey, madame, are you sure you don't want a carpet or a fine fur? I'll make you a special price, because you've got nice eyes," he went on, as he followed her, making grotesque faces.

He made a face that was so sly and so lewd that Léa started to laugh.

"Poor Raphaël, you're as mad as a hatter. I don't know why I stand here putting up with your nonsense."

"Because, my dear, I make you laugh, and my incoherent babbling takes you out of your lethargic adolescence. It's time to grow up, my beauty. We live in troubled times."

They walked in silence for a few minutes. Raphaël stopped at the corner of the Rue de Grenelle and the Rue des Saints-Perès.

"Would you like to come to my place for tea? A friend has lent me a delightful apartment on the Rue de Rivoli. There is a charming view of the Tuileries gardens."

"I'd love to, but I'm afraid I can't. The friend I'm staying with is ill. She'll worry: I've been gone for more than three hours."

"What about tomorrow? Please come. I'll lend you some of my favorite books. It's important to love the same books when you want to be friends."

Léa found herself warming to him in spite of herself. She did not understand why.

"I'll come if I can. I promise."

He scribbled his address and telephone number on an envelope.

"I'll be expecting you tomorrow any time after four. If you can't make it, call me. I'm counting on you."

"Perhaps," she said, slipping the envelope into her pocket. She ran all the way home.

Léa was still fumbling with her key when the door opened and there was Camille, hastily dressed in a navy blue suit which emphasized her big stomach and made her drawn face look even paler.

"Here you are, at last," she cried, leaning against the wall for support.

"What are you doing out of bed?"

"I was going to look for you," she murmured, sliding to the floor in a faint.

"Josette, Josette, come quickly!"

The young maid came running and let out a shriek when she saw Camille lying unconscious on the floor.

"Come! Help me! Don't stand there like an idiot!"

Puffing and panting, Josette helped Léa carry Camille to her room and lay her on the bed.

"Undress her. I'm going to give her an injection."

When Léa returned, syringe in hand, Josette was pulling the covers over Camille, who was now wearing only a flimsy pink silk slip.

Once the injection was over, Léa anxiously examined Camille's poor face with its pinched nostrils. She had never taken so long to come round.

"Why did you let her get up?"

Josette, who was crouching at the foot of the bed, burst into tears.

"It's not my fault, mademoiselle, I was getting the tea ready in the kitchen. I left Madame listening quietly to the radio when, all of a sudden, I nearly broke the teapot she gave me such a fright. She was standing behind me, barefoot, her eyes all wild, repeating over and over: 'I must go and find Léa. I must go and find Léa . . . ' I tried to get her back to her room, but she pushed me away, saying: 'Start packing, the Germans are coming.' I was scared, I thought she'd heard it on the radio. I ran to pack while Madame got dressed. That's when you arrived. Tell me, mademoiselle, are they really coming?"

"I have no idea. Call Doctor Dubois. Tell him to come at once."

"Very well, mademoiselle."

Léa leaned over Camille and tried to revive her with smelling salts. Supposing the Germans do come, she thought, and began to feel panicky.

"Mademoiselle, the doctor isn't in and they're not sure when he'll be back."

"Léa . . . " Camille slowly opened her eyes. "Léa, you're here . . . I was so afraid you'd gone . . . On the radio . . . they say the government's leaving Paris . . . " she stuttered, clutching Léa's arm.

"Now calm down, I've just come in and I didn't see any Germans in the streets. Everything's quiet, you're the one who's getting all worked up about nothing. Laurent wouldn't like to see you being so unreasonable. Rest now and try to sleep. Doctor Dubois will be here soon," Léa lied.

"Fogive me. I'm so frightened when you're not here."

By the time Camille fell asleep, it was nightfall and the doctor still had not arrived.

Léa felt hungry and went into the kitchen in search of something to eat. The cupboard was bare. There were just a few dry biscuits. She stormed out to scold Josette and found the maid sitting in the darkened drawing room, with her coat on, ready to leave, her suitcase at her feet.

"What are you doing, and why are you wearing your hat and coat indoors?"

"Mademoiselle, I want to leave. I want to return to my parents in Normandy."

Léa stared at her aghast. "You want to desert me when I have a sick woman on my hands!"

"I'm frightened, mademoiselle. I'm too frightened . . . I want to go home."

"Home! The Germans have already arrived at your home. If not today, they'll be there tomorrow. You'd be better off going up to bed."

"But . . ."

"Be quiet. Tomorrow you'd better get some food in. Good night."

Léa left the room. Josette sat bewildered and sobbing.

At six o'clock the following morning, Léa was wakened from a restless sleep by the front doorbell. She assumed it was Doctor Dubois. She grabbed her kimono and got up from the sofa in Camille's room, where she had spent the night. Yawning, she opened the door.

A man in a mud-stained uniform, a dirty face with several days' stubble on his chin, was standing before her.

"It's only me. You're not awake yet, are you, my dear? May I come in?"

Léa stood aside to allow François Tavernier to enter.

"Don't look at me like that, Léa. Do you think I'm a ghost?"

"Almost. Where have you been these last few days? I called you several times."

"As you can see from my outfit, I haven't exactly been out wining and dining."

"Stop mocking me. You were supposed to call me and I've been waiting."

"How good of you. Come and let me embrace you for being so faithful."

"Go away. You're filthy!"

"What do you expect, my dear? War isn't very clean. But a soldier is always allowed a kiss from a beautiful woman." François Tavernier pulled Léa towards him and kissed her in spite of her reluctance. Sensing her repulsion, he let her go again.

"How is Madame d'Argilat?"

"Ill. Very ill."

"The doctor?"

"We've been waiting for him since yesterday. Do you have a car we can travel in?"

"Yes. I haven't just been waging war for the last few days, I've hunted down a car in perfect working order. Will you be able to drive it?"

"I'll have to."

"I've sent a reliable man to get it. You'll have it in two days' time."

"Two days!"

"The car is in Marseilles."

"I should have listened to Papa and taken the train."

"It did occur to me. But it would have been impossible for Madame d'Argilat to travel lying down."

The doorbell rang again.

"Oh! Doctor," cried Léa as she opened the door.

Doctor Dubois was barely more presentable than François Tavernier. His clothes were crumpled, he was unshaven and his red-rimmed eyes betrayed his exhaustion.

"I couldn't come sooner. Would you kindly make me some coffee?"

"I'd be grateful for a cup too," said François.

"I'll go and see if there is any. Josette is so frightened that she won't go out to the shops."

As she feared, there was no coffee, milk or bread.

"I'll deal with this," said François, who had followed Léa into the kitchen. "I know a café near here. I used to go there often. The owner will do me a small favor. I'll be back by the time the water's boiled. Meanwhile, would you run a bath for me? I haven't time to go home."

When he returned, he was carrying a large paper bag full of freshly ground coffee, a bottle of milk, a can of chocolate, a pound of sugar, and, wonder of wonders, a couple of dozen croissants still warm from the oven.

François insisted on taking Camille's tray in to her himself. She forced a croissant down to please him. He wolfed down five, and so did Léa, while the doctor ate three. Satiated, they were all silent for a while.

Léa was the first to speak; she said to François: "If you want your bath while it's hot, you had better get a move on."

"I haven't got time. I have to give my report to General Weygand. Then I have a meeting with Marshal Pétain."

"Dressed like that?" Doctor Dubois could not help blurting out.

"Why not? It's the uniform of all those who are being massacred through the government's carelessness, of the troops who are fleeing, wandering aimlessly in search of leadership, and whom they are trying to keep away from Paris at all costs."

"And then what are you going to do?" asked Camille.

"Then, madame, I'm going to lay down my life for France," he replied theatrically.

"François, be serious. I would be quite upset if anything happens to you."

"Dear Madame d'Argilat, thank you for those kind words. I promise to attempt to stay alive. Doctor, do you think our friend is up to travelling?" he asked, turning towards the doctor.

"It seems most unwise to me—as much because of her heart as for the child. However, if the bombing starts again . . . God help us. I'll give her a prescription for stronger medication and will try to come back tomorrow."

"Madame, mademoiselle . . . The Germans are occupying Dieppe, Compiègne, and Rouen, and even Forges-les-Eaux where my godmother lives!" cried Josette, bursting into the room, clutching an uneaten piece of croissant.

François Tavernier grabbed her arm and marched her out of the room faster than she had entered it.

"Little fool! Are you trying to kill your mistress?"

"Oh! No, sir," sobbed the distraught maid, "but I'm thinking of my mother, my father and my little brothers."

"I know you are, dear. In two days' time, you'll be able to leave Paris with Madame d'Argilat and Mademoiselle Delmas. You will go to the south. It'll be peaceful there," he said in a soothing voice, while he stroked her hair.

"Yes, sir."

"Thank you, Josette, you're a good girl. You have two days to pack for the journey. Here, buy yourself a pretty dress."

"Oh! Thank you, sir," exclaimed Josette, almost comforted as she pocketed the bills he held out.

Léa and the doctor were coming out of Camille's room.

"If you want so see Marshal Pétain and the cabinet, you'd better hurry. On the radio they've just announced their immediate departure for Touraine," said the doctor, in hushed tones as he wiped his glasses. "I'll see you tomorrow."

The door closed behind his suddenly hunched figure.

"Why did you let Camille listen to the news?" asked François.

"I can't stop her," Léa said, drawing her kimono tighter.

"Be brave. The worst is yet to come. Kiss me." In a spontaneous gesture, Léa flung herself at him, putting her arms around his neck as he leaned towards her.

Their lips met with such passion that it was painful. The tears running down Léa's cheeks gave their kisses a salty taste. He removed her clasped hands from his neck and without letting her go, drew slightly away from her. How beautiful she was, swaying before him to the rhythm of her grief!

"Do you love me a little?"

She shook her head in reply.

François's rugged features contracted with pain. What did it matter, after all? He would have to be satisfied with kisses. He drew her towards him once more. His hands disappeared beneath the kimono. When he stepped back, Léa's tears had stopped.

"I have to leave you, dear friend," he said, "thank you for such a delightful welcome. I'll see you soon, take care of Camille. *Au revoir.*"

Léa watched him leave without a word. She ran her finger absently over her moist lips.

Léa and Josette had completely forgotten that it was Sunday. Most food shops were closed. They had to go to the market at Saint-Germain where, after a long wait, they managed to buy a dozen eggs, a chicken, a rabbit, a large sausage, some cheese, two pounds of apples and, after a lot of haggling, a huge ham.

Exhausted but proud of their purchases, they set off for home, each holding the handle of the heavily laden basket. Léa's purse was virtually empty.

The weather was splendid. There were not many people in the streets: a few little old ladies, carrying string bags filled with scanty provisions, tramps, *concièrges* sweeping the pavement outside their flats out of habit; two policemen rode past on creaking bicycles, and then a car, piled so high with a mattress, a wardrobe, and a swarm of wriggling children that one wondered how on earth it was possible to drive it. The Rue de Rennes looked like a long river of molten lead with deserted banks. Suddenly, trucks turned into the Boulevard Saint-Germain. On one of them, Léa noticed bundles of hastily packed files beneath a badly secured tarpaulin.

She put dust covers over the furniture and then started packing. As she was putting away Camille's raincoat, she found the envelope on which Raphaël Mahl had scribbled his name and address in one of the pockets. She remembered with irritation her promise to go and see him or else to telephone.

Through the open window overlooking the trees on the boulevard, the sun streamed in invitingly. Everything seemed so peaceful, so summery: the only sound was the chattering of the sparrows and the cooing of the pigeons.

Suddenly, Léa slammed down the suitcase lid, picked up

a light black woollen cape which she slipped over her short, black silk dress with red polka-dots. She paused in front of the Venetian mirror in the hall and put on her black straw hat. She softly opened Camille's door—she was asleep, thank goodness. In the kitchen, Josette was preparing food hampers for the journey.

"I have to see someone, I won't be long."

"It's unwise, mademoiselle, to go out alone."

Léa didn't reply.

Except for a few cars and loaded vans, Paris seemed deserted. As she crossed the river, she noticed dense black clouds going up into the air coming from the Grand Palais. Intrigued, she hastened her step. The Tuileries gardens were as empty as the streets.

Against the background of the sky, Léa could make out the perfect cross formed by the Obelisk and the top of the Arc de Triomphe, gleaming white in the sunshine. Her heart pounding, she stopped as she recalled the little chapel at Verdelais in the storm. She suddenly wanted to be back there, at the foot of that cross, where she had prayed as a child and cried as a young girl. Her emotion was so strong that she tottered.

"My God," she murmured.

A prayer to the God of her childhood welled up inside her. She found herself making the sign of the cross in the face of so much beauty. She tore herself reluctantly from her reminiscences. She reached the Rue de Rivoli where Raphaël Mahl was staying, without meeting a soul.

He opened the door dressed in a white woollen African robe. He seemed surprised to see her.

"Did you forget that you made me promise to come to-day?" she asked.

"Forgive me, my dear friend, but you see I'm in the middle of packing."

"You're leaving?"

"As quickly as I can. The advance of the Germans has cost me my job at the radio station. The head of the station is expecting the order to evacuate the premises any day—or should I say any moment—now."

"To go where?"

"To Tours, no doubt. That's where the Government has fled. I'll take you there if you wish."

"Don't be stupid. I'm leaving myself in two days."

"Where will we be two days from now? Come and sit down. Ignore the mess. Would you like some tea?"

"I'd rather have a cold drink."

"I don't think I have anything, unless you drink whisky. The owner of this flat left two cases of it."

"All right. I've never tried it."

"Make yourself at home."

Léa looked about her. The drawing room was full of Chinese curios, some of which were exquisite, like the long lacquered chest the color of scarab wings. Others were hideously ugly, like the gaudy statuettes. She walked over to the windows which opened out on to the balcony overlooking the Tuileries gardens. Raphaël came over and joined her carrying two glasses containing an amber-colored liquid.

"I drink to your beauty."

Léa bowed her head, smiling, and raised her glass. She took a sip and grimaced.

"Don't you like it?"

"It's got a funny taste."

"Have some more, you'll see, you soon get used to it."

They drank slowly, leaning on the banister. A sickly smell of dense smoke made them wrinkle their noses.

"What is it?" asked Léa.

"It's been going on all day. Let's go back inside." They settled down on a low sofa covered with cushions.

"Have you any room in your suitcase?" he asked.

"Yes, but it depends what for?"

"Yesterday I promised to lend you some books that I consider to be the best literature has to offer." He picked up three volumes from the sofa and faltered slightly as he held them out to Léa. "No, I won't lend them to you, I'll give them to you. This may be the last time we'll see each other. You will keep them as a souvenir of me.

"Here's *Twilight of the Gods* by Elemir Bourges, for which

145

I would gladly trade all of Flaubert's work. *The Life of Rancé*, although perhaps you are a little young for this sort of thing. It is a book for the mature, a companion for old age. Well, you can read it later, when the time is ripe. And *Chéri* by the great Colette. The heroine, an admirable figure of a woman, has the same name as you. Contained in this book is all the greatness and all the sorrow of woman. May you be like her." He continued, "Do you like poetry?"

"A little."

"A little is not enough. Read Nerval. He expresses the most profound despair. He is a poet reflecting the mood of France."

How different Raphaël Mahl was now from the casual carpet or fur dealer, from the journalist and the Parisian pederast! Léa understood that, in giving her these books, he was revealing an intimate side of himself to her.

"Thank you," she said simply, giving him a kiss on the cheek.

He stood up.

"Darling, if I were to have loved a woman, I'd have wanted her to be like you," he said.

Léa looked at her watch. "I must go, it's past six o'clock."

"I'll walk you home. It is not advisable for a young and beautiful woman to be alone in the streets in these times."

"But there's nobody about."

"Precisely! That's why it's dangerous. Believe someone who knows all about dark alleyways. Bad boys always hide in quiet places. It is better to avoid such encounters unless one enjoys them. Give me your books, I'll make a package of them for you."

He pulled an exquisite red silk embroidered shawl from the top of a high black lacquered cabinet inlaid with ivory, and wrapped up the three books.

"Here is a pretty bundle that goes perfectly with your outfit," he said, holding out the silken parcel as he opened the door.

"Aren't you getting changed to go out?" asked Léa in surprise.

"Didn't you tell me Paris was empty? And even if there

were people everywhere? Don't I look good like this? African costume has always seemed the height of chic to me. All I need is a headdress."

Outside, the mildness was spoiled by the smell of smoke. Raphaël took Léa's arm.

"Let's walk along the embankment. Perhaps it's the last time that I will walk here."

Two of the little bookstalls along the river were open, one belonging to a fat woman of indeterminate age, and the other to an old man with tired eyes. They greeted Raphaël as a regular and seemed not to notice his unusual dress.

"You're open today? You can't have had many customers."

"I'm afraid not, Monsieur Mahl. Even the bravest have fled. Such a shame, to abandon such a beautiful city."

"You should do likewise."

"Me, monsieur? Never! I was born here in a courtyard in the Rue des Grands Augustins, I went to school at Saint-Michel, I lost my virtue in the shadow of Saint-Julien-le-Pauvre and I was married at Saint-Severin. My deceased wife, who was the daughter of a second-hand dealer from Belleville, is buried at Père-Lachaise. My eldest son has got a good stall opposite Notre-Dame and the youngest, when he comes back from the war, will take over for me. When we people are uprooted from Paris, we wither and die. So we stay. Isn't that right, Germaine?"

The fat woman, whose skin was as weatherbeaten as a seaman's, noisily agreed: "Absolutely!"

At these decisive words, Léa and Raphaël took their leave.

The grotesque carved figures on the Pont-Neuf were tinged pink by the rays of the setting sun. Overloaded cars went past heading towards the Boulevard Saint-Michel. The clock struck seven.

"We must hurry, I'm late."

They arrived at the Boulevard Raspail having exchanged few words. Like two good friends, they kissed outside the door and wished each other good luck.

The following morning, Camille received a letter from

Laurent. He was near Beauvais, not far from Paris. It was a very beautiful city, he said, with a magnificent cathedral.

"What's the date on the letter?" cried Léa.

"June 2nd. Why? Oh! My God! Beauvais has been bombed to the ground since then," stuttered Camille, sinking to the ground.

Léa was too overcome herself to think of helping the sick woman.

"Léa," she begged.

Léa was so stupefied that she did not hear Camille. Finally, her numbness wore off and she was able to give Camille the attention her condition required. When the crisis was over, the two women fell into each other's arms and cried for a long time. That is how Doctor Dubois found them. He himself seemed ten years older than when he had left them the previous day. In spite of his fatigue, he managed to find the words of comfort they needed to hear.

On Tuesday, the 11th of June, the inhabitants of the apartment in the Boulevard Raspail were ready to leave Paris. All they needed now was the car.

A long night of waiting began.

By Wednesday morning, Léa could no longer stand the tension. She preferred to go out, and said she would go to the Gare d'Austerlitz and find out if there were any trains running. Wearing sandals, she set off at a brisk pace, passing groups of people trailing baby carriages, pushcarts and even wheelbarrows laden with their treasures: clock, vacuum cleaner, sewing machine, barometer, goldfish bowl, mattress, a portrait of an ancestor or a wedding photograph, a birdcage containing a scrawny canary or a pair of turtledoves, a china doll, faded carpets . . . So many wan-looking children, women with tired faces, weary old folk. Where had they come from? From the suburbs, from the north, from Belgium? At the Boulevard Saint-Michel, some of them joined the stream of people heading towards the Luxembourg gardens while others, like Léa, continued on their way to the station. A dense crowd was packed on the pavements surrounding the Gare d'Austerlitz. The most fantastic rumors were spreading among the people stuck there.

"The Germans are in the suburbs . . . "

"No, they're in Antwerp . . . "

"They've blown up the oil storage tanks around Paris . . . "

"They've bombed Versailles . . . "

"There are no more trains . . . "

"They're closing the station!"

That was true.

A railway worker, perched on the roof of a car behind the gates inside the station waiting room, addressed the crowd with the aid of a megaphone. After repeated requests for silence, the crowd was almost quiet.

"As a security measure, the gates will be closed until five o'clock this evening . . . "

Cries of protest arose from all sides.

"Quiet . . . let me speak . . . Quiet . . . "

The cries died down.

"In order to ensure the departure of passengers already inside the station . . . "

"What about us?"

"Everyone will leave. . . . We are putting on additional trains from the Gare d'Austerlitz and the Gare Montparnasse. At the moment, a train is leaving Paris every five minutes . . . you will all get away . . . be patient . . . "

Léa threaded her way with difficulty among the people lying on the pavement amidst their baggage. As she passed the Jardin des Plantes, she noticed that the lawns had been invaded by impromptu picnickers. She crossed the gardens to go through the back streets in the hope that there would not be so many people. A man accosted her and followed her some way babbling nonsense that soon turned into obscenities. Then he suddenly disappeared.

The smell of potatoes frying reminded Léa that she had not had any lunch. She went into the Dupont-Latin restaurant which was nearly empty, and hungrily ate her fill, and drank a beer followed by coffee. Feeling better, she set off again, slowly making her way through the crowds heading up the Boulevard Saint-Michel.

It was already four o'clock in the afternoon.

Chapter 14

The car arrived at five o'clock in the morning. The driver, a young man, was completely exhausted. He fell asleep at the kitchen table, in front of a cup of coffee that he did not have the energy to drink.

Meanwhile, Léa, with Josette's help, carried the luggage down and settled Camille comfortably in the back, insisting she felt all right. Léaving Josette to guard the car, she went back upstairs to waken the driver who was still dazed after such a short sleep. A hot cup of strong coffee helped him regain his senses.

On Camille's instructions, Léa switched off the gas and the electricity, wondering, as she locked up, if she would ever come back to this apartment.

In the street, the driver finished loading the suitcases and a huge trunk on to the roof of the car.

"My name's Antoine Durand. I'm going to drive you as far as Etampes, where I'm to meet up with some friends. Thanks to Monsieur Tavernier, we have fifty litres of gas and a safe conduct pass enabling us to leave Paris by the Porte d'Orléans."

"Why do we need a safe conduct for the Porte d'Orléans?" asked Léa.

"I don't know, mademoiselle. Civilians who wish to leave Paris are being diverted to the Porte d'Italie."

It took them three hours to reach the Porte d'Orléans, which was guarded by soldiers who were directing the crowds to the Porte d'Italie exit from the city. Thanks to their documents, an officer let them through. There were a lot of hold-ups and they had to go through another checkpoint before reaching the main Orléans road. Except for army vehicles, the road was completely empty. After Montlhéry, they started passing the first pedestrians. There were women in bedroom slippers, or in high-heeled shoes, trailing hastily dressed children or pushing perambulators where a baby's head was just visible among the bundles. Young boys and girls pulled carts that were much too heavy for them. On some of them an elderly or sick person was perched. Among them were a number of deserting soldiers; they were helmetless and looked haggard. Some carried suitcases, others guns, and they hung their heads and tried to avoid military checkpoints.

The car threaded its way at a snail's pace through the constantly swelling traffic. This consisted of bicycles, motorcycles, horse-drawn carts, ox-carts, vans, delivery tricycles, fire-engines, cars so old it was a wonder they could move at all, and even hearses. They crawled past Arpajon. A soldier directing the traffic told them that passing was forbidden. Léa showed him the safe conduct pass. He shrugged, letting them by.

At crossroads, a sailor here and an airman or an infantryman there tried to create a semblance of organization among the exodus. The driver managed to overtake twenty or so buses carrying prisoners and their guards by cutting through a field alongside the road. Which prison were they from? Antoine was soon obliged to get back on to the road. They continued the slow crawl under a scorching sun which burnt people's faces and caused cyclists and pedestrians to be drenched in sweat.

A man was standing on the grass in front of his little garden, holding a dented aluminum mug, two buckets of water at his feet which be banged to attract attention, calling to the refugees: "Come on, open your purses! Two francs a bottle," while his wife handed out glasses or bottles to thirsty travellers and took their money.

"How disgraceful!" said Camille.

"You'll see worse than that before the journey's over,"

responded the driver wearily.

Finally they arrived at Etampes. It had taken them nearly six hours to travel thirty miles.

The inhabitants of the little town had joined the refugees. All that remained open was a hotel selling coffee, bread and cheese, which the evacuees fought over. It took more than two hours to get through the town. The young man was dropping from exhaustion, he drove like a robot and his head often slumped on to his chest. Suddenly, he realized they were out of Etampes. This seemed to awaken him and he stopped the car.

"I can't take you any further. I think you should take the secondary roads."

"You're not leaving us!" cried Josette.

"I have my orders. I'm not allowed to proceed beyond here."

At that moment, the dreaded humming could suddenly be heard above the noise of engines, children crying and the tramping of thousands of feet.

"Quick, get out," shouted Antoine opening the car door, "lie down in the ditch."

With Léa's help, Camille got out of the car, clutching her stomach in a futile gesture of protection. She lay herself down in the dusty grass in the ditch, alongside Josette, who was trembling from head to foot, and an elderly couple who were huddled together.

The planes flew so low that those on the ground could see the pilots quite clearly, before they flew off into the cloudless sky. A few people started to emerge, their fear dispelled. Suddenly the German planes turned around and machine-gunned the long, motionless line of fugitives lying flat on the ground.

Léa was splattered with dust from the bullets hailing down on the tarmac. Again and again the planes came back. When the murderous din ceased, there was a long silence and then the first groans, the first cries, the first shrieks could be heard, while a thick black nauseating smell of burning human flesh mingled with rubber and gas shrouded the disaster.

Josette stood up. Dazed and covered with blood, she

swayed giddily. Camille, unhurt, slowly got to her feet. Near-by, the elderly couple didn't move. The young woman shook the old man's shoulder. He rolled over and Camille saw that the same bullet had killed him and his wife. Clenching her fists, Camille stifled a scream. Fighting down her revulsion, she bent over and closed their eyes. Antoine had not been injured. But as soon as Léa stood up, everything started swimming. If it had not been for Camille, she would have fallen.

"Darling, you're hurt!"

Léa touched her forehead and her hand was covered with blood. She felt very strange, but was not alarmed.

"Let me see," said a man in his sixties with a shock of white hair, "I'm a doctor."

He took out dressings and compresses from his black bag.

"It's only the arch of your eyebrow, it's not serious. I'm going to put a tight bandage on it. That should stop the bleeding."

A little dizzy, Léa let him take charge.

Léa sat down on the bank, looking with her dressing like a wounded veteran. She surveyed the scene before her. Many cars were burning, but theirs was still intact. Lifeless bodies were strewn everywhere. The injured lay groaning and call-ing for help. It took several hours to clear. Nobody thought about eating. At eight o'clock in the evening, Léa took the wheel, for the driver had disappeared. At Camille's insistence, Léa agreed to take on board an old woman who had lost all her relatives.

For mile after mile, they were greeted with a panorama of death and destruction. At nightfall, with the blood from her wound running down her face and feeling exhausted, Léa left the road at Angerville in the hope of finding an open café or restaurant. Nothing. Everything was closed. She stopped the car just outside the village. Refugees were sleeping everywhere—in doorways, in the church, in the school, in the square, and even in the cemetery. The four women got out of the car. It was a mild, starry night, and the air was pungent with the smell of hay. Josette opened a food hamper and they hungrily set to.

They woke at dawn to discover they had a flat tire. Léa

was not able to loosen the wheel and went off in search of a mechanic. The garage, like everything else, was closed. Outside the church, nuns were distributing milk to children. Léa asked them where she could get help.

"My poor child, there's nobody left. All the able-bodied men are either at the Front or they've fled: the mayor, the notary, the doctor, the firemen, the schoolmaster, the bakers—they've all gone. There's only the priest, and he's a very old man. Only God, my child, has not abandoned us."

Turning to Léa, she said: "Come, child, let me change your dressing."

She removed the blood-soaked bandages with expert hands, and cleaned the wound which followed the shape of Léa's eyebrow. She applied a thick compress with the aid of adhesive tape.

"It doesn't look bad, but you need a couple of stitches."

"I won't be permanently scarred?"

"Don't worry," said the nun with a girlish laugh, "that won't stop you finding a husband."

Léa thanked her and made her way back to the car. Three times she asked men who were struggling under heavy loads to help her, but they pushed her out of the way without even answering. When she reached the edge of the village, she sat down despondently.

"Léa!"

She was too weary to register surprise at being hailed in these unfamiliar surroundings. She looked up. Standing before her was a dirty bare-headed soldier with a bushy beard. His hair was long, his uniform gray with dust, his boots spattered with mud and his helmet was dangling from his knapsack. He wore a bag on each shoulder and was standing there, rifle in hand, staring at her.

Léa stood up. Who was this man? How did he know her name? And yet . . . that look . . . his blue eyes . . .

With a cry, she flung herself at him. His rifle fell to the ground as his arms swept up his old friend.

"Mathias . . . Mathias . . . "

"You . . . it really is you," stuttered the young man showering her with kisses.

"How wonderful to meet you! What on earth are you doing here?"

Before replying, he picked up his rifle.

"I'm searching for my regiment. I was told they were near Orléans. And you? What are you doing on the road? I thought you were safe at Montillac."

"I'm with Camille d'Argilat. She's pregnant and she's sick. We couldn't leave any earlier. I'm so glad I've bumped into you: our car has broken down."

Camille, Josette and the old woman greeted their arrival with great relief.

"Léa, I was so worried that something had happened to you," said Camille.

"I couldn't find anyone to help me in the village. Luckily I met Mathias. Do you remember Mathias Fayard, the head storeman's son?"

"Of course. How are you, Mathias?"

"As well as can be expected, madame," he sighed.

After drinking some coffee still hot from the thermos, Mathias changed the wheel.

The church clock struck nine just as he finished.

Mathias drove, hoping to reach Orléans by taking small country lanes. The women felt comforted by his presence. Camille, Josette and the old woman slept. Léa's hand rested confidently on the young man's thigh.

Along the narrow white road stretched a procession of people and vehicles moving at a snail's pace. At the roadside were abandoned cars, some of them burned out, dead horses and dogs, freshly dug graves in the fields, various items of furniture, kitchen utensils, wheelchairs, empty suitcases, all bearing witness to recent air raids. In front of them, an ancient motor car, heavily overloaded with two mattresses on the roof, broke down. Mathias got out and helped push it off the road. A woman with a baby in her arms and two small children clutching her skirts stood watching the scene and cried. Mathias got back into the car and moved off again.

By the time they stopped for lunch, they had covered twenty miles.

At the little village washhouse, they were able to refresh themselves, which made them all feel a little better. Camille was still pale and her face drawn. She did not complain, although from time to time beads of sweat broke out on her forehead. The old woman, whose name they did not know, kept nodding, beneath her widow's hat, repeating endlessly: "Michèle, take care of the children: Georges, Loïc, come back . . ."

"Shut her up," exploded Léa. "Shut her up."

Camille put her arms round the hunched shoulders of the old woman.

"Don't worry, madame, Georges and Loïc are with their mother."

"Michèle, take care of the children ..."

Camille wearily covered her eyes with her hand that had become so thin she had removed her wedding ring for fear of losing it.

"You don't know how to deal with people who are sick in the head," said Josette tapping her forehead with her finger. She took the old woman's arm and shook her mercilessly. "You'd better shut up, or we'll leave you by the roadside. You'll see your Georges and your Loïc all right— in hell!"

"Josette, aren't you ashamed of yourself, talking to a poor old woman like that? Let her go," cried Camille.

Reluctantly, the red-faced girl obeyed. For a while, everyone ate their hard boiled egg or their slice of sausage in silence, while the pathetic procession continued to wend its way under the burning sun. Even the old woman said nothing: she was drowsy.

"It's time to move," said Mathias.

It was night when they reached the outskirts of Orléans. There was not a shop, not a house open. The inhabitants had fled. The main street had been bombed.

A violent storm suddenly broke, further hampering the progress of the masses of people marching towards their unknown destination. Everyone sheltered themselves as well as they could, and some had no qualms about breaking down the doors of abandoned houses. The storm stopped as suddenly as it had begun. Dark shadows emerged from the looted houses carrying clocks, paintings, vases, chests and other treasures. They did not even try to conceal their spoils. The plunderers had begun their sinister work.

"I'm afraid we'll have to spend the night in the car," said Mathias. They had not moved an inch in the last hour.

"Mademoiselle! Mademoiselle! Madame's fainted!"

"Well, what can I do about it? Try and get her to swallow her medicine."

Josette took the phial Léa held out and poured the mixture into the cup from the thermos flask. Slowly Camille came around.

They crept forward a few feet.

The crowd moved down the main street like a flock of sheep. There were people on either side of the car, in front and behind, their heads bowed under the weight of their burdens and their exhaustion. Were it not for the noise of engines and cart wheels, and the slow marching of thousands of feet, they would have looked like a herd of ghosts marching towards some obscure destination in the black night.

To their right, the street was almost empty. The suffering and fear were so oppressive that the crowds huddled together instinctively. As for the drivers of the carts and cars, they fell asleep in their seats. They reached a crossroads and Mathias turned, advancing slowly in the dark, the headlights extinguished for fear of planes. They arrived in a district that had suffered in a recent air raid. A smell of damp soot and musty cellars rose from the blackened ruins. In spite of the closeness, Léa shivered. They stopped in a little square surrounded by linden trees, which the bombs had spared. They got out of the car and stretched their stiff legs. They all went to relieve themselves behind the trees.

Josette helped Camille to lie down on a patch of grass.

"I'm cold," murmured Camille.

The maid returned to the car for a blanket and covered her. Camille thanked her with a sad smile, her hands clenched over her stomach.

"Do you need anything else, Madame?"

Camille shook her head and closed her eyes.

The old woman with no name went wandering off down a rubble-filled street. "Michèle, take care of the children . . . "

Mathias and Léa walked around the square, their arms around each other's waists.

They came to a little garden where the air was heavy with the sweet scent of roses. Mathias pushed open a little wooden gate. They found themselves under a rose arbor with clusters of what they guessed to be white roses climbing everywhere. They sat down on a wide bench on which someone had left some cushions and took deep breaths of the fragrant air.

How far away the war seemed at that moment!

All they had to do was close their eyes and it felt like Montillac—the stone bench still warm from the afternoon sun, looking out over the vineyards and leaning up against the wall where the climbing rose bowed under the weight of so many fragrant white blooms. It was a compulsory resting place on those long summer evenings when the setting sun gilded the old stone buildings, the roof tiles on the outhouses and the wooden planks of the shed. It was the moment when a feeling of peace rose up from the earth and was shared by all the inhabitants of Montillac.

Mathias held Léa closer. For the first time in ages, Léa felt safe, in the arms of her childhood friend. She recalled their romps in the hay, their games in the long grass in the meadows, their drunken merriment during the grape harvest, their horse rides through the vineyards, their bicycle races down the hill, when they went to explore the grottoes at Saint-Macaire and the dungeon of the château at Cadillac. She shuddered.

Their lips met violently, their teeth clashed, their breath mingled. They poured into their kiss all their passionate lust for life. Mathias's strong rough hands with his filthy nails practically tore off Léa's flimsy blouse. Her white silk slip was clinging to her skin. The straps slipped off her shoulders revealing her breasts. Her nipples presses against Mathias's sweaty khaki shirt. The rough cloth made them harden, while, with a groan, Mathias plunged down to take them in his mouth. Gently, Léa pushed his head away.

"Please stop, Mathias."

"Why?"

"You're too intense," she replied.

"Don't you want any more?"

"Yes, I do. But wait."

They were so sure they had their whole lives in front of them as they lay on the wooden bench in their crumpled clothes, their heads flung back, intoxicated by the smell of the roses!

The clock struck two.

"Léa, you need some sleep."

Without bothering to adjust her slip, Léa stretched out on the bench and put her head on Mathias's thigh. She fell asleep at once. For a long time he tenderly watched her sleep. All around them was darkness. Only Léa's white breasts glowed faintly. To avoid temptation, Mathias pulled up her slip and buttoned her blouse. Then, he lit a cigarette.

Camille awoke from a restless sleep with a start and wondered for a second where she was.

It was very dark and the linden trees cast menacing black shadows around her. Her child was moving, and she felt full of joy, in spite of the pain. She sat up, leaning against the tree trunk. It is too quiet, she thought, clutching her stomach.

At first, Camille could make out a distant rumbling: a storm perhaps. She listened. The storm was getting closer . . . the rumbling was getting louder. A shadow came swooping down from the sky above her.

"Madame, Madame, the planes!"

The words were hardly out of Josette's mouth when the horror began: a hail of bombs fell so close to the little square that the ground shook and the ruins collapsed. There was explosion after explosion, and great flames leaped up, and the linden trees were silhouetted against a backdrop of fire.

Mathias made the women leave the car, where they had run for shelter, and dragged them to the emptiest part of the square.

"The gas," he whispered in Léa's ear as she struggled.

"It sounds as if the bombs are falling on the road where

we were earlier,'' hiccuped Josette.

Close by, the bombing continued. They could hear the machine guns rattling.

"My God, where is the anti-aircraft?'' groaned Mathias.

He could not know that there was no longer an anti-aircraft unit at Orléans. The rumbling of the planes grew fainter . . . and then came back again. Flying low, the planes circled the town again. A huge bomb came crashing down, destroying the last remaining houses, a garage and the Hotel Saint-Aignan. A shower of stone, metal and fire rained down on the long procession of refugees.

The little square which had been so peaceful was now full of people wandering around, their clothes torn to shreds and their faces contorted with terror. Women, wild-eyed with panic and fear, were carrying maimed little bodies and beings without hands, arms and faces. A nightmarish creature, stripped naked by the explosion, hopped by with astonishing speed on one slipper-clad foot while from the bleeding stump dripped a dark trail of blood. Léa and her companions stood transfixed with horror as they watched the poor wretches flee. A fire engine raced past with screaming sirens, flooding them with light as it hurtled past. A van drew up near them.

An elderly man wearing a helmet from the Great War got out: "Anybody injured?''

"No, we're all right, thank you,'' said Mathias.

"But you're a soldier. You're a youngster. Come with us. We're all old and not very strong,'' said the man, pointing to the others in the van.

"Don't go, Mathias,'' cried Léa, clinging to him.

"It's wrong of you, mademoiselle,'' scolded the old man. "Hundreds of poor souls are buried alive under the houses there. We must go and help them.''

"He's right, Léa, let him go,'' said Camille.

"And what about us? What will become of us?''

"You're young, too. Come and help us.''

"I can't. My friend here is ill.''

"Let's move! People are dying while we stand here talking.''

Mathias drew Léa to one side. "They are soldiers of the

161

home guard. I must obey them. Get into the car and try to reach the bridges."

"But we're not going to leave you here."

"I have to do my duty, whether it's at the Front, or here."

"But we've lost the war!" screamed Léa.

"That's no reason. Don't cry. We'll meet again. Take my rifle, you never know. Look after yourself. I love you."

The three women watched mournfully as Mathias took his kit out of the car and got into the van, which drove off toward the fires.

Léa put her head on her arms and, resting on the hood of the car, sobbed. She put Mathias's rifle in back near Camille.

"Mademoiselle, we must leave," said Josette, supporting Camille who looked even more haggard.

"You're right, crying won't get us anywhere," she said, tearing off her dressing which had come unstuck in the heat.

Together they helped Camille onto the back seat.

"Thank you," she murmured. "Where's the old woman?"

"She's been gone for a long time, Madame," said Josette, pointing towards the fire.

Camille, only semi-conscious, lay groaning. Josette was leaning out of the window guiding Léa through all sorts of debris: jets of water from burst pipes and pieces of burning wood falling from the houses.

"Careful, there's a big hole on the right!"

Léa only half avoided it and the jolt made Camille cry out and Josette swear. Behind them, a building came crashing forward and stones rained down on the car which was suddenly covered with a thick coat of dust.

"I can't see anything," wailed Léa.

Brought to a standstill amid the roaring flames which seemed to surround them, Léa tried to get the windshield wipers to work—without success.

"Get out," she ordered Josette, "and wipe the windshield."

"No, madamoiselle, I'm too frightened," stammered the girl and burst into tears.

162

Léa raised her hand and grabbed her by the hair.

"Get out! I'm ordering you to get out."

The blows rained down and she did not even try to defend herself.

"Stop it. Léa, I beg you, stop it." Camille weakly tried to restrain Léa. "I'll go, give me the cloth."

"You're mad, you can't stand up. If you want to make yourself useful, pass me a blanket."

Outside, the draft created by the fire enveloped Léa. With the help of the blanket, she managed to get rid of most of the dust. Suddenly, she heard a shout from behind, and then, above the roar of the flames, the noise of a body thudding to the ground close by. She whipped around ready to strike with the blanket. Her arms stopped in mid-air . . .

Silhouetted in the glow of the flames, Camille was standing clutching the barrel of Mathias's rifle, staring at the ground. At her feet lay a man, his face covered in blood. Near him, the long blade of a butcher's knife gleamed in the firelight. Numb with astonishment, Léa leaned over the man and shook him. He was motionless. Slowly, she raised her head and looked at the woman who had just saved her life as if she were seeing her for the first time. Gentle Camille had not flinched at killing! How, in her weak state, had she found the strength? Léa gently took the rifle. Then, as if that was what she had been waiting for, Camille fell to her knees beside the body.

"My God, is he dead? I had no choice, do you understand? I saw him go for you with his big knife raised . . . he was going to kill you. After that, I don't remember . . . "

"Thank you," said Léa with such warmth that she was taken aback for a moment. "Come, let's get into the car. We don't want to stay here."

"But I've killed a man!" cried Camille, biting her knuckles.

"You had no choice. Come !"

With uncharacteristic tenderness, Léa helped Camille to her feet. In the car, Josette, who had witnessed the whole incident, sat open-mouthed.

"Help me, or I'll kill you too," spat Léa.

Zombie-like, the girl got out of the car.

"Hurry!"

As soon as she was settled inside the car, Camille fainted.

"Take care of her. Well, what's the matter with you? Get in."

Josette stood staring at the ground.

"Mademoiselle, he's not dead," she whispered.

Indeed, the man was getting to his feet, brandishing his knife and muttering: "Bitches . . . doing that to me . . . whores, I'll get you."

"Quick, get in."

While Josette dived into the car, Léa calmly took a step back, cocked the rifle as Mathias had shown her earlier and, still retreating, she aimed and pulled the trigger. The recoil from the rifle bruised her shoulder. A few feet away from her, the man stood dazed for a second before falling back with his arm still raised.

Léa stood motionless still clutching the rifle, staring at him as he keeled over.

She felt a burning hand in hers. Camille . . . what was she doing there? Couldn't she stay quietly lying down in the car? She had enough problems as it was without the additional burden of having to look after Laurent d'Argilat's wife. Laurent . . . he was probably dead at this very moment: things must be even worse at the Front than they were here. Yes, but he was a man, a soldier, he had a gun. A gun . . . but she had a gun too! Hadn't she just killed a man? Her father would be proud of her. Wasn't it he who had taught her to aim when they were hunting and at the village fairs? Of course he would be proud of his daughter.

"Léa . . . "

Nobody gets the better of Pierre Delmas's daughter: That taught him, the dirty pig. He looked a mess now with his brains hanging out of his head.

"Come on, Léa, calm down. It's over. We've got to go on."

Of course she knew they had to go on, but go where? All around, everything was in flames; in fact, the air about them was very hot. She wiped the sweat that was pouring from her forehead with her dusty hand. Her wound ached and suddenly she felt sick. Camille supported her as she leaned on the car and vomited.

"Feel better?"

Léa replied with a groan. Yes, she felt better, but she didn't want to hang around any longer.

"This time, he's well and truly dead," said Josette as the two women clambered back into the car.

When dawn broke, they were in the square known as Place Dubois. The houses were intact. A first-aid post had been set up there. Dozens of injured people, most of them suffering from burns, were lying on the bare ground. Nuns with blood-stained habits were tending them.

Léa called from the car. "Please, sister, where can I find a doctor?"

The nun, whose gray hair was visible under her headdress, stood up painfully. "There aren't any left, child. There's just us and our mother superior. We are waiting for ambulances to take the wounded to the hospital."

"Where is it?"

"I don't know, we're from Etampes."

Léa looked around her, bewildered. Luckily, Camille had fainted again and could neither see nor hear what was going on. Léa stopped a young fireman—he looked almost like a child—who was running past.

"Excuse me, how do I get to the bridge?"

"The bridge? You'd better be quick! The bridges are going to be blown up. It takes hours to get from one end of the town to the other. From here, your best bet is to try and reach the Maréchal-Joffre bridge."

"How do I get there?"

"Go down the Rue de Coulmiers or the Rue Maréchal Foch. Then turn into the Boulevard Rocheplatte. Cross over and take one of the streets off it."

Then, taking no further notice of her, he hurried off.

How long did she drive around that district of Orléans, moving forwards, going backwards, avoiding obstacles—heaps of rubble and barriers of barbed wire set up by the army forcing her to turn back—with Camille still unconscious in the back of the car? Her back, her shoulders and her arms ached and her wound throbbed, and the heat . . .

Since the killing of the unknown man with the knife, Josette had been quiet, darting brief admiring glances at Léa, helping as best she could, and not hesitating to get out of the car energetically to remove a wooden beam, a piece of furniture or any other obstacle from their path. She felt reassured by Léa's decisive action.

"Mademoiselle, I'm hungry."

It was true they had not had anything to eat for hours, but how could anyone feel hungry under such circumstances?

They reached the Rue de la Porte Saint-Jean which was full of distraught people. Since crossing the Boulevard Rocheplatte, they had come across the refugees again. There was the most incredible tangle of horses, pushchairs, ambulances, ragged soldiers, sinister-looking men who were often drunk, elderly people being carried on charitable shoulders and children lost in the chaos, calling for their mother. Léa could have switched the engine off and the car would have moved on its own, pushed by the crowds of people surging forward. Camille opened her eyes at last, only to close them immediately.

"Oh no! Not again!" cried Léa, fearing she had lost consciousness once more.

With a great effort, Camille opened her eyes. "Josette, give me my medicine and a little water, please."

The water in the thermos, though warm by now, tasted wonderful to her.

"More," she said thirstily.

As she raised the cup to her lips, her eyes met those of a little boy who was walking alongside the car. He was pale and drawn, and kept passing his tongue over his parched lips.

"Here," she said, holding the cup out of the open window.

He grabbed it without thanking her and drank eagerly, then he passed the cup to a young woman in a black suit which must once have been very elegant. She did not drink but gave it to a pretty little girl of four or five.

"Thank you, madame," she said.

Camille opened the door. "Get in."

After a moment's hesitation, the woman pushed her

children in first as well as a very dignified old woman with magnificent white hair wearing a black straw hat.

"My mother."

Then she herself got in.

"Camille, you're out of your mind. Get those people out!"

"Please don't say anything, darling. Just think. This car is half empty. It's a miracle no one has taken it from us before now. Now there's no more room and we've chosen our passengers ourselves."

Sensing the truth of Camille's argument, Léa held her tongue.

"Thank you very much, both of you. My name is Le Ménestrel. Our car broke down at Pithiviers. Some good people took pity on my mother and offered her a place in their car which was already full. The children and I walked alongside. But then, unfortunately, their car broke down too."

"How did you end up in this part of Orléans if you've come from Pithiviers?" asked Josette suspiciously, studying a map on her knees.

"I don't know. Some French soldiers directed us to Les Aubrais and after that I don't know. There was a dreadful air raid during the night in which we lost our new friends."

Camille doled out food. The pieces of stale bread were devoured ravenously. The children ate the few remaining apples. The old woman and the little girl fell asleep.

A big van piled high with files, with several children perched on the roof, stopped. Smoke was pouring out everywhere and it would not start again. Shouts and curses could be heard. Fortunately, a high carriage entrance opened and volunteers were able to push if off the road. It was at that moment that the planes reappeared, flying very low. Screaming, the crowd tried to escape from the death trap formed by the narrow street.

"Move, get a move on . . . let me through . . . get out of the way, you bitch . . . be careful of the children . . . Papa . . . Mummy . . ."

Up in the sky, the pilots were having their fun. They looped the loop, flew upside down and righted themselves, dropping their death ration each time they passed. Bombs fell on the Rue Royale, the Rue de Bourgogne, Place Sainte-Croix and in the Loire River. A stone's throw away, in the Rue du Cheval-Rouge, an artillery convoy was annihilated. The assassins in the sky were doing a thorough job.

A youth who had lost one arm bounced off the hood splattering the windshield with blood. He picked himself up and ran ahead calling for his mother. Half a dozen or so people fell, flattened by machine-gun bullets. One of them watched in astonishment as his intestines fell out of his stomach and landed on his thighs. Madame Le Ménestrel buried her children's heads against her to protect them from these scenes of horror, while their grandmother prayed with her eyes shut.

Camille and Léa, as well as being terrified, were enraged at the massacre. Not far from them, a car went up in flames. The occupants, hair and clothes burning, leaped out, shrieking. One of them was knocked down and trampled by a horse that had bolted, dragging a cart that crushed everything in its path. The poor creature was screaming when a cartwheel broke his legs. He attempted to get up but the flames swept over him and soon there were no more cries. It was not long before he was just an amorphous mass.

"I don't want to die like that!" wailed Josette, opening the door.

"No!" shouted Camille and Léa in unison.

Josette took no notice. Panic stricken, she ran among the bodies, treading in pools of blood. She fell over and picked herself up again, looking for a way out of the confused mass of people and vehicles.

The street sloped steeply. It seemed to Léa that the plane was flying up the street, heralded by the rattle of bullets glancing off the road surface. Standing alone amidst the carnage, while every other living creature lay flat on the ground, Josette watched the deadly plane swoop down towards her.

A mute cry escaped from Camille's twisted mouth as she sank on to Madame Le Ménestrel's shoulder.

The impact of the bullets sent Josette flying backward. She fell with her arms outstretched and her skirt flew up. Her eyes were wide open and she was smiling as if, at the moment of death, all her fears had left her. Blood poured out of the gaping wound in her throat. Léa rummaged for a handkerchief in her pocket with which she might try and stop the bleeding. Unable to find one, she ripped off her blouse and rushed to put it over the ghastly wound. But it was no use; Josette was already dead.

"It's my fault, if I had let her go back to her parents, she would still be alive. Poor girl, she was the same age as me." Léa tenderly stroked the flaxen hair that was matted and sticky with blood, speaking to the dead girl softly, as her mother used to speak to her when she was unhappy: "Don't be afraid . . . it's all over . . . there . . . go to sleep . . ."

She gently closed her eyes. Then, she dragged the body out of the way so that Josette would not be hit again, or trampled on, and leaned her up against a door.

The sirens did not sound the end of the air raid, for there was no longer anybody to operate them. Gradually, the survivors sat up, dazed, and took in the dreadful scene: there was nothing but burned-out cars, twisted and burned bicycles, mutilated and charred bodies, lost children, mute with terror, mothers screaming, their faces contorted with anguish, men embracing a dead wife or mother, women going round and round in circles, their clothes in tatters, their hands covered with blood, the wounded crying for help.

"Quickly, we must clear the way to the bridge," commanded a fat man wearing the Legion of Honor badge on his jacket.

Léa, forgetting that she had no blouse, began to help clear the street. Madame Le Ménestrel joined her.

"Go back to the car, get the gun and make sure no one steals it," ordered Léa.

"You can rely on me," she replied fiercely.

For hours, Léa dragged bodies and cleared debris of all kinds out of the way. She was covered with blood and filth. Soldiers who had deserted from the Seventh Army assisted the rescuers.

"But . . . am I seeing things? Is it not Mademoiselle

Delmas herself?"

There was only one person in the world who would still have the strength to joke in such circumstances.

"François," she cried, throwing herself into the arms of a grimy, bearded Tavernier, standing before her in uniform. "Oh! François, it's you . . . take me away from here, quickly . . . if only you knew . . . "

"I know, darling, I know. Where is Madame d'Argilat?"

"Over there, in the car."

"How is she?"

"Not well. Josette is dead."

As they approached the car, Madame Le Ménestrel, who did not recognize Léa immediately, aimed the rifle at them.

"Don't come any closer."

"It's me, madame, with a friend who is going to help us."

"Forgive me. Earlier on, two awful men wanted to take the car. They only went away when they realized I was going to shoot. But they said they would be back with their friends. It's terrible what they're doing: they're taking money and jewelry from the dead."

Night had fallen by the time François had managed to open a heavy wooden gate. Léa, who was at the wheel, drove into a big courtyard with a gigantic plane tree in the middle. François closed the gate with the help of an iron bar. Apart from the broken windows, the house was intact.

"I'm going to see if we can get in," said Madame Le Ménestrel, after helping her mother out of the car. "Stay with your grandmother, children."

François and Léa carried Camille, who was still unconscious. She was breathing lightly, in gasps.

"I've managed to open the door. We can put your friend in bed. Children, see if you can find some candles!"

The boy and girl raced up the steps. Camille was installed in a room on the ground floor.

"I'll look after her," said Madame Le Ménestrel. "Is there water?"

There was no water, either in the kitchen or in the bathroom. François noticed a well in a corner of the courtyard. The clanging of the bucket against the stone shaft reminded Léa of the well at Montillac. How far off it seemed. Would she ever see her home again? As if in answer, the bombing started up again, but this time in another district.

François carried several bucketsfull into the house. Sitting on the steps with her chin cupped in her hands, Léa watched him.

"Phew! There you are, the ladies will be able to wash themselves. Now it's our turn."

He filled another bucketful of water, placed the bucket on the edge of the table and began to undress. Soon he was naked.

Léa could not take her eyes off him; she found his broad tanned chest beautiful as it gleamed with perspiration in the moonlight. He had narrow hips, long hairy legs and his pale genitals peeped out from the curly dark hair.

"Well what are you waiting for? Take off those filthy rags. You look awful."

Léa obediently removed her grubby skirt, her torn slip and her panties.

"The water feels a little cold at first, but you'll see, it feels good afterwards. I've found a piece of lavender-scented soap and some towels."

He poured some of the water over her head and shoulders. The water felt so icy, she could not help letting out a gasp. François lathered her from head to foot scrubbing vigorously as if he wanted to remove her very skin and with it the memory of the blood that had made her so dirty. Léa let him take over, moved to feel his hands rubbing her breasts, brushing against her intimate parts. He left her covered with suds while he poured the rest of the water over himself and held the soap out to her.

"Your turn."

She had never imagined that the surface of a man's body was so vast or that his muscles were so hard. He moaned softly at the touch of her awkward little hands. In the dark, the young girl felt herself blushing as she felt his erect penis. She knelt down to soap his legs.

"This is how I've always dreamed of being with you one day."

Léa did not reply. She rubbed his thighs and then his calves. He reached down and put his hands under her arms to lift her up.

"Stop. I enjoy seeing you at my feet but I prefer you proud and stubborn."

He drew her towards him and their soap-covered bodies slithered together. They sought each other's lips. Léa's whole body became tense. François grew even harder. He doused water over both of them washing them clean.

The bombing, which had died down, started up again. They did not move; it was as if they felt protected by their desire, even when a bomb fell close to the house, starting a fire that made their bodies glow in the light from the flames.

"Make love to me," she murmured, "I don't want to die without knowing what it's like."

François wrapped her in a bath towel, picked her up and carried her up the stairs, went into one of the bedrooms and put her down on a big bed with a crucifix hanging above it.

"I bless this war which has given you to me," he said, penetrating her gently.

Léa was so aroused that she felt no pain, just an increased desire to feel him go even deeper inside her. Her pleasure was so intense that she cried out. François watched her writhing beneath him, stifling her cries with his hand. She let out a long moan when he withdrew and came on her stomach. A half-hour later, still trembling, she fell asleep.

François Tavernier could not pretend he was not in love with this little girl. But what of her? Was she in love with him? He knew that what had just happened meant nothing. She was a sensual creature. She would have made love with any man in the present situation. François knew enough about women to be sure of that. It was only her lust for life and the recent events that had thrown her into his arms. He felt unbearably sad. She stirred in her sleep and snuggled up to him. Once more, he wanted her. He took her gently, sliding into her orifice which sucked at him like a mouth. She woke, moaning. And her pleasure grew more and more intense; every cell in her body tingled.

The sun was already high when Léa was awakened by the sound of a spoon clinking in a bowl. François, clean-shaven, his hair damp, wearing the dirty trousers of his uniform, was leaning over her.

"It's late, lazybones. Time to get up. I've found some tea and biscuits and I've made you a proper breakfast."

What was she doing in bed, naked, with a man who was not Laurent? Suddenly, she remembered and blushed.

"Don't blush! It was wonderful! I've brought up a suitcase. I think it's yours. I'll leave you to get dressed and have your breakfast."

What had she done? She had been unfaithful to Laurent and behaved like a bitch in heat. If only she had not enjoyed it so much. At the memory of it, she shivered. So that was love, that excitement in every inch of her body, that miracle which made you forget everything, even the war. She recalled the horrors of the previous day; Josette was dead. And what about Camille whom Laurent had entrusted to her care?

Léa got out of bed and felt herself blushing once more as she caught sight of the crumpled bloodstained sheet. She removed it and shoved it into a wardrobe. A terrible cramp in her stomach reminded her that she had not eaten for hours. Without bothering to get dressed, she wolfed down the tea and biscuits prepared by her lover. She looked out of the open-shuttered window. In the courtyard, Francois was pouring into the gas tank the contents of the cans that the driver had taken the precaution of stowing in the trunk. The children were chasing each other, laughing in the sunshine, under the gentle gaze of their grandmother, who was sitting in a wicker chair looking most dignified with her hair in a neat bun. Nearby, Camille was also sitting up, watching the children with a smile. Madame Le Ménestrel was going back and forth from the house to the car, carrying bundles. It was a fine day and in the courtyard of the Orléans house there reigned an atmosphere of holiday excitement on that Sunday, the 16th of June, 1940.

A distant air raid siren wailed, on the other side of the Loire, no doubt. Then, very quickly, the planes appeared.

"Hurry, they're bombing the bridges. If they're blown up,

we won't be able to get across," said François, coming into the room.

Without worrying about her nakedness, Léa opened a suitcase, took out some underwear, a blue cotton shirt-dress and a pair of white leather sandals.

"Here, you can take it back down to the car," she ordered, closing the suitcase.

Without taking any further notice of François, Léa got dressed. François stood rigid, pale with anger, watching her. He grabbed her arm roughly and pulled her towards him. "Don't order me about like that!"

"Let me go."

"No, not until I've said one thing, you stubborn creature. One day you'll be begging me on your knees to love you."

"Never."

Had they made any progress since they had left? All around them, there was nothing but chaos.

"Hurry, the Germans are coming, the bridges will be blown up."

The heat was unbearable, as it had been the previous day. At last, they reached the river. The Engineer Corps was guarding the bridge, trying to control the crowd. They were ready to prohibit access to the mined bridge as soon as the blasting order was given. But they were so few that they did not stand much chance of containing this human tide. It took half an hour to get across.

The planes returned yet again, causing some people to fling themselves to the ground, others to push and shove, knocking over those in front in order to advance a few yards. Bombs slid into the river, splattering the twelve arches holding up the bridge, and those on it, with mud. A shell fell on the quay. Part of the embankment slid into the water, taking with it a deluge of stones, sand, cars, bicycles and people.

It was a descent into hell. The planes came back three times without succeeding in blowing up the Royale Bridge or the Joffre Bridge; however, they machine-gunned all those who happened to be crossing. One woman climbed over the parapet and jumped into the void in order to escape the bullets. There was hardly any water at that particular spot. A driver was hit at the wheel of his car, which stopped dead. A group of fifteen or so toughs lifted the car and with a yell of "Heave, ho!" threw it over the side of the bridge with no thought for the passengers still inside. The injured were dying, trampled by hundreds of feet. They trudged through the vilest sludge underfoot. At last, the planes flew off.

"Keep going," said François to Léa, "I'm going to try and find the officer in charge."

"You're not going to leave us alone!"

Without replying, François got out of the car and fought his way through to the soldiers on guard.

"Marchand!"

"Tavernier! What are you doing in this hell-hole?"

"Too long and too depressing to go into that now. Is it true the bridges are going up?"

"They should have been blown up ages ago. The Germans were at Pithiviers and Etampes yesterday, they can't be far from Orléans now. I haven't even received the necessary amount of explosives, and I've had to divide them between the two bridges. If I had known, I wouldn't have put seven hundred and fifty kilos under the railway bridge."

"Lieutenant, Lieutenant, I think I can see a German tank on the Châtelet embankment!" cried a young soldier who was standing on an armored car looking through a pair of binoculars.

"Good Lord!" cried Marchand, jumping on to the car and snatching the binoculars.

"Damn, they're heading for the George V Bridge. Give the blasting signal, quickly, the Germans are on the bridge."

Albert Marchand, his forehead covered with beads of sweat, followed the progress of the three armored vehicles through the binoculars. Their progress was impeded by the crowd of refugees. The Germans shot at the dozen or so guards. They had reached the middle of the bridge when a series of explosions was heard, then an enormous creaking: one of the arches at the northern end had collapsed into the river, taking with it all who had been on the bridge.

For a few seconds it was impossible to see anything.

It was half past three.

When the smoke cleared, Marchand, still riveted to the binoculars, cried: ''Good Lord, they got across, they're heading towards Sully.'' He looked frantic as he slid down to the ground. ''Keep the people back, we'll have to blow up the Joffre Bridge.''

''But, Lieutenant, not all the people who are on it will get across in time.''

''I know, but we have no choice. Take your positions and don't hesitate to shoot.''

The sixteen soldiers advanced, pushing the refugees out of their way.

''Get back! Get back! We're blowing up the bridge.''

The crowd, who had already seen part of the Royale Bridge collapse, stopped.

''Even more reason to hurry,'' shouted a man who charged the barrier formed by the soldiers. A shot rang out: the man fell.

The crowd gaped and muttered in astonishment and anger. French soldiers shooting their fellow countrymen. But the pressure from behind was increasing. Soon the front rows gave way. A little car jolted forwards knocking over two old men who fell into the no-man's land between the soldiers and the bridge. The car accelerated and ran over one of them. It was like a signal, the crowd charged forward. Three shots were fired that hit nobody. Then the soldiers were engulfed by the crowd.

Immediately after the Royale Bridge was destroyed, François Tavernier rushed off in search of the car that was carrying all that was most precious to him. It was not on the Barentin embankment. He elbowed his way on to the bridge. The car was there, creeping forward at a snail's pace. When Léa finally caught sight of him, she felt uplifted. ''Thank goodness you're here! I thought you'd abandoned us.''

François took over from Léa at the wheel. ''They're going to blow the bridge up,'' he said in a low voice.

''Oh!''

''Shh, there's no need to frighten the others, we're going

to try to worm our way through."

A soldier was walking close to the car.

"Pass the word on to a few people who seem responsible: the bridge is going up. Tell them to hurry people along—but calmly."

The soldier looked at him blankly. His face was grimy and expressionless. He was exhausted and dazed, plodding forward like a beast of burden. Suddenly, he let out a yell, pushing the people in front of him out of the way: "The bridge is going up! The bridge is going up!"

The crowd surged forward as if it had been whipped. They only had another ten yards or so to go before they reached the other side of the Loire. Like animals at the approach of an earthquake, forgetting all human dignity, they fought, and the law of the jungle reigned. Woe to those who fell: they were crushed to death.

There were a few more explosions. Then, with a terrible din, the second bridge collapsed.

It was only half an hour since the Royale Bridge had given way.

Léa and François stood by the car surveying the catastrophe, unable to take their eyes off the horrific scene. How many people had been on the bridge? Three hundred, five hundred, eight hundred? More, perhaps?

Down below, in the river, survivors were trying to clamber up the tangled heaps of bodies, iron and masonry. The injured who had fallen on to the pillars were calling for help, while others were drowning in the deep swirling water. A baby's body was roasting on the hood of a burning car.

"Let's get away from here," said François, pushing Léa into the car.

A pall of black smoke·hung over the Loire.

The car turned into the Avenue de Candalle amid the debris. At Saint-Marceau, French machine guns were firing towards the embankments. As they approached Notre-Dame-du-Val, Camille begged them to stop.

"Not now," grumbled Léa.

"Please, I'm going to be sick."

François pulled over and Camille stumbled out.

"Let me help her," said Madame Le Ménestrel, also getting out.

"Thank you," said Camille, wiping her mouth on the grubby handkerchief she held out.

Leaning on each other, they returned to the car. Camille got in.

"Mummy, we want to go the toilet," said the little boy.

"All right, darlings, hurry up."

They walked a few yards from the car. The little girl crouched down while her brother fumbled with his fly. Suddenly, a shell came whistling through the air and landed a few yards from them. The occupants of the car saw the mother and her two children being tossed into the air like rubber balls. They were riddled with shrapnel. It looked as though they were moving in slow motion as they fell softly to earth again, landing in the dust, graceful even in death.

With a cry of terror, the old woman leaped out of her seat and raced towards her daughter and her grandchildren. She ran from one to the other with outstretched arms. François leaned over Madame Le Ménestrel's body and raised her head. Even dead, she seemed elegant. Her little girl, still clutching her doll, was lying across her legs. The child seemed asleep while a red stain was spreading across her pink dress. Further away lay the little boy with his head almost severed from his body and his tiny little penis poking out of his trousers.

Camille went from one to the other endlessly repeating: "It's my fault, it's my fault . . . " She collapsed, overcome by tears.

Léa took her by the shoulders and shook her, spoke to her and finally slapped her, which stopped her sobs. "No! It's not your fault! You had nothing to do with it! Come back to the car."

"Come, madame, you cannot stay here," said François to the grandmother.

"Léave me alone. I can't abandon them here. I must bury them."

"It's too dangerous. You'll be killed."

"That's all I ask of the Lord, sir. In taking them from me, He's taken away all that I lived for."

"I can't leave you here alone, madame."

"You must, sir. Remember the two young women who are with you. Remember the child one of them is carrying. They need you more than I."

"I beseech you, Madame."

"Don't argue."

François reluctantly made his way over to Léa and Camille, whom he picked up in his arms. How light she is, he thought. Putting her gently down on the back seat, he took the wheel.

"Are you coming?" he asked Léa who stood motionless, unable to take her eyes off the three bodies.

Planes flew overhead, but did not drop any bombs.

At Saint-Marceau, the French soldiers had stopped shooting. On arriving in Orléans by the Faubourg de Bourgogne, the Germans encountered no resistance. They cut down a tree to make a crossing over the railway bridge, which had not been blown up. Towards four o'clock in the afternoon, the first tank crossed the Loire, using the roads, and joining those who had managed to cross the George V Bridge before it went up.

In spite of the brave resistance put up by the soldiers of the Orléans garrison, who had nothing but an old machine gun supported by a pile of bricks with which to defend the bridge, the Germans, superior in numbers and in ammunition, forced them to retreat down the Avenue Dauphine, leaving their dead. The Germans set up three small field pieces at the bridgehead.

The first enemy detachments reached the Croix Saint-Marceau just before five o'clock, and set up machine guns at every road junction. The few inhabitants left in the area emerged from their cellars and stared at the victorious soldiers in open-mouthed astonishment. They had been told the enemy army was starving, and that their uniforms were in shreds, their boots worn out. A middle-aged woman could not help going over to a young officer and feeling his jacket. The latter smiled and said politely: "Good-day, madame."

Dumbfounded, the woman burst into tears, and hurried

away, saying: "They lied to us."

Meanwhile, the French soldiers entered Orléans via the Faubourg Bannier.

"Be careful. The Nazis are here."

"That's impossible," exclaimed a lieutenant, "they're behind us."

He hardly had time to order his men to take up defense positions before the motorized German troops appeared on the scene. After a short exchange of gunfire, the lieutenant and two of his men were killed. The French soldiers surrendered. The Germans took their prisoners to a temporary camp at la Motte-Sanguin and mounted a machine-gun guard. In the course of the evening, they were joined by other captured French soldiers.

The cries of the wounded calling for help rang out everywhere. The artillery thundered, fire raged, the rattle of the last French machine guns died down while madmen who had escaped from the asylum at Fleury threaded their way among the debris shrieking with spine-chilling glee. Escaped French prisoners looted the few shops spared by the flames. There was no water, no electricity and no bread. There was no mayor, and no town council, only an abandoned city in ruins.

The first night of the long occupation of Orléans was beginning.

Chapter 15

They drove down country lanes and arrived, late that night, in a small village called La Trimouille. Camille was lying in the back of the car with her face streaming with cold sweat: she was delirious. In a square, near a river, refugees slept on the ground. In one of the streets, the door of a café opened, and a pale yellowish light filtered out. The place was full. François stopped the car and got out. The smell of beer, smoke and filth assailed him.

"A beer," he ordered, leaning against the bar.

"I've run out."

"A brandy, then."

"No brandy left either."

"Rum?"

"Nothing, I've got nothing left, not even lemonade; they've drunk it all."

"So what can you offer me?"

"I can give you an anisette."

"Anisette it is."

François had never enjoyed an anisette so much. He ordered another one, which he took to Léa, who was sitting on the step outside the open door. She took the glass and drained it thirstily.

"Did you ask where we can get hold of a doctor?"

"Not yet. How is she?"

Léa shrugged in silent response.

François went back into the café.

"Can you tell me where I can find a doctor?"

"None left. Old Vignaud's dead and his substitute has a broken leg. You'll have to go Montmorillon or to Blanc. There are emergency hospitals there."

"Is there a hotel?"

The man burst out laughing.

"A hotel! He wants a hotel! There are several, but you won't even find a floor to sleep on. They're bursting at the seams. They are so full that orders have come from you-know-where forbidding civilians to go beyond Montmorillon. There are fifty thousand people roaming the streets."

"What about Blanc?"

"It's the same story, only they've had air raids too, and the major has had the bridge mined."

"Hurry, François, Camille's going to die!" said Léa as she came over to François.

A hush fell at Léa's entrance.

"Is there an invalid with you?" asked the proprietor.

"Yes, a young woman who's in an advanced stage of pregnancy."

The proprietor's wife, a fat surly-looking woman, came towards them, wiping a glass.

"I might be able to help you. When you get to Montmorillon, go over the old bridge, and immediately on your right, you'll find the Rue du Puits-Cornet. The fourth house on the left is where my second cousin, Madame Trillaud, lives. Tell her that Lucienne sent you. She'll help you if she can."

François shook the woman's hand warmly. "Thank you so much, madame, thank you."

"You're welcome," she mumbled.

Crossing Montmorillon was an unforgettable experience. The streets and squares were congested with all manner of vehicles. Churches had been transformed into dormitories, as had schools and the town hall.

After going around in circles for ages without meeting anyone able to help them, they found the old bridge and the narrow street, the Rue du Puits-Cornet.

Léa was about to give up hammering on the door when

it opened a fraction.

"What's going on? You shouldn't be disturbing people at this hour."

"Are you Madame Trillaud? Lucienne, your cousin, sent us."

The door opened.

"Lucienne? What does she want?"

"Nothing. She said you might be able to help us. My friend is ill."

"What's wrong with her?"

"She's pregnant, but she's been unconscious for hours."

"Poor thing. Come in."

François carried the limp Camille into the little house.

"My house isn't very big, especially as I've got family who arrived from Paris yesterday staying. There's only my bedroom."

"But, madame . . ."

"Don't fuss. You can't go anywhere else. We women have to help each other. Come, help me change the sheets."

Soon, Camille was in Madame Trillaud's bed, wearing one of her nightdresses, similar to the one the good woman was wearing herself.

"That's not all. We've got to summon a doctor. Poor devils, they don't stop for a minute with things as they are. I'll go to Doctor Soulard's first. If he's not back, I'll go to Doctor Rouland's. He's a bit strange, but he's a good doctor."

She threw an old coat over her shoulders.

"I won't be long. In the kitchen, you'll find some coffee by the stove and bread in the bread bin. There's no butter left, I'm afraid. There are a few jars of jam on top of the cabinet in the pantry; take one."

François was sitting at the large kitchen table with its blue gingham tablecloth, watching Léa dunk her third slice of bread and strawberry jam into her bowl of coffee. There were purple rings under her eyes, and she was pale with exhaustion.

"You're not eating," she said with her mouth full, squinting at her slice of bread and jam.

He pushed his bread towards her with a smile.

"Thank you," she said, snatching it as though she feared he would change his mind.

Léa drained her bowl and leaned back in her chair, sated. "I was starving."

"I noticed. You ate like a hungry horse."

The clock struck two. Léa sat with her elbows resting on the table. Her chin was cupped in her hands, she was dreaming. What was she doing in this strange house, in this hell hole, with a dying woman, far away from those she loved? Her parents must be out of their minds with worry. She noticed that Travernier was staring at her.

"Stop looking at me like that."

"Can't we be friends for once? Remember, we have been lovers."

Léa, furious, got up and removed the bowls, which she stacked on the drainboard. As she brushed past François, he barred her path.

"You're stubborn. Why do you fight me? You don't love me? Fair enough. But you like making love. So don't pretend you don't. Do you know, love-making is the best remedy against fear? Yesterday, little girl, you were very lucky, I don't mean to boast: it takes most women years to discover sexual fulfillment. You're made for love, Léa, don't fight the feeling."

While he was talking, his hands burrowed under Léa's skirt. His fingers found the moist orifice which they gently probed.

Léa's eyes were half-closed and her breath came in short gasps as she let François take over. Waves of pleasure came over her. Without removing his hand, François laid her on the table, unzipped his trousers and opened her legs to penetrate her. As on the previous evening, Léa's orgasm was long and intense. For a while they remained locked together, motionless, beyond time, feeling their two hearts pounding. When François lifted himself, they both felt a final shudder of pleasure. François adjusted his clothes, helped Léa to her feet and held her tight for a long time, murmuring endearments into her hair.

"My beautiful love . . . my darling . . ."

Her body lulled, she let her lover's gentle voice soothe her.

When Madame Trillaud came back with the doctor, Léa was smoothing her dress.

"This is Doctor Rouland."

"So where is the patient?"

Madame Trillaud led him to the bedroom. Léa followed.

As soon as he saw Camille, the fatigue which marked his face and caused him to stoop seemed to leave him. He pulled back the blankets and examined her carefully.

"How long has she been like this?" he asked as he removed the stethoscope.

"I don't know," said Léa, "since six o'clock this evening."

"Has she been unconscious this long before?"

"Not as long, no. But she often faints and for quite a long time. The doctor who looked after her in Paris said that she should stay in bed, as much for the baby as for her heart."

"Show me the medicine she's taking."

Léa went out and fetched Camille's bag from the car. She showed the doctor the prescription and the medicine.

"Yes, that's fine, but it's not strong enough. I'm going to give her an injection for her heart, but I can't guarantee anything. She should be in the hospital, but there isn't a hope of finding her a bed."

A few seconds after the injection, Camille opened her eyes, too weak to look around her. François sat on the edge of the bed and took Camille's fragile hand in his.

"Everything's all right now, Camille. You must rest."

"The children, my God, the children . . . " she groaned.

Doctor Rouland drew Léa to one side.

"Are you a relative?"

"Yes," Léa lied.

"Her heart could give up at any time. We must tell her husband, her parents. God, I'm talking nonsense. Her husband's probably at the Front, and goodness knows where her parents are."

"I was taking her to her father-in-law's near Bordeaux."

"It is out of the question for her to travel. If she gets over this attack, she must stay put until after birth."

"You mean we've got to stay here?"

The doctor did not reply. He was preparing to give Camille another injection. Camille's eyes were soon closed again. the doctor started packing away his instruments. He looked haggard and gray with fatigue.

"Someone must stay with her around the clock. As soon as she wakes up, give her three drops of this in a glass of water. In an emergency, you can give her up to ten drops. I'll come back tomorrow."

"Don't worry, Doctor," said Madame Trillaud, "I'll look after her: I'm used to invalids."

"Goodbye, Madame Trillaud, you're a good woman. You go and get some sleep," he said, turning to Léa, "you look as though sleep wouldn't hurt you, either."

François accompanied the doctor to the old bridge. When he returned Léa was sleeping on the back seat of the car. He stood looking at her for a long time. He was moved: when she was asleep, she looked just like a petulant child. He carefully settled down in the front to sleep.

Léa was dragged out of her sleep by the noise of women shouting as they did their washing in the river. There were about ten of them, kneeling on the bank beating their laundry. Nearby, François was sitting on an overturned boat, watching the river bubbling over the stony bed. Further off, long trails of flowery algae were caught in the current. Madame Trillaud appeared on her doorstep and clapped her hands: "Breakfast's ready!"

In the sunny kitchen, the smell of coffee mingled with that of freshly toasted bread made Léa's nostrils quiver. White china bowls with a red band round the edge were waiting for them on the spotless blue gingham tablecloth.

"Come and eat before it gets cold. There's no butter, I'm afraid, but there's some quince jelly. Let me know what you think of it."

"How did our friend sleep?" asked François.

"Very well. When she woke up earlier, I gave her the drops. She smiled sweetly and then went back to sleep."

"How can we thank you for everything you're doing for us?"

"Please, think nothing of it. But if you're staying for a few days, I would ask you for a contribution, as, unfortunately, I'm not very well off."

"That goes without saying, madame," said Léa, devouring her slice of toast and jam.

"Have you listened to the news?" asked François, pointing to a cumbersome radio sitting majestically on the sideboard among family photographs, a bunch of roses in a blue vase and large engraved shells from the Great War.

"No, I was afraid of waking everyone up, and besides, it doesn't work very well."

"I'll see if I can do something about that."

"Do you know anything about radios?"

"A little."

"Where can I wash up?" asked Léa.

"Upstairs, next to my bedroom. It's not very comfortable, it's a little primitive. But I've put out clean towels. Take the kettle full of boiling water. There isn't any running water. Your husband has taken your luggage upstairs."

"He's not my husband," retorted Léa with a violence that surprised Madame Trillaud.

"I'm sorry. I thought he was."

Doctor Rouland came back at eleven o'clock. He was pleasantly surprised at his patient's state of health. Léa had washed Camille and brushed her hair and she was sitting propped up by pillows. Her face had lost its sunken look of the previous day. Only the dark rings under her eyes and her expression betrayed her suffering.

"I'm very pleased with you," said the doctor, after examining her. "It's not as serious as I feared. But I absolutely forbid you to move. I'm going to send you a nurse: she'll give you the injections I'm prescribing. Be a good patient, and then you'll soon be well."

"When can we set off again?"

"For the moment, you mustn't even think about it."

"But Doctor . . . "

"No buts. The life of your child is at stake, and so is yours. It's already a miracle that you haven't lost your baby. Be patient, you only have two months to go."

Doctor Rouland went down to the kitchen to write out his prescription. The large room was full of the Parisian relatives who were helping their aunt prepare lunch, describing their journey for the umpteenth time or watching François repair the radio.

"I think it's working now."

After a bit of crackling, they heard a voice.

"Marshal Pétain will address the nation."

A hush fell over the room. It was half past twelve on the 17th of June, 1940.

"People of France, at the request of the President of the Republic, I am taking over the leadership of the Government of France as of today. I am convinced of the loyalty of our admirable army, which is fighting against an enemy superior both in numbers and in arms with a heroism worthy of its long military tradition. In putting up such splendid resistance, they have done their duty by our allies. Certain of the support of the war veterans whom I am proud to have commanded, certain of the faith of the entire nation, I offer my services to alleviate the misfortunes of our country.

"In this hour of trial, I am thinking of the wretched refugees wandering the length and breadth of France in utter misery. I wish to express my compassion and my concern for their plight. It wrings my heart to say to you today that we must give up the fight. Last night, I spoke to our adversary and asked him if he was prepared to join with me, as another soldier, to seek an honorable means of bringing an end to the hostilities. Let all French citizens rally round the Government of which I am the head, during this ordeal, and silence their distress in order to obey their faith in the destiny of their country."

When the quavering, broken voice stopped, everyone was sitting with bowed head. Tears were streaming down many faces, tears of shame for the most part, but gradually a sense of relief also came over them.

François's expression was grim and hard. He switched off the radio and, without a word, left the house.

One phrase from the entire speech had stuck in Léa's mind:

" . . . we must give up the fight." The war was ending and Laurent would return. She raced up the stairs two at a time to break the news to Camille, who burst into tears.

"But why are you crying? The war's over, Marshal Pétain said so. Laurent will come back."

"Yes, but we lost the war and to those brutes."

"We lost it ages ago."

"No doubt, but I prayed so hard . . . "

" . . . that you thought God would hear you. Prayers! You don't win wars with prayers. You win with planes, tanks and leadership. Have you seen any of our planes in the sky? Have you seen any of our tanks on the roads? And have you seen our leaders out there, in front of the troops? All those we've met were running away. Have you already forgotten that colonel, scared out of his wits, in his limousine full of baggage, saying: 'Make way, make way, I have to get to my post.' His post, eh? To Spain, more likely! And our soldiers, have you seen our fine soldiers? Their uniforms are rags, they're dirty, their boots are worn out and all they can think about is escape from the fighting."

"You exaggerate, I'm sure most of them fought honorably. What about the ones who were defending the bridge at Orléans. All over France, everywhere, men have fought, and fought honorably, and many of them are dead."

"For nothing."

"No, not for nothing. For honor and to stop the animals."

"For honor? Don't make me laugh! Honor is an aristocratic invention; it's a luxury few of us can afford. The worker, the peasant, the tradesman floundering in the mud, with bombs and bullets raining down on him, doesn't give a damn for honor. All he wants is not to die like a dog. He wants it to stop, no matter how or why, but to stop at all costs. He never wanted this war, he doesn't understand it."

"It's true, he never wanted this war, but it's not true that he wants it to stop at all costs."

"Poor Camille, I think you deceive yourself about human nature. You'll see whether they're glad the war's over or not!"

"I can't believe that. Leave me alone, will you? I'm tired."

Léa shrugged and went downstairs.

" . . . he'll be our salvation . . . "

" . . . do you realize, he's offering his services to save France . . . "

" . . . he's a true patriot . . . "

" . . . with Marshal Pétain in charge, we have nothing to fear . . . "

" . . . we'll be able to return home . . . "

" . . . about time too. Things will get back to normal . . . "

"I'm afraid Hitler may be very harsh with us." Doctor Rouland's remark caused a stunned silence.

"What makes you think that, Doctor?"

"Because he has won everywhere, and no doubt he hasn't forgotten the stringent conditions of the 1918 peace treaty."

"That was fair enough. They lost the war!"

"As we have done today."

François came back to Madame Trillaud's very late that night, very drunk. She sat in the kitchen waiting for him, knitting.

"Madame Trillaud, I think I got a bit carried away celebrating our defeat. Shall I tell you something about Germany, madame? Germany is a great country, and Hitler is a great man. Long live Germany, long live Hitler. . . . "

"Will you be quiet, you'll cause a riot," she said, making him sit down. "I'm sure you haven't had any food. You're going to have a bowl of cabbage soup. There's nothing like it for making a man of you again."

"You're very kind, Madame Trillaud, but believe me, Germany . . . "

"Yes, I know. It's a great country. Eat your soup, it's getting cold."

After swallowing the last mouthful, he slumped onto the table with his head nearly in his plate. Gently, his hostess slid it away.

"Poor man," she murmured as she switched off the light.

The following morning, when Madame Trillaud came downstairs, she found François freshly shaven, his hair combed, making the coffee.

"Good morning, madame, you're too early. I wanted to have breakfast ready and surprise you. This morning, I managed to obtain milk, butter and fresh bread."

"Good morning, sir. However did you do that?"

"Yesterday when I was doing the rounds of all the cafés in Montmorillon, I made many friends. I apologize for my behavior last night. Will you forgive me?"

"Don't mention it. I've already forgotten. I'm sure my late husband would have got drunk too."

"Thank you, madame. How is the patient?"

"Much better. What she needed was peace and quiet."

"Let's eat; the coffee's ready. Today I'm going to the town hall to find out where my regiment is. Otherwise, I'll go back to Paris."

"You're going to leave these two ladies alone?"

"Mademoiselle Delmas is quite capable of looking after herself without me. Yesterday, the phone wasn't working. Perhaps they'll have repaired it by now. In that case, I'll call her parents to tell them where she is. Can you direct me to where I can buy some underwear, shirts and a suit?"

"There's not much choice here. Try Rochon's or Guyon-neau's. One is in the market square and the other is on the corner of the main street and the boulevard."

"One other thing: do you know of a house or an apartment my friends could rent?"

"There's nothing at the moment. The first refugees moved into the few places there were to let. But things will be clearer in a couple of days. People are already talking about returning to their homes. Meanwhile, the ladies can stay here."

"That's kind of you, but we've even taken your bedroom."

"Bah! At my age, you don't need much sleep. A mattress in a corner is sufficient."

"It's reassuring to meet a good person like you."

"Hello," said Léa, coming into the room dressed in her kimono, her hair dishevelled and her eyes still sleepy.

"Hello, love. Did you sleep well?"

"Not really. Camille was tossing and turning all night."

"How is she this morning?" asked François.

"Fine, I suppose, since she's hungry."

"That's a good sign. I'll take a tray up to her," said Madame Trillaud, rising from her chair.

"Sit still, madame! I'll do it," said François getting up in turn.

He skillfully arranged a pretty china cup, a basket of thinly sliced bread, a pat of butter, sugar and jam on the rustic wooden tray. He added a bowl of cherries and a rose from the blue vase as a final touch to this appetizing meal. Feeling rather pleased with himself, he showed the tray to the two women for their inspection.

"Not bad, eh?"

"It's lovely," asserted Madame Trillaud.

"You don't think she'll eat all that, do you?" teased Léa.

"You've forgotten the milk and the coffee," said their hostess, putting a little jug of milk and a large pot of coffee on the tray.

"I don't think I'd make a very good maid."

In the kitchen, Léa was shelling peas under the amused eye of her hostess and the admiring gaze of a pimply cousin.

"Don't wait for me for lunch. I'll look after myself," said François coming into the room.

"Where are you going?" asked Léa.

"To look for a garage for the car. Then to the town hall. Then to buy some clothes and phone your parents and Monsieur d'Argilat."

"I'm coming with you," cried Léa, abandoning the peas.

"You're not ready. Meet me at the post office if you like."

"But . . . "

He was already out of the door. Léa sat down again and resumed shelling peas, in a furious temper.

When François came back, at five o'clock, wearing a baggy navy blue suit, Léa was ironing a dress and listening to the radio.

"Where were you? I looked everywhere for you."

"Well, you didn't look very hard! It's not a very large town. I spent three hours at the post office trying to get through to Paris and then to your parents. I managed to speak to them, but we were cut off very quickly."

"How are they?" cried Léa, putting down her iron.

"They're well. They were worried about you. I reassured them."

"I would so like to have talked to Mummy."

"We'll try again tomorrow from Doctor Rouland's place. I met him as I was coming out of the post office and he said I could use his phone. Can you smell something burning?"

"Damn, my dress . . . it's all your fault . . . "

François burst out laughing.

"What have they been saying on the radio?" he asked, twiddling the knobs.

"Nothing, it's so boring. There isn't even any decent music. Look at my dress, what am I going to do?"

"You could sew a pocket over it."

"What a good idea!" exclaimed Léa delightedly. "But I haven't got any material like that," she added, peeved.

"It's a white dress, so put on a colored pocket with matching buttons, it'll look lovely."

Léa looked at him in amazement.

"That's not a bad idea at all. I didn't know you were interested in fashion."

"I'm interested in everything. I'm not like you."

"What's that supposed to mean?"

"That you haven't even noticed that I'm wearing the latest Montmorillon fashion."

"Oh, it suits you very well," she said glancing at him with indifference.

"Thank you. Coming from you I feel flattered."

"Stop fiddling with those knobs."

"I'm trying to get the BBC to find out what developments there have been in the war. Perhaps the English are better informed than we are."

"*This is the BBC . . . General de Gaulle is speaking to you . . .*"

"Who is General de Gaulle?" asked Léa.

"Be quiet, I'll tell you later."

"*The leaders who have been at the head of the French*

Army for many years have formed a government. On the pretext that our army has been defeated, this government has approached the enemy with a view to ceasing the hostilities.

"It is true, we were, we still are, overwhelmed by the enemy's superiority in mechanical engineering, both on the ground and in the air. It is the tanks, the planes and the tactics of the Germans that took our leaders by surprise, rather than their sheer number, and that is why they are in the state they are in today.

"But is that the last word on the subject? Is that the end of all hope? Is our defeat final? No!

"Believe me, I know what I am talking about, and I am telling you that all is not lost for France. Those same things that beat us, could one day bring victory. For France is not alone! France is not alone! France is not alone! We have a vast empire behind us. France can join forces with the British Empire, which controls the sea and is continuing the struggle. France can, like the British, have unlimited access to the huge industrial resources of the United States.

"This war is not restricted to the unfortunate territory of our country. This war will not be decided by the battle for France. This war is a world war. All the errors, all the delays, all the suffering cannot alter the fact that there are, in the universe, all the necessary means eventually to crush our enemies. Although today we are struck down by their superior mechanical strength, in the future we will be victorious through superior mechanical strength. The future of the world depends on it.

"I, General de Gaulle, at present in London, invite French officers and soldiers who are on British territory or who intend to come here, with their weapons, to contact me. Likewise, I invite all engineers and skilled workers in the arms industry who are on British territory, or who intend to come here, to join me. Come what may, the flame of French resistance must not be extinguished, it shall not be extinguished.

"Tomorrow, I shall broadcast again from London as I have done today."

François was pensive as he switched off the radio and began pacing up and down the room. In a corner, Madame Trillaud, who had come into the room unnoticed at the beginning of the speech, sat wiping her eyes on the corner of her apron.

"What's the matter, madame?" cried Léa.

"Nothing . . . they're tears of joy."

"Joy?"

"Yes, this General . . . what's his name?"

"De Gaulle."

"Yes, that's it, de Gaulle . . . he said that the flame of French resistance shall not be extinguished."

"So, what does that mean? He's in London, not France. The Germans are here, not in England. If he wants to continue the struggle, he'd do better to come back instead of deserting his post like a coward."

"You're talking nonsense, Léa," said François. "You don't know what you're talking about. De Gaulle is a brave and sincere man, I met him when he was Minister of Defense. He must have thought long and hard before broadcasting that appeal, which makes him an outlaw—a man who is used to obeying orders according to military tradition."

"Are you going to join him?" asked Madame Trillaud.

"I don't know. It all depends on what happens next. First, I've got to join my regiment. I won't be eating here this evening, I'm having dinner with the mayor."

"What about me?"

"You? You can look after Camille like a devoted friend," he said mockingly.

The following day, Léa spoke to her parents on Dr. Rouland's telephone. She cried when she heard Isabelle's gentle voice and her father's, gruff with emotion. And what a joy to hear Ruth's accent once again! She was even delighted to exchange a few words with Sabine and Laure. She had so many questions to ask, about the estate, her uncles, her aunts and cousins. She suddenly discovered that she loved them all. She wished she could tell her mother about the horror of the air raids, about Josette's death and the killing of the man who wanted to rob them, about the look on the grandmother's face as she stood staring at the bodies of her daughter and grandchildren, and Camille's illness, and her affair with François. All she could do was repeat: "Mummy, Mummy, if only you knew. . . ."

"Darling, as soon as it's possible, Papa and I will come and get you."

"Oh! Yes, Mummy. Do come. I miss you so much, I've got such a lot to tell you, I've been so frightened. I've often thought of you, I said to myself: 'What would Mummy do?' I didn't always do what you would have done. I behaved selfishly, like a spoiled child. Oh! Mummy, I love you so much! I was so afraid I'd never see you again when everything was burning all around us. The bombs, it's so awful, they kill children, poor people . . . Mummy . . . "

Léa was sobbing so hard she couldn't go on. Gently, François took the receiver out of her hands and gave Pierre Delmas his daughter's address and Doctor Rouland's telephone number.

After thanking the doctor, he took Léa out.

It was pitch dark; no lights were shining in the congested streets. The air was mild. As they crossed the old bridge, Léa remarked: "I can smell the water."

She loved the smell of the river mingled with the fragrance of wild herbs, the smell of fish and mud. They were outside Madame Trillaud's house.

"I don't want to go in. Let's go into the countryside. It's not far, just at the end of the path."

"As you like," shrugged François.

Léa took his arm.

They walked slowly between two stone walls behind which were kitchen gardens. At the end of the path, they went past dilapidated old houses with all sorts of refuse on the doorstep. A stench of pig sties made them hasten their pace.

The walls gave way to hedges. Some of these were in flower and the air was perfumed. They followed the path for a while as it became increasingly narrower. Léa led François towards a little meadow where there was a hut standing at the foot of a huge oak tree. When she pushed open the door, they were overwhelmed by the pungent smell of hay.

"It's my house, I discovered it yesterday. I feel so at home here, it's so peaceful and smells so good, it reminds me of Montillac. I came back today with my books," said Léa dropping down into the sweet-smelling hay.

François remained standing, motionless, trying to guess what this unpredictable girl expected of him. He was afraid of doing the wrong thing and making her cold and distant again. He had been so pleasantly surprised by her attitude since they had left Doctor Rouland's office. All he wanted to do was take her in his arms. Not to make love to her, but for the pleasure of holding her to him, even though he knew she loved another.

"Don't stand there twiddling your thumbs, come close to me. Anyone would think you were afraid of me."

There's some truth in that, he thought as he lay down beside her.

They were quiet for a long time.

"Why don't you kiss me?"

"I thought you didn't like it."

"I don't know. Take me in your arms."

At first, his kisses were gentle, his caresses tender.

"Harder! Kiss me harder!"

They made love again and again, all night, until they were exhausted. Then they fell asleep in each other's arms, their naked bodies showing signs of bites and scratches, and dried hay clinging to their clammy skin.

They awoke to the patter of rain. They were cold. François put his blue jacket round Léa's shoulders. They were soaked through by the time they arrived back at Madame Trillaud's.

"I was worried. Where were you? You mustn't scare me like that. Look at the state you're in, you'll catch your death of cold. Monsieur Tavernier, it's very naughty of you. The child's shivering. As if it's not enough with one invalid here," scolded the good woman.

She pulled a blanket out of a cupboard and wrapped it

round Léa, whose teeth were chattering. She made some mulled wine. François's jacket, draped over the back of a chair in front of the stove, steamed.

"Here you are, here's a shirt and a pair of trousers that used to belong to my husband. Go and change."

François took the clothes without a word.

That afternoon, François announced to Camille and Léa that he intended to depart.

"Where are you going?" asked Léa sharply.

"Paris."

"You're going to leave us to fend for ourselves?"

"You're safe here. Madame Trillaud has promised to look after you and she's going to try to find you a suitable place to stay until Doctor Rouland thinks it safe for Camille to travel. Do you have enough money?"

"Yes. That's no problem."

"Monsieur Tavernier, Monsieur Tavernier, come quickly, General de Gaulle is going to speak on the radio again," cried Madame Trillaud from the bottom of the stairs.

"I'd like to hear him," said Camille.

François leaned over the bed, swept Camille up in his arms and gently carried her downstairs. In the kitchen, he placed her in their hostess's wicker armchair. There were ten other people in the room listening attentively to the voice that came to them from a free country to bring them hope.

"*At this moment in time, every French person understands that the ordinary forms of power have disappeared. Faced with confusion, faced with the dissolution of the Government, which has fallen slave to the enemy, faced with the impossibility of relying on our institutions, I, General de Gaulle, a French soldier and leader, I realize that I speak in the name of France.*

"*In the name of France, I formally declare the following: it is the duty of every Frenchman still bearing arms to continue the resistance struggle. To lay down arms, to abandon a military position, to agree to hand over any piece of French soil to enemy control, would constitute a crime against the nation.*

"At this moment in time, I speak, above all, for French North Africa, for an intact North Africa.

"The Italian armistice is nothing but a crude trap. In the Africa of Clauzel, of Bugeaud, of Lyautey and of Noguès, anyone who has a sense of honor has a duty to refuse to accept the enemy's conditions. It would be intolerable that the panic of Bordeaux should cross the sea. Soldiers of France, wherever you are, stand up and fight!"

During the night, François Tavernier left the little town.

Chapter 16

When the armistice was signed on the evening of the 24th of June, 1940, Léa and Camille fell into each other's arms. For both of them, the first thing that came into their minds was: the war is truly over. Now Laurent will come back. Then doubt, fear and shame set in. To be precise, it was Camille in particular who felt ashamed; for Léa, all that the armistice meant was a return to normal life. She was so keen to live, she refused to admit any negatives of the situation. The war was over, period. Everything was going to be as it was before.

She knew she was deceiving herself. Nothing would ever be as it was before; there had been all those wasteful and horrible deaths, that man she had killed. The memory of that incident gave her nightmares that made her sit up in bed and scream. It took all Camille's maternal gentleness to soothe her. Without realizing it, Camille used the same words as Isabelle Delmas at these moments.

"It's nothing, darling. I'm here. Don't be afraid. It's over. You're safe. Go back to sleep."

And Léa would go back to sleep, snuggling up to Camille, murmuring: "Mummy!"

No, nothing would ever be the same again. During the terror of the war, she had become a woman. She was unable to forgive herself for that so easily. She had been trying to contact Montillac since the 19th of June, with no luck. Finally, on the 30th of June, she heard her father's voice. No doubt, it was the distance, the bad connection, but Pierre

Delmas's voice sounded like that of a very old man. He sounded hesitant, bewildered, as he repeated incessantly: "Everything's fine, everything's fine . . . "

When Léa asked to speak to her mother, there was a long silence at the other end.

"Hello . . . hello . . . don't hang up."

"Hello, Léa?"

"Ruth, I'm so glad to hear your voice. How are you? Put Mummy on, I'm afraid we'll be cut off. Hello, can you hear me?"

"Yes."

"I want to speak to Mummy."

"Your mother's not here. She's in Bordeaux."

"Oh! What a pity. I so wanted to speak to her, it would have done me so much good. Give her a big kiss from me. Don't forget to tell her I think about her lots, I love her so much. I'll try and call again later in the week. Hello . . . hello . . . damn, we've been cut off."

As she replaced the receiver, Léa had a strange feeling of foreboding. It was so strong that her forehead was suddenly covered with beads of sweat that made the scar above her eyebrow itch.

"I must go home," she muttered as she got up from the armchair in Doctor Rouland's office.

Just at that moment, the doctor came in.

"Did you manage to get through to your parents?"

"Yes, thank you. When will Camille be able to travel?"

"Not before she gives birth. It would be too dangerous."

"I have to return to my home. It's important."

"The health of your friend and her baby are certainly more important."

"How would you know? I'm sure I'm needed there. I must go."

"Is somebody ill?"

"I don't know, but I have to go. I feel it, do you understand?"

"I understand. Calm down. You know very well that you can't leave."

"But you're here, Doctor, and so is Madame Trillaud.

Besides, Camille must be much better because you've allowed her to get up."

"That's not enough. It's purely your presence that stops her from giving in to panic. She's so fond of you that she hides her uneasiness and worries from you. Just because I allowed her to take a few steps doesn't mean that her condition is no longer serious. What's more, she is so exhausted that she's likely to give birth prematurely. Please, be patient."

"I've been patient for weeks and weeks. I can't take any more. I must see my mother."

Léa sank into the armchair, covered her head with her hands and whimpered like a child. "I want to go home. Please let me go home!"

Skillful as he was when it came to treating his patients, Doctor Rouland was at a loss when confronted with tears, especially those of a pretty girl. He eventually came to grips with himself and prepared a sedative which he persuaded her to drink. His nerves were shot and he too drank a mouthful.

"Dry your eyes . . . crying won't help . . . you'll make yourself ill."

When Léa went back to Madame Trillaud's, the good woman took one look at Léa's distraught face, felt her burning hands and made her go to bed. During the night, her temperature rose to 104° F. Madame Trillaud got the doctor, but he didn't know how to diagnose Léa's illness.

For the next three days, Léa was delirious. She kept calling for her mother, Laurent and François. Then, her temperature disappeared as suddenly as it had arrived, leaving her thin and weak. During those three days, Camille did not leave Léa's bedside for a second, in spite of the doctor and Madame Trillaud's admonitions.

A week later, Léa, completely back to her old self, was swimming in the river.

That evening, Camille said to her: "Doctor Rouland thinks I can go back to Roches-Blanches without any risk."

"Is that true?" exclaimed Léa.

"Yes, if we drive slowly. One of Madame Trillaud's cousins is going to check the car and get us gas. We can leave as soon as you're ready."

"That's wonderful, I'll get to see Mummy again at last!"

Camille looked at Léa with an expression of pure goodness.

"It's true that she seems to love me," thought Léa, "If she knew how I feel about Laurent . . . "

"Madame Trillaud, we can leave. Camille is strong enough to travel!" she cried rushing toward their hostess who was coming into the kitchen carrying a huge basket full of vegetables.

The good woman faced Camille in astonishment.

"But, child . . . "

She stopped in mid-sentence when Camille signalled to her to be quiet.

"We are leaving tomorrow, Madame Trillaud. Doctor has given us his consent."

A frown spread across the face of the woman who had nursed her as a mother during those three days. "Why didn't he say anything to me before he left?" she asked suspiciously.

"He must have forgotten. He has so much on his mind."

"I didn't know he'd gone away. Where did he go?" asked Léa.

"To Brittany to fetch his mother, who is alone now, since her youngest son was killed at Dunkirk."

"I didn't know he had lost a brother in the war," said Camille.

"He doesn't talk about it, but I know it's a great sorrow to him. That boy was like a son to him."

"Please tell him how sorry Léa and I are to hear it."

"You'd do better to wait until he returns so you can tell him yourselves."

"No. We must go back home. I want my child to be born in my family's home."

"The roads aren't safe."

"Madame Trillaud, don't worry, everything will be all right," said Camille taking her hands in hers. "Promise you'll come and stay with me for as long as you like. You will always be welcome."

"I'm going to miss you, Madame Camille. I found such a lovely house for you, with a garden, by the river. You know, the house with red and white shutters on the other side of the river; it belongs to a grain broker who only comes for a few days each month. They rent out half of the house. Some Paris bankers lived in it, but they've gone."

"Now the town is deserted. It's eerie. There's nobody left in the streets," said Léa. "I'm going to pack."

The following morning, in spite of Madame Trillaud's tears, Camille and Léa set off, taking with them baskets full of food. Even Léa had a lump in her throat as she said goodbye to this woman who had so generously opened her heart and her house to them.

"When things settle down, I'll come back with Laurent and our child," said Camille, comfortably installed on the back seat.

"I hope I never see this place again," said Léa as they crossed the old bridge.

Early that afternoon they reached Nontron, a small town in the Limoges region. There was little traffic on the roads, but, here and there, in the ditches and by the roadside, abandoned or partly destroyed vehicles reminded them that the refugees had been on these roads.

Léa helped Camille get out of the car and found her a seat in a pavement café.

"Order me a cold lemonade. I'm going to inquire about vacant rooms at the hotel across the street."

"Why?"

"So you can rest. You look tired."

"No. There's no need. Let's go on. We can rest later."

"Are you sure you're all right?"

The waitress arrived at that moment and Camille was spared the need to answer.

"Two cold lemonades, please. do you want anything to eat?" asked Léa.

"Thank you. I'm not hungry."

"Neither am I. This heat kills one's appetite."

After washing up at the pump in the courtyard of the café, they set off again.

In Perigueux, they were stopped by French gendarmes

who were worried at the sight of two unaccompanied young women in such a big car with so little luggage. Any vehicle that was not carrying mattresses on the roof was suspicious! It was only when they saw how weak Camille was that they allowed the women to continue, with words of advice: "You'd do better, little lady, to drive to the nearest hospital if you don't want to give birth on the way."

Camille thanked them and went back to the car gritting her teeth.

They drove for a while in silence. They went over a bump and Camille let out a groan. Léa turned around.

"Do you feel bad?"

Camille shook her head, with a pathetic smile. Léa pulled over to the side of the road.

"Where does it hurt?" she asked, climbing in beside Camille.

"Everywhere," murmured Camille under her breath.

"Oh no! What have I done to deserve this?" Keep calm, keep calm, she told herself. "Let's go to the nearest village and find a doctor."

They did not find a single doctor in the few villages between Perigueux and Bergerac. In Bergerac, the three doctors Léa searched for were away.

When she returned to the car, Camille was still in great pain. Fortunately, they had no trouble finding a hotel room. It was not very comfortable, but it would do for one night. Léa had dinner brought up to the room and made Camille swallow a few spoonfuls of broth.

As soon as her head touched the pillow of the sagging bed, Léa fell asleep. As for Camille, she did not close her eyes all night. She fell asleep at dawn, but then she was so restless that she woke Léa. Feeling irritated, Léa got up. It was six o'clock and the weather was cloudy.

Léa washed quickly and went downstairs. She went to look over the town while she was waiting for the hotel café to open so she could have some breakfast. As she passed the post office, she thought she ought to try to telephone her parents to tell them they were on their way. She had not been able to get through before they left because the lines were dead, once again. Although it was early, there was already a long line of people waiting to telephone at the post office. At last, it was Léa's turn, but after the operator had made several attempts, she heard her say: "I can't get through. Try again later."

It was nearly eleven o'clock when she left the post office, feeling thoroughly demoralized. As she walked past a shop window, she caught sight of her reflection and had difficulty recognizing herself. What would her mother and Ruth say if they could see her like this, dishevelled and with her dress in tatters? At the recollection of the two women's scoldings, she felt a surge of joy. Soon, she would be able to see them. How gladly she would put up with Ruth's lectures and her mother's tender admonitions! Soon, in a day at the most, she would fling herself into their arms.

Camille was dressed and lying on the bed waiting for Léa. To hide her pallor, she had put rouge on her cheeks. But as she was not accustomed to wearing make-up, she had overdone it, which made her look like a doll whose face had been clumsily painted. However, she deceived Léa.

"I see you're looking better this morning. Do you feel well enough to leave?"

"I'm fine," said Camille, biting her lip as she stood up.

She managed to go down the stairs clutching Léa and the rail, then cross the hotel foyer and get into the car. The effort was excruciating. She lay down on the seat. Léa went back to get their luggage, change her dress and brush her hair.

Now Léa was on home ground. The names of the towns and villages were music to her ears: Sainte-Foy-la Grande, Castillon-la-Bataille, Sauveterre-en-Guyenne, La Reole. Léa was of two minds. Should she take Camille to her father-in-law's or to Montillac? She turned around to ask Camille what she thought. The back seat was empty.

"Camille, Camille?" called Léa, coming to a halt.

She opened the door, and stepped back as she found herself face to face with a woman with bulging eyes who had fallen between the seats and was biting on the blanket.

"My God! Camille . . . " Now what was the matter with her?

"The baby . . . "

What about the baby? The baby . . . what did she mean?

"The baby . . . " Camille gasped, raising her head.

Oh no! Not now! Couldn't the wretched baby wait a bit? Léa looked about her in panic. Nothing but miles and miles of countryside and a storm brewing. She must keep calm. How long did it take to give birth? Léa had to admit that she did not have the faintest idea. Isabelle had never discussed things like that with her daughters.

"When did it start?"

"Yesterday, but it stopped this morning . . . earlier on, I felt something tear inside my stomach. That's when I fell. I was all wet."

Her thin, distorted body was racked by another contraction. Camille was unable to repress a cry which disfigured her poor face as make-up mingled with the sweat and ran down her cheeks.

The pain eased and Léa tried unsuccessfully to lift her back on to the seat.

"I can't, I'm sorry."

"Be quiet and let me think! The next village is Pellegure. We'll ask for help there."

"No! I want to go to Laurent's house, or to your parents."

"Do you think you can hang on for another fifty kilometers?"

"Yes."

Léa would remember those fifty kilometers all her life. It was at Saint-Maixant that she saw the first German uniforms. She was so startled at the sight that she nearly drove into a ditch. At the foot of the Verdelais hill, there was a road block. A soldier signalled to her to stop.

"Es ist verboten weiter gehen."

In her astonishment, Léa forgot every word of German that had been painfully taught her by Ruth.

"I don't understand."

An officer came over and laboriously translated: "It is forbidden to go any further. Have you an *Ausweis?*"

"Ausweis?"

"Yes. Permit."

"No, I'm going home. It's at the top of the hill," she said pointing to Montillac.

"*Nein,* no *Ausweis,* no go on.*"*

"I beg you, look, my friend is giving birth . . . baby . . . " she said pointing to the back of the car.

The officer peered in.

"*Mein Gott! Wie heissen Sie?*"

"Léa Delmas."

"*Gehoren Sie zur Familie der Montillac?*"

He signalled to a soldier to clear the way and mounted a motorcycle that was leaning up against a tree.

"Come, I shall accompany you."

Léa had imagined her homecoming differently: they would all be there to greet her, to make a fuss over her and celebrate her arrival. But today, nothing of the sort happened; everything was deserted, the farm, the outhouses, the house, the barns, even the animals seemed to have disappeared. Everything was quiet. Too quiet.

"Mummy! Papa! It's me!"

In the dining room, in the drawing room, in her father's study, the curtains were drawn as if there was blinding sunshine. Léa had to face the fact: no one was at home. Outside it was getting dark. In the kitchen, the German officer was waiting, supporting and encouraging Camille.

"*Wo soll ich sie hinlegen?*"

"To my room."

Léa led the way upstairs. The room smelled musty. She went to get some sheets from the linen cupboard. The German helped her make the bed. Camille lay moaning in the armchair where he had put her down. They laid her cautiously on the clean sheets which smelled of lavender.

"*Ist der niemand da?*"

"I'm going to call the doctor."

She galloped down the stairs two at a time. Her father's study was a mess and she had difficulty finding his address book. She could not get a reply from Doctor Blanchard's number, or from any of the local doctors, who were all friends of the family. A cry rang through the old house. Where on earth were they all? A fresh cry brought her running out of the study. She noticed in passing a black-edged postcard and wondered who had died.

In the kitchen, the officer was busying himself. He had lit the stove and was heating several pans of water.

"Kommt der Arzt?"

Léa shook her head—if only the doctor were coming—and went upstairs to Camille. She managed to undress her, leaving just her slip on, and then she sat down beside her, held her hands and wiped her brow. Camille thanked her between contractions, and tried to repress her shrieks.

The German came in carrying a basin of hot water. He had taken off his cap and his jacket and rolled up his sleeves. Léa suddenly noticed that he was young and handsome. A long lock of blond hair fell across his forehead, emphasizing his youth.

"Berugigen Sie Sich: es wird schon gut gehen," he said soothingly, leaning over Camille and trying to put her at ease.

He stepped back when he saw the expression of sheer terror that crossed Camille's face. She tried to sit up and pointed at the Nazi badges decorating the young man's shirt.

"Don't be afraid," said Léa getting her to lie down again, "he helped me bring you here."

"But he's German . . . I don't want a German to touch me, or to touch my child! I'd rather die!"

"That's exactly what will happen if you don't calm down. I don't know what's going on, but there isn't a soul around."

An even stronger contraction prevented Camille from replying, then another, and then another.

"Holen Sie Mal Wäsche."

Léa did as she was told. "Will you know what to do?" she stammered, returning with a pile of towels and two big aprons.

"Mein Vater ist Arzt, ich habe ein paar Bücher aus seiner Bibliotheck gelesen."

While he was putting on an apron, Léa washed her hands. If only Mummy would come now, she thought. I know I'm going to faint.

"Na, wie sagen Sie es aus Französisch: courage!" he said in an effort to be friendly.

209

Then, turning to Camille: "Be brave, madame, the baby is coming."

When Ruth, dressed in black from head to toe, pushed open the door of the bedroom, she had to hold on to the doorpost to stop herself from falling over. There was a German—she recognized the boots and trousers—holding in his arms a tiny baby wrapped in a towel and yelling vociferously.

"Das ist ein Junge," he said proudly, holding out the little boy.

Léa flung herself into her governess's arms. "Oh! Ruth! You're here! Where's Mummy? I needed you so badly."

"Good-day, madame," said the officer in the best French he could manage, bowing, his face red and covered with sweat. With a beaming smile he added:

"All is well. The baby is small but very strong."

Without replying, Ruth leaned over Camille. Looking worried, she stood up and ran out of the room.

A few seconds later, Doctor Blanchard hurried in, wearing a black suit, followed by Bernadette Bouchardeau wearing mourning clothes.

"Doctor! Quickly!"

"What's going on?"

The doctor understood at once.

"Bernadette, take care of the child. Ruth, go and get my bag. You'll find it in my car."

"Doctor, will she die?"

"I don't know. Her heart seems weak. What's this soldier doing here?"

"He helped me get Camille home and he delivered the baby."

Since Bernadette Bouchardeau had taken the new-born baby from him, the young man had been standing in the middle of the room, looking rather awkward, wiping his hands on his apron.

Ruth returned with the doctor's bag and spoke to him in his own language.

"Wie bedanken uns, mein Herr ..."

"Leutnant Frederic Hanke."

"Léa, see the lieutenant out. *Auf Wiedersehen, mein Herr.*"

Frederic Hanke removed the apron, bowed stiffly and followed Léa out as he put his jacket on. In the passage, they bumped into Sabine and Laure, who were both dressed in black. They fell into each other's arms.

"Laure, little Laure, I'm so happy to see you . . . even you, horrid Sabine!"

"Oh! Léa, it's awful!"

"What's awful? Here we are together again, Camille's baby is fine, the war is over, well nearly . . ." she added, looking at the German.

"What's he doing here?" whispered Laure.

"I'll explain. Where are Mummy and Papa?"

"Mummy?"

In the kitchen, Raymond d'Argilat, Jules Fayard, the head storeman, Amélie Lefèvre and Auguste Martin, her steward, Albertine and Lisa de Montpleynet, Luc and Pierre Delmas and their neighbors, were all drinking large glasses of sweet yellow wine from the estate.

All these people were clad in black. The women had raised their veils.

When she caught sight of them, Léa's delight at seeing her father froze. Why did she suddenly feel so cold? Behind her, Sabine and Laure were crying and the German was buttoning his uniform. When he had finished buckling his belt, from which hung a black leather holster containing his pistol, he put on his cap, stepped forward, clicked his heels in front of Pierre Delmas and left without a word.

In the courtyard the motorcycle started up with what seemed like a tremendous roar. As long as he could be heard, nobody moved.

In the kitchen, a ray of sunshine emphasized the contrast between the black clothes and the white walls. On the big table with its blue linen tablecloth that was a little worn in places, the flies were getting drunk on the wine that ran down the sides of the bottles. The big clock chimed five o'clock. Ruth and the doctor came in and still nobody moved. Léa strained to hear. Why was she taking so long? Didn't she know her daughter was waiting for her?

"Mummy," she heard herself say. "Mummy? Mummy . . . " the word screamed inside her head. No, not that . . . not her . . . let them all die, but Mother . . .

"Papa? Tell me . . . where's Mummy? It's not true, is it? It's somebody else."

Léa looked around the room, trying to see who could be missing. Plenty of people were absent: Uncle Adrien, cousins . . .

Her sisters sobbed even louder. They all looked down. On her father's cheeks—how he had aged!—there were tears. Ruth held out her arms to hold her.

Chapter 17

For nearly a week, Léa remained in shock; she was unable to cry, unable to speak. She ate what was put on her plate, and slept curled up in the little bed in the children's room. She took the tablets prescribed by Doctor Blanchard and sat on the terrace for hours at a time staring in front of her. Neither her father nor Ruth nor her sisters were able to get through to her. At the sight of Léa, a motionless thin little figure looking towards the path to Verdelais as if waiting for someone, the old nurse felt a pang of anguish.

It was the discovery of an old pink silk blouse that had belonged to her mother in one of the trunks in the children's room that brought on Léa's liberating tears. On hearing her sobbing, Camille, in a white nightdress, dragged herself out of bed and, with the same tone of voice as Isabelle, found the words that soothed her grief a little.

Drunk from crying, exhausted from sobbing, Léa fell asleep in Camille's arms.

When she awoke, much later, she splashed some water on her face, drew her hair back and went into her mother's room. Isabelle's perfume still hung in the air of the shuttered room. Near the carefully made bed, a bunch of roses had lost the last of their petals. Léa knelt down by her mother's bed and laid her cheek on the white piqué bedspread. Her tears flowed gently.

"Mummy . . . my darling mother."

Her father came in and knelt down by his daughter.

"Tomorrow morning, we'll go to the cemetery together."

Turning to him, she said. "What happened."

"Let's go into my study, I can't bear talking in here."

In the study, Pierre Delmas gulped down two glasses of port, one after the other. Sitting on the old sunken leather sofa, Léa waited.

"It happened on the night of the 19th of June. Your mother had gone to Bordeaux to the office of the Women's Catholic Action League, of which she was a member, to help distribute food and supplies to refugees. She was to spend the night at your Uncle Luc's. Shortly after midnight, there was an air raid. Bombs fell all over the city, near the docks, in the Bastide district, in the Avenue Luze, in the Saint-Seurin district. Ten fell between the Rue David-Johnston and the Rue Camille-Godard, Rue des Remparts, near the station, Avenue Alsace-Lorraine, in a trench shelter in the Damours quarter, where a number of people died. One bomb fell near the hotel which houses Marshal Pétain and General Weygand's offices, where the regional commander is staying."

Léa had difficulty controlling her impatience. Who cares where the bombs fell? What she wanted to know was how her mother had died.

Pierre Delmas poured himself another glass.

"Your mother came out, with a group of others, from the Catholic League building to go to the nearest air raid shelter. She was in the street when a bomb fell in the Rue Ségalier, wounding her in the head and in the legs. One of the first people on the scene was a journalist from Paris who carried her to the hospital and got in touch with me. When I arrived, she was unconscious. She did not come round until the eve of her death, which was the 10th of July."

"Did she say anything for me?"

Pierre Delmas drained his glass before answering, in a voice that had become somewhat husky: "The last word she uttered was your name."

A thrill of joy ran through her. So, before she died, her mother had thought of her!

"Thank you, God," she murmured, throwing herself into her father's arms.

"We ought not to cry, my darling: at night she comes back and talks to me."

Léa looked at him in amazement. "Yes, Papa, I believe she's still with us."

Léa left the room without noticing her father's smile of absolute conviction.

The following day, when Léa and her father returned from the cemetery, they found Frederic Hanke and another officer talking to Ruth. It was a heated discussion judging from the old woman's furious expression.

"Good-day, gentlemen," said Pierre Delmas, coldly. "What's the matter, Ruth?"

"These gentlemen intend to move in with us. Apparently, they have a requisition order."

"But that's impossible!" exclaimed Léa.

Unfortunately it's true. Frederic Hanke's gesture seemed to convey as he pointed to the piece of paper Ruth was holding.

"We don't have room. We're sheltering relatives from Paris and Bordeaux."

"I'm sorry, sir, but we have our orders. I'm Lieutenant Otto Kramer. I need two suitable rooms for Lieutenant Hanke and myself. We will try to disturb you as little as possible." The officer spoke perfect French.

"That will be hard," mumbled Léa.

"You can't stay here, we are in mourning," said Ruth, unable to conceal her anger.

"Please accept our sincerest condolences. May we explore the house?"

Pierre Delmas gave the lieutenant his room and moved into his wife's room.

"Take my room, you know where it is," said Léa to Frederic Hanke.

"I don't want to drive you out, Fraülein."

"*Es ist schon gemacht,*" she replied, emptying the drawers and refusing to recognize his attempt at conciliation.

"I swear I couldn't do anything about it. Our orders come from Bordeaux."

That was the beginning of a difficult time. Early in the morning, the Germans went down to the kitchen where Lieutenant Kramer's orderly prepared their breakfast. Sabine, who was a nurse at the hospital in Langon, had to get up early and she often met them by the stove where the water was being heated. Gradually, they began to exchange a few words, and once, she even agreed to share their breakfast, which was more copious, than hers. The rest of the day, they were not to be seen: they were in Langon or Bordeaux. In the evening, they made sure they came back late.

Albertine and Lisa de Montpleynet were very appreciative of their courteousness. The person who could least stand their presence was Camille, who was having difficulty recovering from the birth. Knowing the Germans were under the same roof sent her into hysteria that exhausted her. Doctor Blanchard, who was treating her, was against her going back to Roches-Blanches, saying that it was too far for him to visit her daily. The child, a delightful little boy, whom his mother named Charles, was healthy and developing normally, but because he was underweight, he needed to be watched carefully. Camille had to resign herself to the situation. Each weekend, her father-in-law, Raymond d'Argilat, came to spend two days with her and his grandchild, the sight of whom helped him to bear his son's absence and the lack of news.

Thanks to Lieutenant Kramer, the whole family was able easily to obtain passes to the unoccupied zone. Isabelle's death had disrupted the life of the household. Ruth soon noticed that supplies in the larder had rapidly diminished: no more oil, soap, chocolate, coffee, little sugar, jam or preserves. She, Léa and Sabine decided to cycle to Langon to shop.

Langon lay in a blistering heat, its streets practically deserted, the cafés nearly empty or full of German soldiers drinking beer and looking profoundly bored. All the shops had been looted: there was nothing to be had for love or money at the grocer's, the shoe and clothes shops. Nothing in the baker's and the butcher's windows. A few dusty bottles were all that was left in the wine merchant's: the Germans had been there and taken everything for themselves or to send back home to Germany.

"Even the ironmonger has made a fortune," said Madame Vollard, the grocer's wife, who had been serving the Delmas family for years. "The bookseller, who used to complain that the people of Langon never read, hasn't got a single book left on his shelves, not even a pencil. Business was wonderful for two days. Now it's rations for everybody."

"But what are we going to do. We've got nothing left in the cupboard!" wailed Léa.

"That would not have happened when your mother was alive. You know, I saw her the day before the bombing. In spite of rationing, I managed to fill up her baskets. But today . . . "

"You've got nothing to sell us?"

"Not much. What do you need?"

"Everything! Coffee. Soap. Oil. Sugar . . . "

"I've got no coffee. I do have some chicory: it's very nice with milk. I got some butter in this morning. I can let you have two litres of oil and three kilos of sugar. I still have a little chocolate, some noodles and some sardines."

"Give us everything you can. What about soap?"

"There's some of that too. Have you your ration books?"

Back at Montillac, Sabine and Léa gathered the family together in the drawing room.

"We'll have to take steps now unless we want to die of hunger," said Léa. "We'll have to dig over the little meadow, near the wash-house, and plant a vegetable garden, buy some more hens, rabbits, pigs . . . "

"Oh! no," Laure interrupted her, "they stink."

"You'll be glad enough to eat ham and bacon."

"And a cow, for milk," added Lisa.

"That's all very well," said Sabine, "but what about meat and groceries?"

"We'll come to some arrangement with the butcher in Saint-Macaire: he's your mother's godson. As for groceries, Sabine goes to the hospital in Langon three times a week, she can stop at Madame Vollard's. But until the vegetable garden starts producing, things will be scarce."

"By that time, Marshal Pétain will have everything back to normal," said their Aunt Bernadette.

Bernadette Bouchardeau had not gone back to Bordeaux. She had gratefully accepted Pierre Delmas's hospitality. Her son, Lucien, had run away to join General de Gaulle, leaving a letter to tell her where he had gone. She had not heard from him since and vowed eternal hatred for the deserter in London as she called him. When it was announced on the 2nd of August that he had been sentenced to death in absentia, she was pleased.

At the end of August, a letter from Germany informed Raymond d'Argilat that his son, Laurent, was a prisoner in Westphalenhof in Pomerania. He was taken into captivity after being wounded. Alive! He was alive! Both Camille and Léa's eyes shone with joy.

"I won't see my son again," said Raymond d'Argilat.

"Come, come, my friend, don't spoil our pleasure. You're talking nonsense. Laurent will be home shortly," said Pierre Delmas.

"It'll be too late for me."

His conviction worried Pierre Delmas, who studied his friend closely. It was a true he had aged and grown very thin in the last few weeks.

On the 2nd of September, a man rode up to Roches-Blanches on a bicycle and asked for Madame d'Argilat.

"What do you want with her?" asked the old head storeman.

"I have news of her husband."

"Of Monsieur Laurent! Oh! How is he, sir? You know, I knew him when he was a child," said the old man with emotion.

"He's well, I hope: we were prisoners together. He gave me an envelope to deliver to his wife."

"Madame d'Argilat isn't here, she's at Montillac, near Langon. Monsieur d'Argilat senior is there too."

"Is it far?"

"About twenty miles."

"Well, what's a few miles more or less?"

"Still, you have to be careful: the estate's in the occupied zone. My son will go with you, he knows the way well."

The two young men arrived without any trouble late that afternoon. The traveller was immediately introduced to Camille.

"Good day, Madame. I am Second-Lieutenant Valéry. I was captured at the same time as Lieutenant d'Argilat. He was wounded in the legs and wasn't able to escape. He gave me this envelope for you. Forgive me for taking so long to accomplish my mission. Have you heard from him?"

"No . . . only that he is wounded and a prisoner in Pomerania."

"Thank God he's alive!"

"Are you fond of him?"

"He is a kind, brave man. All his men loved him."

"But you escaped?"

"Yes."

"What are your plans?"

"I'll go to Spain, and from there to North Africa."

"How?"

"There's a network in Bordeaux. A Dominican friar is in charge."

"A Dominican?" asked Léa who was present. "What's his name?"

"I have no idea. The meeting place is in a dockside bar."

"Léa . . . ? You're not thinking of . . . ?"

"Of course not! The lieutenant can't stay at Montillac, it's far too dangerous . . . "

"Two German officers are staying here," Camille added.

"How will you get to Bordeaux?" Léa asked.

"By train."

"The stations are all being watched, and there are no more trains this evening. You will sleep in my room."

"No, in mine," said Camille. "No one dares disturb me because of the baby."

"You're right. Tomorrow morning, I'll go to the station

with you. Meanwhile, don't say anything to the others: there's no point in worrying them. You must be hungry, sir,'' said Léa.

"I would like something to eat."

Léa came back from the kitchen with a tray of cold meat, cheese, bread and a bottle of wine. The young man devoured it with an appetite that made them smile.

"Forgive me," he said with his mouth full, "I haven't eaten for two days."

"We're going to leave you to get some sleep. Thank you very much for bringing me my husband's letters."

The two young women left the room.

"Let's go on to the terrace," suggested Camille.

"Are you strong enough?"

"Doctor Blanchard advised me to get some exercise. Since I've had news of Laurent, I've been much better, and these letters brought by the lieutenant tell me that I'll see him again soon."

On the terrace, Camille sat on the iron bench, under the arbor where the last of the wistaria was dying, opened the fat envelope and began to read:

My beloved wife, God willing, Second-Lieutenant Valéry will give you these letters written in one of my rare peaceful moments. You may find them rather boring, but I am in such a state of weariness and depression that I find it hard to get out of this absurd daily routine. I want you to know that I think of you and our child constantly. It is you who give me the strength to continue hoping.

My darling, forgive me for being so brief, so dry, but I have seen so many of my friends, my companions, dying beside me. The world must know that they fought bravely. Do not forget that, for we are probably outnumbered by those who will say that the French soldiers fled before the enemy. Unfortunately, in some cases, that is true. I saw them, those who sacked Reims, throwing their rifles into the ditches so they could run faster, I saw them, and I shall never forget. But I've also seen humble heroes get themselves killed rather than retreat. Those are the ones who must be remembered.

Take care of yourself. God bless you, and Léa too. Near Veules-les-Roses, 15th June 1940. P.S. I enclose my diary.

Poor Laurent, thought Camille. She took out the staple that held together the bundle of pages covered with his small handwriting in pencil, and settled down to a long read. As usual, she read several passages aloud to Léa.

Tuesday 28th May 1940
I met Houdoy at the local bar. He's exhausted. He's travelled l50 miles with his horses in four days. Many of his horses are injured. I spent the rest of the day looking for food at the neighboring farms.

Wednesday 29th May 1940
I rode with Houdoy and Wiazemsky. We talked all night. We went through Congis, Puisieux, Sennevières, Nanteuil, Baron. At six o'clock in the morning, we stopped to rest at a farm. After a few hours' sleep, we examined our equipment and our weapons before approaching the Front. The colonel came to see us. We leave at 11:30.

Thursday 30th May 1940
We went through Senlis at about one o'clock in the morning. We arrived at 7:30, after thirty miles. The squadron is bivouacking in a field. It's difficult to find water.

Friday 31 May 1940
Assemble at one o'clock in the morning, departure at 1:30. A short stage of fifteen miles to Bois-du-Parc, where we bivouac. During the day, I drove my lorry into Beauvais in search of supplies. All's quiet in the town; the shops were open. I bought a local paper. Left at 4 p.m., with the job of setting up the next bivouac at Equennes. At l0 p.m. the camp was packed up when a message arrived from the colonel telling me we can no longer use that billet. We set off aimlessly.

Monday 3rd June 1940

While I was having breakfast with Wiazemsky, we saw a plane crash into the woods behind the Third Squadron. There was a general rush. Luckily, the pilot was alive. He's English, a strapping fellow of six foot. The colonel ordered me to drive him back to his base, five miles outside Rouen. On the way back, I stopped at Gournay-en-Bray to buy some sandwiches and chocolate. The shops are bursting with goods, and the whole town seemed peaceful. I had dinner at headquarters. They're talking about sending us to Forges-les-Eaux. Went for a walk in the woods with Yvan Wiazemsky whose conversation I enjoy more and more. There isn't anybody more likeable in the whole regiment, I'm captivated by him. He's good-looking, well built, charming, in spite of his big ears. He has a slow gait and a faraway look in his eyes. He's extremely intelligent and kind-hearted. He's taken me under his wing, so to speak, insisting we be on first-name terms and offering a welcome friendship. He and Houdoy are my best friends here.

Tuesday 4th June 1940

A quiet uneventful day. It's difficult to get hold of hay.

Wednesday 5th June 1940

I'm writing by the light of a candle stuck to an upturned crate. After stocking up on food, early as usual, I went to the village barber's for a shave and a haircut. My chin was still covered with lather when Wiazemsky bounded in waving the order from the brigade: "The enemy attacked along the Somme this morning, with fairly heavy forces and they managed to break through in several places." We know what that means. It's dreadfully hot. Hundreds of planes fly overhead. Shells are exploding not far from us. I obtained authorization from the captain to resume my duty as liaison man and to follow the commander with my trailer and driver. We left at about 2 p.m. and overtook the regiment in a cloud of dust. Several times, I met with the vanguard. At about

4 p.m., we stopped at Hornoy, which is still inhabited, and I ransacked the bars to find drinks for the head-quarters staff. We set off again and got caught in an unbelievable hold-up at Belloy. The inhabitants were being evacuated. The squadrons were stuck. An officer said that General Maillard wanted to see the colonel urgently. Four of us went, the colonel, Creskens, Wiazemsky and I. With the help of a map, the general explained that the Germans are very close and that he intends to attack the Fourth Hussars at Warlus with tanks. They crossed the Somme this morning. It's a matter of stopping the enemy as they march down towards Beauvais. The colonel dictated orders for the squadrons to set up camp and ordered me to leave immediately to fetch ammunition and mines from Agnières. I left at once, at about 6 p.m. By the time I got back, the German tanks were very close, driving around the outside of the village, between the lines. I learned that Chevalier's truck had been blown up—he drove over a mine just outside Hornoy. It was almost dark, and there was shooting from all sides. I found Chevalier wandering in the dark with a serious back wound. He was brave and didn't complain. I waited with him for the doctor, who told me that the wound is serious. I shook Chevalier's hand as he was evacuated to the rear.

I went back to HQ at Bromesnil, where Houdoy is stationed with his horses and his men. He informed me that we are once more under General Contenson's orders. It's 11 p.m. and I am going to snatch a few seconds' sleep.

Thursday 6th June 1940
At 2 a.m. HQ was moved to Fresneville, while the squadrons took up positions on the line. At dawn, I met with Navarre at the Château d'Avesnes. A group of low-flying bombers took us by surprise. We tumbled out of the car and rushed for shelter behind a wall. The planes machine-gunned the car as they flew overhead. I saw the bullets rip through the bodywork. In the end they

withdrew. We set off again for Arguel.

It's eight o'clock. All's quiet at HQ, in spite of the pressure of the German tanks. The regiment has moved during the night.

A little later, I left for Hornoy. There, I met a lieutenant from the engineers who told me there was no point in trying to continue planting mines. The village is surrounded. The gunfire has been getting closer. I asked him if he was planning to abandon the village, and he replied: "Certainly not." I offered my help. I caught three Senegalese marksmen fleeing. I saw them again an hour later. It was horrific, all three of them fell, flattened by a burst of machine-gun fire. I was bent double by a wave of nausea. If it hadn't been for my zeal, those three might have been deserters, but they would have been alive. Bullets whistled past from all directions. I picked up a rifle lying beside a lifeless body and I shot: from the bushes came a cry. A man stood up, bareheaded. There were less than ten yards between us. I was struck by his youth and his fairness. A jet of blood spurted from his open throat. His eyes were wide open and he fell looking at me. A shout saved my life: "Lieutenant! Lieutenant! Don't stand there!" I instinctively threw myself to the ground, just in time. Stones hit my back. There were two overturned motorcycles on the road. Nearby, their riders lay blown to bits. One of the bikes was intact: I took it in the hope of getting back to HQ. At 4 p.m., I made my report. I didn't even have time for a breather before I was ordered to drive my supply trucks to Sénarpont. I distributed two days' worth of rations to the squadrons. It's 9 p.m. I'm exhausted.

"Here, you read," said Camille handing Léa the pages. "I've got to see to Charles, he's crying."

Léa took the diary and continued reading.

Friday 7th June 1940
I'm at Rohin-Cabot's HQ and the German attack on the entire Front is apparent. The air raids are twice as fre-

quent, the German offensive has become more savage. I have been up to the second floor, where Colomb had just been killed; Kéraujat and then Rohin-Cabot were wounded.

At 8:30 p.m. the colonel, having lost contact with Séze, sent me to get confirmation of the order to withdraw. I made a rapid tour in the middle of air raids.

By dawn, we ended up at Campneuville (fifteen miles). It was tough going: desolate countryside, many houses destroyed. At 5 a.m. the colonel assembled everybody. We were totally cut off. We decided to try to find our way to the Seine, and cover the retreat of the Alpine Division with the Fifth Cavalry Division. The regiment fell into step painfully. The colonel informed me that his men had been without food for forty-eight hours. I offered to have a few animals slaughtered, requisition the bakery and get in a stock of cider. Wiazemsky and I brought back 500 kilos of bread and 1,600 liters of cider. For the rest, the squadrons had to fend for themselves.

Sunday 9th June 1940, Monday 10th June 1940, Tuesday 11th June 1940
The regiment organized a resistance on the Auvilliers-Mortimer line. German infiltration is reported everywhere. At about 5 p.m. we received orders to retreat. Extremely difficult withdrawal. Saint-Germain, which was our only viable way out, is occupied. When the Third Squadron arrived, there was a street battle and Dauchez was killed. The Germans withdrew and we went through with the Second and Fourth Squadrons.

I had time to kill three animals which we doled out, then set off for Château ? where HQ had been set up. We organized a new defense strategy. We learned that we were totally surrounded. I took the Fourth Squadron, the only one that's still intact, to reinforce the Third Squadron and I set up my HQ in Stern's shelter. I had time to find out that Séze had been captured at Bellencombre with three platoons, and . . . it was hell.

Cazenove, who tried to organize support on my left, was killed, and then it was Chambon's turn. He fell beside Audox with a piece of shrapnel in his throat. Then Stern was seriously wounded. The Fourth Squadron was crushed by German tanks: Echenbrenner was killed, Luirot, Branchu, Novat and Sartin wounded.

I assembled the survivors and took them to HQ in the quarry under the cliff. The German tanks came within 200 yards and machine-gunned us for three hours with 37s and incendiary bullets. Our ammunition trucks grouped at the edge of Veules-les-Roses, were blown up one after the other. The sky was set alight. The horses were magnificently calm. A feverish night of waiting. I soothed my impatience by writing these notes in the shelter of the cliff, by the light of a candle shielded by a greatcoat stretched over two rifles wedged in the pebbles. It's been quiet for a while. I can distinctly hear the tide coming in. On the other side of the water, in England, is freedom, perhaps life. I think of my beloved Camille, of our child who may never know its father, or magnificent, passionate Léa, of my father, of this French land invaded by the enemy, of all my dead friends who died so that France might be free and whose sacrifice will have been in vain, of that German soldier I killed—I who hate violence. A strange feeling of peace comes over me. The night is still, beautiful. The smell of the sea mingles with the warm smell of the horses.

Camille, with little Charles in her arms, walked over to the window that looked out over the estate and tried to make the baby laugh as she fought back her tears.

Léa, enthralled, continued reading:

Wednesday 12th June, dawn
We discovered that only three English ships were able to sail (one had run aground on the beach and the other sank as it left the port). Wiazemsky was taken prisoner during the night, Mesnil has vanished. There are just a few men left from the Fourth, under Dumas, Pontbriand and myself, and fifty or so men out of the 226 there were

at the beginning. Commander Augère has given me the cliff to the northeast of Veules as my section, with my back to the sea. I dispersed my men and I climbed to the top. About two miles to the east, the south and the west, columns of tanks were maneuvering.

Around midday, we were hit by round after round of 37s and tracer bullets. Ravier and a number of men were wounded. My men and I were returning fire until 4 p.m. Wounded in the legs, I fell to my knees. Then we ran out of ammunition and locked ourselves in a barn to wait for nightfall. But an hour later, German soldiers burst into our shelter, machine guns in hand. I flung down my empty revolver and came out, supported by two of my men. They took us to a sunken lane where we found the survivors of the regiment.

We were evacuated to the country hospital in Germany where I am today.

Second-Lieutenant Valéry has told me of his plan to escape. I am stuck with my leg wounds, so I'm entrusting him with these notes and a letter to my wife. God be with him.

The last lines swam before Léa's eyes. She could feel Laurent's pain in her own body. Between the lines, she cound sense all the sorrow he had suffered. Where was he now? Were his wounds serious? He didn't say anything about them. Camille came back carrying little Charles. She had been crying again.

"Don't cry like that. You'll make yourself ill. Here's Ruth: go back in with her," said Léa, handing the pages back to her. Camille hid the papers in her dress pocket.

"Camille," scolded Ruth, "you've been crying again. You're most unreasonable. Think of your son. Come along, come indoors."

The young woman allowed Ruth to steer her indoors without a word.

Léa remained alone with the baby. The countryside around betrayed nothing of the misfortune that had befallen it. Léa contemplated it with tender anxiety as if it were the face of a beloved mother suffering from a perhaps incurable disease. Everything seemed as it had always been. The vines shimmered in the evening breeze; in the distance, a dog barked, while on the road, young children were shouting at play.

Chapter 18

Early next morning, before the Germans and Sabine were up, Léa drove Second-Lieutenant Valéry to Langon station where they waited until seven o'clock for the first train to Bordeaux. The Second-Lieutenant registered his bicycle, and went through customs and the checkpoint without any difficulty: his false papers were not discovered. Meanwhile, Léa was anxious to observe how carefully the German soldiers and the French gendarmes inspected the passengers' papers. On impulse, she left her blue bicycle with the station master who had known her since she was a child, and bought a round trip ticket to Bordeaux.

"Haven't you any luggage?" a gendarme wanted to know.

"No, I'm going to Bordeaux for the day to see one of my aunts who is feeling poorly."

Léa got on to the train just as the whistle blew.

The journey was interminable. The train stopped for a long time at every little station. It was nearly ten o'clock when they chugged into Bordeaux. Léa tried to find Second-Lieutenant Valéry, but there were so many people on the platform that she found herself in the arrival hall without having spotted him.

"Léa."

She jumped. Gazing at her, looking elegant as always, stood Raphaël Mahl.

"Raphaël, I'm so pleased to see you again!"

"Not as glad as I am to see you, my dear. I've missed you more than any other of the beautiful women I know in Paris during this absurd period.''

''You always exaggerate.''

''Let me look at you. You seem even more beautiful than ever.''

Heads turned to look at them.

''Careful, people are staring.''

''Well, our beloved France has certainly taken a memorable clobbering.''

''Be quiet,'' begged Léa.

''Come. Let's get out of this station. Where were you headed?''

''I don't know.''

''Wonderful. Join me for lunch. A lunch just like 'in the old days.' What do you say?''

''If you like.''

''Don't sound so sad. With your black dress, anyone would think you'd lost your father and your mother.''

''My mother's dead.''

''Léa, I'm so sorry!''

A chauffeur-driven car was waiting outside the station. Raphaël held the rear door open and Léa stepped inside.

''To the newspaper offices,'' he said as he got in.

For a few moments they drove in silence.

''Tell me what happened.''

''Mummy was killed in the air raid on the 19th of June.''

''I was in Bordeaux then. I'd been following the Government from Tours. After an air raid that killed sixty people, I wanted to leave France. I had a reservation on the *Massilia* and then I bumped into Sarah Mulstein, who was trying to get her father out of France. They had their visas, but the ship was full. I gave him my reservation.''

''That was very generous of you.''

''No, I couldn't leave such an exceptional conductor as Israel Lazare at the mercy of the Germans.''

''What about Sarah?''

''I don't know. On the 20th of June, Bordeaux was declared an open city; on the 21st of June, the armistice was signed; on the 25th there was a national day of mourning declared by Pétain; on the 27th the Germans waltzed into

Bordeaux and, on the 30th of June, the Government packed their bags. You have no idea of the turmoil. As for me, I went back to Paris on the 29th. At the radio station, which was occupied by the Germans, I was informed that my presence was no longer required. Through a stroke of luck, some friends of mine found me a job as a journalist for *Paris-Soir*. That's why I'm back here. I'm working as a reporter.''

The car stopped outside the offices of the local paper where Raphaël Mahl had an appointment. He led Léa into a dark office with piles of newspapers everywhere.

''Make yourself at home. I won't be long. There's plenty to read. You may learn something,'' he said, indicating the newspapers.

He came back thirty minutes later and took Léa to lunch at the Chapon Fin.

''Good-day, sir, your table is ready,'' said the headwaiter, bowing.

''Thank you, Jean. What's good today?''

''We haven't got much, Monsieur Mahl,'' he said adjusting Léa's chair. ''I can give you *foie gras* with a bottle of Château d'Yquem, roast lamb with baby vegetables or stuffed chicken. Or there's sole.''

''Very good, and what about dessert?''

''Strawberry charlotte with raspberry purée or chocolate profiteroles.''

''I must be dreaming,'' said Léa, ''I thought that restaurant meals were restricted.''

''Not all restaurants, mademoiselle. Not all.''

''We'll have the *foie gras* and a bottle of Sauternes. How about the lamb, my dear? It's delicious. Then bring us a bottle of Haut-Brion, and make sure it's a good vintage.''

''I'll send the wine steward over.''

''There's no need. Tell him to serve the Sauternes right away.''

''Very good, monsieur.''

''Do you come here often?'' asked Léa, looking about her.

''From time to time. Prices are really exorbitant. But all the good restaurants are exorbitant these days. When the Government was here, I often used to go to Chez Catherine, an excellent restaurant, run by Monsieur Dieu, the great chef and book lover. I had an argument with him over which year Norden's *Journey to Egypt and Nubia* was published. He insisted it was 1755 and I swore it was 1757. It turned out he was right."

"Look. German officers are dining here too! Look over there!"

"What's so strange about that? They don't all live on sauerkraut. I know of more than one who's a great connoisseur of vintage wines."

"No doubt, but all the same, it upsets me."

"Get used to it, my dear. Otherwise join General de Gaulle in London. Mark my words, the boys from Berlin are here to stay."

The wine waiter cautiously brought over a bottle of Château d'Yquem 1918.

"The wine of victory," he whispered to Raphaël Mahl as he showed him the bottle.

"Be quiet," Raphaël hissed back, glancing hastily around the restaurant.

"Pour some, quickly," said Léa holding out her glass, "that I may drink to victory!"

An amused smile hovered on Raphaël Mahl's lips.

"Why not. To victory!"

"To victory!" cried Léa at the top of her voice as she raised her glass.

Their glasses clinked in a silence which made Léa's laughter ring out all the louder.

"Monsieur, mademoiselle, please," mumbled the owner, who had come rushing over as he glanced anxiously over to the table occupied by the German officers.

One of them stood up, bowed towards Léa and raising his glass of champagne said: "And I drink to the beauty of French women."

"To the beauty of French women!" cried his companions also getting to their feet.

Léa went red with anger and wanted to get up. Raphaël restrained her.

"Sit down."

"I don't want to be under the same roof as these animals."

"Don't be ridiculous. Don't attract any more attention than you have already. It's unwise. Think of the safety of your family."

"Why do you say that?"

Raphaël lowered his voice.

"I told you I was here as a journalist. I'm investigating an underground network involved in smuggling certain people out to Spain or North Africa who want to join de Gaulle."

"So, what does that have to do with me?"

"You? Nothing. But I have reason to believe that a certain Dominican friar is the brain behind this network."

"A Domin—"

"Yes, a Dominican, like your uncle Adrien Delmas, the famous preacher."

"But that's absurd. Uncle Adrien isn't interested in politics."

"That's not what they're saying in Bordeaux circles."

"What do you mean?"

"They haven't forgotten his role in the Spanish Civil War. It should be my duty as a good French citizen to denounce him to the authorities."

"You wouldn't!"

"I don't know. Eat your *foie gras*. Isn't it delicious?"

"I'm not hungry."

"Come on, Léa, how can you take me seriously? You know I'm teasing."

"I don't think it's funny."

"Eat."

Hunger got the better of her. She ate slowly.

"It's good, isn't it?"

"I suppose . . . " replied Léa.

"Do you know we're sitting at the same table as Home Secretary Mandel was when he was arrested?"

"No. I didn't know he'd been arrested. I thought he left on the *Massilia*."

"He did leave, but he was arrested on Marshal Pétain's orders. I was eating at the table next to this one. He was finishing his meal in the company of the actress, Beatrice Bretty, when a colonel in the gendarmes came to his table and insisted on a word with him. Mandel stared at him and went on eating his cherries. After a moment, which seemed endless to me, he stood up and followed the gendarme. Eating cherries on the 17th of June 1940! They were to become the symbol of the corruption of the régime. The colonel took him into his office and informed him of his arrest, together with that of his former collaborator, General Bürher, chief-of-staff of the colonial troops."

"Why was he arrested?" asked Léa.

"Pétain was persuaded that they were plotting to prevent the armistice."

"What happened in the end?"

"It turned out all right for Mandel. His successor as Home Secretary, Pomaret, went to plead the case before the Marshal and Alibert, the Lord Chancellor: the one who called Mandel simply "the Jew." Previously, Pomaret had been very severe with the Marshal, accusing him of having committed a serious error in letting this business go too far. That is when Pétain ordered Mandel and Bührer's arrest. Bührer cried and complained that he had been arrested in front of his officers in spite of his five stars. As for Mandel, he said with great dignity, 'I shall not lower myself to offering an explanation. It is up to you to give me one.'

"To everyone's astonishment, Pétain shut himself up in his office and returned shortly afterwards with a letter that he read out loud: 'Minister, after hearing your explanation . . . ' 'I did not give any explanations,' replied Mandel, 'you will have to cut that bit out.' And Pétain rewrote the letter which became a lame letter of excuses that Mandel read out that evening to Lebrun and a few others. It's rather amusing, isn't it?"

"It's incredible," said Léa, shaking her head. "How do you know all that?"

"I heard Pomaret telling the story."

"Who started the rumor about the conspiracy?"

"A certain Georges Roux, a writer, lawyer and contributor to *La Petite Gironde*. He was arrested and released again very quickly."

"Bordeaux must have been very strange during that time," said Léa, twirling her glass of Haut-Brion in front of her eyes.

"I've never seen anything like it. Imagine: two million refugees in this town. Not one room left. At the Hotel de Bordeaux and the Hotel Splendide, people were renting armchairs in the foyer. The whole of Paris was in Bordeaux. You kept bumping into friends and acquaintances all over the place. You ended up forgetting the exodus and only remembering the pleasure of meeting old friends again.

"In the street cafés, people formed and reformed the Government. Queues at the consulates got longer as more and more people tried to get passports. Ministers advised Rothschild to get out, although nobody believed the Germans would get as far as Bordeaux. Restaurants opened their doors at ten o'clock. In the afternoon, I would linger chatting with someone or other: Julian Green, Audiberti or Jean Hugo. In the evening, I would roam around in search of a kindred spirit.

"There's nothing like times of trouble for encouraging debauchery. After all, you don't know what tomorrow holds in store, so you may as well enjoy today. And then you look for a means of escape, through depravity or alcohol, when you're the helpless spectator at the fall of your own nation. I never thought I would witness such cowardice. We are the feeble old inhabitants of an old tribe that has been disintegrating from the inside for the last two hundred years. It's something we have to come to terms with."

"But I don't want to come to terms with it. I'm not one of those old people you're talking about."

"Perhaps not you. But where are those vigorous young men who should be defending you? I saw them knocking terrified civilians out of their way as they went, throwing away their rifles in order to run faster, fat, pot-bellied, bald before their time, dreaming only of paid holidays, security and retirement."

"And what have you done? Where's your uniform, your rifle?"

"Oh! As for myself, my dear, like all those of my ilk, I hate firearms" simpered Raphaël. "We queers only like uniforms

235

to add a bit of spice to our love affairs. So, look at them, look at our charming occupying forces: blond, tanned, at the same time virile and gentle, like young Roman gods. They make my mouth water."

"You're disgusting!"

"No, just realistic. The delicate flower of French youth is either dead or captive, so I'm forced to turn to the Germans. Take my word for it, my dear friend, you ought to do likewise, otherwise you'll be an old woman before the end of the war. "Gather ye rosebuds while ye may . . . ""

"Forget all that and tell me about your work."

"You nosey little thing, you'd like me to tell you more about that Dominican friar, wouldn't you? It's a secret, my pet, that's not for your pretty little ears. Look at this strawberry charlotte. Doesn't it make your mouth water? And these profiteroles? I could eat myself sick on them. Well, well, hello old fellow—"

"Mahl! You're in delightful company! Introduce me."

"Of course! Léa, meet my friend Richard Chapon, the editor of *La Petite Gironde*. Richard, Mademoiselle Delmas."

"How do you do. I'm delighted to meet you, even in such bad company," he said winking. "Don't hesitate to ask if I can be of service to you. I would be happy—"

"Thank you, monsieur."

"See you later, Mahl. I have something to discuss with you."

"See you later, this afternoon."

They finished their meal in silence. The restaurant gradually emptied. Léa was not used to drinking so much and she felt a little dizzy.

"Come, let's go for a stroll."

Outside, the weather was hot and close.

"When shall I see you again, Léa?"

"I don"t know. You're in Paris, I'm here. You seem happy and relaxed, I'm not."

"What's the good of disillusioning you, little girl? I have my moments of happiness, but never total happiness. I am tormented by a sharp, confused and profound suffering that never leaves me. When I was twenty, I wanted to write a

236

sublime book. Now I'd be satisfied if I wrote a good book. Léa, that book is inside me. My work as a writer is the only thing I really love, and it's the only thing that I can't realize. Everything distracts me and lures me away.

"I'm ambitious for future glory," he continued, "but I have no ambition on an everyday level. I get bored with everything so quickly. I love everybody and nobody, rain and sunshine, town and country. Deep down inside me I'm nostalgic for what is good and honorable, for laws that I've never taken any notice of. Although I'm annoyed by my bad reputation, I'm weak enough to be proud of it. My downfall, you see, is that I'm not totally depraved, I'm generous to the point of extravagance, out of cowardice more often than not; that I've never pretended to be half-virtuous, that is, like everybody else deep down; that I prefer bad boys to those hypocrites who claim to be respectable, when they're hardly more honorable than I am. I don't love myself but I wish myself well."

His last sentence made Léa laugh.

"I'm sure you'll be a great writer."

"What does it matter! We'll see. Perhaps I'll be famous after I'm dead. . . . But I'm talking about myself all the time: you're the one who's interesting. Come to Paris, don't stay at Montillac."

"My father needs me."

"Now that's nice. What a good little girl you are! Family feeling is a beautiful thing. And, on the subject of families, tell your Dominican uncle to be careful. In my article, I won't reveal all that I found out, but somebody else might very well do so."

They were walking arm in arm. Léa clutched his arm and turned her shining eyes towards his.

"Thank you, Raphaël, I won't forget."

"Thank you for what? I haven't said anything. I'm going to say goodbye to you here," he said pointing to the church of Saint-Eulalie. "If you're a believer, light a candle for me. Goodbye, lovely friend, don't forget me. If you need to get in touch with me, write to me care of the Gallimard Bookshop, Boulevard Raspail. They'll forward it."

He kissed Léa with an emotion that he did not try to conceal.

"The Rue-Saint-Genès is just around the corner," he said over his shoulder, and with a final wave of the hand, Raphaël disappeared.

Léa went into the church. After the baking heat outside, the coolness of the church made her shudder. She automatically picked up a candle, dropped a few coins in the box, and lit the wick. Candle in hand, she walked over to the statue of Saint Theresa, to whom her mother was particularly devoted. Mummy . . . she sat down in front of the altar and let her tears flow . . . "The Rue-Saint-Genès is just round the corner" . . . Why had he said that? What was there in the Rue-Saint-Genès? The name rang a bell but she could not think why. It was irritating not to remember. A priest and a monk walked down the aisle past her. Uncle Adrien! Rue-Saint-Genès was where Uncle Adrien lived, or rather it was where the Dominican monastery was. She understood why Raphaël had brought her here. She had to warn her uncle and quickly.

It was so hot outside that the Rue Saint-Genès was deserted. The door of the monastery opened at once.

"What can I do for you, my child?" said a very old monk.

"I'd like to talk to my uncle, Father Delmas. I have a message for him. I am Léa Delmas."

"Father Adrien has been away for a few days."

"Who is it, Brother Georges?" asked a tall monk whose austere expression was softened by a splendid crown of white hair, as he came into the hall.

"It's Mademoiselle Delmas. She wants to see Father Adrien."

"Good afternoon, child. You must be one of Pierre Delmas's daughters. I knew your mother well. She was a wonderful woman. May God give you the strength to bear your sorrow."

"Thank you, Father."

"Your uncle's not here," he added. What important message do you have for him?"

"He must . . ." Léa stopped in mid-sentence without

238

knowing why.

"He must what?"

She was unable to tell him the reason for her visit. She suddenly felt inexplicably wary.

"I am your uncle's superior: tell me why you wish to talk to him."

"My father needs to see him, it's urgent," replied Léa hurriedly.

"Why?"

"I don't know."

The monk stared at her coldly. Without blinking, Léa returned his gaze.

"As soon as he returns, I shall tell him of your visit and your father's wishes. Goodbye, child. God bless you!"

Outside, a light wind had stirred up, but it brought no relief. Léa could feel her black dress sticking to her skin. How could she contact Uncle Adrien? And where was Second-Lieutenant Valéry? Hadn't he mentioned the docks? But which ones? Léa stopped, demoralized. The only person who could tell her was Raphaël. With great difficulty, she found the Rue de Cheverus and the beautiful building where the office of *La Petite Gironde* was. She was told that Monsieur Mahl had just left for Paris.

"Who wants to see that scoundrel?" said a voice from one of the offices.

"A young lady, monsieur."

"A young lady to see Mahl? Will wonders never cease! Show her in."

Léa went in, reluctantly. There was nobody to be seen.

"I'm over here, I've just dropped a pile of books."

The voice came from underneath a table, the top of which could not be seen for mountains of books, papers, letters and files. Léa bent down.

"But it's Mademoiselle Delmas! Just a sec and I'll be with you."

Richard Chapon stood up, his hands full of books; he gave up trying to find room for them on the desk and put them on the armchair.

"Were you looking for Mahl? He's left. I'm surprised that a young lady from such a good Bordeaux family is a friend of somebody like him. No doubt one must keep up with present-day customs. Perhaps I can stand in for him?"

Léa hesitated. How should she phrase her question without arousing the editor's suspicions? Could she trust him?

"How can one find a means of getting out of France?" she burst out.

An expression of profound astonishment came over Richard Chapon's face, followed by a fleeting look of anguish. Slowly, he went over and closed the door.

"And Mahl's the person you wanted to ask?"

Léa sensed that she should reply cautiously. She put on her most ingenuous face.

"Since he's a journalist, I thought he would know the possibilities."

"Anything's possible, but I'm astounded to hear that question from the lips of a young girl. Who do you know who wants to leave France?"

"No one. I just wanted to satisfy my curiosity."

"You're very young and very ignorant, mademoiselle. You ought to know that in our present situation, you don't ask certain questions 'just because you want to know.'"

"Well let's not talk about it any more, then," Léa said, sounding playful. "I'm sorry I disturbed you."

"Dear mademoiselle, your disturbance is most welcome," he bantered in a tone of mock sophistication. "Is it important?" he whispered, restraining her hand on the door knob.

"No," she muttered, and then, changing her mind: "Can you tell my uncle, Adrien Delmas, to be careful?"

"The Dominican?"

"Yes."

"Don't worry. It'll be done."

"Thank you very much. Goodbye."

"Léa darling, we were so frightened! Where have you been?" cried Pierre Delmas clasping Léa to him.

The whole family, who were sitting in the drawing room listening to Sabine play, leaped up when Léa walked in.

Camille stared hard at her with shining eyes. Ruth blew her nose vigorously. Lisa waved her chubby little hands, Albertine cleared her throat, Bernadette heaved a great sigh, Sabine frowned. Only Laure carried on, flicking through a book.

"I went to see Uncle Adrien in Bordeaux."

"In Bordeaux, with all those Krauts!" exclaimed Bernadette.

"Aunt, stop calling the Germans Krauts! They don't like it," said Sabine, whose irritation seemed rather excessive to Léa.

"Krauts they are and Krauts I'll call them."

Sabine shrugged.

"Why didn't you say you wanted to go and see uncle?" her father said. "I'd have come with you. Your mother would have been pleased to see him too."

An embarrassed silence fell on the group. Léa looked at her father. She was hurt and surprised. Poor Papa, how he had changed! He seemed so fragile, at times his expressions were almost childlike. He—their natural protector—seemed himself as if he needed to be protected.

"I'm sorry, Papa."

"Please darling, don't do that again. I was worried. Did you see your uncle?"

"No, he wasn't there."

"He wasn't there for Isabelle's funeral either," grumbled Bernadette.

"You haven't eaten, you must be hungry," said Camille. "I'll get you some dinner. Are you coming to the kitchen?"

Léa followed Camille and watched her take some eggs out of the icebox.

"Is an omelette all right?"

"Fine," said Léa sitting down at the big table.

"Well?" asked Camille as she broke the eggs into a salad bowl.

"At Langon, the second-lieutenant had no trouble; and I don't think he did at Bordeaux either. I bumped into Raphaël Mahl at Bordeaux station. Do you remember, I told you about him? I had lunch with him. I thought he was telling me that Uncle Adrien could very well be the Dominican in question."

"That doesn't surprise me," said Camille putting a sliver of butter into the frying pan.

"I don't understand. Aren't we supposed to obey Marshal Pétain's orders? Isn't he France's savior, the father of the nation, as Aunt Lisa and Aunt Bernadette call him?"

"I don't know either, but I think that every French person's duty is to fight the enemy."

"But how? What are we supposed to do?"

"I don't know yet, but I'll think of something. Eat up," she said as she put the omelette in front of Léa.

"Thank you."

"The grape harvest is coming. Your father hasn't said a word about it."

"It's true. I'd forgotten. I'll talk to him tomorrow."

She ate in silence for a while.

"Don't you think Papa's been behaving oddly recently?"

Part of the harvest was lost because they did not have enough hands to pick the grapes, although everyone at Montillac took part in the harvesting. But the women were not used to the rough work and, in spite of their willingness, they were slow and clumsy. Only Léa and Ruth achieved a great deal. Camille, whose poor health was incompatible with heavy work, helped old Sidonie and Madame Fayard to drive the ox-cart and prepare the meals.

Léa had to take charge of the organization of the grape harvest as Pierre Delmas had shown total indifference to the proceedings. Even Fayard, the head storeman, who was still without news of his son, had not shown his usual competence. Monsieur d'Argilat had been able to do nothing more than offer advice, as at Roches-Blanches he himself was in a difficult situation.

Léa had haughtily refused friendly offers of help from their German "lodgers" in spite of Sabine's entreaties, and had watched, with mounting anger, as the grapes rotted on the vines.

Everything was going badly that autumn of 1940. Léa and Ruth had combed the countryside looking for pigs, rabbits, hens and ducks to buy. All they had found were a few scrawny hens, half of which died, and a pig which turned out to be expensive to feed.

Léa knew nothing of her family's financial situation. She had always assumed her parents were rich. He father informed her that the greater part of their fortune was in the West Indies and that certain investments he had made before the war had been disastrous.

"So we haven't much money left?" she asked incredulously.

"No," he said, smiling, "except for the rent from the property in Bordeaux."

"What does that come to each month?"

"I don't know, ask your mother, she deals with all that."

"Ask your mother." How many times had she heard that phrase? Several times a day, it seemed. At first she had not taken any notice except of the pain she felt. But, as time went by, she began to feel a fear that she dared not speak of. Everybody else in the household felt the same way. One day, gathering her courage, Léa broached the subject to Doctor Blanchard during one of his visits to Camille.

"I know. I've prescribed some medicine for him. We must be patient. He's in a state of shock. I don't know if senility is setting in."

"But it seems to be getting worse all the time. He's completely in his own world. I'm frightened."

"Come, come, keep a grip on yourself. You and Ruth are in charge of the household. I'm not depending on Madame Camille as she'll be able to go back to Roches-Blanches soon."

"Already?"

"Aren't you pleased? I thought you found it difficult to put up with her being here."

Léa shrugged irritably. "Not at all. Camille is useful and I gave my word to Laurent that I would care for her."

"Have you heard from him?"

"Yes, a letter saying that he had recovered and asking for shoes, underwear and tobacco. We sent him a parcel yesterday. It was a job finding shoes. It was Sabine who got hold of them. She won't say how but they are beautiful crêpe-soled shoes."

Chapter 19

Christmas 1940 was one of the saddest occasions ever for the Montillac household.

Three weeks earlier, they had buried Monsieur d'Argilat, who died in his sleep after an illness which nobody had realized was so serious. As he had predicted, he died without seeing his son again. When he was told of his best friend's death, Pierre Delmas remained dazed for several days. It was Léa who had to deal with the necessary formalities. She wrote to Laurent to break the bad news to him and to ask what she should do about the estate. She had a violent argument with Sabine, during which she accused her sister of being useless in the house because she was so wrapped up in the hospital when her family needed her.

"I do as much as you do. Who brings home meat when there isn't any to be had anywhere? Oil? Sugar and twenty bags of coal? If I stayed here dragging the plow as you do, we wouldn't have food on the table!"

It was true, Sabine was right. If it weren't for her, the family would have nothing but turnips, potatoes and chestnuts gathered by Léa, Ruth and Laure to live on. But how did she manage it? And how come she never needed any money, saying that her wages as a nurse were enough? Léa had her suspicions, for as well as buying vital provisions, Sabine often bought herself a skirt, a blouse, a scarf and even a pair of shoes. She had promised to get Léa a pair from the hospital cooperative.

Léa had tried, on many occasions, to get her to take an interest in Montillac's future, to ask what she thought about the way the estate should be run while waiting for their father to get over his grief. All she could get out of her was an indifferent reply.

"Everything you're doing is fine, little sister."

"But it's your business too, it's our land, we were born in this house. This is the house that Mummy loved and that she decorated."

"I've never understood what you find so wonderful about this old place or, worse still, the countryside, it's deadly boring!"

Léa remained speechless at this outburst and, as she used to do when they were children, she flew at her sister ready to fight. Sabine managed to duck a blow and took refuge in her room. Relations between the sisters had been strained ever since.

Despite the planes that were constantly heard coming over from Bordeaux, Ruth had decorated the traditional Christmas tree in the drawing room, as she did every year. She hung streamers and glass balls which Isabelle Delmas had carefully kept wrapped in shoe boxes since the birth of her eldest child. It was the first time that she did not lay the wax figure of the baby Jesus in the crib. It was up to Camille to carry out this symbolic gesture.

Estelle and Madame Fayard surpassed themselves and made the most sumptuous Christmas dinner. Forgetting the good simple fare of the cook, whom they had been obliged to get rid of for economic reasons, they had cooked a huge turkey, a gift from Sabine. Then there was cabbage, slowly cooked in the juice from the bird, chestnut purée, and a Christmas pudding, Estelle's masterpiece. A few good bottles of wine from the estate completed this festive meal.

It was so cold that they decided to forgo midnight mass and have dinner early. Although they were still in mourning, everyone had made an effort with their dress: a scarf, a necklace, a flower added a splash of color to all the black.

After the meal, the whole family went into the drawing

room, which was warm and brightly lit by the candles on the tree and the fire roaring in the hearth. Camille gave Léa a magnificent pearl necklace which had belonged to her mother.

"Camille, how exquisite! I can't take it."

"Please, darling, I want you to have it."

Léa was ashamed of her simple present: a pen-and-ink drawing of the baby—which Camille hugged delightedly.

"It's the best present you could give me. May I send it to Laurent?"

"It's yours. Do what you like with it."

Sabine and Laure each had a pretty gold bracelet, Ruth a brooch with a sapphire in it, Lisa a lace collar, Albertine an old edition of *Pascal's Thoughts,* and Bernadette Bouchardeau and Estelle received silk scarves. As for Pierre Delmas, Camille gave him a box of his favorite cigars.

Ruth and Bernadette gave gloves, scarves, socks and sweaters that they had knitted. Everyone had gone out of the way to give pleasure to the others within the limits of their means. The Montpleynet sisters gave their nieces some warm fabric to make coats out of. During the euphoria that generally follows the opening of Christmas presents, they had all, for a few moments, forgotten their sorrows, their fears and the war, as they listened to Sabine play a Bach fugue.

For the first time, Léa thought of Isabelle without rebellion and without tears. A hand squeezed hers. She did not withdraw her hand even though she recognized Camille's bony fingers. Sabine stopped playing. There was a burst of applause from the hallway before those in the room started clapping. They all turned round: there in the hall were Frederic Hanke and Otto Kramer. Sabine got to her feet and walked over to them as they came into the drawing room.

"Mademoiselle your daughter insisted that my comrade and I come in," said Lieutenant Kramer. "We took the liberty of coming downstairs to listen to Bach," he added addressing Pierre Delmas. "My mother is a fine musician, she adores Bach. May I wish you a merry Christmas, in spite of the war."

He clicked his heels and headed for the door.

Much to everyone's surprise, Camille suggested: "It's Christmas Day. Let's forget we're enemies. Have a drink with us."

"Thank you, Madame Camille," replied Frederic Hanke.

"*Heilige Weinacht!*" said Camille.

"Happy Christmas!" they answered.

"Lieutenant, you were saying that your mother is a musician. What about you?" asked Lisa.

"He's one of the best pianists in Germany," volunteered his companion.

"Don't pay any attention to my friend. He exaggerates."

"But Lieutenant . . ."

"Quiet, Frederic!"

"Lieutenant, please play something for us," urged Sabine.

They all stared at her. She bowed her head, blushing furiously. They all knew about Sabine's passion for music. She would never miss a single concert in Bordeaux. She had been to hear *Samson and Delilah* and Ravel's *Bolero* at the beginning of the concert season, in spite of Ruth and her aunts' protests. But to ask a German officer to play!

"With your father's permission, mademoiselle, I should be delighted to oblige."

"Do play, Lieutenant. My wife loves music," said Pierre Delmas drawing on his cigar, his face flushed and a faraway expression in his eyes.

Otto Kramer sat down at the piano.

"I bet he plays Wagner," Léa whispered to Camille.

He played several pieces for piano by Debussy. Everyone was touched by his thoughtfulness. When the last note faded away, there was a few seconds' silence before they applauded heartily. Camille noticed a look of pride and happiness on Sabine's pretty face.

Later they learned that on the following morning, Laurent d'Argilat and a companion escaped from the camp of Westphalenhof. The two men had managed to get away with the help of two comrades during wood-gathering duty outside the camp. The two accomplices had reported sick and then left the infirmary to join the little group after their guards had counted them. When Laurent and his friend arrived in the wood, they hid among the branches. It was bitterly cold, snowing and the sky was dark. The guards cut short the wood-gathering duty and counted the prisoners: everybody was there. The little group set off back to camp.

Wild with joy and excitement, Laurent and his companion got to their feet and raced toward their freedom. The snow was deep. After half an hour, they stopped for breath and removed their prison uniforms. During his long hours in captivity, Laurent had made himself a black jacket from a Dutch gendarme's hussar jacket. Under this, he wore two woolen pullovers sent by Camille. Lined leather gloves, Sabine's shoes and a coalman's cap completed his outfit. Their rucksacks contained sleeping bags and food. They set off in the direction of Jastrov station, which was twenty-five miles away.

That night, they slept in a workman's roadside hut. The following evening, they walked through the village of Jastrov. The Christmas decorations were still up in the streets, and couples with their arms around each other were on their way to the village ball. They passed the doorway of a bar: there was a warm haze of alcohol and tobacco and they could hear the strains of an accordion. . . . They hurried toward the station in the hope of finding a providential train. But the only ones that came were going in the opposite direction. Frozen, they took refuge in a carriage that was in a siding. Their sleeping bags were not warm enough to keep out the bitter cold, and they shivered until dawn.

At the end of that long night, they got on a train to Scheindemühl without buying tickets. They spent six days traveling in freight cars hunched up among sacks of potatoes, cattle or gravel. Sometimes, they traveled on a passenger train, still without tickets, and tried to blend in with the crowds. Laurent's knowledge of German got them out of trouble on several occasions and they managed to avoid arrest. That is how they reached Frankfurt-on-Oder and then Cottbus, Leipzig, Halle, Kassel, Frankfurt-on-Main. They crossed the Rhine at Mainz, hidden in the brakeman's cabin.

Their adventure came to an abrupt end at Bingerbrück, in front of the train timetable, when a policeman spoke to

Laurent's companion. Unable to speak a word of German, he could not get out of his predicament. They did not arrest him at once, suspecting that he had an accomplice. Laurent saw him from a distance, quietly sitting down, and was walking over to him when, suddenly, his companion leaped up and ran to a passing freight train. The two men managed to heave themselves up on to a flat car while the policemen ran along the platform shouting. Unfortunately, the train stopped and the Germans, revolvers in hand, arrested them. Without further ado, they were taken to the station police bureau. The atmosphere changed when Laurent answered their questions in perfect German. They were given hot broth and meat, and the police expressed their admiration for their performance. Then they were locked up in the municipal prison and, the following day, heavily guarded by three stalwart officers, they were escorted back to the Westphalenhof camp.

They were interrogated by an intelligence officer. Then they were sentenced to thirty days of solitary confinement. Nine days had passed since their escape.

On their release, they had a lecture from Colonel Malgorn, who was in charge of the prisoners of the camp, on the selfish nature of their enterprise, and the dire consequences that they had been spared due to the generosity of the camp commander. He advised them to meditate on the true meaning of their present duty: to behave like good prisoners was the most effective contribution they could make to Marshal Pétain's policy, a pledge that a "European France" would soon be established.

Their punishment over, they joined their unit, but not for long, for they were soon taken to another more secure camp.

It was more than seven months since they had been taken prisoner, on a summer's day, on a French beach.

Chapter 20

Winter was interminable. There was a shortage of fuel and the huge house was chilly and cold. They ate in the kitchen where there was the warmth of the ancient kitchen range on which Ruth and Estelle cooked. They were all hungry, in spite of the provisions that Sabine sometimes brought from Langon.

In this wine-growing region, nearly everybody suffered from hunger and cold during the harsh winter of 1940-41. The French railway workers watched, enraged, as entire cars full of meat, flour, vegetables and wood left for Germany.

However, at Montillac, everybody made sacrifices so that they could send parcels to Laurent. In February, they received a card informing them he had been transferred to Colditz.

In March, Albertine and Lisa announced that they intended to go back to Paris. The two spinsters were used to city life and could not stand the country any more. The rest of the family tried to stop them, but it was no use. Only Isabelle Delmas could have persuaded them to stay.

Spring brought a little relief to the estate. Vegetables had been planted in the part of the field that Léa and Ruth had ploughed. Léa passionately tended every green shoot that appeared. The success of the kitchen garden became, in her eyes, a matter of greater importance. It had cost a lot of backache, sore muscles, chapped hands, and hunger that she had vowed never to have to experience again. The vineyards, which were a constant source of worry in the region, became less of a burden when Fayard, who was now manager of the estate, heard from his son: Mathias was a prisoner in Germany, but would be home soon. The Marshal had given his word.

Fayard's love and gratitude to Pétain knew no bounds. Here was a leader who cared about the fate of the unfortunate prisoners of war! France was in good hands! Work, the family, the nation, that was where the future lay. This veteran from the Great War set to work with renewed enthusiasm. There was only one thing that marred this enthusiasm: he had trouble getting used to the presence of Germans at Montillac. Each time he caught sight of a uniform was an unpleasant surprise.

Mathias Fayard was released in May. When she saw him, Léa smiled again for the first time since her mother's death. When the young man hugged her, an intense thrill aroused her numbed body. Ignoring Ruth's disapproval and Camille's amusement, Léa prolonged their embrace. As for Mathias, he stared at her unable to believe his happiness. He found her changed, she was more womanly; beautiful, a wilder beauty than before with a new security in her eyes.

"You're thin and filthy, you look like a tramp. Come with me, I'll run you a bath."

"But, Mademoiselle Léa, he can have a bath at our place," said old Fayard chewing his moustache.

"It's all right, Fayard, everything my daughter does is fine. Her mother was just saying to me this morning . . . "

"Look, Papa . . . "

Without giving Mathias's parents a chance to speak, Léa dragged him up the stairs into the children's rooms. They fell into each other's arms and rolled among the cushions.

"You're alive, you're alive," was all Léa could say, over and over.

"I couldn't die because I was thinking of you."

They touched each other, inhaling each other's odor as if to convince themselves that the other really was there. Léa buried her head into the boy's neck and nibbled at it.

"Stop it. I'm filthy and I might have lice."

At the word "lice," Léa pushed him away. Mathias knew

what he was doing when he mentioned those little creatures. Léa had never, since they were children together, been able to bear the idea of lice. At the mere mention of them, she felt an uncontrollable disgust. He laughed as her horrified expression.

"You're right. Wait here, I'll run your bath."

The bathroom off the children's room was the oldest and biggest one in the house. They seldom used it, as the enormous bathtub took up all the hot water. There were double wash basins and there was a dressing-table with faded flowered chintz skirts. A cane chaise-longue completed the furnishing while the tall window facing due south had a white cretonne curtain. For Léa this practical room held all the charms of her childhood memories. It was in this huge bathtub that, every evening, Isabelle used to bath her daughters, amid laughter, shrieks and splashing! Sometimes, their father, disturbed by the noise, would come upstairs and pretend to be angry. Then, the girls' excitement would reach its peak, and they would fight for the privilege of being dried by Papa. Laure, the youngest, was often the lucky one, much to Léa's annoyance. She would have liked to be the only one to be wrapped in the enormous bathrobe and carried into the bedroom all bundled up.

Léa poured the last of her mother's lavender bath salts into the stream of running water. The hot perfumed steam that rose up upset her so much that she burst into tears. She fell to her knees on the bath mat and rested her head on the enamel rim, and gave free rein to her sorrow.

"Léa!" Camille entered and saw her destraught. She knelt down beside her and stroked her hair.

"What's the matter, darling?"

"Mummy . . . "

Her profound and childlike despair made Camille dissolve into tears too. That was how Ruth found them.

"What's the matter? An accident?"

"No . . . no . . . don't worry, Ruth. Just an excess of grief," said Camille getting to her feet.

She splashed cold water on Léa's face with a motherly gesture.

"Madame Camille, Lieutenant Kramer is downstairs. He wishes to speak with you."

"What's he doing here in the daytime? And why does he want to see me?"

"I don't know, but he looked rather grim."

"My God! I hope nothing has happened to Laurent."

"What do you think can happen to Laurent! He's a prisoner. He's not in any danger," said Léa, drying her face.

"Come with me, I don't dare go down alone."

"Let's brush our hair first, look at us. If he sees that we've been crying, he'll be suspicious."

"You're right."

The two young women tried to conceal the traces of their crying.

"Ruth, would you tell Mathias that his bath's ready," said Léa smoothing her skirt. "He's in my room."

The lieutenant was standing waiting in the drawing room. He bowed as they entered the room.

"You wish to see me, monsieur."

"Yes, madame. I have some regrettable news: your husband has escaped."

Camille remained absolutely impassive.

"You know nothing about it, of course?" continued the officer.

She shook her head.

"And when did it happen?" asked Léa.

"At Easter."

"And you've only just found out about it?"

"No, we were told three weeks ago."

"Why have you waited so long to tell me?"

"We've been keeping a watch on the house and on Roches-Blanches in case he was thinking of coming home to join you."

"Would you have arrested him?"

"I would have done my duty, madame. Sadly, but I would have done it. As I am your guest, and feel respect and liking for you, I insisted on warning you myself."

"What will happen if he is recaptured?"

"This is his second escape. In future, he is likely to be treated with great severity."

"But isn't it natural to try to escape when you're a prisoner?" retorted Léa angrily.

"I agree, mademoiselle: if I were a prisoner, I would try to escape. But I am not. We have won the war and . . ."

"For the time being," Léa interrupted.

"Yes, glory is fickle, but, at present, no country is strong enough to challenge the Third Reich."

"Not even America?"

"Not even America, Madame d'Argilat. Allow me to give you a word of advice. Should your husband manage to avoid detection, encourage him to give himself up."

"I would never do anything of the sort."

"Madame, I'm telling you this for his sake and for yours. Think of your son."

"It's because I'm thinking of my son, monsieur, that I would never tell my husband to do such a thing."

Lieutenant Kramer looked with compassion at the frail young woman facing him.

Clicking his heels, the lieutenant saluted and went out of the room.

Camille and Léa remained silent and motionless for a long time.

"Don't let him come here," they both thought.

"We must tell Uncle Adrien," said Léa.

"But how? Except for a brief appearance at the beginning of February, we haven't heard from him."

"Before he left, he told me that in an emergency we could leave him a message with a man named Richard Chapon in Bordeaux. I met him through Raphaël Mahl."

"I'll come with you."

"No. If we both go, the lieutenant will be suspicious. I've got an idea. Tomorrow, Papa and Ruth are going to visit Laure at boarding school. I'll tell them that I want to see my little sister."

Léa left the room and in the hall she bumped into a tall young man reeking of lavender, who took her in his arms.

"Stop . . . Oh! it's you . . . I'd forgotten all about you."

"Already? I've only just arrived and already you've forgotten me—that isn't very nice of you."

"No, Mathias, that's not it. It's . . . I'm sorry, I can't tell you. Meet you at the Cross in an hour."

When Léa joined Mathias, it was beginning to rain. They took refuge in one of the chapels and there, snuggled up together, they told each other what had happened to them since they had parted in Orléans.

Léa told him everything, including the killing of the man who wanted to rob them, but she said nothing of her relationship with François Tavernier.

As for Mathias, after helping to rescue the wounded in Orléans, he had wandered among the ruins and the refugees looking in vain for Léa. He ended up with a group of soldiers under the orders of a young lieutenant and they fought near the cathedral. All his companions were killed except for a corporal, and the two had been taken prisoner. They were dumped in a temporary camp surrounded by barbed wire near the church of Saint-Euverte, and then at la Motte-Sanguin.

The following day, he helped fight the fire which ravaged Orléans for five days. He cleared rubble, carried the wounded away and buried the dead. He joined the 18,000 prisoners in the Pithiviers camp after walking there on foot and in the company of a pathetic band of captives. They slept on the ground, in the mud and were left unfed, filthy and covered with lice. They were no longer even aware of the stench they gave off. Some of them had not changed their shirt or socks for a month. They would fight over a crust of stale bread, a ladleful of barley soup in a makeshift pot, a cracked old bowl or an old tin can.

Mathias, his head lowered, told Léa the whole story . . . the thirty grams of horsemeat they were allowed from time to time, their joy when the French Ladies Guild brought them a few blankets, the *foie gras* sandwiches distributed by the Red Cross, a bar of carnation-perfumed soap a young girl had given him, the hope of being freed soon and the disappointment, the general feeling of confidence in Marshal Pétain. He told her about the one-franc packet of tobacco that was being sold for a hundred francs, the growing demoralization, the church services that were attended by an increasing number of prisoners: a hundred out of 18,000 at the beginning of June, 2,000 out of the 2,500 who were left by the beginning of August.

He told her that he had been among those 2,000, praying to see her again. He told her with anger in his voice how cowardly they had all been when escape was so easy, how overjoyed when the armistice was announced, how disappointed when they heard the clauses about the cessation of hostilities, especially paragraph 20 which said that: "All French prisoners of war will remain in German camps until peace is fully established." He recalled the long hours of inactivity spent going over and over what it was like "in the old days," dreaming up, with hunger in their bellies, gargantuan menus, and dreaming of women. Fortunately for him, harvest time came. He was one of those young farmhands sent all over France to replace the men who were away.

"I never thought I would be so happy to lift sheaves of corn, stripped to the waist under a burning sun. At last, there was enough to eat."

He had written to Léa and to his father from a farm in the Beauce region. Neither letter arrived. When he received no reply, he tried to run away by "borrowing" clothes from the owner of the farm. He was caught after he had covered eighteen miles, and packed off to Germany in a cattle truck. He only stayed two weeks in a prison camp before being sent to a forestry development where he had been forced to work until he was liberated.

He did not understand why he had been freed: he had no family obligations. The only plausible explanation was that there was no more work, the forester no longer needed him and the camps were overpopulated. It was also at the time when the Vichy Government was doing what it could to secure the release of prisoners of war. He had been lucky. And even luckier to find Léa safe and sound.

"What are you going to do now?" she asked.

"I'm going to work, my father needs me terribly."

"Yes, of course, but what about the war?"

"What do you mean, the war?"

"There are people who continue to fight."

"You mean in North Africa?"

"Yes, and General de Gaulle."

"You know, I heard about de Gaulle two days ago on the train. A lot of people think he's not very responsible and that we should remain loyal to Pétain."

"Yes, but what do you think?"

"You know, for the time being, I can only think of one thing: I'm home and I'm holding the woman I love. Let de Gaulle wait," he said smothering her with kisses.

Léa pushed him away good humoredly.

"I don't like you talking to me like that."

"Come on, my love, you're not going to tell me that you're interested in politics and that you're a Gaullist?"

"You don't understand. It's more than politics. It's a matter of freedom."

The young man burst out laughing.

"Well that's the last thing I would expect to hear: the lovely Léa Delmas holding forth about freedom, flirting with de Gaulle, no longer trying to seduce young men. What happened to make you change so much?"

Léa stood up angrily.

"What's happened? I've seen women and children dying atrocious deaths, I killed a man. My mother, whom I thought was safe here, was killed in an air raid in Bordeaux, Laurent is lost God knows where. We've got no money. There's hardly anything to eat. The Germans are occupying our house and my father . . . my father's going mad."

Léa's fist hammered the walls.

"Forgive me for being so clumsy. I'm here now, I'll help you."

He kissed her face, her head, seeking the smell of hay that used to linger in her hair after their romps in the barn. He buried his head in her neck where he inhaled the vanilla smell of her skin. He hugged her passionately. While his fingers fumbled impatiently at the buttons on her blouse, his teeth

257

were already biting her lips.

Léa did not move; Mathias's rough caresses stirred memories in the depths of her body. She told herself that she shouldn't, that she loved Laurent, that she was mad and careless, but any resistance was overcome from the start, she so yearned to feel a warm body against hers, to feel a man inside her. She heard herself moan, babble words that made no sense. Quickly, quickly, let him take her . . . what was he waiting for? She flung off her underwear impatiently and offered herself to him, shameless and magnificent.

"Come! Eat me!" she commanded.

The boy stared at her tuft of pale curly hair framed by black suspenders holding up her black cotton stockings, setting off the fragile whiteness of the insides of her thighs. He buried his face in the sweet-smelling moisture. His questing tongue made Léa moan again and again.

For a second, her eyes opened and met the face of Christ falling under the weight of his cross. The statue seemed to come to life, and the son of God was giving her a knowing wink. She let out a cry and climaxed as Mathias kissed her. Her erect nipples sent a delicious pain through her body. She jerked his head away from her stomach and hungrily kissed that mouth that had given her pleasure, intoxicated by the taste.

'Take me,' she said, spreading her legs.

She moaned again when Mathias forced his way inside her.

"I love it!" she screamed suddenly.

Outside, the rain cascaded down. It was dark, like winter. In the open-air chapel under the trees, a half-naked boy and girl slept at the foot of a group of stone figures whose pale faces seemed to protect them.

The following day, Léa went to Bordeaux with her father, her Aunt Bernadette and Ruth, on the pretext of going to see Laure and buying seeds for the vegetable garden. After an uncomfortable lunch at her Uncle Luc's, where he went on about how fortunate France was in having a leader like Marshal Pétain, she asked to be excused in order to do her shopping.

"I'll come with you," said Laure getting to her feet.

"There's no need, I won't be long," replied Léa.

"Can I come too?" asked their cousin, Corinne.

Léa looked imploringly at Ruth.

Ruth had always been wary of what she called "her little one's mad ideas," but she had always maintained that Léa would always land on her feet and that she needed more freedom than her sisters.

"Léa has a vitality, an instinct for survival that overcomes everything. Woe to anyone who gets in her way," she had said to Adrien Delmas the last time she saw him.

In spite of her misgivings at that moment, she came to Léa's aid.

"Laure, don't you have to go to the bookshop? You and I could go there with Corinne while Léa goes off to buy the seeds. She'll meet us when she comes back."

The words were hardly out of Ruth's mouth when Léa hurried out of her uncle's house. Fortunately, the lawyer's house was not far from the office of *La Petite Gironde* in the Rue de Cheverus, and the bookshop was in the Rue Vital-Carles, also around the corner from the newspaper.

Adrien had said that if she needed to contact him she could do so through Richard Chapon. She was greeted by the same employee as before, who told her that the editor was out and he did not know when he would be back.

"But it's urgent," insisted Léa.

"Perhaps he's got too many urgent things to do, mademoiselle."

On seeing Léa's look of despair, he added: "Go and see his friend, the priest at Sainte-Eulalie, he might be able to help you."

Saint-Eulalie? That was close to the Dominican monastery, where Raphaël Mahl had left her. She decided to go there.

"Thank you, monsieur."

The weather had clouded over and it was cold. Léa turned up the collar of Isabelle's old mackintosh and pulled her felt hat down over her ears before starting to run, clutching her shoulder bag.

She stopped, breathless, at the foot of the steps to the

church. As she pushed open the door, drops of rain fell.

A few women were praying at the altar where a little red light was burning. For the sake of appearances, she knelt down near the sacristy and thought about what she was to say and do.

"Léa, what are you doing here?"

She jumped and almost let out a scream as she felt a hand on her shoulder. A man with a huge moustache, wearing a brown suit and holding his hat, was looking at her.

"Uncle Adrien!"

"Shhh! Follow me."

He headed for the door.

It was raining outside. Adrien Delmas put his hat back on and, taking Léa's arm, led her swiftly away.

"Why are you dressed like that?"

"A Dominican's robes are too attention-getting in certain places. Thank the Lord I've met you. The church has been under observation by the Gestapo for the past few days. If I hadn't seen you go in, God knows what might have happened."

"I was looking for you."

"No doubt. But don't come round here again. What's the matter?"

"Laurent's escaped from Germany."

"How do you know?"

"Lieutenant Kramer told Camille and me."

"When did he escape?"

"At Easter."

The rain was lashing down and they stopped for shelter in a doorway opposite the cathedral.

"Has Camille heard from Laurent directly?"

"No."

"So what do you want me to do?"

"I . . . Camille's afraid that Laurent may try to join her. The house is being watched. What should we do if he makes it home?"

Two German soldiers were standing in a doorway, laughing, not far away.

"Bad weather in France," said one of them looking peeved.

"Yes, but good wine," retorted the other one.

Without consulting each other, Léa and her uncle left their shelter. They walked in silence for a few moments.

"I've got to go to Langon next week to see one of our brothers in hospital. At the same time, I'll come to Montillac. I've got to make a few contacts in the area."

"Can't I go instead?"

While they walked, Adrien held her close to him.

"No, my love, it's too dangerous. You already know too much for the safety of both of us."

"I want to help Laurent."

"I'm sure you do. But the best way to help him is not to attract attention. By the way, how's your father?"

Léa heaved a great sigh.

"I'm worried he's changed so. He's not interested in anything. It's been even worse since Monsieur d'Argilat died. All the time he talks about Mummy as if she were still with us. He stays in his study alone, or sits on the terrace and talks to himself. When you want to keep him company, you feel as if you're in the way. 'Go away, can't you see I'm talking to your mother.' It's awful, Uncle Adrien. I'm afraid for him."

"I know, child, I know. What does Blanchard say?"

"He won't discuss it. He gives him pills that Ruth makes him take regularly."

"Part of him is dead, and pills won't bring him back to life. We must pray to God . . ."

"God! You don't still believe in God, do you?"

"Hush, Léa! don't blaspheme!"

"Uncle, I don't believe in God any more and, I'm sorry to say, neither does anyone at Montillac, except perhaps poor Camille.

"Don't say such terrible things."

They were walking past the ruins of a bombed building in the Rue des Remparts.

"Why didn't you come to Mummy's funeral?"

"I couldn't. I wasn't in Bordeaux. Where are you going now?"

"I've got to meet Ruth and Laure at the bookshop."

"That's just round the corner. I'll leave you here. I don't

want them to see me dressed like this. Do as I say. Don't try to reach me at the monastery or at *La Petite Gironde*. The newspaper is being watched. I'll get in touch with you. In any case, I'll be at Montillac early next week. Till then, be careful. If, God forbid, Laurent should turn up, tell him to go to your mother's godson at Saint-Macaire. He knows what to do. Tell Laurent to say: 'The dominoes have been moved.' He'll understand."

"The dominoes have been moved."

"Yes."

They said goodbye. The rain had stopped.

At the bookshop, an assistant told Léa that the Delmas ladies had just left. Luckily, the seed merchant in the market place was open and had a few packets left. He even had—the height of luxury—tomato plants and lettuce seedlings.

At Uncle Luc's, Laure gave her a frosty reception. She was getting ready to go back to school

"I had something important to tell you," she whispered, "but it'll have to wait till next time."

"Don't be silly, tell me."

"No, that's your hard luck."

"I'll come with you."

"Don't bother." Laure paused for emphasis. "Ask Sabine if she enjoyed herself at the concert the other evening. Goodbye."

Chapter 21

"Uncle Adrien!"

Léa was kneeling in "her" vegetable garden clutching a handful of weeds. She was wearing a black peasant blouse with blue and white flowers and a big straw hat on her head. She stood up.

Accompanied by Camille, the Dominican came over to her, hitching up his white robe. Léa flung herself into his outstretched arms.

"I'm so happy to see you again, Uncle."

"He's seen Laurent, he's in Bordeaux!" gabbled Camille.

"In Bordeaux!"

"He wanted to come and see me, but your uncle stopped him."

"For the time being, he's safe."

"Where? I want to see him."

"You can't for the moment, it's too dangerous. Soon, I hope I'll be able to tell you when you can join him."

"Quickly, I hope."

"How is he?" asked Léa.

"He's exhausted. After his escape from Colditz, he hid in Switzerland. He fell seriously ill there and was not able to write. In a few days' time, I'll get him into the unoccupied zone."

"Does he need anything?"

"Nothing for the moment. Next Thursday, I'm coming back to Langon to see Father Dupré at the hospital. I'll come out here to tell you how Camille can see Laurent. Meanwhile, please don't move, don't say a word. If by chance I can't come to Montillac, I'll leave a message with Sabine. She's in charge of Father Dupré's ward.''

"Is it wise to entrust her with such a mission?" said Camille lowering her head.

Léa and her uncle looked at her in surprise.

"Why did you say that?"

"Isn't Sabine Léa's sister? Don't you all live under the same roof?

"I know, but . . .''

Adrien and Léa exchanged bemused glances. Why this reluctance, this sudden wariness? It was so unlike Camille.

"She might lose the message . . . or be arrested by the Germans," she stuttered, blushing scarlet.

"Camille, you're hiding something from us. Why do you distrust Sabine?"

"No, no, it's nothing. I'm simply afraid for Laurent."

Father Delmas paced back and forth and then returned.

"I'll put an address in the binding of *The Path to Perfection* by Thérèse d'Avila. But I'm sure so many precautions are unnecessary and I'll come and give it to you myself."

They went back towards the house, still chatting.

Pierre Delmas was sitting on the stone bench looking out over Bellevue and Verdelais Hill. His chin was resting on his hands and he leaned on a thick gnarled wooden walking stick. A vague smile hovered on his lips and he stared straight ahead of him.

"Well, brother, taking it easy?" joked Adrien.

"Rather. Isabelle made me move all the furniture in her room. I'm exhausted."

"Papa, Mummy is . . .''

"I do sympathize, Monsieur Delmas, there's nothing as tiring as moving furniture," Camille butted in.

"No, there isn't," he replied, delighted. "Isabelle just won't realize that I'm getting old . . .''

Léa turned away with tears in her eyes.

Camille and Sabine were sitting on the lawn that sloped down to the terrace watching as little Charles took his first tentative steps.

"He'll be walking in a month's time," said Sabine.

"That's what Sidonie and Ruth think too. They say that a baby who isn't fat learns to walk sooner."

"Won't Laurent be pleased to see him? It's odd that you haven't heard from him since his escape."

Camille bit her lip.

"If he hadn't run away, no doubt he would have been released like Mathias," Sabine went on as she picked up the child, who shrieked with laughter and wriggled.

He was a beautiful child; he was very fair and looked like both his father and his mother. He was growing fast and was never ill. Camille watched over him with an animal protectiveness. She looked lovingly at him as if she was afraid she might lose him from one minute to the next. He was cheerful and never cried. Everyone adored him, except Léa, who couldn't help feeling jealous, even though, from a very early age, he showed a liking for her.

"Are you going to read the book that Uncle Adrien gave you? *The Path to Perfection*—it doesn't look much fun."

"No, it's not much fun but perhaps it's useful in giving one the strength to live."

"Maybe you're right," said Sabine, subdued.

Camille sensed her change of mood but pretended not to notice. She played with her son and laughed at his antics.

"Motherhood suits her," thought Sabine.

It was true on this Whitsunday, that Camille d'Argilat looked radiant. When the fine weather came she cast off the black winter mourning clothes she had been wearing for her father-in-law and her brother and because there was a shortage of material, and today she was wearing one of her old pale blue linen dresses that set off her eyes, her tanned face and her hair which the sun had lightened. She was so slim that she looked like a frail adolescent. Sabine, sitting nearby, seemed older, more womanly, although she was the same age.

Sabine had changed a lot since she began working at the hospital in Langon. She had become more feminine, more seductive, fussing over her hair, wearing too much make-up—in the opinion of Ruth and her Aunt Bernadette—and dressing well, in spite of rationing. She was wearing a red silk dress with blue polka dots and a tight belt which looked as though it came from a good couturier's and not from the little dressmaker in Langon who she said had made it.

"Tomorrow, I'll be seeing Laurent," Camille was thinking.

Léa was in a foul mood. She had met Mathias at Saint-Macaire, at the house of a friend who was out for the day. Mathias was overjoyed at the prospect of a day away from Montillac, far from Ruth's prying and from his parents' anxious curiosity. He had not been able to see Léa for a second since their lovemaking in the chapel at Verdelais. He suspected she was avoiding him. But when on Thursday evening she had come into the farm kitchen, very pale, and asked him to come with her, he had been surprised.

He followed her into the barn and there, without saying a word, she threw herself into his arms and lay there trembling like a lamb. He kissed her unyielding lips gently and laid her in the hay trying to warm her. Her arms, locked round his neck, were stiff as those of a corpse. He had difficulty prying open her thighs, she was pressing them so tightly together, and it took all his patience, in spite of his desire, to penetrate her. She cried out in pleasure as others cry out in pain.

Mathias was left with a strange bitter taste after this encounter.

To rid himself of this feeling, he had prepared a high tea just like the ones Léa used to love in the old days: strawberry tart, sweet white wine, cherries in brandy, caramel cream. It had required a great deal of ingenuity to obtain all these luxuries. The humble old house was fragrant with the scent of white roses that he had put everywhere. Léa smiled when she saw how much trouble he had taken. Playing at master of the house, he held a glass of wine out to her.

"Let's drink to our happiness."

Léa emptied her glass in one gulp.

"More Please. That tastes good."

Mathias refilled her glass with a smile.

Léa inspected the room, glass in hand, pausing for a long time in front of the fireplace. On the mantelpiece, there was a view of Lourdes painted on a piece of bark, a rather moth-eaten stuffed ferret, a post-office calendar, a bunch of roses and some yellowed photographs.

"Your friend's place is nice and cozy," she said slowly. "Where's the bedroom?"

There was a hint of annoyance in Mathias's expression. He could not get used to Léa's offhand attitude to their sexual relationship. Without realizing it, he actually would have preferred her to be more coy. He had the unpleasant feeling that it was she who called the tune, and he did not find that natural or enjoyable. As far as he was concerned, it was now clear that she would become his wife. Could it be otherwise? When she entered the bedroom, Léa almost burst out laughing, it was so much like Sidonie's room: the same high walnut bed with a white cotton bedspread and an enormous red satin eiderdown. Above it, there was a big black wooden crucifix decorated with palm leaves; opposite the bed, on either side of the window, were two portraits of countryfolk dressed up in their Sunday best, and near the door was a huge wardrobe.

Léa removed her sandals without bothering to undo them. The coolness of the tiled floor was pleasant underfoot. She put her glass on the bedside table and began to undress, humming to herself as she did so.

Mathias pulled back the covers and the bed, with its white sheets, seemed enormous. Léa lay on the bed, naked.

The sheets smell of lavender, she thought with a slight pang.

"Give me a drink."

"You drink too much," said Mathias coming back with the bottle.

Léa sipped her drink slowly as she watched Mathias undressing.

"You should strip to the waist when you work. You can see a line where your shirt ends and it looks as though your sun-tanned face has been stuck on to a body that isn't yours. It looks ugly."

"I'll show you if it's ugly," he said, lying down beside her and pulling her towards him.

"Wait! Let me put my glass down."

As she leaned over him, he caught one of her breasts in his mouth while his fingers squeezed the other one.

"Ouch! That hurts."

"Too bad."

They rolled on top of each other, laughing and shrieking under the impassive gaze of the family photographs.

Perched on the edge of the crumpled bed, Léa was devouring the tarts, the fruit and the cream and drinking more wine, which was beginning to make her feel dizzy. She was naked, her hair was disheveled and she had shadows under her eyes. Mathias watched, enchanted.

"Don't stare at me like that!"

"I can't help it. You're beautiful."

"That's no reason to stare."

"When you're my wife, I'll stare at you as much as I like."

Léa's hand, which was about to put another tart in her mouth, stopped in mid-air.

"Whatever are you talking about?"

"Marrying you, of course."

"We're not getting married."

"Why not?"

Léa shrugged.

"Aren't I good enough for you?"

"Don't be silly. I just don't want to get married, that's all."

"Every girl wants to get married."

"Perhaps, but I'm not every girl. Please let's not talk about it any more."

"No. I want to talk about it. I love you and I want to marry you," he said squeezing her arm.

"Let me go. You're hurting me."

Mathias tightened his hold.

"Let me go!"

"Not till you promise to marry me."

"Never! Never!"

He raised his hand to strike her.

268

"Go ahead, hit me . . . go on then . . . what are you waiting for?"

"But why won't you?"

"I don't love you."

Mathias turned pale. "What did you say?"

She leaped up and began to scramble into her clothes.

"Mathias, don't be angry with me, I'm fond of you . . . I've loved you a lot but . . . not as your wife."

"But you're already mine."

Léa finished doing up the buttons on her dress. She looked at Mathias who was still sitting naked on the crumpled sheets with his legs dangling over the edge of the bed and his head bowed. A lock of hair hid his face and Léa felt a surge of tenderness for him. He looked so like that little boy who used to bow to her every childish whim! She sat down beside him and laid her head on his shoulder.

"Look, be sensible. Just because we've been to bed together, it doesn't mean we have to get married."

"What's his name?"

"What do you mean?"

"Who's your lover?"

"I don't know what you're talking about."

"Do you think I'm stupid? Do you think I didn't notice that you weren't a virgin?"

Her faced burning, Léa stood up and began rummaging for her shoes. One was at the foot of the bed and the other under the wardrobe. She got down on all fours and tried to fish it out. But Mathias was faster and he snatched the sandal.

"Will you answer me? Who is it?"

"You're getting on my nerves. It's none of your business."

"Bitch . . . I didn't want to believe it, I said to myself, 'Not her, she's a nice girl . . . perhaps it was her little fiancé, she wanted to be nice to him before he left for the war . . . I can't hold it against him . . . ' but now, I can see it wasn't Camille's poor brother who taught you all that . . . you slut . . . and I wanted to make you my wife . . . like your sister, the Nazis' whore, the Nazis' whore . . . "

The unhappy lad collapsed on to the bed sobbing.

Léa felt the blood drain from her face. She stared blankly straight ahead of her.

They remained like that for a long time, she motionless, he crying. He was the first to get hold of himself. He was suddenly afraid of Léa. He wiped his wet cheeks on the sheets and went over to her. Her face was ashen and her eyes were abnormally round. With a great effort, she turned towards him and asked in a dull voice: "What did you say?"

Mathias regretted his outburst.

"Nothing, I was angry."

"Repeat what you said."

"Nothing, honestly, it was nothing."

" . . . like your sister, the Nazis' whore . . . "

Then, bending like a blade of wheat in the field under the scythe, Léa swayed to the floor. Mathias accompanied her fall and on the red tile floor he attempted to assuage the effect of his words.

"No, don't say anything, hold me tight . . . how could you believe . . . ?"

"Forgive me . . . "

" . . . that I . . . "

"Be quiet," he stuttered, stopping her mouth with kisses to prevent her from speaking.

"Sabine . . . oh! now I understand . . . Papa . . . poor Papa, he mustn't find out . . . Mathias, what am I to do?"

"Don't think about it, my love . . . perhaps I'm wrong."

Unconsciously, Léa returned his kisses and she rubbed against him as she felt him growing hard. Once again they made love.

Léa did not want Mathias to see her back to Montillac. She pleaded an awful migraine and went to bed without dinner. As she was going up the stairs, she met the two German officers who saluted and stood aside to let her pass.

Alone at last in the disorder that she loved, Léa fell on to the cushions. So what she had vaguely suspected was true:

270

Sabine, her sister Sabine, was the mistress of a German. Which one? Otto Kramer, of course. Love of music!

There was a knock at the door.

"What is it?"

"It's me, Camille, may I come in?"

"Yes."

"My poor darling! It's true that you don't look well. I've brought you an aspirin."

"Thank you," said Léa taking the tablet and the glass of water.

"It's sweet of you to drive me into the unoccupied zone tomorrow. Laurent will be pleased. He's so fond of you."

"Have you noticed anything strange about Sabine recently?"

"No, what do you mean?"

Léa looked at her suspiciously. "Your reluctance the other day, why was that?"

Camille blushed and said nothing.

"Do you think so too . . . that she and the lieutenant . . ."

"Be quiet, it would be too ghastly."

"But has it crossed your mind?"

"It's not possible . . . we must be mistaken."

"And if we weren't?"

"Then it would be dreadful," exclaimed Camille in a low voice, burying her face in her hands.

"We'll have to get to the bottom of it, I'm going to ask her."

"Not now . . . not before I've seen Laurent."

"Who would have thought it of Sabine?"

"Let's not judge her. We don't know for sure. And if it is true, it's because she loves him."

"That's no reason."

"It's the best reason."

Léa looked at Camille in horror. What! What on earth did this prude know about love and passion? The image of Camille tottering forward but determined to kill in order to defend her came back to her. She wasn't shy then, and perhaps in love . . . the idea was unbearable: imagine

Camille giving rein to her unbridled passion in Laurent's arms . . . no!

"You don't know what you're saying. You forget that he's German."

"Oh no, I'm not forgetting. For weeks . . . "

"You knew! And you didn't say anything to me . . . "

"What could I have said? It was only an impression. Certain looks between them, nothing definite."

"Even so, you should have told me. Ah! If only Mummy was here! Do you think the others suspect anything?"

"I've no idea. Put it out of your mind until you're certain. You need sleep. We'll leave early tomorrow. I've had the engine checked; everything's in order. Léa, I'm so happy! In a few hours, Laurent and I will be together again!" She misunderstood Léa's pained look. "Forgive me darling, I'm thoughtless and selfish. One day you'll meet a nice boy who'll make you as happy as you would have been with my brother," said Camille, kissing her tenderly.

Léa undressed in a furious temper, and slipped on a nightdress that was too short and made her look like a little girl. In the bathroom, she cleaned her teeth and brushed her hair half-heartedly. In the mirror she caught sight of her reflection: her face was obstinate and drawn. If she looked like that tomorrow, Laurent wouldn't think she was very beautiful. A brilliant smile effaced her scowl, her eyes shone, she bit her lip and her breasts swelled. . . .

"Here's to the two of us, Laurent."

They crossed the demarcation line into the unoccupied zone without any problem. The car kept up a good speed on the deserted road, as if it too was intoxicated at being in the free zone.

After La Réole, Léa took a little lane on the left. Very soon, a trimmed hedge appeared. For a few seconds she drove on the gravel of a wide avenue lined with rose bushes, and then she pulled up in front of the terrace of a large turn-of-the-century house which was characterless and unattractive. Léa switched off the engine. The only sound to be heard was the singing of the birds and little Charles's burbling. He had just awakened. A tall figure limped into view. Léa and Camille both leaped out of the car. Camille gave Léa the baby and ran towards the man shouting, "Laurent . . ."

Léa hugged the baby tighter. He had his tiny arms around her neck. She would have liked to be able to tear herself away from the spectacle of the two bodies locked in embrace, but she was incapable of moving. After a time, which seemed interminable, the couple came towards her hand in hand. Laurent was looking at her with such warmth that she almost dropped the baby to throw herself at him, but Camille took Charles from her and held him out towards his father. He took him awkwardly and stared at him incredulously.

"My son," he stuttered as a tear ran down his cheek and disappeared in the bushy moustache which made him look older.

Cautiously, he kissed the little face.

"Charles, my son."

"Without Léa, neither of us would be here today, Laurent."

Laurent handed Charles back to Camille and drew Léa towards him.

"I knew I could depend on you. Thank you."

He rested his lips on her hair, near her ear.

"Thank you," he murmured fervently.

Léa was overwhelmed with a desire to shout out her love.

"Laurent, Laurent, if only you knew . . ."

"I know, it was very hard, Adrien has told me everything. You were very brave."

"No I wasn't, I'm not brave," protested Léa, "I just didn't have any choice, that's all."

"Don't listen to her, Laurent, she was marvelous."

"I know."

A man and a woman in their sixties joined them.

"Camille and Léa, I want you to meet Monsieur and Madame Debray, my hosts. They take great risks to hide escaped prisoners like myself."

"No, Monsieur d'Argilat, it is an honor for us to assist our soldiers," said Monsieur Debray with feeling.

"We are only doing our duty," said his wife softly.

"This is Camille, my wife, and my son Charles."

"Charles? That's a little careless of you, madame, are you not aware that Philippe is the fashionable name these days?" teased Monsieur Debray.

"Fashions come and go, monsieur. I'm very happy to be able to thank you for all you've done for my husband."

"Don't mention it. You would have done the same in our shoes. It's our way of continuing the struggle and of being closer to our son."

"Our son was killed at Dunkirk."

Camille tried to say something.

"Don't say anything, words are useless. Come, let's go indoors. Who is this lovely young lady?"

"Mademoiselle Delmas, Léa Delmas, our very dear friend to whom we owe our happiness."

"Welcome, mademoiselle."

They stayed in that hospitable home for three days. On the second day, Adrien Delmas came to join them in civilian dress. Her uncle's presence eased the horrible jealousy that was tormenting Léa. She could not bear to see Camille's radiant face and Laurent's tender solicitude.

Laurent was one of the first prisoners of war ever to escape from Colditz. That citadel, once a royal castle, rose 120 feet on a steep pinnacle overlooking the little pink sandstone and brick town on the right bank of the Mulde.

He had realized very early on that his only chance of escaping was during the walk. He confided in three of his comrades who helped him collect supplies, clothes and a little money.

One afternoon, as they were going down for their walk, Laurent noticed that the façade of a three-storey building above the path the prisoners took to the park was being renovated. A door that was usually shut was now ajar.

Because of the steep slope, the cellar was in fact the first floor in relation to the path. He looked up through the rusty bars over the narrow openings at ground level and saw that there were store-rooms. He had to act quickly: the door might be closed again at anytime. On the way back from the walk, with his little luggage hidden under his overcoat, he made up his mind. He whispered to his neighbor: "Now's the time."

His comrade slowed down the whole procession.

"Stay calm. Stare straight ahead of you."

The guard in front did not turn around once. Laurent, in the third row, could see the hairs on the back of his thick neck. Behind him were a few more rows of prisoners and the rear guard.

In three strides, he dived into the cellar doorway. He expected to feel a bullet in the back any second. He could hear his companions' footsteps receding. With thumping heart, he rolled up his blue trousers to turn them into knickerbockers of a sort, exposing his long thick white woolen socks. He took off his old canvas jacket and kept on only his heavy beige Aran pullover that Ruth had sent. With the collar of his blue shirt turned down over the neck of his pullover and his jaunty cap, a little hold-all carrying the bare essentials and his comfortable crêpe-soled shoes, he hoped to pass for a healthy German hiker. Two minutes had passed. There were no shouts, no calls, no barking dogs.

Leave the damp cellar, jump over the little wall, go back on the path, above all don't run. He had repeated the plan so many times in his mind. The only real danger was the guards on the covered walkway around the fortress.

His plan was simple: he wanted to get back into the park by crossing—with the help of a fallen tree—the little river that separated the fortress from the place where the prisoners took their walk. Then he would climb over the wooden fence that surrounded the German soldiers' athletic field, and from there he would scale the high stone wall behind the fence, using the slightly protruding stones as footholds. He was delayed by the presence of German soldiers playing ball on the field. He had to stay hidden in the cellar where, several times, he thought he had been discovered: two children came and played marbles on the main path, soldiers walked past keeping close to the walls of the house, a couple walking their dog stopped in the open doorway for a long time. Laurent was most afraid of the dog.

When they finally moved on, Laurent was sweating profusely in spite of the damp cold of the cellar. Surprisingly, the guards had not yet discovered his disappearance. In two hours' time, there would be a roll-call. Laurent finally got out of the cellar and did everything according to plan. When he reached the foot of the wall, he turned around: in front of him was the empty park; to his left was the huge fortress that looked even more menacing in the twilight. On the covered walkway, the sentries stood out as black silhouettes against the pale evening sky. If one of them were to look in his direction, then he would be done for.

He calmly began his slow climb. In spite of the wound in his leg that still bothered him, he reached the top without any difficulty. He jumped into the void below; his fall was softened by dead leaves on the ground. He had escaped from the Colditz fortress.

Down below was a road, the road to freedom. The loose stones on the slope had made a terrible noise as he landed. He could hear voices on the road. Laurent tidied his appearance, wiped off the mud from his shoes. The voices drew nearer. He walked past two officers from the citadel and their wives, engaged in an animated conversation, who had not taken the slightest notice of him. He looked like an average German. As if it were a game, he returned an old man's smile and greeted a group of young people with a booming *Heil Hitler*. When he reached the main road, he allowed himself the luxury of turning around to contemplate the solid mass of Colditz castle. He was overwhelmed with a feeling of great pride: he had defeated the massive and subtle surveillance network that surrounded this prison.

Three days later, he crossed the border to Switzerland at Schlaffhouse. In the evening, he boarded a train at Rochlitz, penniless. When he arrived in Berne, he fell seriously ill. He stayed in the hospital for several days and wrote long letters to his father and his wife, which never arrived. Only the letter he sent to Adrien Delmas, miraculously, slipped through the net of censorship. The monk contacted him through a Swiss Dominican, who provided him with identity papers and money.

A mild, peaceful afternoon was drawing to a close over La Réole, where Laurent and Léa had come to do some shopping. Camille was not with them, she had stayed behind to look after Charles. It was the first time they had been alone together. Madame Debray had recommended a baker's in the Rue des Argentiers whose bread was reputed to be the best in the region and who still sold flour. They got lost in the back streets and ended up near the castle of Quat'Sos which overlooked the Garonne Valley. They walked past the Benedictine abbey. The air was sweet with the fragrance of the linden trees. Léa wanted to go into the church. In the chapel of the Virgin Mary, Laurent paused for a long time. Léa went up to him, took his hand and laid her head on his shoulder. He kissed the top of her curly head. She could feel the pulse of the man she loved. When she raised her face to his, their eyes locked and they were unable to look away. Their lips brushed. This slight contact was enough to set fire to their entire bodies. A door slammed nearby, bringing them back to reality: the spell was broken.

Laurent gently pushed Léa away.

"No . . . don't let me go."

"Léa . . . this is crazy. We mustn't . . . I mustn't . . ."

"Be quiet. I love you."

Once again, she pushed her body against his. He grabbed her hips and pulled her to him.

"I love you."

Léa snaked up and down, caressing his erection with her belly. He pushed her away so violently that she stumbled.

"Stop it!" he cried.

She looked at him triumphantly and walked towards the door. He followed her with his head bowed.

"Come on, hurry up, the baker's will be closed."

The shop hadn't closed, but only because Madame Debray had sent them they were able to come out with a four kilo loaf of bread and a sack of flour.

They had left their bicycles near the station. They rode back, each lost in their own dreams, totally indifferent to the beauty of the surrounding countryside. In a short time they arrived at the Debrays' house.

As soon as they appeared, Camille came running up to them.

"Where were you? I was out of my mind with worry."

"What did you think happened to us? We visited La Réole," said Léa unmoved by Camille's concern.

During dinner, Léa was cheerful and amusing, talking wittily about anything and everything, encouraged by Adrien and Monsieur Debray, who found her entertaining.

While they were drinking a cup of awful coffee in the garden, Adrien told Laurent: "I've found the person we've been looking for. A certain Jean Benazet from Verilhes near Foix. We're meeting him tomorrow afternoon at the Café de la Poste in Foix. He'll give you the underground route to get you to North Africa."

"So soon!" exclaimed Camille.

"Please, darling. You'll come and join me as soon as its possible."

"But I want to go with you!"

"It's out of the question. Think of Charles. He needs you."

Madame Debray got to her feet and placed her hand on Camille's shoulder. "Don't undermine your husband's morale with your tears. By continuing to fight, he's doing his duty. Be brave. Would you like to stay here? My husband and I would be delighted to have you here with us."

"It isn't possible," said Laurent, "Camille must take my place at Roches-Blanches. I had a letter from Delpech, our manager, and he tells me that not only is the house occupied by the Germans, but that the vineyards are in a terrible state."

"Like Montillac," said Léa.

"Like everywhere in the region," added the Dominican.

"What do you intend to do?" asked Monsieur Debray.

"I really don't know. I can't stop thinking about my poor father. I wonder what he would have done. The trials and tribulations of this poor land fill my heart with sorrow and anger. I used to be for the unity of nations, for a united states of Europe, but now I'm a nationalist, something I thought completely stupid before the war. I did not realize I was so French or that I loved my country so much."

"Thanks to young men like you my friend, we will try to re-establish honor and freedom in this country," asserted Monsieur Debray vehemently.

"Do you really think so?"

"If I didn't, my wife and I would have killed ourselves the day we heard Pétain announce that he had asked for peace! It felt as though our son were being killed all over again. We cried and prayed to God for guidance. The following day, we heard His answer through General de Gaulle's voice."

For a few seconds, nobody spoke. The only sounds were the calls of the various birds and the cries of the swallows chasing each other in the sky. Adrien Delmas broke the silence.

"What we need is more people like you. All around there is nothing but cowardice, confusion, compromise, disgraceful denunciations, perverse informing, the acceptance of servitude. Gifted writers, like Brasillach, Rebatet and Drieu, academics, businessmen, soldiers and even—may God forgive them—priests, are prostituting their talents to serve a vile ideology. They're like weak animals: they lie down on their backs baring their stomachs for the enemy's boots to trample on. . . . I despair."

"But your faith in God will restore your faith in humanity," interrupted Madame Debray.

"No doubt: my faith in God . . ." he trailed off as he stood up.

Léa, who was bored by the conversation, also got to her feet. She was surprised by her uncle's tone of voice. She thought she could detect hatred and disillusionment. Had he lost his faith? "That would be strange," she thought, "a monk who doesn't believe in God!"

"Uncle Adrien, you look miserable," she said tenderly, as she joined him under a big chestnut tree.

He lit a cigarette but said nothing.

Léa watched him out of the corner of her eye: he was not only miserable, but he was desperate. A shyness that went back to her childhood prevented her from consoling him. To change the subject and dispel her distress at seeing him like this, he who was so strong in his faith questioning the existence of that God for whom he had given up everything, she asked: "Do you know if Lieutenant Valéry got to Morocco safely?"

"He did."

"What about Laurent? Do you think he will be all right?"

The Dominican looked at her intently. He was not mistaken: the little one was still in love with Laurent d'Argilat.

"Everything will be all right. The man who will take him across the border is trustworthy. When he gets to Algiers, he'll meet his comrades. Camille and the child will soon be able to join him."

Léa turned pale but did not falter.

"You must be delighted that everything is working out for your friends," he added with a hint of irony.

"Overjoyed," she snapped, turning away. "Excuse me, I'm tired. I'm going to bed. Goodnight, Uncle."

"Goodnight, God be with you."

Léa ran into the house.

Alone in her room, she did not see how she would be able to see Laurent on his own before he left. Lying naked on the bed, she went over every second they had spent at La Réole in the Chapel of the Virgin Mary in the Church of Saint-Pierre. At the memory of their bodies touching, she shuddered and her hand found its way between her thighs, giving rise to a pleasure that left her feeling furious with herself. She fell asleep at once with her arm over her face.

It was an interminable day.

Very early the previous day, Adrien and Laurent had taken the train to Toulouse, where they had to change trains for Foix. Their farewells had been suitably heartrending, thought Léa with irony. However, she had managed to slip a letter into Laurent's hand; his sudden blushing did not escape either Adrien or Madame Debray's notice. But she did not care: the main thing was that he should know she loved him and that she should be able to tell him again.

"Once again I'm entrusting you with all that is most dear to me," he said as he kissed her.

At last, there were footsteps on the gravel drive. They were indeed Adrien's. Léa restrained herself from running up to him to question him.

Madame Debray was there and she had not stopped watching her since the previous evening.

"Did everything go well?" cried Camille, breathless from running with one hand on her thumping heart.

"Yes, very well."

"When does he leave for Spain?"

"Tonight. He won't be alone; there are seven or eight of them."

"If you knew how frightened I am, Father," said Camille.

"Don't be afraid, everything will be all right."

"I hope so, but what about me, what am I supposed to do in the meantime? Isn't there anything I can do in France? Father, you're doing something, and so are Monsieur and Madame Debray. I want to help too."

The Dominican was moved by the fragile young woman's offer of help.

"Your first duty is to resist despair and to be extremely careful. There are very few of us involved in action, as you can see for yourself. We must wait until people lose faith in Marshal Pétain. They're already wavering, but many men and women, no less patriotic than you or I, are reluctant to break the law. In London, certain officers are hostile to de Gaulle. Many of them are wary of the British. When they fired on our navy at Mers-el-Kebir, the British seriously jeopardized good relations between our two countries. Be patient. As soon as it's possible, I'll contact you to give you news of Laurent and tell you when you can join him. Meanwhile, there is something you can do for me: drop a bundle of letters at Saint-Emilion. There's a slight risk involved when you cross the demarcation line."

"Where must I drop off the bundle?"

"At Monsieur Lefranc's, Château-du-Roy Alley. Give him this copy of the Brittany guide book. He'll understand. Then, forget all about it and go back to Roches-Blanches. Come here, Léa, let's walk a little, I have to talk to you.''

As she followed Adrien down the garden path, her heart was thumping. She had been dreading this conversation.

"I must leave this evening. I'm taking the six o'clock train to Bordeaux. Tomorrow, you will drive Camille to Saint-Emilion and then to Roches-Blanches. From there, go home as quickly as you can via Cadillac, where you will give these three letters from the Canon to Monsieur Fougeron who works at the town hall."

"Is that all?"

"Yes. Oh no! I forgot: Laurent gave me this to give you."

Léa's cheeks turned red as she took the tattered envelope from her uncle.

"Thank you."

"Don't thank me. I'm not doing it for you but for him. Even if I disapprove of his writing to you, I agreed to do it because I could sense that he is suffering."

Léa looked down and said nothing as she fingered the envelope: there was no seal on it. She glanced at Adrien.

"Don't worry, I haven't read it."

Chapter 22

Léa had no trouble crossing the demarcation line at Saint-Pierre- d'Aurillac. The letters were hidden in the baby's little suitcase.

At Saint-Emilion, Camille gave the *Guide to Brittany* to Monsieur Lefranc. Then later at Roches-Blanches, Delpech had been overjoyed to see Camille and her son.

It was the first time that Léa had been back there since that engagement party which had marked the end of a happy era. She had only one desire: to spend as little time there as possible. After splashing some water on her face and hands, she tore herself away from Camille's fussing and carried on her journey. She had never imagined for one moment that she would feel the slightest regret on parting from Camille. And yet she had flung herself into her arms with genuine sorrow before setting off again.

She arrived in Cadillac just before the town hall closed. On the steps, two German soldiers strode past her, laughing. At the counter, a clerk was writing in painstaking copperplate handwriting: it was Fougeron. Léa gave him the letters and he asked her to post a parcel in the free zone. She did not have the chance to utter a word: when the German soldiers returned, Léa quickly slipped the parcel into her bag.

From that day on, she regularly carried letters from one zone to the other. To do so, she had to ask Lieutenant Kramer for a special pass, saying that she had to supervise work on her father's estates in Mounissens and La Laurence near Saint-Pierre-d'Aurillac. Thanks to her visits to the farms, the menus at Montillac improved. What is more, they were able to send food parcels to Albertine and Lisa, who had written that they were nearly starving to death in Paris.

Laure was back from boarding school for the summer holidays, determined not to go back now that she had her school certificate. She was a pretty sixteen-year-old, frivolous and coquettish, and a great admirer of Pétain. She collected portraits of him in any shape or size. She had not forgiven Léa for hurling a photograph of her idol, which she had proudly placed on the piano, onto the floor of the drawing room.

She complained to her father, whose reply had made quite an impression her: "Your mother would have done the same."

Since then, she made a great show of walking out of the room every time Léa tuned into the BBC in London. As for Sabine, nobody really knew what was going on in her mind. When she was off duty at the hospital, she could be heard playing the piano all day and she wandered around looking so happy that Ruth said: "I shouldn't be surprised if the little thing was in love."

With whom? That was the question Léa did not want to answer. She watched her sister closely for a few days and noticed nothing suspicious in her behavior. However, once, she came downstairs earlier than usual to have her breakfast and bumped into Lieutenant Hanke in the darkness of the staircase. He greeted her loudly.

"Good morning, Mademoiselle Léa."

"Good morning," she snapped.

When she entered the kitchen, Lieutenant Kramer was finishing his breakfast. He stood up and bowed as she came in.

"Good morning, Mademoiselle Delmas, you're up early today. No doubt you're going to visit your father's estates in the occupied zone?"

Why were there three bowls on the table, and why was one of them full?

Not long after Laure, Uncle Luc's children, Philippe, Corinne and their little brother Pierrot, arrived at Montillac. The old house rang with shouts and laughter once again. Because of the presence of the Germans, they were a little short of room.

Léa was pleased to see her cousin Pierrot again. At fourteen, he already behaved like a man. As in the old days, he slept in the children's room with her.

At mealtimes, the arguments were so heated that Bernadette Bouchardeau would rush to close the windows.

"Do you want the whole world to hear you? We'll all be arrested!"

The table was clearly divided into three camps. The staunch Pétainists: Bernadette, Philippe, Corinne and Laure, who could not find words strong enough to condemn those cowards who betrayed the Marshal and therefore France; the Gaullists, or at least those who did not accept occupation: Léa and Pierrot; and the don't-knows for various reasons: Pierre Delmas, Sabine and Ruth.

The former advocated the collaboration as Pétain had asked for on the 30th of October 1940. It was the way, they said, to restore order, dignity and religion to their country, which had been corrupted by Jews and Communists; the Gaullists said that the only way France could retrieve her honor and liberty was by following General de Gaulle.

"A traitor!"

"A hero!"

The don't-knows said little: Ruth out of tact, Pierre Delmas out of indifference, and Sabine . . . Sabine? Nobody knew. Often, when the discussion became too heated, she would leave the table.

One day, unable to contain herself any longer, Léa followed her. She found Sabine crumpled up on the iron bench, sobbing her heart out.

"What's the matter?"

She sobbed even harder.

"I'm fed up with hearing about the war, Pétain, Hitler, de Gaulle, rationing, the Russians, the unoccupied zone, the occupied zone, England and . . . and, I've had enough. I want to be left in peace . . . I want to love whoever I

285

choose, I want . . . I wish I was dead. . . ."

Gradually, Léa's sympathy for her sister's unhappiness gave way to irritation and disgust. When crying makes you look as ugly as that, you do it in private, she thought.

"Look at yourself! If there's something the matter, say so. If your lover's making you so miserable, leave him."

"What do you know about my lover? You're the one who rolls in the hay with a farmhand while thinking all the time about another woman's husband. If my lover wanted to, he'd have you all a— It's none of your business, it's nobody's business. I hate you all! I never want to see you again!"

After spitting out these words, she fled. Léa watched her stumbling figure receding in the distance as she ran through the vineyards and disappeared behind Valenton.

Léa had been teasing, she was not really thinking. The violence of Sabine's outburst left her stunned and speechless.

Léa remained motionless, looking out over this familiar landscape while a little sentence kept going round and round in her mind:

"If my lover wanted to, he'd have you all arrested." However, as always, the tranquil beauty of the fields, the woods, the slopes, the vineyards, the villages and the darkness of the moors in the distance soothed her and silenced the awful refrain in her head.

The following day, Sabine announced she was going to stay with a friend in Arcachon. Léa remembered that Laure had advised her to ask Sabine if she had enjoyed the concert. Léa had been astonished. Her younger sister had then muttered vaguely that it wasn't important, that she had forgotten about it. When Léa nagged her, she finally admitted: "I thought I saw her with Lieutenant Kramer. But it couldn't have been him because the man she was with was wearing civilian clothes."

Léa was no longer in any doubt: her sister was having an affair with a German and was probably his mistress.

She told Camille, who had come to spend a few days at Montillac before the grape-picking began. What should she do? Should she tell her father?

"Don't do anything," Camille advised her, "it's too serious.

Only Sabine or Lieutenant Kramer can tell you if it's true."

"But those words . . . "

"She said them in the heat of the moment."

Léa realized that while Sabine was in Arcachon, Lieutenant Kramer was hardly ever at Montillac.

When autumn came, everybody went back to Bordeaux, including Laure, who had found the country "deathly boring." Léa, who had handed the responsibility for the vineyards over to Mathias and his father, was delighted to see them all leave. All the more so because feeding so many people, despite additional ration tickets, was quite a job. She was not too worried at the thought of the oncoming winter, thanks to the jars of vegetables from her kitchen garden and the farmyard full of hens and rabbits . . . not to mention the two pigs. The only thing that she fretted over was the scarcity of money.

Wine sales were just enough to pay those who worked in the vineyards and, even then, not everybody. Fayard had not been paid for six months. Léa had learned, through Camille, that Laurent had stayed in Algiers for only a few weeks. Now he was in London. She was delighted that Camille no longer talked about joining her husband.

Despite her love for Laurent, she continued to sleep with Mathias. Each time their love-making was more violent and more disappointing. Each time she swore would be the last, but after a week, or a fortnight, she would go and meet him in the barn, in the vineyards or in the old house in Saint-Macaire.

On the 21st of October, a German officer was killed in Bordeaux. On the 23rd of October, 1941, fifty French hostages were executed in the public square.

Léa felt increasingly stifled. She was intensely bored and in vain she sought relief in her father's library. No author found favor with her: Balzac, Proust, Mauriac—they all seemed tiresome. At night, she suffered horrible nightmares: either her mother rose sobbing from amidst the ruins, or the man she had killed crushed her in a disgusting embrace. During the daytime, she was subject to sudden fits of tears, which left her feeling exhausted. Montillac was a burden. She wondered whether it was necessary to work so hard to keep it all going, and if there was any point in wanting to hang onto this land now that she was the only one who cared, since neither her father nor her sisters took any interest in it.

Someone else, however, did love it to the point of wanting to own it: and that was Fayard. Since his son's return, he had become his old self again, but there was a bitterness that so far he had managed to conceal, until one day, he said to Léa straight out: "All this is too much for a young girl like you. Poor Monsieur Delmas has gone a bit soft in the head, he'll have to be put away soon. You need a man to run an estate this large. Advise your father to sell. I've got some savings and my wife has just come into an inheritance. Of course, there won't quite be enough, but your father will agree to give it to you as a dowry."

Léa looked at him frostily. She realized that during all the years he had worked on this land, he had only one thing in mind: to own it. The present circumstances were to his advantage. Had Isabelle Delmas been alive, he would never have had the audacity to make such a suggestion. Moreover, he had just made it quite clear that he knew about her intimacy with his son.

"You're silent, I see. You're afraid you'll have to leave the house? But you only have to say the word and it's yours for ever. Marry my son."

She had difficulty containing her anger.

"Does Mathias know about your wonderful plans?"

"More or less. He says we shouldn't think about things like this at the moment."

Léa felt as though part of the weight that oppressed her had lifted.

"You're mistaken, Fayard. It is out of the question for me to sell to you or to anyone else. I was born on this land and I intend to keep it."

"You've no more money and I haven't been paid for six months."

"Our financial affairs have nothing to do with you. As for

288

your salary, you will be paid by the end of this month. Good night, Fayard."

"You are wrong, Mademoiselle Léa, to respond this way," he said in a threatening voice.

"That is enough, I have nothing more to say on the subject. Goodnight. Leave me now!" The last was a command.

Fayard went out grumbling to himself.

The following day, Léa wrote to Albertine asking her to lend her the money owed to Fayard. Her aunt sent it by return mail and Ruth was dispatched to take the money to the head storeman. That was when a violent argument broke out between father and son and at the end of it Mathias made up his mind to volunteer to go and work in Germany. Léa begged him to change his mind, saying that she needed him, that to go to Germany was to betray his country.

"No. You don't need me. You're thinking of Montillac when you say that. Well, I don't give a damn about Montillac," he said. He'd obviously been drinking.

"That's not true! It's just because you've had a lot of wine that you talk this way!" she cried.

"Oh yes, it is. I'm not like my father. I want you with or without the land. But I've finally realized you don't love me. You are just a bitch in heat who needs to screw from time to time . . ."

"Shut up. Don't be so crude."

"If you knew how little I care whether I'm crude or not. Nothing matters to me any more. So whether I'm here or in Germany . . ."

"But if you really want to leave, why not join General de Gaulle?"

"I don't give a damn I tell you. De Gaulle, Hitler, Pétain, they're all the same to me: military. I don't like the military."

"Please Mathias, don't leave me."

"You'd almost think she meant it! Oh look, she's crying! So, you'll miss poor Mathias, will you, my beauty? Poor Mathias and his big cock?"

"Shut up!"

They were in the little pine woods near the kitchen garden

where Mathias had come to tell her of his decision.

With a violent gesture, he pushed her to the ground. She slid on the pine needles. As she fell, her skirt flew up, showing a white expanse of thigh above her black woolen stockings. He fell on top of her.

"All you're interested in, you bitch, is my cock inside of you! Don't cry. I'm going to give it to you one more time!"

"Leave me alone! You stink of wine."

Léa only pretended to struggle. Drunkenness unleashed Mathias's strength. The smell of the pine needles, warmed by the brilliant sunshine that winter afternoon, reminded her of their childhood games when they used to roll around at the foot of the trees. She was so agitated by these memories that she stopped resisting him and offered herself to his probing member. Mathias misunderstood her apparent submission.

"You really are a whore."

He humped away, grunting like a pig, trying to hurt her, to punish her for not loving him. They both groaned in pleasure.

How long did they lie locked in each other's arms, crying? They were visible from the kitchen garden. The cold and the discomfort of their position brought them back to sad reality. Without saying a word, they stood up, tidied their clothes, shook them to get rid of bits of mud, removed pine needles from their hair and after exchanging a look which expressed all their sorrow, both went off in different directions.

That night, Mathias took the train to Bordeaux. He was scheduled to leave for Germany on the 3rd of January 1942.

Chapter 23

The Fayards' dog had followed Léa on her walk. They were both resting at the foot of the Borde Cross which overlooked the plain. It was a bright sunny day and a cold biting wind made Léa's cheeks glow. She was wrapped up in a huge shepherd's cloak as she sat staring into the distance with a faraway look in her eyes. In Saint-Macaire, the bells tolled the end of vespers: it was Sunday. Suddenly, the dog pricked up its ears and got to its feet growling.

"What's the matter, Courtaud?"

The dog started barking and ran towards the path. "It must be a rabbit or a field mouse," thought Léa. She sank back into her daydreams.

A stone came to rest nearby. Léa looked round. In an instant she was on her feet.

"Uncle Adrien!"

"Léa!"

They hugged each other joyfully.

"Whew! I'd forgotten how steep the climb up here was," he said, dropping down on to the grass, breathless. "Unless it's old age," he added, gathering the folds of his robe.

"What are you doing here? When did you arrive?"

"I just got here and I was looking for you. I'm glad to find you away from the house so we can talk."

"Laurent?"

"No, it's nothing to do with Laurent. He's well . . . at least he was last time I saw him."

"Last time you saw him? Is he in France then?"

The priest hesitated and then said, "Yes. He was parachuted on a flight from London."

"Where is he?"

The Dominican did not reply.

"Does Camille know?"

"I don't think so. Listen to me carefully, Léa. This is important. Lives are at stake! I know you've been acting as regular postman between the two zones, and your blue bicycle is a familiar sight to those who still hope. You've proved, on several occasions, that you lack neither courage nor presence of mind. I have a very important mission for you. I can no longer go to the unoccupied zone. I also have a message that must to be delivered in Paris. You'll go in my place"

"Me?"

"Yes, you. Tomorrow, you'll receive a letter from your Aunt Albertine asking you to come to help her look after her sister."

"Is Aunt Lisa ill?"

"No, but you need a valid pretext for leaving. You will take the night train tomorrow. You will travel second class. Here's your ticket. When you reach Paris, phone your aunts from the station. Be careful what you say to them. Then take the metro and go straight to the Rue de l'Université via the Rue du Bac . . . "

"But . . . "

"I know, it's a long way round, but that's the way you'll go. Once you're there, find an explanation for your visit. If Lisa could spend a few days in bed, that would be perfect. In the afternoon, go for a walk in the area, do your shopping at Bon Marché, go window shopping. On the way back, go past the Gallimard Bookshop on the Boulevard Raspail. Do you know it?"

"I think so."

"Look at the window display and then go into the shop. Flick through the books displayed on the table in front of the cash desk. Then look at the books on the shelves and stop in front of the letter P as in Proust. Take down volume two of his *Remembrance of Things Past*. Inside you will find a publisher's leaflet advertising new publications. It will seem a little thicker than those sorts of leaflets usually are. Replace it with this one."

Léa took the pale green leaflet on which were printed titles of books.

"This one's thick too."

"Yes, it contains a message which absolutely must be delivered. Then, you will put the book back in its place on the shelf. Pick up any book published by Gallimard and go to the cash desk and pay for it."

"Is that all?"

"No. You will enter the bookshop on the dot of five o'clock, and leave ten minutes later. You may not, for one reason or another, be able to switch the leaflets. In that case, return the following morning at eleven o'clock. If there is a problem on that occasion, go back to your aunts, where you will receive further instructions. Is this all clear?"

"Yes. What must I do with the other leaflet?"

"Put it inside the book you have just bought. The following day, if all goes well, you will go and see the film *We Kids* by Louis Daquin at the noon performance at the cinema in the Champs-Elysées. Sit in the next to last row, next to the center aisle. Before the end of the film, slip the book under your seat and leave. If that's not possible, do it at the four o'clock showing. Two days later, you are to go to the Grévin Museum at three o'clock. Someone will come up to you by the painting of the Royal Family at the Temple and say: 'We won't go to the woods any more,' and you will reply: 'The laurels have been cut.' He will drop a booklet about the museum and you will pick it up and he'll say: 'Keep it, you may find it interesting.' Thank him and continue your visit, looking at the guide from time to time."

"And then?"

"Then go home to your aunts. The following day, you will take the morning train to Limoges. There will be checks at Vierzon station. When you reach Limoges, leave your suitcase in the check room. Take a trolley outside the station and get off at the Place Denis-Dussoubs. You'll see a cinema, the Olympia. On the corner of the square and the Boulevard

Victor-Hugo, there's a bookshop. Go up to a stout woman in her sixties in a gray smock and ask her if she's got The *Mysteries of Paris* by Eugène Sue. She will reply that she's only got *The Mysteries of London* by Paul Féval. She will hand you a copy and you will slip the the booklet from the Grévin Museum inside. Give the book back to her and say you're sorry but you don't want it. When you leave, take the Rue Adrien-Dubouche on your right and go into the church called Saint-Michel-des-Lions, because of the two stone lions by the door. Walk around the church.'' He paused to smile. ''By the way, there's nothing to stop you praying while you're there. When you leave, take the Rue Clocher and go past the Nouvelles Galeries store and the Hotel Central in the Place Jourdan. Then take the Avenue de la Gare. It will be about five o'clock. There's a train for Bordeaux at about half past five. Your Uncle Luc will be waiting for you at Bordeaux. You will spend the night at his house. He knows nothing. He thinks you have been looking after your aunt. The next day, you will go back to to Montillac where you must try and forget all this. Is that perfectly clear?''

''I think so.''

''Repeat the instructions.''

Léa repeated the sequence of what she had to say and do without a single mistake.

''Everything should go smoothly. Don't fret when you cross the demarcation line. Your papers are in order. If checked, don't panic. If you have any trouble in Paris, call or get a message to François Tavernier . . . ''

''François Tavernier!''

''Yes. You remember him? You met him at Camille and Laurent's engagement party.''

''I can trust him?''

''It depends what for. Some people say he's collaborating with the Germans. Others say he's an intelligence agent. Let them think what they like. I can count on him. So, if you're in any trouble, leave a message for him at the Ritz Hotel. He'll get back to you.''

Léa shivered.

''You're shivering! I'm completely mad to keep you sitting here so long. Get up, you'll catch cold. We can't have you falling ill now."

Back at Montillac, they found the whole family in the drawing room in front of a log fire, drinking hot chocolate and eating an enormous brioche.

"Whose birthday is it?" exclaimed Adrien as he came into the room.

"It's thanks to Sabine," said Bernadette Bouchardeau, "one of her patients gave her these treats to thank her."

As she sipped her chocolate, Léa could not help darting worried glances in her sister's direction. Should she tell her uncle of her suspicions?

Everything went according to plan. They took the train to Bordeaux together and, without looking back, Léa got on to the Paris train alone.

The Montpleynet sisters were so overjoyed to see their niece that they were not surprised at her sudden arrival. Their happiness knew no bounds when Léa took a ham, a dozen eggs and a kilo of butter out of her case. Lisa, the greedy one, had tears in her eyes, even the dignified Albertine seemed moved and as for Estelle she kissed Léa on both cheeks and called her "our angel girl," before carrying the food to the kitchen.

The three women had a lunch consisting of a thin soup, a few miserable potatoes and a little ham.

"If it weren't for you, the menu would have been even more pathetic!" sighed Lisa with her mouth full, pointing to the soup tureen.

"We shouldn't complain, sister, there are those who are worse off than we are. Thanks to the little money we have left, we can occasionally afford to buy meat or poultry on the black market."

"True, but we never eat cakes any more."

Her childlike remark made Léa and Albertine laugh.

After lunch, Léa announced that she was going out for a walk.

When she came out of the metro, Léa paid little attention to what was going on around her. It was only when she reached the Boulevard Saint-Germain that she became aware of the quietness. There were no cars, only a few bicycles and cycle-taxis. Pedestrians were few. A gleaming Mercedes, with two German officers embracing two women with bleached blond hair and fur coats, drove slowly past. Léa stared at the car, and pulled her coat, which was not warm enough, tighter round her. She wished she had worn a pair of Claude's trousers that Camille had given her. She had thought that they were not smart enough for Paris.

The few pedestrians hurried past, their faces set and their heads down to protect themselves from the gusts of icy wind.

She walked quickly up the Boulevard Raspail. When she reached the Hotel Lutetia, she slowed down. German flags were flapping all along the façade. Even thought it was no novelty for her—Bordeaux also showed signs of occupation—her stomach turned. In the Rue de Babylone, the wind nearly blew her over.

It was warm inside Bon Marché. Most of the counters were bare. "Do some shopping," Adrien had said, giving her some money. Léa was only too pleased to. But what was she to buy? Practically everything was rationed. At the stationery counter, she bought some coloring pencils and a tin of paints and at the perfume counter she bought some Chanel toilet water. She wandered through the shop for an hour; then she went up to the tea room and drank a hot beverage that was supposed to be tea. At last, half past four came. If she walked slowly, she would be at the Gallimard Bookshop at five.

It seemed to Léa that everyone in the bookshop was staring at her. She would never have believed it could be so difficult to take a book down from the shelf and look natural. And that young assistant could not take his hungry black adolescent eyes off her! The titles swam before her eyes.

"So, you're looking for a good book?"

Before she swung round, Léa replaced volume two of *Remembrance of Things Past.*

"It's you!"

"Yes, it's me! Wasn't it here that we met for the first time?"

"Raphaël, that seems such a long time ago," she said holding out her hand.

"Hello, lovely lady from Bordeaux. How strange! Every time we meet I feel the same pang, the same nostalgia. Alas, sweet friend, that I am not otherwise . . . I would have loved you so," said Raphaël covering her hand with little kisses.

"Will you ever change?" she asked, withdrawing her hand.

"Why should I change? I've already told you, I like myself the way I am: a Jew and a homosexual."

"Why don't you use a loudspeaker?" she retorted with embarrassment."

"Oh, I'm among friends here. Everybody knows me. Aren't I one of their authors? Little known, but esteemed! That charming young man with dark hair at the cash desk is a mine of information, he's read everything, even my books. At sixteen! Incredible, isn't it? Remind me what your name is." This last directed to the young assistant.

"Jean-Jacques, monsieur."

"Jean-Jacques, that's it. Well, young Jean-Jacques, have you located that book I'm looking for?"

"Not yet, monsieur, but it'll only be a matter of days until I do."

"As soon as you have it, bring it to my hotel in the Rue de Saints-Pères, and I'll give you a taste of a very old and very rare port," he said tweaking the boy's cheek. The latter looked insulted and amused. Turning to Léa, Raphaël asked, "Did you look at his eyes? What fire! Forgive me, sweetheart, I'm neglecting you. What are you doing in Paris? Last time I saw you, you were standing in front of a church in Bordeaux. By the way, how are the Dominicans in that good city?"

Léa had difficulty in repressing a shudder and replied more sharply than she intended: "Very well."

"I'm glad to hear it. But you haven't told me what you're doing here."

"One of my aunts is ill and the other is tired: I'm here to help them a little."

"What a good little girl. . . . Naturally, this evening you'll have dinner with me."

"It's not . . . "

"Rubbish! I'll come and pick you up at half past six. One eats early in Paris these days. Tell me where you're staying."

"Sixty-five Rue de l'Universite. But I assure you . . . "

"Not another word. I've found you again, I'm keeping you. Dress up for this evening I'm taking you out into the big wide world. First, we'll have dinner at Tour d'Argent. Then we'll go to a sophisticated reception where you will be the star attraction."

"How can I get rid of him?" wondered Léa. Now, it was too late to switch the leaflets.

"Please, for friendship's sake, do accept."

"Very well, come and pick me up later."

"Thank you. You have no idea how happy you make me."

Was he a spy? Léa kept wondering to herself as she hurried back to her aunts. No, it was impossible! Didn't he try to help me in Bordeaux? As long as there was no one in the bookshop tomorrow. What shall I wear this evening? She felt guilty worrying about her appearance when she had not even managed to carry out her simple mission. But she could not help mentally running through the clothes she had brought with her. She had nothing suitable to wear to the Tour d'Argent.

"Really Léa, you're not thinking of having dinner with a gentleman whom we don't even know!"

"But Aunt Albertine, you will meet him because he's coming to escort me."

"Maybe, but it's not proper."

"Please, Aunt! It's the first time in ages I've had a chance to enjoy myself in Paris."

Albertine looked lovingly at her favorite niece. It was true that the poor child had not had a particularly happy time of it. She suffered as they all did but she was so young. She needed to have some fun.

"Have you got an elegant dress to wear?"

"Unfortunately, I haven't."

"I'll talk to Lisa and Estelle and see if we can find something for you. Thank goodness I didn't sell my fox fur."

Lisa and Albertine unpacked old ball gowns from their trunks. The newest of them was from the 1920s.

"What about this, what is it?" asked Léa, unfolding a black tulle skirt with lace insets.

"This one belonged to mother."

"It's very pretty," she said slipping it on over her skirt. "Once it's been ironed it'll make a perfect skirt. And this top?"

"You can't possibly wear that, darling, it's completely out of date!"

"Estelle, would you help me? We'll soon see whether it's out of date or not."

That was how Léa caused a sensation when she walked into the Tour d'Argent. She wore a high black lace collar which set off her long neck. Her blouse was from another era, with sleeves that billowed at the wrists, while the folds of her long skirt surrounded her chair. She wore her hair up, with a jet comb for decoration, a style that gave her a very sophisticated look. Elegant women wearing heavy make-up turned to stare enviously at this young girl; there was just a hint of powder on her pale face, and her clear eyes were emphasized by a touch of mascara on her eyelashes. The men also stared at her with somewhat different feelings. Those who knew Raphaël Mahl and his dubious reputation were astonished that such a distinguished young lady should appear in his company.

Léa felt a great sense of pride and satisfaction at the attention. She congratulated herself on not having a fashionable dress and thus distinguishing herself from these other women whom she instinctively felt to be of a different species. Raphaël was of the same opinion, and he complimented her with his usual exuberance.

"You're the most beautiful of them all. Look how everybody's staring at you, especially the women. It's so funny. Where on earth did you dig up that outfit? The other women look like tarts beside you. Thank you for being so beautiful. Waiter, champagne. A good vintage."

"Very good, monsieur."

"We must celebrate our reunion in fitting style. I found your dear aunts absolutely charming. I thought one of them was ill?"

"She's better," said Léa hastily.

"I'm delighted to hear that. Ah! Here's the champagne. Because of the war, there's no light, so you can't admire Notre-Dame, the Seine and the Ile Saint-Louis; but I promise you the food will compensate for the lack of view. This is one of the oldest restaurants in Paris and one of the most famous."

Léa looked at her companion. He had changed since their last meeting: he had grown fat, his dinner jacket was straining at the seams in places. He had the muddy complexion of someone who goes to bed late too often; he seemed worried and was chain smoking.

"Give me one."

"I didn't know you smoked," he said, offering her the open packet.

Léa took a cigarette with a golden filter. The waiter leaned over to give her a light.

"Thank you," she said, blowing out the smoke.

"Do you like it?"

"Where do they come from? It tastes funny."

"They're Turkish. The messenger boy at the Crillon gets cartons of them for me. I can get you some if you're interested."

"Thank you, but I'm sure they're beyond my means."

"Who's talking about money, my lovely? You will pay me for them later."

"No thank you. I'd rather have a good pair of shoes."

"If that's what you want, I can get them for you too. Tell me what you want; boots, shoes, sandals? I can supply anything. Do you want a sable coat, silk stockings, cashmere sweaters, a camel-hair coat? I can get all of those for you."

"Are you a black-marketeer?"

"That, my beauty, is my secret. On the whole, my clients are not particularly interested in knowing where things come from. They're content just to pay and . . . "

The wine steward served their champagne.

"Let's drink to your beauty and my prosperity."

Léa bowed her head but did not reply. She emptied her glass in two gulps.

"My dear friend, you should savor this wine, it's not lemonade. What would you like to eat? They have no scarcities here."

"I would like shellfish, lots of shellfish, and that famous duck dish they talk so much about."

"What an excellent choice, I'll have the same."

Shortly afterwards, a large platter of oysters, sea urchins, mussels and clams arrived. Then they ate the famous duck dish, followed by a Brie that was beautifully ripe, and a huge portion of chocolate cake. When she had swallowed the last mouthful, Léa leaned back in her chair, to the amusement of the people on the neighboring tables.

"Mmmm . . . that's the first time in months that I've had enough to eat."

"I should hope so. You ate enough for four."

"Are you criticizing me?"

"No, it's a pleasure to watch you eat. You obviously enjoy it. It's delightful."

"Do you think so?" she asked with a frown. "I'm ashamed. Give me a cigarette and tell me who all these people are, apart from the Germans of course."

"These people are the same as before the war. See and be seen has always been the rule for the Parisian set. Everyone who's anyone is here, my dear. Or they go to Maxim's or Fouquet's or Carrère or Le Doyen—it's the thing to do."

"I don't believe you."

"Look at those two women over there, between that distinguished-looking German officer and that handsome man with bluish hair."

"He looks like Sacha Guitry."

"He *is* Sacha Guitry. On his right is the famous pianist Lucienne Delforge. She's the one who said: 'If I were asked to define collaboration, I would say that it's Mozart in Paris.'"

"I don't see the connection."

"Because you don't have a sense of humor, darling. The other lady is Germaine Lubin, the great Wagner specialist. See that German officer? He's Lieutenant Rademacher, who heads the censorship department. Unless he passes it, no play, no show can be put on in Paris. Over there, at the table by the window you have Albert Bonnard, Bernard Grasset and Marcel and Elise Jouhandeau. There's Arletty over there: the most beautiful woman here apart from you . . . "

A man wearing a cloak lined with red satin draped casually over his dinner jacket came over to their table. He was still young-looking with sharp features and firm nervous hands. He was followed by a very handsome young man also wearing a dinner jacket.

"Raphaël, what are you doing here! I'm glad to see that business is still so profitable!"

"Things are better, much better. I seem to be enjoying a special good spell at the moment. Léa, let me introduce a dear friend of mine: Monsieur Jean Cocteau."

"Jean Cocteau . . . How do you do, monsieur. I enjoyed your last play very much indeed."

"Thank you, mademoiselle. I didn't know that my friend Raphaël knew anybody as charming as yourself."

"Jean, this is Mademoiselle Delmas who comes from Bordeaux."

"Bordeaux! Such a delightful city! Nowhere else does boredom have that aristocratic elegance. Even the little toughs in the Quinconces area are in a class of their own. Can I give you a lift somewhere? A friend has been kind enough to lend me his car and chauffeur."

"It'll be a squeeze."

"Oh! I'm sorry old fellow. I wasn't thinking. This young lady's presence is so distracting. Mademoiselle . . . I'm sorry, I don't remember you name."

"Delmas."

"Mademoiselle Delmas, allow me to introduce the most remarkable dancer in Paris, indeed in Europe: Serge Lifar."

The young man, looking slim and elegant in his midnight-blue dinner jacket, gave a curt bow.

"Where are you going?" asked the poet.

"To my friend Otto's place."

"What a coincidence, we're going there too. Come, or we'll be the last to leave."

The door of a sumptuous dark limousine was held open by a German chauffeur. Léa drew back.

"Come come, dear friend! There's no danger. You're in safe hands and the place we're going to is one of the most famous in Paris. I've known celebrities who will stoop to anything to get themselves invited there."

Léa sat between Jean Cocteau and Raphaël. The dancer, still sulking, sat next to the chauffeur.

They drove along the deserted embankments in silence. The night was clear and cold, and the dark mass of Notre-Dame seemed to be watching over the city. Seeing it reminded Léa of when she had arrived in Paris with her father. It seemed such a long time ago. . . .

They turned into the Rue des Saints-Pères and took the Rue de Lille. A few seconds later, the car turned into a huge entrance guarded by German soldiers and drew up by the main steps of a mansion.

Jean Cocteau gallantly helped Léa out of the car.

"Where are we?" she asked.

"In the mansion that Bonaparte gave to Josephine."

They reached the top of the steps. There was a swish as the curtains over the glass doors parted. They were engulfed by a stream of light, warmth and perfume. Liveried servants relieved them of their coats. Léa reluctantly parted with her fox-fur cape. She was dazzled by all the glitter, and looked around with childlike delight. Her pleasure was slightly marred by a feeling of unease which she tried in vain to ignore.

"Where are we?" she asked again.

"You don't know? This is the German Embassy."

Léa felt as though she'd been punched in the stomach. She drew back. Raphaël gripped her arm and steered her towards the brilliantly lit reception rooms.

"I want to leave!"

"You can't do this to me." he hissed. "Anyhow, it's too late. Here's the ambassador."

He was a handsome man, still young, wearing a dinner

jacket which hid his slight paunch. He hailed Jean Cocteau.

"My dear friend, it is always a pleasure to entertain a famous poet."

"Your excellency . . ."

"Introduce your friends to me."

"Your Excellency, this is Serge Lifar, of whom you have already heard."

"Of course. I adore the way you dance, monsieur."

"Your Excellency."

"The journalist and writer Raphaël Mahl."

"I know this gentleman," said the ambassador walking past him without holding out his hand.

Raphaël blushed slightly and bowed stiffly.

"Who is this ravishing young lady—the future leading lady in one of your masterpieces?"

"Allow me to introduce Mademoiselle Léa Delmas. Léa, this is His Excellency Monsieur Otto Abetz, the German ambassador to Paris."

Léa did not dare refuse the hand he proffered. The ambassador took her informally by the arm and said, in perfect French: "Come with me, mademoiselle. I should like you to meet my wife. She is French too, and I'm sure you two will get along very well."

Madame Abetz greeted Léa with great charm. "My dear, your dress is most original. You must give me the address of your couturier."

Then, without waiting for a reply, she went off to welcome some new guests. Léa was left alone in the middle of the room, while elegantly perfumed people laughed, chatted and milled around her. Nearly everybody stole a glance at this slim young girl whose strange billowing black dress emphasized her pallor. Léa felt herself stiffen under their gaze. She was thankful that the length of her dress concealed the ugly old black shoes she was wearing that had once belonged to Lisa. She did not even attempt to hide her curiosity as she watched the crowd. Everyone appeared to be lighthearted, relaxed, glad to be there. The luxurious dresses of the women and their glittering jewels contrasted brightly with the men's black suits.

"It's extraordinary, isn't it?" Raphaël murmured in her ear.

"What's extraordinary?"

"All those people paying court to the enemy."

"What about you. What are you doing?"

"Oh me! I'm just a worm and, anyway, I like winners."

"They might not be the winners forever."

"Not so loud, sweetheart," he said looking all around with a worried frown. "Do you think," he went on, murmuring in her ear, "that the people here have any doubt that the Reich will achieve total victory?"

"I hear that in Russia, the German troops are losing more and more men."

"Shhh! You'll get us both arrested. That's something you ought not to know and you certainly shouldn't discuss it. A word of warning: listen to French radio rather than the BBC. It's less dangerous."

They stopped by the buffet table. Léa helped herself to three *petit-fours* and ate them one after the other.

"I feel as though I'm back in the days when I used to go to cocktail parties on the Left Bank. I could put away huge quantities of smoked salmon and caviar canapes. They would keep me going for two days. Here, have a drink; otherwise you'll choke."

The strains of a waltz reached their ears. It was coming from another room.

"The ball has begun. What a pity I'm such an appalling dancer. I should have loved to sweep you up in my arms to the sound of a Viennese waltz. Come have a look round the house. I'll show you Josephine's boudoir."

The little room was so crowded that they gave up the idea of trying to get in. They sat down in a drawing room that was somewhat secluded. On the table was an exquisite Chinese vase that had been made into a lampstand. The lampshade gave off a soft dusky pink light that made Léa's hair and complexion glow. A rather stout man of average height walked past them.

"Well, well, well, it's my dear editor in person."

"You do get around, don't you? Is this young beauty with you? Introduce me."

"Léa, this is Monsieur Gaston Gallimard, the great publisher and great lover of women. This is Mademoiselle Delmas."

"Don't believe a word he says, mademoiselle," he said as he sat down beside her.

"Gaston, would you come over here for a second? The ambassador wishes to have a word with you."

"Excuse me, mademoiselle, don't run away, I'll be back. Coming, Marie."

"Isn't that Marie Bell?"

"Yes, that's her. Charming woman. It's a very literary evening tonight. As well as our friend Cocteau, there's Georges Duhamel, Jean Giraudoux, Robert Brasillach, the handsome Drieu, La Rochelle, Pierre Benoît deep in conversation with his friend Arno Breker . . . "

"The sculptor?"

"Yes, he's here to prepare for his big exhibition in May. Look there are two of his less gifted colleagues, Belmondo and Despieux, who've just gone over to join him. Over there are Jean Luchaire and Edwige Feuillère . . . "

"That's enough! Stop name-dropping; it's depressing. . . . "

"Would you care for the next dance, my dear?"

Léa looked up.

"François . . . "

She shouted his name.

"Francois . . . "

She leaped up.

"Léa . . . "

They stood staring at each other in disbelief, not daring to touch.

"It's a strange place for us to meet again," murmured François. "How beautiful you are! Let's dance."

It was a long time since Léa had had such a pleasant dream: waltzing slowly in the arms of a man she desired and who obviously desired her too. It was a delightful feeling to let herself be carried away! The important thing was not to wake up, not to open her eyes. She clung to François. She forgot where she was, the people all around them, Germans, French, she forgot the mission which had brought her to

Paris and she even forgot Laurent. All she wanted was to be a woman in the arms of a man who wanted her.

"My dear friend, I can't say I blame you for dancing on even though the music has stopped!" said Otto Abetz, placing his hand on François Tavernier's shoulder.

François stared at him blankly and, without replying, led Léa away.

"Ah! Only the French can love like that," muttered the ambassador gazing enviously after the couple.

In the entrance hall, Raphaël came up to Léa.

"Are you leaving?"

"Yes," answered François, "Mademoiselle Delmas is weary, I'll see her home."

"But . . . "

"Goodnight, monsieur."

"Goodnight, Raphaël."

François held open the door of a Bugatti that was parked in the courtyard.

There was not a soul in the blacked-out streets of Paris. The Place de la Concorde looked like a film set, and the trees on the Champs-Elysées stood tall with their bare branches.

"Where are we going?"

"I don't know," he said pulling up and stopping the car.

He lit his cigarette lighter and moved the flame backwards and forwards across Léa's face. The tension was unbearable. The flame died down and they fell into each other's arms. Their lips soon tasted of salt and blood which only goaded their desire.

If it had not been for the appearance of a German patrol, who asked François for his papers but then apologized and went away, they would probably have made love in the car.

"Are you staying at your aunts'?"

"Yes."

"At the moment, I'm staying very near there, at the Hôtel du Pont-Royal. Shall we go there?"

"Yes."

*   *   *

"Léa, your aunts will be out of their minds with worry, it's five o'clock in the morning."

"I'm so comfortable, I don't want to move."

"You must, my darling."

"Yes, I suppose I must."

Léa drowsily put her clothes on.

"This is madness," he thought.

"I'm ready."

"Let's hope your aunts aren't waiting for you on the doorstep. You'll have some difficulty explaining the bags under your eyes and the state of your hair."

"True, I look as though I've just been dragged out of bed," she said looking at herself in the mirror.

Everyone was sound asleep at the Rue de l'Université. Léa and François were unable to part on the landing.

"I've thought of you so often, my love, these last few months. You must tell me all that's happened to you."

"I'm sleepy."

"Go and get some sleep, sweetheart. I'll pick you up for dinner tomorrow."

After a last kiss, Léa closed the front door. She found her way to her bedroom like a sleepwalker. She fumbled impatiently with the hooks on the lace collar. She pulled her thick nightdress from under the covers. There was a hot water-bottle inside. As the room was cold, and she was shivering, she slipped the nightdress on.

The sheets were lovely and warm, thanks to Aunt Lisa's hot water bottles. Léa was asleep before her head touched the pillow.

"Oh, no! Switch off the light, close the curtains," groaned Léa burrowing under the blankets.

"But, darling, yesterday you said you had to go on an errand this morning. So I thought it was time to wake you."

An errand? What errand? Oh, damn, the leaflet!

She threw off the covers and jumped out of bed.

"What time is it?"

"About half past ten, I think."

"Half past ten . . . Oh my God, I'm going to be late."
She rushed into the bathroom and washed. Then she put
on a pair of thick stockings, a woollen petticoat, a skirt and
a bulky sweater.

"You're not going out without any breakfast?"

"I haven't got time. Where's my bag?"

"There, on the armchair. What a mess!"

"I'll staighten up later."

The leaflet, where was the leaflet? There it was . . . what
a fright she'd given herself!

"At least have a cup of tea."

Léa gulped down a mouthful to please her aunt.

"Wrap up well, it's very cold this morning," said Albertine coming into the room while Léa was putting on her coat
and a thick red woollen scarf.

She fiddled with her black beret as she clattered down the
stairs.

She stopped running a few yards before the bookshop.
It was two minutes to eleven. She was still panting when
she pushed open the door.

The shop was empty except for three sales clerks. One
of them went out and the other went downstairs. There was
just the dark-haired young man with the intelligent and enquiring eyes, who was writing out cards. He looked up.

"Can I help you?"

"No thank you, I'm just looking."

She paused, as she had done the day before, by the shelf
of authors beginning with the letter P.

On entering the shop, she had felt nervous and worried,
but when the moment to take down the volume two of
Remembrance of Things Past came she was perfectly calm
and relaxed. She took the book and began to flick through
it. The leaflet was there. She automatically checked that it
was thicker than normal and deftly slipped it into her coat
pocket. Still holding the book, she turned round and took
a few steps while pretending to read it. The young man was
still engrossed in his cards. Without hurrying, she inserted
Uncle Adrien's leaflet and put the book back on the shelf
in the most natural way.

There were still no customers in the bookshop.

Léa picked up a book bearing the famous Gallimard logo from the table and read the first few lines.

"*Carrying the exercise books of his forty-two pupils in his leather briefcase, Monsieur Fosserand imagined that he was the poet Virgil emerging from Hell through the main exit of Clichy metro station. He marvelled naïvely as he surfaced in this strange land where he could see there was much to be learned.*"

She looked up and met the young man's eyes.

"It's an excellent book, I recommend it," he said, walking over to her.

"All right, I'll buy it on your recommendation. I haven't read anything by this author."

"That's a mistake. You should read everything by Marcel Aymé."

"Thank you, I'll remember that if I like this one."

Léa paid for the book and left the bookshop.

"Goodbye, mademoiselle. See you soon."

There were still no other customers. It was almost eleven fifteen.

Despite the spring sunshine, it was very cold. As she walked past the Hotel du Pont-Royal, Léa recalled the events of the previous evening. She blushed.

"I must think," she kept saying over and over to herself as she opened her bedroom door.

A huge basket of white flowers took up the whole top of the chest of drawers. Léa smiled, removed her shoes, stretched out on the bed, drew the eiderdown over her and closed her eyes. She opened them again and looked at the envelope resting against the basket.

It was half past three when she came out of the metro at the top of the Champs-Elysées. She tried hard not to look at the heavy ads around the central island from which a policeman was directing the thin stream of traffic.

It was a fine afternoon. Despite the cold, a lot of people

were strolling along the avenue. The lines outside the cinemas were growing. *We Kids* was showing at the Normandie. Léa joined the line. The documentary on youth camps was interminable. As for the news, it was all about the "exploits of the glorious soldiers of the Third Reich," crowds greeting Pétain, the joyful departure of young voluntary workers, an elegant wedding in Vichy, an extract from a play by Montherlant, Maurice Chevalier singing for the prisoners in Germany and the latest spring fashions. Léa thought the film would never end. When it was finally over, she pretended to drop her glove and slipped the book under the seat. She got up and left without looking back.

She felt as though everyone in the Champs.-Elysées was staring at her. Any second, she was expecting to hear: "Follow me, mademoiselle."

Seated at the rear of the theatre, she was sure she had recognized the dark-haired young man from the bookshop. She fought back the impulse to run.

The train was packed. Léa was wedged between a German soldier and a fat girl wearing an overpowering perfume. She changed trains at Concorde, and so did the fat girl.

It was half past six when she reached her aunts' apartment. The first thing she heard was Lisa's guffaw, followed by Albertine's more ladylike laugh. Who on earth could be amusing the Montpleynet sisters? She went into the bedroom. It was the only room in the house that was more or less decently heated by a stove which now took the place of central heating. François Tavernier was sitting in an easy chair rubbing his hands together and warming them over the stove. He stood up at Léa's entrance.

"Léa!" cried Lisa. "Why didn't you tell us you'd met Monsieur Tavernier? . . ."

". . . and that you were having dinner with him?" added Albertine.

"I didn't have time to tell you this morning."

"Did you thank Monsieur Tavernier for his lovely flowers?"

"Don't mention it, mademoiselle."

"Excuse me, I'll just go and get changed."

"Don't. You look fine as you are. We're going somewhere very simple. Simple but good."

"I'll just brush my hair, then I'm all yours."

Léa came back a quarter of an hour later. She had changed and wore a hint of eye make-up.

"Don't bring her home too late, dear monsieur. These days we're so afraid."

"Have a good evening, pet, and enjoy your food," said Lisa with greed in her voice.

When they reached the second floor of an ordinary block of flats, in the Rue St. Jacques, François rang the doorbell using a discreet code. There was no indication that it was a restaurant. The door opened a fraction and then it was flung wide open.

"Monsieur François!"

"Hello Marcel. Still in good shape?"

"Mustn't complain. You're lucky. I've just received a side of beef. I also have quail."

"Whatever you think's best. It will be delicious, as always."

"What do you say to a Chablis for aperitif?"

"Fine. Give us a quiet corner."

"Well, the only place I can think of is the bedroom," he said not daring to look at Léa.

"Fine. Put us in the bedroom."

The place was not without charm. The Andrieus had converted their four-roomed apartment into a clandestine restaurant. Their clientele of regulars jealously kept the address to themselves.

Their immediate neighbors, who were obviously in on the secret, were generously rewarded for their discretion.

Twelve guests could be served comfortably in the family dining room. There was an eighteenth-century sideboard, a serving table with a red gingham tablecloth and the walls were covered with faded flowery wallpaper. There were some awful paintings of rustic scenes and the room was lit by a feeble glow from a hanging light. The plates were of heavy white china and the glasses were large. None of the cutlery matched and the whole effect was warm and homey.

This quaint provincial tone was set by Madame Andrieu, a stout, jolly woman who was in her element in the kitchen. She was as much loved for her generosity as for her culinary skills. She was from Saint-Cirq-Lapopie in the Lot region and she was warm and generous as people from that area are reputed to be. She came from a large family who were always sending her truffles, *foie gras,* all sorts of fowl, abundant supplies of sausage, a marvelous Cahors wine, walnut oil, the most wonderful fruit, the freshest vegetables, delicious little goat's-milk cheeses and even a little tobacco grown in secret.

Of course, they had had to bribe a few people to guarantee regular deliveries. But "only Frenchmen" repeated Monsieur Andrieu proudly, when asked by what miracle he had managed to obtain strawberries when there weren't any to be had even at Maxim's or any other of the top restaurants.

You could be sure you would never see a German uniform at the Andrieus's. Most of their clients were well-to-do retired people, academics, writers, wealthy merchants and a few well-known artists. Sometimes there was the odd rather more disturbing character or a vulgar sort of woman, but Madame Andrieu's outspokenness soon discouraged them.

Before the war, the couple had run a little restaurant near Montparnasse, specializing in dishes from the Quercy region, and François had been a regular customer. They immediately warmed to this generous, unpretentious client and soon became the best of friends. At the end of the previous year, a bomb had brought their prosperity to a sudden end. Overnight, they lost everything they had.

It was Tavernier who found them the apartment in the Rue Saint-Jacques. They furnished it cheaply from the flea-market. Like most French people, they had heaved a sigh of relief when the armistice was announced. Their only son would now come home. Madame Andrieu very soon realized how useful her family in the south could be. Her uncles and cousins became their suppliers again, a role they played before the war. François intervened a couple of times on their behalf and the clandestine restaurant had been running successfully for a year.

313

They were so popular that they had to set up tables everywhere: six in the living-room, three in the passage and even one in the Andrieus's bedroom. But that table was specially reserved for close friends.

The table in the bedroom was lit with candles in a rather pretty silver candelabrum. A matching candelabrum stood on the chest of drawers, which was used as a serving table. The bed was hidden—out of modesty, no doubt—behind a Chinese screen which seemed out of place in these simple surroundings.

Before they sat down, François had to go and kiss the owners' grandson, who was his godson. It was a ritual he could not get out of without hurting these good people's feelings. Léa burst out laughing when she saw him with a baby in his arms.

"It doesn't suit you at all. I didn't know you liked children."

He smiled at her while the baby drooled all over his shirt.

"I love them. Don't you?"

"Not at all. I find them noisy and irritating."

"One day, perhaps, you'll change your mind."

"I don't think so," she said sharply.

He handed the child back to his mother.

"Congratulations, Jeannette. My godson is becoming more and more handsome."

The woman blushed with pleasure.

"My husband will come to take your order."

The flickering flame from the candle seemed to bring the dragons on the screen to life and give Léa's features a softness which was belied by the look in her eyes. François studied her face in silence.

"Stop staring at me like that."

"I've often tried to conjure up your face these last few months."

The son of the house came in at that moment, bottle in hand.

"Here I am Monsieur François. I'm sorry to keep you waiting, but as usual, every table is full this evening."

"How are you René?"

"I'm fine, Monsieur François. Would you like some *foie gras,* country ham and stuffed gooseneck to start with?"

"Very good."

"For the next course, Mama's making you a chicken fricassée with girolle mushrooms and potatoes sautéed in goose fat; followed by walnut oil salad and, for dessert, chocolate mousse."

"Oh, yes!" exclaimed Léa.

"Perfect. Give us a bottle of Cahors as well."

"Very well, Monsieur François. Taste this Chablis," he said offering him a glass.

"Mmm . . . not bad at all!"

"It's not, eh?"

René poured some wine for Léa, filled up François's glass and left the room.

They drank for a moment in silence.

"Tell me what you've been up to, but, first, tell me how Madame d'Argilat is."

"She's fine. She had a little boy and named him Charles."

"And her husband?"

"Laurent? He escaped twice, the second time successfully. He's now in London with General de Gaulle."

Léa said that with a mixture of pride and defiance, but instantly regretted it. François Tavernier could read her face like a book.

He drank two glasses of wine, one after the other. He had to speak to her, but what could he say? He could not bear his own fear and her wariness. How could he make her understand?

"Léa . . ."

She slowly looked up.

"Yes?"

"Laurent has certainly done the right thing in going to join de Gaulle. It is very brave of him. But you ought not to tell anyone. Not even me."

"Especially you, you mean."

He smiled wearily.

"No, you can tell me everything. I won't betray you. However, I had a shock yesterday when I saw you come

315

in with that toad, Raphaël Mahl."

"He's an old friend. Why do you say he's a toad? After all, he moves in the same circles as you."

"True, you've got a point. But you're wrong about him. He's a toad for several reasons: one of them is that he has no compunction about denouncing his friends to the Gestapo for money."

"I don't believe you."

"If you see him again, which I advise you not to, ask him. He's a total pervert as well as being profoundly masochistic, I'm sure he'll give you an answer, and, as he's a very precise bastard, all the details."

"It's not possible. That would be too base."

"Anything's possible with him. Did he not take in a Jewish child . . ."

"You see, he's not so bad."

". . . and take him back to the orphanage after a few months when he found him dull. He fleeced several people who gave him their savings to be able to cross to the unoccupied zone. He smuggles gold, currency and heroin. The French police have arrested him twice. They've had to let him go both times."

"How do you explain the fact that he's invited to all the literary salons or that his books are published?"

"He isn't invited anywhere. The people you met yesterday evening use him, that's all. Otherwise only black market dealers take an interest in him. As for his books, they were published before the war. Believe me, keep away from him. He taints anyone who comes near him."

"But, in Bordeaux, he warned me that my uncle . . ."

Léa stopped in mid-sentence and took a sip of wine while she regained her composure.

"I know what your Uncle Adrien does, but you shouldn't know anything about it."

"What do you know about my Uncle?"

"Nothing. Forget it. So what did your friend Raphaël do that was so admirable?"

"In Bordeaux, he gave his place on the *Massilia* to Sarah Mulstein's father."

"That's true, I admit. She told me about it. I was surprised. Sarah's like you, she has a soft spot for him. She says he's not all bad."

"Is Sarah still in Paris?"

"Yes. She won't leave. She's tired of running away."

"But she's mad."

"I know, I tell her every time I see her. But something snapped inside her after her father's death."

"I didn't know he was dead."

"In Algiers. The Vichy police imprisoned him."

"Why?"

"Because he was a Jew and a foreigner. He couldn't take being imprisoned. He was a very tired old man who only lived for music. One morning, they found him dead in his cell. He'd hanged himself."

"Were you very fond of him?"

"Yes. He was remarkable. Something of the best of humanity died with him."

Jeannette came in carrying two plates piled high with food.

"I hope you enjoy the meal!"

Léa stared at her plate. She felt slightly sick and brushed her hand across her forehead.

"I know how you feel, Léa. For the time being, I can't tell you anything. You would have to love me blindly to trust me. But I'm perfectly aware that that's asking a lot of you. It's too soon. Eat. These days, good cuisine has become a rare pleasure."

"Not for you, it seems."

"Do you want to continue with the Chablis, or would you prefer Cahors?"

"Cahors."

He stood up, took a glass from the serving table and poured her some red wine.

At first, Léa picked at her food, but gradually the *foie gras* and the velvety wine revived her healthy appetite.

By the time she had carefully wiped her plate with a piece of bread, she was feeling more amenable.

"You're like a little animal, Léa. All you need is food and love to make you forget the world."

"Don't think it's that simple," she said with her mouth full.

Marthe Andrieu came in wiping her hands on her white apron, followed by her son who was carrying a dish with a silver lid. She proudly removed the lid.

"Just smell this, Monsieur François. That smell is enough to knock me over, it brings back the whole region to me. I can see my poor mother in front of the enormous stove in the farmhouse kitchen tossing the mushrooms, crepes, girolles and horns of plenty. Nobody knew how to cook mushrooms like my mother."

"Except you, my dear Marthe!"

"Oh! No, Monsieur François, my mother's were ten times more delicious."

He smiled and tasted the dish that had been prepared with such love and skill.

"Madame, I've never eaten anything as good as this," said Léa wiping her chin.

The cook smiled with satisfaction and said with a knowing wink at François: "It's a good sign when a pretty girl enjoys good food. . . . I'll leave you to it, I've got people waiting."

Léa alone ate most of the chicken, the girolles and the potatoes. She also drank a lot. She was so engrossed in the pleasure of eating that she had completely forgotten her cares. She did not object when her companion's legs wound themselves round hers beneath the table, nor when he stroked the inside of her wrist.

By the time the salad arrived, they were well into the second bottle of Cahors.

When she had polished off the rich, creamy chocolate mousse, Léa felt that life was worth living.

François had to restrain himself more than once from pouncing on her and carrying her over to the bed behind the screen. After the meal she had pushed her chair away from the table and was leaning back. She crossed her long legs and her lace petticoat peeped out as she savored this moment of total well-being with half-closed eyes.

She observed the man who was her lover through her eyelashes. She loved his strength and his eyes which could change from dark to light, from gentle to hard, love to hatred. She looked at his chiselled features, his beautiful mouth, that could kiss so well. She shuddered at the memory of the previous night. "I want him," she thought. "I want him now."

"Let's make love."

François smiled. He had been waiting for her to say that, but he wisely did not say so. In his amorous adventures, he had met few women who were so naturally gifted in love. She loved with spontaneity and heathen joy that she had surely not inherited from her mother or learned at her convent in Bordeaux. What was more, she had never shown the slightest fear of becoming pregnant. Was she ignorant or just reckless?

The bed was a dark shadow behind the screen. He laid her gently on it and softly kissed her eyelids, her lips and her neck. She let him take over. Suddenly she threw her arms around him and bit into his lip.

"Hurt me! Take me like in Montmorillon."

Gladly, he raped his willing victim.

François had asked the Andrieus to prepare a basket of their choicest preserves, which he gave to Léa for her aunts.

"Give them this with my regards."

"Thank you."

"When will I see you again?"

"I don't know. I plan to leave in two days."

"So soon!"

She was touched by the disappointment in his voice when he said that. She answered him gently: "I can't leave my father alone for long. His health has deteriorated terribly since Mother's death."

"I understand. If you see your uncle, give him my best."

She suddenly remembered the Dominican's advice: "If you get into serious trouble, call or get a message to François Tavernier." What use could someone who seemed to be eating out of the Germans' hands be to her?

"I'll remember. Especially since he told me to find you if I was in trouble."

His face relaxed in a smile of pleasure.

"He's right. Tell him also that nothing's changed."

"Good night, I'll tell him. Thank you for the wonderful dinner and for this," she said indicating the basket. "Aunt Lisa's going to be thrilled!"

Léa spent the following day in bed, shut up in her room with an upset stomach.

The following day, still pale and unsteady, she went to the Grevin Museum. Everything happened just as Adrien had said it would. When she returned to her aunts', Sarah Mulstein was waiting for her.

"François Tavernier told me you were in Paris for a few days. I wanted to see you again," she said kissing her.

How she had changed! She was still as beautiful, perhaps even lovelier than before, but she seemed to have undergone a profound internal transformation, which totally altered her expression and her eyes. Léa had the strange feeling that she was possessed by somebody else. As if she could read her thoughts, Sarah said: "I've changed so much recently that I hardly recognize myself."

"François told me about your father. . . . "

"Yes. I'd rather we didn't talk about it, if you don't mind."

"What about your husband?"

"I hope for his sake that he's dead by now."

Léa could taste bile in her mouth.

"After they tortured him, he was sent to a concentration camp, I don't know which one."

Sarah was silent for a long time. Nobody spoke.

"François told me you were fond of Raphaël Mahl: so am I in spite of all I know about him. However, be careful, he's someone who hurts even those he loves."

"But you go on seeing him?"

"When you've reached the point I've reached, what can he do to me? I see him because he fascinates me. I'd like to understand where that bad side comes from, and his ruthlessness. Why is he so self-destructive? Why does he despise himself? Why his taste for humiliation combined with such arrogance? I know he's capable of doing good, for no special reason, for fun, and, the next minute, deride that good deed as if he wanted to punish himself for a moment of kindness.''

"Why don't you leave France?"

"I don't know. I love this country. I'm tired of running. And then, I don't want to go too far from Germany because I keep telling myself, although it's completely illogical, that my husband might be released."

"At least go over to the unoccupied zone."

"Perhaps I will. François wants me to stay with some friends of his."

"Where?"

"In Eymoutiers, a little town not far from Limoges."

"I'm going to Limoges tomorrow. Why don't you come with me?"

"What will you do in Limoges?" asked Albertine.

Léa regretted her carelessness, but it was too late. She improvised an explanation.

"Papa has a customer who owes him money and he asked me to see him."

"You should have told us."

"I'm sorry, Aunt, I didn't think to mention it. What do you say, Sarah, will you come with me?"

"Why not? It makes little difference where I am."

A sudden long ring at the front door made the four women freeze. The door opened to reveal François Tavernier.

"What a fright you gave us," cried Sarah, "You sounded like the Gestapo."

"That's why I'm here. You can't go back to the Donatis': they've just been arrested."

"No!"

"You must leave. I've brought you an identity card and a pass so you can cross to the unoccupied zone."

"But I can't leave like that. I haven't got my clothers or my books . . . "

"I know, Sarah, but there's no time. There are no more trains for Limoges this evening and the first is at half past seven in the morning. You must take it. At Limoges you change for Eymoutiers. Now, we've got to find you a place to sleep."

"Madame Mulstein can stay here for the night," said Albertine, "can't she, Lisa?"

"Of course."

François smiled gratefully at the two elderly ladies.

"That's very kind of you. But I must warn you that it could be dangerous," cautioned François.

"Don't talk about that, dear Monsieur Tavernier."

"I'll have a bed made up," said Lisa.

"Don't bother, mademoiselle, I'll sleep with Léa if she doesn't mind. That way it'll be easier to wake up and we won't miss the train."

"Is Léa going to Limoges?" asked François, astonished.

"Yes. I was just asking Sarah to come with me."

"I'm reassured to think you'll be travelling together. The trickiest moment will be the identity check when you cross the demarcation line. It's easier when there are two of you. Léa, may I have a word with you alone for a moment?"

"Come into my bedroom."

Léa sat on the bed and drew the comforter round her.

"I shan't ask what you're going to Limoges for, as I don't suppose you'd tell me. But please be careful. Will you do me a favor?"

"If I can."

"I'd like you to take Sarah to my friends at Eymoutiers. She speaks French very well, but I'm afaid her accent may arouse the suspicions of the French and German police."

"Why do they want to arrest her?"

"Because they're arresting all foreign Jews. Will you do it?"

"Yes."

"Thank you."

The door bell rang again. Léa leaped up to open it. Raphaël pushed past her to get in.

"Where's Sarah?"

Léa leaned against the wall in astonishment. She hoped that Lisa, who had just appeared, would not say anything.

"Who are you talking about?"

"Sarah Mulstein, of course."

"I haven't seen her since 1940. Why are you looking for her here?"

322

"She was fond of you. I told her you were in Paris, I thought she might come and see you. I've been looking for her everywhere for the last two hours."

"Why?"

"To warn her not to go home. The Gestapo are waiting for her."

Léa feigned surpise as best she could.

"Oh! My God!"

Raphaël flopped down on to the hall seat.

"Where can she be? I can't wait outside her front door to warn her. I'm in enough trouble as it is."

"I thought you were hand in glove with those gentlemen."

"Yes, while I'm useful to them. If they learn, for example, that I'm trying to snatch Israel Lazare's daughter from their clutches, I'm the one who'll end up in a concentration camp in her stead."

"Poor Raphaël, you don't expect me to feel sorry for you. After all, they are your friends."

"You're right," he said getting to his feet. "Don't feel sorry for me, I'm not worth it. I'm going. I'll continue to look for her. If you see her tell her not to go near her home. And you, sweetheart, are you still going back to your beloved countryside?"

"Yes."

"Well, *bon voyage*. Think of me occasionally. Farewell."

"Goodbye, Raphaël."

Léa pensively closed the door behind him and listened to the sound of his footsteps die away on the staircase.

"Bravo, you were fantastic," said François putting his arm round her shoulders.

"You see, he's not as bad as you make out."

"Perhaps, but it could be a trap."

"No, I'm sure he was sincere."

"So am I," said Sarah emerging from the boudoir.

"All right, all right. Even so, we must be even more careful. Tomorrow, someone will come to pick you up and drive you to the station. He'll come at half past six, ring the bell and say: "The taxi's waiting." He's a man who has a cycle-taxi. I use him from time to time. He'll have your ticket and he'll stay with you until the train leaves. . . . Sarah, I have to go now. Promise me you won't give yourself away.''

"I'll try, François," she said kissing him. "Thank you for everything."

"As long as you're together, take care of Léa," he murmured.

"I will."

Léa felt utterly confused: who were François Tavernier and Raphaël Mahl in fact? And even Sarah Mulstein? What were they all playing at? And what about herself, dropping books in cinemas, picking up leaflets in museums, taking a train to Limoges with a Jewish woman who was sought by the Gestapo, to go and ask for *The Mysteries of Paris* in a bookshop? It was all crazy. Why had she agreed to carry out Uncle Adrien's mission? She was lost in thought when François's voice made her jump.

"Don't think too much, Léa. It's better if you don't know the answers to some of your questions. Everything is both much simpler and much more complex than you think. Goodbye, little girl, I'll miss you."

Léa felt as though something was being taken from her. She was astonished at herself. She thought: It hurts me to leave him! She offered him her cheek. He kissed her so lightly that she hardly felt it.

It was still dark when the cycle-taxi man rang the doorbell.

Chapter 24

The Germans at the different crossing points on the demarcation line knew Léa by now. They called her *Das Mädchen mit dem blauen Fahrrad*—the girl with the blue bicycle. When she came back from the unoccupied zone with a basket full of fruit on her carrier: strawberries, cherries, peaches or apricots, she never failed to offer some to the soldiers on duty. Often, there were letters that she had just collected from the poste-restante at Saint-Pierre-d'Aurillac hidden under the fruit.

"Well, well, you have got a lot of admirers," the old postmaster always said to her.

Sometimes, for safety's sake, she rolled the letters up and slid them under the seat or inside the handlebars.

One day, a German who was warier than his colleagues, said: "Open your basket and your bag; you're smuggling letters."

Léa burst out laughing and showed him her bag.

"If I wanted to smuggle letters, I'd hide them under the seat, not in my bag!"

"Indeed, that would be a good hiding-place," said the man laughing as he handed her bag back.

Léa had been afraid and her legs were shaking when she got back on her bicycle. The hill seemed much steeper that day. However, she loved these cross-country errands that enabled her to get away from the atmosphere at Montillac. It deteriorated daily due to Pierre Delmas's decline and Fayard's pressure on them to sell the estate, Bernadette

Bouchardeau's moaning about her son, the presence of two German officers which was becoming more and more intrusive, and Sabine's constant grumpiness. She seemed more bad-tempered every day. There was beginning to be a serious shortage of money. Ruth had given Léa all her savings. Before reaching that point, Léa had approached Uncle Luc, the rich man of the family. The lawyer, whose support for the Vichy Government was not secret, advised her to sell the property to Fayard, since her father was no longer capable of maintaining it, and he had no son to step into his shoes.

"But there's me, and my sisters!"

"A woman! As if women were capable of running a wine-growing estate! If you're attached to Montillac, find yourself a husband who's capable of looking after it. That shouldn't be too difficult for a pretty girl like you, even without a dowry."

Léa turned pale at the humiliation but she did not back down.

"Uncle, there are Mummy's estates in Martinique. When the war's over, we'll be able to sell them."

"My poor child, that's all rather uncertain. How do you know they're not being occupied by Communists, or they might have been stolen by the natives. . . . Excuse me, I've got an appointment. Give my regards to your poor father. I'm giving a little party in your cousin's honor next week. Laure and Sabine are coming. Will you join us?"

"No thank you, Uncle Luc, I don't like the people I meet at your house."

"What do you mean?"

"You know very well what I mean. You entertain the captain of the Bordeaux militia, the . . . "

"Be quiet! I'll entertain whom I please. I can see you've been influenced by that poor Adrien whose superior was saying to me only the other day: "I pray to God for our unfortunate brother, that He may bring him back to the path of righteousness and show him what is truly for the good of France." I believe Adrien has betrayed his country and the Church. It's a disgrace for our family to have one of its members in league with terrorists. Thank God, nobody here thinks I share these grievous ideas. Moreover, I have told my friends that if this traitor were to turn up at my house, I should have no hesitation in denouncing him. As far as I'm concerned, my brother is dead."

"Bastard!"

Luc Delmas advanced threateningly towards Léa.

"Do you know who you're talking to?"

"And as far as I'm concerned, you're my dead uncle. I spit on your corpse."

With Ruth's money, she would be able to last out until the grape harvest.

July brought Laure back home. She was bitter because, since Léa's quarrel with Uncle Luc, she was no longer invited to the grand apartment. She spent her days locked in her room, or in Langon with the notary's daughter, who was an old school chum.

Léa had tried hard to get close to her little sister. She was very fond of her, but Laure would not have anything to do with her. To provoke Léa, she would walk among the vineyards with Frederic Hanke, laughing loudly and flirting with him.

That summer of 1942, Camille and her little boy also lived at Montillac. The Gestapo had forced them out of Roches-Blanches. They had confiscated the estate and all property belonging to Laurent d'Argilat, who had been denounced as a secret agent.

Camille had been interrogated at length by SS Lieutenant Friedrich-Wilhelm Dohse in Bordeaux. He wanted to know where her husband was. The young woman told him calmly that the only information she had received was that sent by the authorities. Dohse was not fooled, but he judged it best to let her go, thinking that sooner or later, Laurent d'Argilat would try to get a message to her, or even join her.

Every week, Léa received a letter from Sarah Mulstein who described, with great humor, her life in Eymoutiers. She made Léa laugh with her poignantly funny accounts of the expressions on the faces of the local inhabitants when she walked through the streets of the little town, with the yellow star sewn on to her dress which she wore out of solidarity with the Jews in the occupied zone.

> If I walked about stark naked, they wouldn't be more embarrassed. Most of them look the other way. Only a one-armed old man with a bushy gray moustache, like most of the country folk round here, and a row of medals on his velvet jacket came up to me and took off his big black felt hat and said in a gruff voice: "I'd be prouder of wearing a star like yours than I am of all this scrap-metal I won at Verdun."

In another letter, she derided the harassment of the Jews:

> Having forbidden us to possess radios or telephones, now they're barring us from restaurants, cafés, theaters, telephone booths, swimming pools, beaches, museums, libraries, military installations, exhibitions, markets and fairs, sports grounds, parks . . . I suppose we're also forbidden to make love with non-Jews. The fact is the Nazis dream of one thing: forbidding us to breathe for fear that the air we breathe out might pollute the pure German race.

In her letters, she often mentioned François Tavernier. She spoke of their friendship before the war, of the absolute trust she had in him. She supported Léa's decision to fight to preserve Montillac.

On the 27th of July, the last letter from Sarah arrived. Also in the mail was a letter from Uncle Adrien. She put it aside to read Sarah's letter first. Léa stopped under a tree and tore open the envelope.

> By the time you read this, I'll be back in Paris. The events of the last few days make it impossible for me to stay in hiding while my people are being led to the slaughterhouse. As censorship is operating perfectly, perhaps you haven't heard. Here are the facts as they were told to me by a Jewish friend of mine and a friend of his, who works for the Bureau of Jewish Affairs.
>
> Last Wednesday night, between three and four o'clock

in the morning, French police officers knocked on the doors of thousands of foreign Jewish families, of all origins, and arrested them. Some managed to get away with the help of sympathetic or mercenary policemen, but they were too few, alas. The others, women, children, old folk, men and even the sick were taken away with the few belongings they were allowed to keep with them. The sick were taken away by bus, the others on foot. Parisians looked the other way as they passed. They were confined in the Vélodrome d'Hiver stadium: 7,000 people, 4,051 of whom are children; 6,000 others have been taken to a camp at Drancy. The French police have arrested 13,000 people simply because they are Jews! Apparently, the German authorities are disappointed: they expected 32,000. To avoid being rounded up, several unfortunate souls committed suicide. Women, remembering the pogroms in Russia and Poland when they were children, threw themselves out of windows with their children.

No preparations had been made to provide for such a crowd. They spent a week under the corrugated iron and glass roof which was like a greenhouse in the hot sun. There was no ventilation and each day the stench got worse. There were not nearly enough toilets and those they had very soon became unusable. They had to wade through the most disgusting sludge, and urine was running down the steps. Humiliation was added to their fear.

The sick died for lack of proper care. Only two doctors were allowed inside the stadium but, even with the help of a few Red Cross nurses, they were unable to deal with all the miscarriages, scarlet fever, dysentery. . . . Only about ten people managed to escape. On Sunday the 19th of July, 1,000 people, most of them men, were shut up in cattle cars and sent to Germany.

I know the fate that awaits them, but it is so atrocious that no one will believe me, not even my Jewish friends. And yet, some of these friends have read *Mein Kampf* and the English *White Book* which was published in

France in 1939, which describes the camp at Buchenwald and how it operates in horrific detail. They see it as science fiction. And they had such faith in France!

Why are the French joining forces with what will obviously be one of the greatest disgraces in human history? Why?

I used to feel that, because I speak several languages, because I've travelled widely and because of my cosmopolitan culture, and being neither practicing nor a believer, I was a free citizen of the world. But now all this has happened, I feel Jewish, and nothing but Jewish. I'm going back to my people, even though I am aware that I'm probably going to my own death. This I accept. If it is possible to fight to save some of us from being wiped out, I'll fight. In that case, I may need your help. I know I can count on you.

Take care, my friend. You're young. Think of me from time to time. I love you and kiss you. Sarah.

It was a beautiful summer morning, warm but not too hot, there was not a cloud in the sky and there was the merest hint of a breeze. The fields and the vineyards looked like a patchwork quilt in various shades of green. A few fields were dotted white with sheep. In the distance, the church tower and the roofs of a village completed the gently undulating harmony of the scene.

Léa got up and decided to postpone reading Uncle Adrien's letter until later. She got back on her bicycle to deliver the post to Mouchac, Verdelais and Liloy.

When she arrived back at Montillac, she took refuge in the children's room to read the letter at last. Her uncle congratulated her once again on successfully carrying out her mission in Paris and Limoges. He asked her to listen to the BBC every evening and she would hear a message telling her when to join him in Toulouse. At the main post office, she would find a letter instructing her where to go. She was to leave two days after hearing the message: "The violets are blooming by the cross."

Léa had just finished burning the letter when Camille walked in without knocking.

"I'm sorry to disturb you but was there anything for me?"

"No, only a letter from Adrien," she said, showing her the burnt paper, "and from Sarah Mulstein who has left Eymoutiers."

"To go where?"

"To Paris."

"Paris! She's mad!"

"Here, read her letter, you'll understand better."

It was the 2nd of August when Léa heard the message on the radio. Camille would look after the mail during her absence.

At the post office in Toulouse, she found a terse note instructing her to be at the Basilica of Saint-Sernin at five o'clock that afternoon, having first stopped at the church of Notre-Dame-du-Taur.

The heat was stifling and Léa was hungry and thirsty. All she had in her stomach was a warm lemonade from the station buffet. There were very few people in the streets and in the main square. The little church in the Rue du Taur seemed like an oasis in this hot, white, brick desert. Her eyes took a long time to get accustomed to the dark. She went up to the altar, near which a little red lamp was burning. Snatches of prayer went through her mind: Our Father who art in heaven . . . merciful Mary . . . the Lord Almighty . . . Thy will be done . . . deliver us from evil . . .

She put down the little leather suitcase which had belonged to her mother and knelt, full of the desire to believe still, and to take refuge in God's protection. But all she felt was profound boredom. It was only four o'clock! An old woman came into the church dragging her feet. She paused in front of Léa and stared hard at her, and then she went away grumbling: "That's no way to dress in church."

The heat had made her forget how low-cut her rather short blue cotton dress was. She fumbled in her suitcase for a silk scarf, which covered her head and part of her shoulders. She would be less conspicuous.

Half past four. Léa left the church and headed for the Basilica. It was still as hot; there was not a breath of wind. Her wooden shoes clattered on the cobblestones of the narrow street. Suddenly a door opened in a huge entrance to a sixteenth-century mansion and a man came out, pulled her towards him and pushed her inside the doorway.

"But . . ."

He clamped his hand over her mouth.

"Be quiet. You're in danger."

In the street, there was the sound of running feet and then voices, close by.

"They can't get away now, the bastards . . ."

"Don't cry victory yet. Those Jew-bastards are cunning."

"OK, but the boss is even more cunning than they are."

"Is it true that there are priests who help them?"

"So they say. But I believe they're Communists disguised as priests."

"Yes, but the Dominican they arrested yesterday was a real one all right."

Léa began to tremble against the man who was still holding her.

"We'll have to see. If he is a real one, even though he's a priest, he'll live to regret that he was ever born. He can't have any religion if he's helping the Jews."

There was a long whistle in the street.

"Let's go."

The two men ran off. Then there were shouts, curses, shots and . . . silence.

Léa leaned against the door with her eyes closed.

"Come with me. We'll go through the cellars."

"Please tell me. Was it my uncle they arrested?"

"I don't know. Yesterday, Lécussan and his men set a trap for Jews and those who were helping to smuggle them out of the country. I know there was a priest with them."

"What was he like?"

"I have no idea. Hurry! The district will be surrounded soon."

"One more question. How did you know I'd be coming this way?"

"I had orders to protect you between Notre-Dame-du-Taur and the Basilica. As I passed the Basilica, I recognized Lécussan and two of his men, and I thought they might have been there because of you. Satisfied? Are you coming now?"

"Yes."

"Give me your suitcase," he said sliding the pistol, which he had kept his hand on all the time, under his arm.

They entered the mansion through a little door, went down a few steps and came face to face with a door which the man unlocked. During what seemed like an eternity, they went through a maze of passages that had caved in, broken staircases, going up, then down; they went under magnificant vaults fleetingly lit up by the torch. Léa stopped, breathless.

"Where are we?"

"Underneath the Capitol. In the old part of Toulouse, there are sometimes several floors of undergound passages. Some of them are ill-famed because they served as torture chambers during the Inquisition. But over the centuries, many of them have been used as hideouts. Since the beginning of the war, a group of us have shored up walls, carried out repairs, cleared rubble and dug out openings."

They walked on in silence. Then, they found themselves in a narrow passage where they had to duck and it led into an enormous pink brick room with superb pointed arches. It was lit by torches which had been driven into the sand on the ground.

Léa was stunned. She stood absolutely still and then looked up at the gothic arch and turned slowly around. There appeared to be no other entrance apart from the one they had come through. The flickering light enhanced the splendor and the mystery of the place.

When she looked down, all along one wall she saw tables, crates and camp beds with men stretched out on them. Some of the men were very young and they were poorly dressed.

"Have you finished your inspection?" asked her companion.

"It's wonderful!"

A man came up to them.

"Why have you brought her here?"

"I thought it was the right thing to do, chief; I couldn't let her fall into Lécussan's hands. You know what he does to women?"

"Don't worry, Michel, I'll answer for her."

That voice . . .

"If you'll take responsibility for her . . . "

"I will."

"Laurent!"

With her hands clasped over her mouth, Léa stood there incredulous as she watched the man she loved walking towards her. How he had changed!

"Yes, Léa, it's me."

"Laurent," she repeated in a whisper of disbelief.

He drew her towards him and put his arms around her.

Léa was unaware of anything except the warmth that enveloped her body, his breath on her neck, his voice murmuring her name. The spell was broken when the man called Michel said: "She can stay tonight. She'll have to leave tomorrow."

Who cared about tomorrow. It was this moment that mattered. Now she knew that he loved her, in spite of his question: "How are Camille and little Charles?"

"They're both well. As you know, they've been at Montillac since the Gestapo confiscated Roches-Blanches. Charles is a lovely little boy. He takes after you." She couldn't resist adding, "Like you, I think he loves me!"

"How could anyone not love you? How can I ever repay you for all you've done for us?"

"Don't talk about it. What's mine is yours. I wish you'd get that into your head once and for all."

"I'm afraid you'll get into trouble."

"As long as Captain Kramer is under our roof, there won't be any trouble."

"How can you be so sure? There are so many denunciations these days."

"Who would give us away? Everybody knows and loves us."

"You're so confident! Every day, our comrades are denounced by their neighbors and even their friends.''

"While we were hiding in the rue du Taur, I overheard them saying that a Dominican had been arrested . . .''

"Don't worry, it wasn't your uncle; it was one of his friends, Father Bon.''

"But perhaps they arrested my uncle earlier on the Basilica?''

"They didn't arrest anyone. But there's no doubt that he's been denounced.''

"What am I supposed to do now?''

"Rest.''

"I'm hungry and I'm thirsty.''

"Sit with me.''

Laurent installed her on a crate at a table. A few moments later, he was back with a small dish of pâté, a chunk of bread, a peach, a half-empty bottle of wine and two glasses. Léa pounced on the bread and breathed in its wonderful fresh smell.

"How on earth do you get hold of bread like this? Ours is dark and sticky.''

"We're very lucky as far as supplies are concerned. The farmers from the market in the main square keep us in meat, pâtés, vegetables, cheese and fruit. An old baker in Caraman makes our bread for us and a wine-grower from Villemur sends us wine. We pay them when we can. The network doesn't have much cash. When there are more of us, it'll be a problem.''

"What's that noise?''

"That's our printing press. We print most of the clandestine literature for the Tarn, the Garonne, the Hérault and the Aude regions, as well as pamphlets, fake ration cards, and false identity cards. We're very well organized.''

"But it's dangerous!''

"We're careful.''

"But you're completely shut up. It's like a prison.''

"Don't believe that. We have lots of hidden exits, trapdoors, underground passages and dungeons too. It's like a rabbit warren underneath Toulouse and some of our men know it like the backs of their hands . . .''

"But if they know it, others might know it too," Léa cut in.

"True. That's why we've walled up the easiest and best known entrances."

"What about the one in the Rue du Taur?"

"Tonight, the walls will cave in and block off the opening."

As she talked, Léa spread pâté on her bread.

"This is so good!"

"I've never seen anyone eat like you. It's as though you involve your whole being, body and soul."

"Aren't you the same?" she asked with her mouth full.

"I don't think so."

"That's your loss. Although, at the moment, it's rather lucky for you that you're not like me. You're like Camille, she eats like a sparrow. She's always saying 'I'm not hungry'— it's so irritating to hear that when my stomach is almost always empty."

She smiled and held out her glass.

"Let's drink a toast."

"What are we drinking to?"

"To us," she said raising her glass.

"To us . . . and to victory."

"What about me? Don't I get a drink?"

A shabby, dirty man was standing near them.

"Uncle Adrien!"

"Father Delmas!"

The Dominican burst out laughing at their astonished expressions.

"Hello, my children," he said, taking a seat on one of the upturned crates.

Léa poured him the last of the wine which he quaffed in one swallow.

"I had the fright of my life when I saw the Basilica was being watched. If they had arrested you, I would never have forgiven myself, Léa."

"Michel was marvellous, he managed to head her off in time and bring her here."

Léa couldn't take her eyes off her uncle.

"You know, if I'd seen you looking like that, I wouldn't have recognized you and I'd have run away."

"Don't you like my disguise? It's perfect. I blend in with the crowd of down-and-outers begging on the steps of Saint-Sernin."

It was true. Nobody would suspect this filthy old tramp, with a gray beard and baggy trousers held up with a piece of string, a battered green felt hat and the most ridiculous old boots on his bare feet. Yet he was the elegant preacher whose sermons were famous; the pious Dominican known to the whole of Bordeaux.

"Uncle, I didn't know you had a gray beard."

"Neither did I. It came as a surprise. I didn't realize I was that old. Now listen carefully because I can't stay long. I've got to go. There's a parachute landing tonight. I asked you to come for several reasons. You can stay, Laurent, you're in on this. They're going to step up surveillance on the demarcation line. You're going to go to Caudrot for the mail from now on. The postmistress and her young lady assistant are part of our network. You and Camille will take it in turns, and every fifth time, you'll go together. Sometimes you'll have messages to be delivered in person. When that's the case, Monsieur and Madame Debray will tell you. If one day, you hear on the BBC: 'Sylvie likes mushrooms,' that means, don't go to Caudrot any more, that your cover's been blown. Now, you'll be getting pamphlets and newspapers through the post. You have to distribute them. Have you brought a strong suitcase that isn't too big?"

"Yes. There it is," said Léa pointing to her case.

"Good. What you're going to carry is dangerous. You can say no. If there had been anyone else, I wouldn't ask you."

"What is it?"

"I want you to go to Langon and deliver a transmitter-receiver to Oliver's Restaurant."

"But it's full of German officers!"

"Precisely, that's why it's an ideal place. The day after you get back, put the transmitter in your shopping basket and put the basket on the carrier of your bicycle. It'll be market day. Go early and buy as much as you can lay your hands on: fruit, vegetables and flowers. You will happen to bump into the Olivers' old wine-waiter, Cordeau—you know him.

337

He'll ask after your father and tell you he's got a treat for his old friend's daughter. Go to the restaurant with him and keep talking. When you get there, he'll take your basket from you and disappear with it. When he comes back, it'll be lighter, but it will appear to be just as full. there'll be three jars of potted duck and one of cepes on the top. Will you do it?''

"It makes my mouth water. I'd do anything for the potted duck," she replied laughing.

"Thank him warmly and leave. The hard part will be at Langon station. The stationmaster is a sympathizer, but I'm afraid to alert him."

"I know him, I often take him letters from his son. As soon as he sees me, he manages to keep the gendarmes and the customs officers at a distance. It'll be all right, you'll see. He's the one who looks after my bicycle and he'll help me fix the suitcase on to the carrier."

"I think it should work. What do you think, Laurent?"

"I think so too."

"Cordeau's not the one who'll be using the transmitter, is he?"

"No, a pianist was parachuted in from London yesterday."

"A pianist?"

"Yes, that's what we call someone who transmits messages."

"Where is he?"

"You don't need to know that. Cordeau will be your only contact. If you want to send a message that you think is important, tell him; he'll get it to me and tell you what to do. Is that quite clear?"

"Yes."

"If you are arrested, don't act the heroine, but try and drag out the interrogation as long as possible to give us time to take precautions."

"I'll try."

"One more thing. My underground name is Albert Duval. Use it. Now, I must leave."

Adrien Delmas stood up and for a second he looked deep into his niece's eyes.

"Don't fret, Uncle Adrien, it'll be all right," she said, hugging him.

"God be with you," he said, blessing her. "Goodbye Laurent."

"Goodbye, Father."

After the Dominican had left, they sat in silence for a while. Léa leaned over and whispered to Laurent: "Where's the toilet?"

"I'll tell you, but it's not very comfortable. Take this flashlight. Go down the passage and it's the second corridor on the right and then right again : there's a room and it's in there. You'll see a shovel for covering everything with sand, like cats do."

When Léa came back, Laurent was loading his pistol.

"These cellars are extraordinary. Show me around."

Laurent took one of the flashlights and they went into the little passage.

"Is that the only way out of that room?" she asked.

"No, there's another one. We would use it only as a last resort."

"That's better. I really feel like a prisoner down here, don't you?"

"You get used to this life. But I'm hardly ever here. Come look at the walls."

"What are all the carvings?"

"At various times in the past, this room was used as a prison."

Léa read aloud: "1763, five years already; 1843, Amélie, I love you; long live the king, long live death. Who is this Lécussan fellow you were talking about earlier?"

"He's an ex-naval officer from the Haute-Geronne region. When the armistice was signed, he went to London. After the British fired at the French navy at Mers-el-Kebir, he was imprisoned by the British and then repatriated back to France. He's an arrogant creature, violently anti-British and anti-Communist, but that's nothing next to his fanatical anti-Semitism. To give you an example, the anti-Semitic students from the Toulouse faculty of medicine paid tribute to him by giving him a Star of David made of human skin that had been taken from the corpse of a Jew and carefully tanned.''

"How awful!"

"When he's been drinking, he shows it off and says: 'It's a piece of ass.' That's the delightful character Xavier Vallat has nominated head of Jewish affairs in Toulouse. For the last year he's been hunting Jews and terrorists with a band of characters as despicable as himself, whom he keeps in the lap of luxury."

They walked on in silence for a few seconds.

"This is, in a way, my territory. I've brought a few books, some blankets and an oil lamp down here. I take refuge here when I need to be alone or after a difficult operation," he said, drawing aside a faded curtain.

It was a small room. There was a single cluster of arches and there was soft white sand on the floor. In some places the pink brick walls had been blackened by soot. Léa knelt on the covers, suddenly attentive, and watched Laurent set the flashlight into the sand. He suddenly seemed tired and unhappy.

"Come here."

He shook his head.

"Please come."

He walked towards her, looking reluctant. Léa pulled him closer and he fell to his knees beside her.

"Since I got here, I've been waiting for the moment when I could be alone with you," she said softly.

"We mustn't."

"Why not? You love me and I love you. Who knows, tomorrow you may be captured or wounded. . . . I can't bear the idea of not belonging to you totally, of having a few kisses as my only memory of you. No! Don't say anything. You'll talk nonsense or say something trite. What I feel for you is outside the boundaries of convention. I don't mind being only your mistress. I want you to be my lover if you won't be my husband."

"Be quiet . . ."

"Why should I be quiet? I'm not ashamed of desiring you and telling you so. The war has changed a lot of things and girls behave differently now. Before, I might not have dared

340

talk to you like this . . . although . . . No, I wouldn't have been very different. Like today, I would have told you I love you, that I want to make love with you, and that nothing and nobody can stop me.''

Léa pulled her blue cotton dress over her head. She was naked except for a pair of childlike cotton panties.

Laurent could not take his eyes off her magnificent body. His hands were drawn to her breasts. How could he resist her skillful hands as they unbuttoned his shirt, and then attacked his trouser belt? Suddenly he stood up and backed away.

"Léa, we mustn't.''

She crawled towards him on her knees.

The light outlined her body as she inched forward on her hands and knees on the sandy floor. She was like an animal stalking its prey: her breasts swayed gently from side to side and her back arched. The man who was watching her felt as if he had stepped back to the dawn of time, when primeval woman was choosing her mate.

When her strong sinewy hand gripped him, he no longer resisted. Nor did he push away her mouth as it closed over his penis. He wished she would go on forever, and yet after a time, tore himself away.

Léa cried: "No!''

But her cry of revolt gave way to a cry of victory when at last he penetrated her.

The white sand clung to their bodies making them look like stone statues. Léa opened her eyes first and turned to look at her lover with a mixture of tenderness and pride. He was hers, all hers. Poor Camille! She didn't stand much chance in the face of their passion! Nothing and no one could come between them now! And yet she felt a sense of disappointment which she could not understand. She had never given herself so entirely. It was not only her body she had given to Laurent, but also her soul. It had not been the same with François and Mathias. With them, she had been present in body, but it was only with the man she loved that she felt fulfilled. After his violent climax, he became tender, too tender to satisfy her desire. She would have liked him to take her again. She wanted to feel his hands caressing and hurting her. She wanted him inside her, but a sudden modesty prevented her from asking him.

How beautiful he was with his fair hair, his face with its classic features and his smooth white skin. With his eyes closed, he looked like an angelic child. When he opened them, she was overjoyed.

"Forgive me, my love," he murmured into her neck.

Forgive him? What was he talking about? He must be crazy. She lay on top of him, and was filled with an intense feeling of happiness. They looked deep into each other's eyes for a long while. Léa's whole body trembled as she clung to him.

The sound of voices brought them back to reality.

"Coming," cried Laurent pushing Léa gently away.

She clung to him.

"I've got to go, my love. Do you want to spend the night here? Are you sure you won't be afraid?"

"No. Do you really have to go?"

"I do."

He hastily got dressed. His clothes were those of a farm hand: a mixture of blue and brown with a beret to complete the outfit. He bore no resemblance to the elegant young man of the summer of 1939 who used to take her for long drives along the endless roads of the Landes forest.

"You're beautiful."

That made him laugh. He leaned over her.

"Darling, I want you to know I'll never forget this moment, in spite of the shame I feel for taking advantage of your affection for me."

"But it was me . . ."

"I know, I shouldn't have. I've wronged you and I've wronged Camille."

"But you don't love her! you love me."

"Yes, I do love you. I don't think you can understand what I feel for Camille. She's my sister, my daughter and my wife all at the same time. She's fragile. She needs me and I know that I couldn't live without her. Don't look at me like that. I'm trying to tell you that Camille and I are of the same breed.

342

We love the same things, the same books, the same lifestyle . . ."

"You've already told me. I'll change. I'll love what you love. I'll read your books. I'll live your way. I'll also be your sister, your daughter, your wife and your mistress. I'll be a perfect lady if you want me to. I'll do anything to keep you. I'll—"

"Be quiet! You frighten me!"

"Are you a coward?"

"When it comes to you, yes."

"Don't be. I want you to be strong. I want to be able to look up to you, always."

"I'll try not to disappoint you. Get some sleep. You'll have to be up early in the morning. Promise me you won't do anything foolish."

"Promise. Now, I'm invulnerable. You be careful too: I'd never forgive you if anything happened to you."

They exchanged just one kiss, but they poured everything they could not put into words into it.

Laurent paused with his hands on the curtain and turned towards Léa looking at her.

"Remember, I've entrusted you with Camille's safety. Look after her. I can rely on you."

The sand muffled his footsteps. What silence! Léa had not yet noticed how quiet it was. She laughed nervously to herself.

She burrowed under the blankets.

When she woke up, she felt as if she had only just fallen asleep and that she would never be able to get up, her body ached so much!

Michel, the young man who had brought her to the cellars, took her back to the station and carried her suitcase and car-ryall. He found her a seat in a third class compartment, slid the case under the seat and put the other bag on the rack above her head.

"I didn't put your suitcase up on the luggage rack, I was afraid you might not be able to get it down by yourself and

343

if somebody gave you a hand, they would find it unusually heavy. In the bag, underneath the cheeses and sausages, there are some pamphlets and our newspaper, *Liberate and Federate*. Pass it around the area. It's the 23rd of June issue, in which we published General de Gaulle's declaration. If you haven't read it, do so. It makes stimulating reading."

"Do you want to have me shot?"

"That would be a shame, a pretty girl like you. There are two of our comrades in the train ready to step in if there's any danger. If you see that you're about to be arrested, leave your luggage. They will create a diversion and seize your suitcase. If you are interrogated, say it has been stolen. Do you understand?"

"Yes."

The whistle blew.

"The train's about to leave. Good luck!"

He jumped onto the platform as the train slowly pulled out of the station.

Léa leaned out the window and waved until he was out of sight.

"It's sad to leave one's fiancé," said a voice with a German accent.

Léa turned around. Her legs suddenly felt limp.

But the German officer who'd spoken simply continued on down the crowded corridor. With thumping heart, she came away from the window and went to her seat inside the compartment.

"Langon. The demarcation line. The train will stop for forty-five minutes. Everybody get off the train with their baggage."

Léa let the other people in the compartment off first. How heavy the suitcase was! If only Loriot, the stationmaster was on the platform! She stood on the step trying to find a familiar face among the jostling crowds of people who were waiting, identity cards in hand, to be checked. Suddenly, she saw the German customs officers get on to the train to search the empty compartments. There was an officer with them.

"Lieutenant Hanke!"

"Mademoiselle Léa! What are you doing here?"

"Hello, Lieutenant. I was looking to see if there was anyone I knew to help carry my suitcase, it's very heavy."

"Let me help you. It is heavy. What have you got in there, lead?"

"You're not far wrong! I've got a cannon in little pieces!" she laughed.

"Don't jest about things like that, mademoiselle. Every day we arrest people for smuggling."

"Are books illegal?"

"Some are."

"One day I'll have to ask you which ones."

Meanwhile, they had reached the exit. Léa moved as if to go to the area where they searched the women passengers.

"*Es ist nützlich, Fraulein, das Mädchen ist mit mir,*" said Lieutenant Hanke to one of the women in charge, and since he was an officer she had no reason to doubt that the lady who accompanied him was *bona fide.*

In the ticket hall, Loriot came forward.

"Hello, Mademoiselle Delmas , I'll get your bicycle for you. Hello, Lieutenant Hanke."

"Hello, Monsieur Loriot. I must get back on to the platform. Help Mademoiselle Delmas strap her luggage on," he said giving him the suitcase.

Lieutenant Hanke's French had greatly improved.

The weight of the suitcase and the carryall made the bicycle unsteady and Léa feared it would topple over any moment. Pink-faced and panting, Léa got off and pushed it the rest of the way home. The first person she saw was her father, who seemed extremely agitated. She leaned her bicycle up against the wall of the barn and tried to get her breath back.

"Bastard . . . rat . . . Isabelle will get rid of you . . ."

"What's the matter, Papa?"

"Where's your mother? I've got to speak to her at once."

"But, Papa . . ."

"No 'buts,' get your mother at once! I've something urgent to tell her."

Léa wiped her perspiring forehead. She was suddenly overwhelmed by the exhaustion of the last few hours: her father asking for his dead wife, this suitcase that weighed a ton,

Laurent becoming her lover, Lieutenant Hanke carrying her suitcase, the gothic vaults of Toulouse, her uncle the beggar, the Star of David made out of a Jew's skin, and Camille running towards her with outstretched arms. . . . She fainted at Pierre Delmas's feet.

When she opened her eyes, her head was on Ruth's knee and Camille was bathing her forehead with a damp towel, which she dipped into a basin of water held by Laure. Her father was puffy-eyed with grief and he was weeping and saying to Fayard: "My little one isn't dead, is she? Her mother would never forgive me."

"Don't worry, monsieur," said Ruth, "it's just a touch of the sun. No wonder, riding a bicycle in that heat!"

"It's not serious, Papa, don't worry. Laure, look after him, please."

Léa had passed out for only a few minutes. With Camille's help, she was soon on her feet.

"I'm sorry to have given you such a fright. Ruth's correct. It was the heat. Where's my suitcase and carryall?"

"Fayard went to fetch them."

"Quick, catch him."

They found him in the kitchen.

"I don't know what you've got in there, Mademoiselle Léa, but it weighs a ton. I'll take it up to your room."

"No, leave it. Thank you, I'll take it up myself."

"It's much too heavy for you."

Léa did not dare insist for fear of arousing suspicion. She followed him to the children's room.

"Thank you, Fayard, Thank you very much."

"You're welcome, mademoiselle."

Camille and Ruth came in. Ruth held a glass in her hand.

"Drink that. It'll make you feel better."

Léa did as she was told.

"Now get into bed and get some rest."

"But . . ."

"Don't argue: you might have sunstroke."

"Don't worry, Ruth, I'll take care of her. You go and care for Monsieur Delmas."

346

Léa stretched out on the cushions and closed her eyes to shut out Camille.

"I haven't slept a wink since you left, I was so worried. As soon as I closed my eyes I saw you and Laurent in danger of your lives. It was horrible!"

While she talked, she removed Léa's shoes and gently stroked her legs. Léa wanted to scream. She sat up.

"I saw Laurent in Toulouse."

Camille let go of her leg.

"You didn't! How is he? What did he say?"

Léa was overwhelmed with an impulse to tell her everything. Supposing she told her that she and Laurent loved each other and that they had become lovers? Something in Camille's tired, drawn face stopped her.

"He's fine. He asked me to tell you that he thinks of you and little Charles lots and that you're not to worry about him."

"How can I not worry?"

"I also saw Uncle Adrien. He's given me a mission and new instructions."

"Can I help? Please let me help!"

"I'll tell you how when the time comes."

"I'm worried about your father. He's been acting even more strangely. He keeps cursing and threatening. I've tried to talk to him, to find out what's the matter, but all he does is repeat: 'What will Isabelle say?' I thought for a moment that he'd had an argument with Fayard, but Fayard told me that they hadn't had a quarrel for a week. Ruth has no idea what it's about and neither has your Aunt Bernadette. As for Sabine, she's been on night duty at the hospital for the last three days. Only Laure seems to know what's going on, but she refuses to speak to me and locks herself in her room, but I can hear her crying."

"I'll talk with her."

"Rest first."

"No. I've got a feeling it's something serious. I'm afraid for Papa."

Léa looked for her sister everywhere, but could not find her.

She did not see her until dinner. Laure's eyes were red and puffy. Nobody seemed hungry. Léa could not take her eyes off her father. He seemed to have calmed down, but his silence was almost more worrying than his agitation that afternoon. As soon as the meal was over, Léa took her sister's arm and led her aside.

"Come take a walk with me, we must talk."

Laure tried to draw away, and then resigned herself. Together they went to the terrace. The valley looked like a painting in the evening sun which was still warm. They sat down on the little wall, in the shade of the wistaria.

"What happened to make Papa so upset?"

Laure hung her head. Two tears splashed onto her hands which were resting on her knees.

"Don't cry, little sister. Just tell me what happened."

Sobbing, Laure flung herself around her big sister's neck.

"I'll never dare tell, *especially* not you."

"Why especially not me?"

"Because you wouldn't understand."

"Understand what?"

Her sobs grew louder.

"Tell me, please. Think of Papa."

"It's not Papa who's the problem."

What did she mean? Léa shook her in her irritation.

"Sabine . . ." she stuttered.

"Sabine?"

"Sabine and Otto."

"Sabine and Otto, what do you mean, I don't understand."

"They want to get married."

"Get married . . ."

"Yes. The captain asked Papa last week."

"I see. And Papa refused, of course."

"I knew it. I knew you wouldn't understand and that there was no chance you'd help Sabine. I told her, but she kept saying: 'You're wrong, Léa's experienced, she knows what love is.' But I said it wasn't true, that you didn't know anything about love. That if she wanted advice or help, she should go to Camille."

Léa was surprised at the violence of Laure's feelings.

"Apart from Montillac, you don't love anyone or anything. Poor Mathias realized that. That's why he left."

"Leave Mathias out of this. We're talking about Sabine and her relations with a filthy German."

"I was sure you'd feel this way. You only swear by your General de Gaulle and the terrorists he sends from London to blow up trains and murder innocent people."

"Murder innocent people! How dare you call the enemy that's occupying our country innocent? They starve, deport and kill us. If it weren't for these 'innocent people,' our mother would still be alive, Papa wouldn't be mad, Uncle Adrien and Laurent wouldn't be forced into hiding . . ."

"But they're in the wrong, they're rebels."

"Rebels! Those who are fighting for the honor of France?"

"Those are just words, big hollow words. It's Pétain who represents the honor of France."

"Laure, you're just an ignorant fool. Your Pétain is Hitler's accomplice."

"It's not true: he's putting himself at the service of the French people."

"What a treat for France. What we need is a well-equipped army and a leader who carries on the fight."

"You're insulting a great old man."

"So what? Does being old excuse him for acting so despicably? On the contrary, it makes matters doubly serious. He's using his prestige as a hero of the Great War to make people accept the disgrace of the armistice."

"If it weren't for the armistice, hundreds of thousands of people would be dead, like Mummy, in the air raids."

As she said the word "Mummy," Laure began to cry again. Léa held her head against her shoulder.

"Perhaps you're right. I don't know any more. What would Mummy have done in this situation?"

They sat like that for a while, overwhelmed by their troubles.

"Laure, aren't you shocked that Sabine wants to marry a German?"

"A bit," she admitted, "but since they love each other . . ."

349

"Well, let them wait until the war is over."

"It isn't possible."

"Why not?"

"Because Sabine is expecting a baby."

"Oh no!"

"Yes."

Léa leaped up. In the distance, the moors formed a dark shape on the horizon and Langon was bathed in a light mist which rose from the Garonne.

"Poor Sabine," she murmured.

Laure heard her.

"Help her, Léa, talk to Papa, he'll listen to you."

"I don't think he will. He's too far gone now."

"Please try, please."

"If only Sabine were here, then I'd be able to talk to her and find out precisely what she wants to do."

"Talk to Papa. He must give his consent, otherwise Sabine will kill herself."

"Don't talk nonsense."

"It's not nonsense. She's desperate."

"I promise I'll do what I can. Now, leave me. I need time to think. Go and tell Camille to come out here."

"All right."

Then, after a moment's hesitation, she kissed her sister Laure's cheek.

"Thank you, Léa."

A few minutes later, Camille joined Léa, who briefly told her what had happened.

"I feel I'm to blame. We didn't do anything."

"What could we have done?"

"Shown her more affection, made her confide in us."

"I know her. That wouldn't have made any difference. I'm going to the market at Langon tomorrow and I'll go and see her at the hospital. Depending on what she says, I'll talk to Papa. I'm too tired this evening. Goodnight, Camille."

"Goodnight, darling."

"Here you are, Mademoiselle Léa, let me know how you find

the potted duck," said old Cordeau as he handed Léa's basket back to her.

"Thank you very much. Papa's the one who'll be pleased, you know how much he loves his food."

"Give him my regards and tell him I'd love to see him one of these days."

"I will. Thank you very much. Goodbye, Monsieur Cordeau."

Léa left the restaurant carrying her huge basket covered with a red-striped tea towel. There was a German soldier standing near her bicycle, which was leaning up against a wall.

"It's careless of you, mademoiselle, to leave your bicycle unchained. There are thieves around. Be careful."

"Thank you."

Her hands were shaking as she attached the basket to the carrier with the help of the soldier.

She got on to her bicycle and rode off towards the hospital.

The courtyard was full of ambulances and military vehicles. She asked at the office if she could speak to her sister. They told her she was in the East Building, in the emergency ward. Léa mounted her bicycle. The first person she met was Captain Kramer, who bowed stiffly when he saw her.

"Hello, Mademoiselle Léa. I'm glad to see you to say goodbye."

"Goodbye?"

"Yes, I've had an urgent call to go to Paris. I'll be stationed there. I leave in an hour. My orderly will take care of my belongings. Please give my regards to Madame d'Argilat. She's an admirable woman. I hope her love for France does not incite her to an act of carelessness. Tell your good father that it was an honor for me to meet him and I hope he will reconsider his prejudices. Say goodbye to dear little Laure for me, and to Ruth and your good aunt."

"Are you sure you haven't forgotten anybody?"

"I've just said goodbye to Sabine. She's going to need all your affection. Can I rely on you?"

Not him as well! Men seemed to have a habit of asking her to look after their wives or their mistresses!

"I'll do what I can, but it's not only up to me."

"Thank you. Sabine isn't as strong as you are: she's vulnerable and gullible. Don't judge her. I would have liked to get to know you better, but you always refused any attempts at conversation. I understand you. If I were in your position, I might have done the same. But I'd like you to know that I admire France and the French people. One day our two fine nations will join together to make one and bring peace to the world. That's why we must join forces."

Léa was hardly listening to him. The sad thing was he was sincere.

"Don't you agree?"

"I might believe it if you weren't occupying our country and if you didn't persecute helpless people. Goodbye, Captain Kramer."

Léa walked into the waiting room carrying her basket. The nurses were grouped at the other end of the room. Léa walked towards them.

Surrounded by her friends, Sabine was sitting at the table crying with her head cradled in her arms.

"What do you want?" asked a nurse.

"I'd like to speak to my sister, Sabine Delmas."

"There she is. I hope you can calm her down."

"Can you leave us alone?"

"Of course. Back to work, girls! Mademoiselle Delmas will take care of her sister."

When all the nurses had left the room, Léa sat down beside Sabine, who had not moved.

"Come Sabine, let's go home."

She had said just the right thing. The poor lovesick girl's shoulders stopped shaking and a shy hand sought hers and squeezed it.

"I can't. What will Papa say?"

Her childlike voice touched Léa more than she could have imagined.

"Don't worry, I'll deal with it. Come on."

"I have to change."

"Where are your things?"

"In the closet over there."

Léa opened the closet and took out her sister's flowery

rayon dress, her handbag and her shoes. Sabine was getting dressed when the matron come in.

"Have a rest, dear. You can have tomorrow off."

"Thank you, madame."

The two sisters rode the two miles from Langon to Montillac without exchanging a word. Léa pushed her bicycle up the hill as she had done the day before, while Sabine stood up to pedal. "She could at least wait for me," thought Léa.

In the kitchen, Camille and Ruth were making lunch.

"Have you seen Sabine?"

"Yes, she said she was going up to bed," said Ruth, tossing potatoes in the frying pan.

"Look what I've got to go with the potatoes."

"Potted duck!" exclaimed the two women in unison.

"It's a present from old Cordeau."

"Old Cordeau?" asked Ruth. "He's not usually that generous."

"He was today and we're going to have a feast. Papa will be thrilled!"

"Why will I be thrilled, daughter?" said Pierre Delmas, coming into the kitchen.

Léa got the shock of her life when she saw him. Her father was usually meticulous about his appearance. Today he was unshaven, his ragged shirt hung out of his trousers which were stained and covered with streaks of mud. How he had changed overnight!

He's realized that Mummy is dead, thought Léa.

She fought down a desire to take him in her arms, to console him, to tell him it wasn't true, that Isabelle would walk in any minute now with a basket of flowers on her arm with her big straw hat that kept the sun off so well. The memory was so poignant that Léa looked away. She realized that, deep down, she had not accepted Isabelle's death either, and now that her father accepted the truth she was separated from her mother forever.

The jar of potted duck slipped out of her hand and smashed on the tiles with such a loud crash that they all jumped.

"How clumsy you are, darling," said Pierre Delmas bending down to pick up the broken glass.

"Leave it, monsieur. I'll clean it up," said Ruth.

Léa could not hold back her tears and Pierre Delmas noticed she was crying.

"Come, come, it doesn't matter. We'll wash the pieces. We can still eat them. Come and blow your nose like when you were little."

To become a little girl again, sit on his knee, cuddle up to him as if to hide away, to blow her nose in her father's handkerchief and feel his big arms round her, inhale the familiar smell of tobacco, wine-cellars, leather and hair that was sometimes mingled with her mother's perfume, that was all she wanted at that moment.

"Papa . . ."

"It's all right, darling. I'm here now."

Was he there, back in the land of the living at last? And for how long?

They all did justice to the potted duck, which Ruth had carefully cleaned, except for Sabine who remained in her room.

Before lunch, Pierre Delmas had shaved and changed his clothes.

During the meal, the family could see that he was once again his old self.

Chapter 25

A few days later, as she promised, Léa tried to talk to her father during one of their after-dinner walks through the vineyards. As soon as she opened her mouth, he stopped her:

"I don't want to hear any more about this unnatural marriage. You're forgetting all too easily that the Germans are our enemies, and the enemies of France. They're occupying our country. Captain Kramer has broken the most elementary law of hospitality."

"But Papa, they love each other."

"If they really love each other, they'll wait for the war to end. I refuse to give my blessing to a union that your mother would have disapproved of."

"Sabine is . . ."

"Not another word on the subject! This conversation makes me feel ill. I'm already very tired."

He sat down on a large stone by the path.

"Do you really have to go to Bordeaux tomorrow?"

"Absolutely, I've got to see Luc to discuss how I can annul the commitment I signed that I would sell to Fayard."

"The commitment to sell! Oh! Papa, how could you do that?"

"I don't know. Since your poor mother's death, he's been nagging me, forever asking me for more money to buy equipment. When he realized we were having difficulties, he offered to buy me out. The first time he mentioned it, I managed to be quite firm and told him I'd fire him if he brought the subject up again."

"Why didn't you say anything to me?"

"You could see for yourself, my pet, that I wasn't thinking clearly. Isabelle wasn't there and I imagined that you were still a child."

"But Papa, it's thanks to me that Montillac is still alive. I've kept it going single-handed. I've been supervising Fayard and the farmhands. I've managed to feed everybody on the vegetables that I grew myself in the kitchen garden. I put Fayard in his place, and now you tell me . . ."

Léa was not allowed to finish. Pierre Delmas took his daughter's hands in his and kissed them.

"I know all that. Ruth and Camille have told me how courageous you've been. That's why I have to annul this commitment to sell. I need a lawyer's advice."

"Beware of Uncle Luc: he's a Pétain supporter."

"I can't believe that. He's always been conservative and a fervent supporter of a strong-arm right. I know he's a rabid Jew-hater and anti-Communist, but to collaborate with the Germans . . ."

"If Uncle Adrien were here, he'd convince you."

"Luc and Adrien have never been able to stand each other. As children, they were already in opposite camps. Both of them were always good Christians, but they knew nothing of forgiveness. Things were better when Adrien entered the monastery, but even then Luc said that it was putting the cat among the pigeons.

"Your uncle's success as a preacher flattered Luc's vanity and snobbery, but then came the Spanish Civil War. Adrien helped the Republicans and denounced the attitude of the French Church and government from the pulpit in the Bordeaux Cathedral. Luc hated him for it. Camille tells me that Adrien is in touch with London and is in hiding in the unoccupied zone. I'm sure that doesn't please Luc."

"He told me that if he knew where Adrien was, he'd denounce him."

"I don't believe a word of that. I'm sure he said that in a moment of anger. Luc has many faults, but he's not a Judas."

"I do so hope you are right!"

"I also hope to have news of Adrien. I've written to his superior to tell him of my forthcoming visit."

"I'll come with you, so I won't have to worry about you."

"As you wish, my pet. Now leave me. I need to be alone."

Léa kissed her father's cheek and left him.

As she walked towards the house that glowed pink in the sunset, trying not to think about the next day, it occurred to her that it hadn't rained in so long that the ground was baked hard. Some of the leaves were turning yellow. She bent down and picked up a handful of dust. "Tomorrow, I'll tell Fayard to get rid of all the bindweed." She went around the little wood and on to the terrace. The evening light enhanced the beauty of the landscape and, as always, Léa was filled with happiness as she looked out over the valley. Sabine was sitting hunched up on the grass in the shadow of the rose arbor, waiting for her. Léa sat down beside her. Sabine looked up. The expression on her face was pitiful.

"Did you speak to Papa?"

"I tried, but he wouldn't listen to me. I'll find a way. I promise."

"It's no use. What will become of me?"

"You could . . ."

Léa faltered; she played with a clod of earth.

"You could go to Cadillac, to Doctor Girard. They say . . ."

"How dreadful! How dare you suggest such a thing? Otto and I both want this child. I'd rather die than—"

"Well then, stop bawling, and tell Papa yourself that you're pregnant."

"No, I could never tell him. I'll run away and join Otto. Perhaps that'll make Papa give in."

"Don't do that. It would make him too miserable. Think of what he's been through since Mummy died."

"What about me. What about what I've been through?"

"I'm sorry, but I don't feel much pity for you."

"What about you and Mathias, and others, no doubt . . ."

Léa protested. "They weren't Germans, my lovers."

"That's too simple. Is it my fault that our two countries are at war?"

"He behaved badly."

"But he loves me!"

Léa shrugged.

Sabine went on:

"I know lots of girls who have German boyfriends. Our cousin Corinne is engaged to Commander Strukell. Uncle Luc was a bit hesitant about giving his permission, but he was flattered when the commander's father, a high-up Nazi, very close to Hitler, came over specially from Germany to ask for his daughter's hand. What's more, the family's very rich and they're from an old aristocratic line. Everything that Uncle Luc could wish for! Corinne's lucky. If Mummy were still alive, I could have talked to her. She'd have understood and helped me."

"You could have confided in Ruth."

"I didn't dare."

"Is that why you chose Laure for a confidante? She's just a kid. Didn't it occur to you that she might be upset by your revelations?"

"No. She hasn't got anything against the Germans, and I needed to talk to someone who wasn't hostile to me."

They both stared at the ground in silence for a long time.

"Sabine, I'd really like to help you . . ."

"I know, Léa, thank you. I feel better now that you know about it. Even though we don't agree about anything, I know I can count on you," she said, kissing her sister on the cheek.

"Tomorrow, I'm going to Bordeaux with Papa; he's going to Uncle Luc's. Perhaps when Corinne's engagement is announced, he'll change his mind. I promise I'll try and talk to him again. But you promise that you won't do anything to upset him."

"I promise," she said, wiping her hands on her dress.

Pierre Delmas came back to Montillac a broken man. According to Luc, it was impossible to annul the commitment to sell because he would have to pay a large sum in compensation, which he simply did not have. What was more, the solicitor had been pessimistic about their chances of selling their estates in the West Indies.

The visit to the monastery in the Rue de Saint-Genènes had also been an ordeal. The father superior made it quite clear that he considered Adrien a terrorist, a traitor and an apostate. He had considered it his duty to inform the mother church in Paris and hoped that they would tell Rome of the activities of this reprobate brother. No, he did not know of his whereabouts, nor did he have any wish to. Adrien Delmas had dissociated himself from the Catholic community by his actions, he was unworthy to be a member of the order of Saint-Dominique and was nothing but a defrocked priest. Every day, he prayed for him, asking God to bring this stray lamb back to the fold. Léa left the pious residence feeling sick.

Afterwards, the announcement of Corinne Delmas's engagement had met with scornful indifference on the part of Pierre Delmas. Luc immediately said:"You ought to allow Sabine to marry Captain Kramer. He is from a family every bit as excellent as that of my future son-in-law."

Pierre Delmas got up to leave and simply replied: "I don't wish to discuss the matter any further. Goodbye, brother."

How many times had Sabine paced the hundred yards or so between the house and the road as she waited for her father and her sister to return? Twenty times? the last train from Bordeaux had long since gone. Old Chombas's cart, which served as a taxi, should have drawn up outside the gates of the estate hours ago. Supposing they had decided to spend the night in Bordeaux? She could not bear another sleepless night of uncertainty.

Since Otto's departure, Sabine had never suffered his absence so keenly. She had already endured so much for this love affair: the contempt of her colleagues at the hospital, of Léa and her father, Camille's pity, Fayard's mockery, the shame of having to meet in secret and the fear of being found out. It was too hard. While he was still there, she felt strong and brave. Without him, she was just a shy, lost little girl.

The rumbling of the cart made her jump. She hid behind one of the big plane trees in the drive, like a child who had been caught out. When she saw her father get down from the cart, helped by Léa, and walk falteringly with bowed head, she realized that, as far as she was concerned, all was lost. She rested her forehead against the bark of the tree, noticed two ants scuttle away panic stricken, and remembered how, as a little girl, she would hide behind that same tree to jump out at her father when he came back from work or from his walk, and she was so excited when he said: "Fee, fi, fo, fum! I smell the blood of a little girl: I think she's hiding somewhere here. I'm, going to look for her and gobble her up . . ."

"No, Papa! No, Papa!" She would scream rushing out of her hiding place and throwing herself into his outstretched arms.

It was over. She would leave tomorrow.

The following day, Léa went to Caudrot to pick up the mail. At the post office, there was a message telling her to go to La Rèole, to the Debrays' house. She found them worried and agitated.

"Could you go to Bordeaux either this evening or tomorrow morning?" asked Madame Debray.

"I don't know. I went there yesterday with my father. I'd have to think of an excuse."

"Find one. It's a matter of life and death for a number of people in the network. Go to 34 Cours de Verdun to the office of Monsieur André Grand-Clement, the insurance broker, and tell him that Léon des Landes's *foie gras* is not very good. He'll reply that he knows that, that he and his wife had food poisoning. Then tell him that you've come for the insurance policy that your father wants to take out. He will show you into his office and you will then give him these documents. They are fake insurance policies which contain our messages. After a while, tell him that you don't feel very well, that you need some air. He will come outside with you. Once in the street, tell him that Superintendent Poinsot is on to him, and that if he hasn't been arrested yet it's on SS Lieutenant Dohse's advice. Dohse has probably infiltrated the network and is waiting until he has all the

360

necessary elements to strike a heavy blow. Tell him not to lose any time in warning the others so that they can take cover. Is that quite clear?"

Léa repeated the instructions.

"Good! The sooner you get to Bordeaux, the better."

"I'll try to catch the six o'clock train. Dohse . . . That name is familiar."

"He's a highly intelligent, formidable character, with a nose like a police dog. He never abandons a lead. Be very careful. . . . As an extra precaution, one of our friends will take you over the demarcation line through the Font-au-Loup forest."

"But the Germans at Saint-Pierre know me. If they don't see me come back, they'll be suspicious."

"If they question you when you cross back over the line, tell them you came back via Saint-Laurent-du-Bois because you wanted to see a friend. I'll make sure they remember you at Saint-Laurent."

"All right."

"Perhaps I was wrong about you, love," said Madame Debray embracing her.

"Perhaps, madame, but does it matter?"

"It does to me. We heard from your uncle yesterday, who asks you to tell your Aunt Bernadette that her son, Lucien, is with him."

"Oh! I'm so pleased. I'm very fond of my cousin, and I was so afraid that something had happened to him. Did Uncle Adrien say anything else?"

"No."

"It's time to leave. Go through Labarthe and wait for the blacksmith. He knows you and will get you across the line without any trouble. Do exactly as he tells you and everything will go smoothly. He'll take you as far as Saint-Martin-de-Grave; you know the way from there. Goodbye, child, God be with you."

The Debrays watched Léa ride off on her blue bicycle and wondered whether they had the right to endanger the life of this very unusual and very beautiful girl.

When they reached the Manchot woods, the blacksmith

told Léa to camouflage herself and her bicycle as best she could. They cut across the woods and the vineyards to get on to the main road which formed the boundary between the occupied zone and the free zone. At the hamlet of Maison-Neuve, the road, which was very straight at this point, was deserted. The blacksmith beckoned to Léa and they crossed the border without incident. They both rode Léa's bicycle to Saint-Martin-de-Grave, and parted at the old mill. Léa had a flat tire at Mouchac and had to finish the journey on foot, cursing as she went.

Camille was playing with her son in the meadow in front of the house. The child ran to greet Léa with outstretched arms. She put her bicycle down and picked him up.

"Hello, Charlie. Hello, pet. Ouch, you're hurting me!"

Th child was hugging her with all the strength in his little arms. Camille came towards them smiling.

"He adores you. I ought to be madly jealous . . ."

She radiated such love and trust that Léa felt uncomfortable.

"Promise me that, if anything happens to me, you'd look after him as if he were your own," said Camille suddenly serious.

"Don't talk foolishness. Why should anything happen to you?"

"You never know. Please, promise me."

Not only did she have to protect the mother at the father's request, but also the child at the mother's request. What about her? Who would protect her? she thought. Aloud she said, "I promise, I'll look after him as if he were my own son."

"Thank you," said Camille. After a moment, she asked, "How did it go with the mail?"

"Fine, but I must go to Bordeaux. Can you find some excuse to give to Papa and Ruth?"

"Don't worry, I'll think of something."

"I'm going to get changed. Will you lend me your bicycle? Mine has a flat."

"Of course."

"Can you tell Aunt Bernadette that Lucien is well and that he's with Uncle Adrien."

"That's good news! I'll run in and tell her."

As Léa came back down stairs, she could hear the sound of raised voices coming from her father's study. Her instinct was to go in, but she would miss the six o'clock train. She left Montillac full of apprehension. It was not hard to imagine the conversation that was taking place between her father and Fayard.

Léa left Camille's bicycle with the stationmaster. As usual, she went through the police and customs checks without a hitch.

In her compartment, there were just two peasant women. Léa stretched out wondering where she would sleep that night. It was out of the question for her to go to Luc Delmas's house. She would see when she got there. She was glad Lucien was with Uncle Adrien. Perhaps Laurent was with them. She missed him.

As always when she thought of Laurent, François came to mind. The closing words of Sarah Mulstein's letter came back to her: "You two are made for each other." How ridiculous! She was made for Laurent and nobody else.

What about Sabine, whom was she made for? Poor thing, if she really did love her German, Léa felt sorry for her, and what she was going to suffer. What would become of her with her child? Léa decided she would have to persuade Papa to let Sabine marry Otto.

The train arrived in Bordeaux.

It was quite a walk from the station to the insurance broker's office. Léa went along the embankment. Several times, German solders tried to waylay this pretty girl in a short white cotton dress whose wooden-soled sandals clattered on the cobblestones. Some even offered to carry her little wicker suitcase which contained the documents the Debrays had given her.

It was almost eight o'clock in the evening when she arrived at the address in the Cours de Verdun. She had to ring three times before the door was opened; the man in the doorway resembled the description she had been given.

'Monsieur Grand-Clement?'

He nodded.

"Good evening, monsieur. I wanted to tell you that Léon des Landes's *foie gras* is not very good."

"I know, unfortunately my wife and I both got food poisoning."

"I wanted to talk to you about my father's insurance policy."

"Would you care to step into my office."

Léa gave him the documents, asked if she could go out for some air. . . . Outside, she gave him the message.

"Thank our friends for this precious information. I'll take the necessary steps to warn our people," said Monsieur Grand-Clement.

"Have you got anything for me to take back to them?"

"No, not now. Rest assured, mademoiselle, as far as your father's insurance policy is concerned," he said rather too loudly.

Two men walked past. They looked like two people enjoying the cool evening air.

"You must leave now! Those are two of Superintendent Poinsot's police officers."

Léa walked straight on and arrived at the Place de Tourny. There, she paused to think. Where should she go? Apart from her Uncle Luc, she did not know anyone in Bordeaux. She walked the deserted narrow street with the distinct impression she was being followed. She arrived in the square in front of the main theatre. There were more people about, soldiers mainly. She stopped in front of the newspaper stand *La Petite Gironde* . . . the name of that newspaper seemed to ring a bell. *La Petite Gironde* . . . Raphaël Mahl . . . Le Chapon Fin . . . the editor, Richard Chapon. She heaved a sigh of relief. That's where she would go.

The cathedral bell tolled nine o'clock when she reached the newspaper office. The porter was familiar from her first visit.

"The paper's closed."

"I want to see Monsieur Chapon."

"He's not here. Come back tomorrow."

"Please, I have to see him." said Léa walking towards the door which she knew was the door to his office. It opened even before she touched the handle. At that very moment, two men came into the hall.

"Gentlemen, gentlemen, the paper is closed," cried the porter blocking their path.

Léa recognized the two men who had walked past the insurance broker's office. One of them brutally pushed the porter out of his way and continued walking towards her.

"Gentlemen, what's going on?" asked Richard Chapon from the doorway.

"We would like to speak to this young lady."

"Do you know these gentlemen?"

She shook her head.

"I'm afraid, gentlemen, I must ask you to leave."

"I'm sorry, but we have to take her away for interrogation," said the one who seemed to be in charge. He showed Chapon an identity card which he scrutinized carefully.

"I'll speak for Mademoiselle Delmas: she'a a friend of mine. What is more, her uncle, Luc Delmas, is an important man in Bordeaux."

"That doesn't concern us. Superintendent Poinsot gives the orders. We just carry them out."

"It's almost dark. Can your questions not wait until morning?"

"No. We've got to take her now."

"Very well, I'll come with you. Dufour, tell Luc Delmas that I'm with his niece."

The police officers' look of annoyance did not escape the editor's notice.

"What are you waiting for, Dufour. Call Monsieur Delmas."

They did not leave the building before making sure that the porter had indeed managed to get hold of Léa's uncle.

A chauffeur-driven Citroën was waiting outside. Léa and Richard Chapon climbed into the back with the police officers.

They drove through the maze of dark streets in silence.

"But this isn't the way to Poinsot's station!" exclaimed Chapon.

"We're going to the Avenue du Marachel-Pétain."

"To number 224?"

"Yes, that's where the superintendent told us to take the young lady."

Léa noticed her companion's anxiety.

"What the matter?" she whispered.

Richard Chapon did not answer.

Léa thought at top speed. She was no longer carrying anything compromising on her. Her papers were in order and her visit to Grand-Clement was plausible. She relaxed a little, comforted by Chapon's presence.

It was so dark that Léa could not even see the building she was taken into. Near the door was a German soldier seated at a desk, writing. He looked up and asked in French: "What is it?"

"It's for Lieutenant Dohse."

"I'll tell him."

"What does this mean? I thought it was Superintendent Poinsot who wanted to see Mademoiselle Delmas."

"Lieutenant Dohse wants to see her too."

The soldier came back.

They went down a corridor at the end of which was a room with double doors padded with black leather. Inside, SS Lieutenant Dohse, a very tall man with black hair, in his early thirties, was standing waiting for them.

"Leave us," he said to the two police officers.

The men left the room.

"Good evening, dear Monsieur Chapon. Why are you here?"

"Well, I'm not here for fun. You can be sure of that. I would rather be at home in bed. I am accompanying my friend, Mademoiselle Delmas, whom your men said they were taking to Superintendent Poinsot."

"That is true. I expect him any minute now. The poor superintendent is so overworked that I sometimes help him out. But please, do sit down.

"And so, mademoiselle, you are the niece of the famous lawyer Delmas? My congratulations! There's a man who knows his duty! One of your cousins is to marry one of our most brilliant officers, is she not? What better way to cement the union of our two great nations? I'm sure you're a good patriot yourself. Am I correct?''

"Of course," said Léa with a smile in spite of the fear she felt welling up inside her.

"I was sure. Many of your fellow countrymen are like you and are a great help to us in hunting down the terrorists. Unfortunately this minority seems bent on causing trouble. Our job is a thankless one. It is often misinterpreted. But our reward is the upholding of law and order and setting the citizens' minds at rest, is it not? No doubt you went to see Monsieur Grand-Clement on family business?''

"Yes. My father wishes to take out certain insurance policies.''

"Didn't he have time to deal with it himself, yesterday?''
Instinctively, Léa gave the right reply.

"Are you having us watched? Is that how you know my father was in Bordeaux yesterday?''

"Watched is an exaggeration. We have a number of our agents in the railway stations who inform us of the arrival of certain people.''

"And why my father?''

"Isn't he the brother of Adrien Delmas whom we strongly suspect to be in the pay of London?''

"Nonsense! He is a priest. My Uncle Luc is also his brother, and you don't appear to be watching him.''

Richard Chapon pretended to have a coughing fit to conceal his smile.

"Mademoiselle, your uncle has given us all the proof we need of his loyalty to Germany, don't you think?''

"I'm sure he has," she could not help replying.

The telephone rang and Dohse answered it.

"Yes, show him in. . . . Here is Superintendent Poinsot, as well as Monsieur Delmas.''

The SS lieutenant greeted the lawyer with deference, and the policeman with marked condescension.

"Believe me, Monsieur Delmas, I'm very sorry to disturb

you. Has Superintendent Poinsot explained that it's simply a routine check that has led to our questioning your niece?"

"Yes, but I find it intolerable that a member of my family should be under suspicion. How can you imagine that this child is interested in anything other than pretty clothes?"

"Unfortunately, these days, young girls are not what they used to be," said Superintendent Poinsot.

"Not the girls in my family, monsieur," said Luc Delmas sharply.

"Excuse me, Chapon, I didn't say hello to you. What are you doing here?" asked Poinsot.

"I wasn't going to let Mademoiselle Delmas go off on her own with two policemen I didn't know."

"Thank you. But what was she doing at your place at nightfall?" asked the superintendent.

"I didn't have time to ask her. Your men didn't give me the opportunity."

"Mademoiselle, what were you doing in Monsieur Chapon's office?"

Léa thought quickly, knowing she had to give a convincing answer.

"I was going to ask Monsieur Chapon for a job."

"A job?" said Luc Delmas and the superintendent in unison.

"One day, he said to me that if ever I needed anything, I could count on him, and as I need to work . . ."

"But why?" asked her uncle, astonished.

"To help Papa."

The four men looked at each other.

"I know about your father's financial problems, but I hardly think your wages would be much help. Still, I congratulate you on your brave gesture."

"I'm touched by your trust, Léa. I think I'll be able to offer you something shortly."

"Well, gentlemen, I think you're satisfied with my niece's answers to your questions. It's getting late and I have to be at court early tomorrow. Come Léa. Your cousins are waiting for you. Poinsot, would you like a lift back?"

"Thank you, monsieur, but I've got one or two things to

discuss with the lieutenant. I'm sorry for this inconvenience. Goodbye, Mademoiselle Delmas, goodby, Monsieur Chapon.''

SS Lieutenant Friedrich-Wilhelm Dohse bowed. ''Goodbye, mademoiselle. Be careful who you mix with, won't you?''

Léa nodded but said nothing. She went out followed by Luc Delmas and Richard Chapon.

As they were getting into the lawyer's car, the editor of *La Petite Gironde* commented: ''You are lucky to be able to drive. I haven't had a car for a long time now.''

Luc Delmas didn't reply.

Richard Chapon went on: ''I must say, I was feeling pretty uncomfortable. If you hadn't been there, we might not have got out so easily.''

''Why not, if she hasn't done anything wrong?''

''With that bunch, you've always done something wrong.''

Again, Luc Delmas did not comment.

''Shall I drop you at your office?''

''Yes, please, if it's not out of your way.''

They had no further words until they reached the paper.

''Goodbye, Léa. You can count on me.''

''Goodbye, monsieur, thank you for everything.''

Uncle and niece drove the rest of the way in total silence. When they entered Luc Delmas's apartment, he said: ''Don't make any noise. Come into my study.''

The dreaded time for explanations had come. Léa went into the austere study with its walls lined with serious-looking books. Her uncle paced up and down for a while with his hands behind his back. Finally, he stopped in front of Léa, who had remained standing.

''Let's get things straight. I only came to get you in order to prevent a scandal which could have affected us. We've got enough trouble with one black sheep in the family, your Uncle Adrien. I hope for your sake that Lieutenant Dohse and Superintendent Poinsot were taken in by your little act with Chapon.''

Despite the hatred and contempt she felt for her uncle, Léa sensed that she ought to convince him.

"But it wasn't an act! I really am looking for a job. We've got no money left at home."

She sounded so sincere that Luc Delmas was taken aback.

"Do you honestly believe your small wage would be enough to save Montillac?"

Léa did not have to force herself to make her eyes fill with tears.

"No, of course not, but it would help. It looks as though the grape harvest is going to be a good one."

"Why are you so determined to keep the place?" he asked more gently.

"You've got your old house with the pine woods near Marcheprime, haven't you? Apparently you're very fond of it."

Léa could see from his face that she had touched his weak spot. This man, whose main preoccupation had always seemed to be to increase his wealth, passionately maintained a humble shepherd's cottage surrounded by woodland which he had inherited.

"Yes, I understand," he said, giving up the fight. "Go to bed."

Léa looked surprised.

"You didn't think I was going to let you sleep in the street?"

Léa's cousin Corinne woke her the next morning with a breakfast tray. She was bright and elegant, with a red and blue silk dress and a fashionable hair style. Léa could not believe her eyes: white bread and jam, butter and, wonder of wonders, croissants! Corinne smiled at Léa's look of ecstasy.

"Don't imagine we have this every day. Thanks to Papa's connections, we're not short of anything, but we only have croissants twice a week."

"I've obviously come on the right day!" said Léa with her mouth already full.

"Yes! Don't eat so fast, you'll make yourself sick!"

"You wouldn't understand. It's so good. And this coffee? Real coffee. How do you manage?"

"I'll give you some. It was given to us by a client of Papa's whose boats go to South America, the West Indies and goodness knows where else. Each time one of his ships comes back, he supplies us with sugar, coffee, cocoa and cloth."

"Cloth?"

"Yes. We can trade it."

"You're well organized."

"One has to be, these days."

She sounded like a little bourgeoise, anxious to maintain a well-run home. In a few years' time, she would be just like her mother, thought Léa, feeling sorry for her German fiancé.

"It's late. You should have wakened me earlier."

"Papa has phoned Montillac."

"Thank him for me. I'll take the four o'clock train."

"Can't you stay till tomorrow? I'd so like you to meet my fiancé."

"I'm afraid I can't. I must get back. Next time."

"I won't insist; Papa tells me you've got a lot of problems. But I do want you to come to the dressmaker's with me for a fitting for my wedding dress. You can't refuse me that."

Léa was relieved when it was time for her train to leave. Her suitcase was full of sugar, coffee and three lengths of lovely fabric. Corinne had insisted on coming to the station with her. Léa had not seen her uncle again.

She was almost home now. Not much further and she would finally be able to walk into the house which was at last rid of the presence of the Germans. She imagined everyone's joy when she opened her suitcase . . .

Camille, Laure, Bernadette Bouchardeau, Ruth and old Sidonie were all sitting round the kitchen table looking overwhelmed when Léa walked in.

"Léa!" cried Laure, hurling herself at her sister.

"Here you are, at last," sighed Ruth looking tired and drawn.

"How dreadful, what a shame!" snivelled Bernadette whose face was puffy and red.

"Poor little thing," murmured Sidonie, holding her stomach.

Léa turned to Camille who stood silently.

"What's going on?"

"Sabine has run away."

"Run away? When? Where?"

"Yesterday evening, we think. We only found out this morning. She left a letter for your father and one for you too," said Ruth.

"Where is it?"

The governess took a crumpled envelope out of her pocket.

Dear Sister,

I'm running away to join Otto. I'm too unhappy away from him. I hope you'll understand. Papa will be very hurt and I'm relying on you to comfort him. Tell Laure that I love her dearly and ask her to forgive me for setting such a bad example. I'll miss Ruth a lot. Please tell her. Give my love to Aunt Bernadette. Ask Camille to pray for me. She knows better than any of you what I've been through. Mention little Sabine to dear Sidonie from time to time and drink her blackcurrant liqueur to my health.

I'm leaving you a heavy burden, but you're strong enough for anything. Whatever happens, you face up to it with courage and pride. I never told you, but I greatly admire how you have kept Montillac going single-handed, even ruining your hands cultivating that land to feed us. The little treats I brought tasted bitter compared to your vegetables.

Another thing, be careful, you and Camille. You ought to know that Otto received several anonymous letters saying that you were smuggling letters across the demarcation line, that you mixed with terrorists and smuggled Englishmen across the line. Otto tore the letters up, but his successor might take such denunciations seriously. I must tell you that I agree with what you're doing. That'll probably surprise you coming from me. It's true, I love a German, but I also love my country.

Léa, you can write to me poste-restante in the Eighth

district in Paris. As soon as I've got an address, I'll let you know. You will write to me, won't you? You won't leave me without news of Papa?

Please don't judge me, darling. Forgive me for running away like this, but I can't face up to seeing you all again. Lots of love, Sabine.

When she finished reading, Léa sat down with quivering lips and a far-off look in her eyes.

"Sabine has gone to Paris."

"To join her German," hissed Bernadette.

Léa darted her such a look that she held her tongue. Then, with a great effort, Léa gave each person their little message from Sabine.

"How did Papa react?" she asked Camille.

"At first he came in fuming, and then sat there forlornly on the bench by the path as if he were hoping she would come back. Then he asked where you were. That's when Uncle Luc telephoned and they talked for a long time. I don't know what they said. Your father got his hat and his walking stick and made for the shrine. We haven't seen him since. Sidonie came to tell us she saw him at the cemetery praying by your mother's grave. She went up and talked to him. He looked straight through her as though he didn't recognize her and signalled her to go away. He seems to have lost his reason again."

"What about since then?"

"Laure went to Verdelais. He's not there any more."

"I went into the church, I went to see people he knew. I came back past the shrine, but I couldn't find him," stated Laure.

"We've got to locate him before it gets dark. There's definitely a storm brewing," said Léa.

The storm broke that evening, just as Léa got back. Nobody had found any sign of Pierre Delmas. Doctor Blanchard, who had been told of his old friend's state, came as soon as he could. Fayard covered every inch of vineyard with his dog and returned soaked. Neighbors who had been helping in the search came back too. They all dried themselves around the kitchen fire airing their opinions and drinking mulled wine served by Ruth. Little Charles was excited to see so many people and he went shouting from one person to another. Around midnight, everybody went home, except Doctor Blanchard.

Léa refused to go to bed and, as soon as dawn broke, she took her bicycle and went out again to search the countryside. She went to all the places where she and her father used to walk when she was a child. There was no trace of him. She sat down in the wet grass at the foot of the cross. The sky was vast and gray with menacing black clouds crushing the landscape. However, in the distance, over the moors and the sea, there was a thin band of light. The weather's going to clear up, thought Léa, before she drifted off to sleep leaning up against the cross.

The cold awoke her. the weather had not cleared and the sky was dark and threatening again. It was no longer bright on the horizon. It began to rain. Léa picked up her bicycle and pushed it along the muddy path. Like the previous evening, the kitchen was full of men in wet clothes. They were silent, too silent. Did it have to be in this warm, cozy kitchen that Léa always learned what she feared most? She looked around her. Their heads were bare and they were staring at their feet.

A terrible pain crushed her heart and a flood of tears welled up in her eyes and stopped behind her eyelids. A soundless cry tore at her throat while inside her a childlike voice called her father's name.

It was the local priest who had found Pierre Delmas's body hunched up in a dark corner of the chapel, where he had no doubt gone to shelter from the rain. His tired old heart, exhausted from grief, had stopped beating.

Chapter 26

Ruth and Camille were worried by Léa's mute, tearless grief.

She had stood contemplating the rigid corpse for a long time where it lay on the divan in the study. It was she who had arranged a lock of his gray hair on his icy forehead, staring with a strange indifference at what had been her father. Who was this shrunken old man with weak hands whose dead body was lying there? Her father was big and strong: when he took her in his arms, she felt protected from the whole world; nothing could happen to her. Her hand disappeared completely in his warm, reassuring grip. Walking through the vineyards with him was like setting off on an adventure, going out to conquer the world. He spoke of the land the way Isabelle spoke of God. For him they were one and the same thing. Only Léa's faith in the land had survived. The land had neither betrayed nor deserted her. When they were all hungry, it was the land that had rewarded her toil. Like her, Pierre Delmas had eked a living out of the soil of Montillac. Father and daughter were of the same breed. And standing before his pathetic remains, Léa knew that it was the image of her father striding through the vineyards that would stay with her forever.

She gave instructions for the funeral to Ruth and her Aunt Bernadette with the utmost calm. She called Luc Delmas and Lisa and Albertine de Montpleynet herself. She asked her aunts to inform Sabine if they saw her.

She told Camille to let their friends and neighbors know.

She went up to her room, changed her dress and came back down again, dressed in one of those black overalls worn by old women, which could still be bought easily at the market.

She took her straw hat down from the hatstand in the hall and tied the ribbons under her chin. The sun had come out again.

"Are you going out?" asked Ruth.

"Yes, I've go to go to La Réole."

"Now?"

"Yes."

Camille came forward.

"Don't you want me to come with you?"

"No, thank you, I need you here. I've got to collect the mail and tell the Debrays what happened in Bordeaux. I also want to ask them to try to get in touch with Uncle Adrien and Laurent."

Léa rode off on her blue bicycle.

Everybody who could, relatives, friends, and neighbors, came to mourn with the Delmas family. In spite of the risk of being arrested, Adrien Delmas was there in his white robe, and so was Laurent d'Argilat. Lucien, to his mother's delight, had come with them. Only Sabine was missing.

When her aunts, dressed in mourning, had told her on the morning of their departure for Bordeaux that they were going to her father's funeral and that they wished to travel with her, Sabine had told them that she would not go for anything in the world. She did not want to be accused of killing him. She had rushed off in tears.

Adrien had insisted on saying mass, which was served by Luc, which he did with the help of a group of other friars. Surrounding the mourners was a small army of ecclesiastics in identical white robes, all saying mass in unison. In the second row of mourners circling the holy men, Léa spotted the bearded face of Laurent. She had *known* he would be there.

During the service, the brothers seemed to have forgotten their differences.

The German authorities in the area were in turn put on

the alert—two prime movers from the French Resistance were expected to come out of hiding and surface for Pierre Delmas's funeral. They put in a Top Priority request to General Headquarters in Paris for extra men, both uniformed troops as well as plainclothes Gestapo. The commandant of the district emphasized that the capture of both Laurent and Father Adrien would be well worth the extra manpower at the funeral.

Léa's grief was compounded by the ominous fear that two of the dearest people in the world to her, her beloved Laurent as well as her Uncle Adrien, would surely be arrested by the hated Germans as they paid final respects to Pierre Delmas.

Not only did the people who had known and respected Pierre Delmas and the Delmas family come, but groups of townspeople from villages and hamlets all around Montillac gathered in the church at Verdelais, overfilling its modest capacity and spilling out into the courtyard. The roads converging on the churchyard grounds were crowded with people in cars and on bicycles, and whole families in horse-drawn carts, as well as others on foot. It looked much like the exodus of civilians during the dark days of June.

Not only were most of the Germans assigned to the area unable to get close to the mourners, but the reinforcements requisitioned from General Headquarters in Paris couldn't get within three kilometers of the area.

The French underground had quietly spread word everywhere. The people came out in droves.

A dozen Germans stood quietly outside the core of family mourners helplessly watching the friars say mass. They were in an awkward dilemma. Their instructions were to take into custody Father Adrien Delmas, whom they were certain was there. But to arrest a small army of Dominican friars in the midst of thousands of superstitious and unfriendly French mourners would surely precipitate an ugly confrontation, which the German High Command in Paris had given strict instructions to avoid at all costs. Berlin was bending backwards to cement relations with the puppet French government in Vichy.

The captain in charge looked at his eleven men, then surveyed the masses of French people surrounding him and simply threw up his hands in a sign of utter frustration. He peered at the many white-robed clergy bobbing and mumbling undecipherable Latin phrases, and with difficulty led his men through the milling masses of mourners towards the road out. "We'll get the sly old priest next time," he muttered to the lieutenant behind him.

Léa was sitting in the front row with the women in the family. Taking refuge behind her lace veil, she was soothed by the monotonous droning of the Basilica choir. She felt guilty at feeling so overjoyed to see Laurent again. For a few seconds she had even forgotten her sorrow. The day before, when he had held her in his arms and hugged her to him for a long time, she had felt a surge of peace and happiness. He had come, risking his life, because he loved her. Léa was so fulfilled, so sure of that love, that she did not even feel envious when she saw him going upstairs to bed with Camille. As soon as her head touched the pillow, she fell into a deep dreamless sleep. And in the morning, Camille's radiant face did not affect her feeling of peace.

She gradually began to realize that now there was no reason for her to stay at Montillac. What was the point of fighting to keep an estate that even her father had given up on? Laure's only dream was to live in the city. Selling the land would enable her to buy an apartment in Bordeaux, or Paris, and to live comfortably for a few years. Or she could rent out the vineyards and keep the house. She would have to ask Uncle Adrien and Laurent's advice.

Sabine would also have to have her say. She was the eldest and had come of age a month ago. There was nothing to stop Léa from joining Laurent in his struggle either. She would live beside him, sharing the same dangers, the same fight. . . . She stood up, unable to pray, knelt down and sat down again automatically, following the general movement.

Suddenly, for no reason, her heart began to race and her neck and shoulders felt terribly hot. She felt an irresistible urge to look around. She turned. There, in the shadows near the column . . . she had the bizarre sensation that her heart was going to jump right out of her chest. She looked back again and tried to concentrate on the altar. Suddenly, she looked around again. It wasn't a ghost: François really was there, watching her. . . . Why did her breasts hurt her so? Why did she feel a shudder in the pit of her stomach? Camille, who was sitting next to her, put a hand on her arm. Léa brushed her away with a gesture of irritation. She bowed her head and lowered her eyelids as if better to quell the tumult she felt rising within her. Images of the most intense, the wildest, the most delightful and the most shameful moments she had spent with the three men who had been her lovers ran through her mind at the most astonishing speed. In vain, she tried to repress these shamelss memories, shocked at having such indecent thoughts in the presence of her father's remains. The ceremony was drawing to a close.

The ritual of accepting everybody's condolences seemed interminable. The procession dispersed in the little cemetery with its steep paths baked hard and cracked by the blistering sun. Léa could feel the perspiration running down her back. Her thick black silk dress clung to her skin. She felt giddy. She suddenly wanted to slide into the open grave and stretch out on the light oak coffin. It must be nice and cool underground. She teetered. A firm hand caught her. It was good to feel that strength flow into her. She closed her eyes and let herself fall against the man. She laid her head on the shoulder she knew she could lean on without fear.

It was François Tavernier. She wasn't at all surprised. Léa had known instinctively that he would somehow be there. François always managed to appear at those moments when she needed him.

"Your father would have been delighted to know that more people showed up at his funeral than showed up at our last late lamented Premier's. All roads to Verdelais are jammed for miles around. It's lucky that I had a Top Priority certificate, along with a short-cut I remembered, that got me here on time and in one piece."

Léa peered quizzically at François as he smoked his little twisted black cigar. "You . . . you brought out all these people to pay final respects to Papa?"

François shrugged. "Not really. I only orchestrated it to keep the Nazis away from your uncle . . . and your precious Laurent. I didn't need to get any coded BBC messages from London to know that these two foolish sentimentalists would be here—and so did the Germans, from the accounts of the staff cars stalled on the road from Paris heading here."

How gently he removed her cumbersome hat and veil, lifted up her damp hair and undid the top three buttons of her dress. If he said, "I'm taking you away from here," she would follow him.

"What are you thinking about?"

"Leaving," she said.

François Tavernier looked at her as if he were trying to read her thoughts.

"Why do you want to leave?"

"There are too many things here that remind me of those who have gone."

"Leave it to time. I'm also hoping time will help me to accomplish my task."

"What task?"

"It's too soon to talk about it."

Camille, Adrien and Ruth were coming towards them.

"We're going home, Léa, are you coming with us?" asked Camille. Then, turning towards François, she kissed him and said: "I'm delighted to see you again, Monsieur Tavernier."

"I too am delighted to see you, Madame d'Argilat. Good afternoon, Father."

"Hello, Tavernier. Thank you for being with us today. How did you know?"

"Ha! Two of Rommel's Panzer divisions couldn't keep you two romantics away from Pierre Delmas's last rites. Even for me it took a lot of doing to rustle up all these villagers to help you two get lost in the crowd."

"Yes, it's only thanks to you that we haven't been arrested yet. But it would not be very wise to hang around here too long. We're leaving again this evening."

"Already!" exclaimed Léa.

"If we stay any longer, we'll be arrested. Not even Tavernier here could help us then. We're going back to Montillac, where I shall speak to Luc and Fayard about how we can protect your rights."

Laurent joined them and shook Tavernier's hand.

"I'm glad to be able to thank you, Tavernier, for all you did for my wife—and for us. I'm indebted to you forever."

"Don't exaggerate. You would have done the same."

"No doubt, but that doesn't stop me from being grateful."

François Tavernier bowed, not without a certain irony, it seemed to Léa. Then, turning to her, he said: "May I accompany you?"

"If you wish."

Leaning on his arm, Léa walked down to the church square where the cars and carts were waiting. She climbed into François's Citroen with Camille, Adrien and Laurent.

At Montillac, a snack was waiting for them in the courtyard, in the shade of the linden trees. Léa, whose thoughts were elsewhere, let Camille, Ruth, her sister and her aunts take care of their guests. She walked down to the terrace holding her glass.

Two men followed her thin black figure with their eyes, as it glided across the grass. François Tavernier looked away first and went over to Adrien.

"Father Delmas, would you show me through the wine cellars?"

"With pleasure, but they're not much compared to some of the famous vintages in the area."

The two men walked off towards the little door leading off the courtyard.

"Will we be alone? I have to talk to you," said François softly.

✳   ✳   ✳

Léa, leaning against the low terrace wall, followed the distant progress of a train crossing the Garonne.

"Camille's worried about your standing here alone," said Laurent tenderly.

"Did she send you over? I'd rather you had come by yourself. Haven't you anything to say to me?"

"What's the point. Let's forget what happened."

"Why should I forget? I'm not ashamed, I love you, and you love me too," she said, taking his arm and leading him towards the little wood, out of sight of the courtyard.

"I'm sorry about what happened. I behaved badly towards you, towards Camille. I don't know how I could have —"

"You could because, like me, you wanted to. You love me, even though you won't allow yourself to. You love me, do you hear? You love me."

She shook him as she spoke. Her hair fell loose from her chignon on to her shoulders, giving her that wild and crazy look that he found impossible to resist. Her flashing eyes captivated him, her parted lips compelled him, her arms were around him, her body clung to his. He gave up the unequal struggle and kissed her waiting lips.

Léa savored her victory and tried to draw out the emotion.

She thought she heard footsteps on the gravel path. She could not stop her body becoming tense. Laurent pushed her away. François Tavernier appeared around the bend in the path.

"Ah! there you are! Your wife is looking for you."

"Thank you," Laurent stammered.

Léa and François watched him stride away.

"You're always around when you're not wanted."

"Believe me, my dear, I'm sorry to have interrupted your tender *tête-a-tête*," he said insolently. "I've always wondered what you see in that man."

"You're always repeating yourself too. What have you got against him? He's marvelous!"

"He's perfect, absolutely perfect. But what can I say? I just can't picture you with a man who's perfect."

"No doubt you find it easier to imagine me with a man like you?"

"In a way. We are very alike, you and I. We have a strange sense of honor which can prompt us to act with absurd courage and make us like what suits us. Like me, you're capable of anything, even of killing, in order to get what you want. Your desire will always be stronger than your intellect and your instinctive wariness. You want everything, Léa, and you want it now. You're a spoiled child and you've no compunction about taking another child's favorite toy—in this case Camille's husband—even though, once you've got it, the toy doesn't interest you any more."

"That's not true."

"Oh yes, it is. But you'd rather bite your tongue off than admit it. What does it matter? It's of no importance if you think you're in love with him. You'll grow out of it."

"Never!"

He dismissed her reply with an off-hand gesture.

"Let's talk about something a bit more interesting. You ought to spend more time in Paris. It would give you a change. Your aunts would be delighted to have you stay with them."

"I don't want to go to Paris. I've got to stay here and deal with my father's affairs."

"They'll fleece you. I've offered your family the services of my business manager, Monsieur Robert. He's a very honest and competent man."

"Why should I accept your help?"

"Because I'm offering it," he said in a gentler voice.

They reached the edge of the estate at the end of the path which ran below the terrace.

"Let's go back."

"No, I don't want to see all those people, I want to be alone."

"I'll leave you then."

"No, not you," she said, clinging to his arm. "Let's walk for a while. Shall we go to La Gerbette?"

Tavernier stared at her in amazement. This little girl in mourning was so full of contradictions!

"La Gerbette?"

"It's a shack were I used to play when I was little. It's half buried in the ground, and it's very cool inside. We keep alfalfa in there for the rabbits, and old tools. I haven't been there for ages."

They walked down through the sloping vineyards and arrived in front of a little tiled roof at ground level. They walked around it. A narrow path which was almost hidden by brambles led to the door, which was locked. François put his shoulder up against it and the rusty lock gave way easily. Half the little room with its earth floor was full of hay. Thick cobwebs hung from the rafters.

"It's not very nice. I remembered it being much larger."

François took off his jacket and spread it on the hay.

"Lie down. I find this place charming."

"Don't tease me. This is where I would hide when Ruth wanted to give me a German lesson. There's a nook behind the manger over there. What fun we had here!"

"You're still a child," he said sitting down beside her.

Léa's childlike expression changed to a provocative one. She looked at François through half-closed eyes as she stretched out with her arms folded under her head, arching her back and thrusting out her breasts.

François watched her with amusement.

"Stop flirting, or I'll stop acting like a big brother."

"But that's how you love me, isn't it?"

"As a brother and also in a different way."

"That doesn't sound like the François I know. So virtuous?"

"I don't like being second best."

"What do you mean?"

"You know very well what I mean."

"So what? Supposing I like it like that. I thought we were so much alike. Don't you want me?"

He leaped on top of her and pulled up her skirt, thrusting his hand between her legs.

"You little bitch, I'm not . . . "

He did not finish his sentence. Léa crushed her lips against his and clung close to François.

"I'd like a cigarette."

"It's not a good idea in here," said François taking a pack of American cigarettes out of his pocket.

They lay there naked, with bits of hay clinging to their sweaty bodies, their legs entwined, smoking in silence. By now it was almost dark inside the shack.

"They'll be getting worried."

Without answering, she got up, slipped on her mourning dress and rolled her underwear and stockings into a ball which she hid under a stone, shook the hay out of her hair and went outside carrying her shoes.

She walked back up towards Montillac without looking back. François joined her halfway up the path. They reached the terrace in silence. Camille was sitting under the wisteria.

As soon as she saw Léa, she got up and hugged her.

"Where were you?"

"I wasn't in any danger. I was with our friend here."

Camille gave them a broad grin.

"Laurent and Adrien have left. They were sorry to leave without saying goodbye."

Léa shrugged. She turned towards the plain, and slipped her hand in the large comforting hand of François. She leaned out and watched the sun's red disc disappear behind Verdelais hill.

They sat there on the terrace for a while, just holding hands. Neither spoke as they gazed at the sky over the vineyards.

"Will you return to Montillac soon?" asked Léa softly. François lit another one of his little black cigars before responding. "It all depends on the fortunes of war, my dear. If it wasn't for the sudden passing of your father I seriously doubt whether we would be sitting here together.

"There is much to be done by many people if France is ever to be freed from our conquerors from the west. It has been a most pleasurable interlude being with you, my dear, but my mission in coming here was to protect Father Adrien as well as your rather reluctant lover, Laurent."

Léa flared up. "He *does* love me!" she exploded.

"Oh hush, little one. Let's not go into all that again. As

I was saying, your uncle and Laurent are both valuable and irreplacable men in the Resistance. With more and more double agents infiltrating the underground we can ill afford to lose anyone.''

Léa peered deeply into François's eyes, as if trying to see into his very soul. Who was he? What was he? ''I know you, and I don't know you. You are able to arouse everyone from the countryside to hide two people from the Nazis, and yet you are on good enough terms with the enemy to hob-nob with the German ambassador in Paris at the highest levels. Really, who are you, François Tavernier?''

The tall man looked at her for a few seconds, then smiled enigmatically. ''You know, dear, I sometimes ask myself the same question, too. When I leave here I have a rendezvous at Gestapo Headquarters in Paris—with Sabine's beloved Captain Kramer. No, don't worry. I won't mention having been at the funeral.''

''Sabine should have been there,'' declared Léa with emotion.

''Now, now, little one. I don't want to be in the middle of any family squabbles, especially when it concerns the Delmas sisters.'' He paused, snuffed out his cigar giving himself a moment before making his next remark. He hesitated only slightly before he spoke. ''Regretfully, I must take leave of you now. But I thought you'd like to know that before we meet again I will also see your occasional hayloft romping playmate Mathias in his work camp in Germany. I want to see what kind of mischief he—or we—can make in the Fatherland.''

With that François gently pressed Léa's hand one last time and strode quickly from the terrace.

She did not stir when François said goodbye, or when Camille called her back into the house. A little later, she heard the noise of an engine, and then once again everything was silent.

A light sea breeze blew through her hair as the first stars appeared. She slipped to her knees by the wall, and merged with its dark mass as her first tears since her father's death gently began to flow.